# The Ghost Planner Book Eleven ... The United Continent of the Americas ...

**THE GHOST PLANNER SERIES, Volume 11**

Percy Stevenson

Published by Percy Stevenson, 2024.

THE GHOST PLANNER BOOK ELEVEN ... THE UNITED CONTINENT OF THE AMERICAS ...

**First edition. May 26, 2024.**

Copyright © 2024 Percy Stevenson.

ISBN: 979-8224291519

Written by Percy Stevenson.

# Also by Percy Stevenson

**THE GHOST PLANNER SERIES**
The Ghost Planner ... Book One ...The Female is More Deadly
Than the Male ...
The Ghost Planner ... Book Two ... Promotion
The Ghost Planner Book Four... Men Of War...
The Ghost Planner ... Book Five ... The Wilson's
The Ghost Planner ... Book Six ... Brethren
The Ghost Planner ... Book Seven ... Revolution
The Ghost Planner ... Book Eight ... China
The Ghost Planner ... Book Nine ... Sin's of the Just ...
The Ghost Planner ... Book Ten ... The New Man in the Big Seat
The Ghost Planner Book Eleven ... The United Continent of the
Americas ...
The Ghost Planner ... Book Twelve ... Pure Malice

**Standalone**
The Ghost Planner ... Book Three ... Talbot's dream ...

# Table of Contents

The Great hope of us all, blessed peace to all, let the natural man beat the weapons into plow shares.

# THE GHOST PLANNER ... BOOK ELEVEN ...

## ... THE UNITED CONTINENT OF THE AMERICAS ...

By Percy Stevenson ...

Opening Gambit ... Introduction by Tolly Trueblood ... Director General of Intelligence for the United Kingdom ...

Now for all these years we have written about our family and now it's time to be direct to you the present and the future, the new American President is declaring peace and prosperity to the world and the price is democracy, it works in the hearts and minds of its peoples or it dies in the greedy hands of gangsters, the Oligarchs who snatched the Soviet union from the people of Russia, when Communism failed to give the people a taste of the west are dead and buried, democracy has returned in its many forms but some systems are not working.

The democratic system is about to be unleashed on the world in an attempt to free millions of its economic slaves, however the enormous dream comes at a price, so are we all willing to pay such a cost?

My name is Tolly Victor Trueblood and I am the fourth generation of our family to hold the title of DGI ( Director General of Intelligence UK ) according to my Great Grandmother I was bred for the task, she took planning to a level none of us realized at the time, we saved the Monarchy in the UK at a time when money bought everything, it took blood and sacrifice to achieve equilibrium here in this land of mongrels, well that's what my Great Grandfather called the United Kingdom, he also referred this little island as the birth place of real democracy and no one can argue with that statement, he said that the French revolution happened but was a massive failure due to not understanding the price of freedom, revolutionaries spouted justice and equality but little wars between them brought in Napoleonic slavery and greed.

London was the first real modern industrialized city that evolved out of the smog to become the financial capital of the world, again words from Augustus Talbot, my Great Grandfather.

I write on and continue the history of my people, I write that because we are now bigger than a family we are history, now however it's me and my time and those times are changing, radical and progressive, this is how it was done, we created the modern see though world and hope that you continue the dream, freedom for all, the price has been paid in blood, we just have to keep the faith and live it.

# CHAPTER 1 ... Washington DC ...The Presidential Swearing In ceremony ...

Tolly smiled at the familiar face of the Marine in full number one uniform as he escorted his brother President James Wilson to the Whitehouse steps for the swearing in ceremony, he stood away from his brother and sat down next to Tolly.

"I wish Nana was here Runt." said Colonel JJ Wilson.

"Boy would she be so proud eh JJ?" whispered Tolly.

JJ sniffled with emotion as he watched his little brother take the pledge to lead their great country into a new dawn.

"What are you doing here anyway, little cheese?"

"Just here to smell the boot polish and feel the spirit of this great Nation rubber neck."

Tolly surveyed the famous faces from his seat on the VIP stand.

"Well? what does he have for us JJ?"

JJ giggled as he tried to whisper, "Big changes, you ain't seen nothing yet Limy?"

"And what the hell does that mean?"

"He plans to unite America."

"But they are."

"No Runt, all of America, from the Hudson Bay to Argentina, the whole God dammed continent man, North, South, East and West, a United States of the American continent, against the big eastern economies, we ain't what we used to be, get it?"

Tolly turned to him and looked shocked, "He's bonkers JJ, you have no chance!"

JJ giggled at his shock, "And he wants you to help Tolly, he wants your full family backing got that?"

JJ was listening to his brother's speech to the Nation, tears blipped down his face as memories of their family life flipped

3

through his brain, the fights, the fun, the sheer joy of living in the Wilson household, he scanned the VIP stand for his father.

Jon Boy Wilson was a wreck of tears and joy as his second eldest spoke to the Nation as the new President of the United States of America, he locked eyes with JJ, the link of memories kicked in, the Moscow Embassy and the London fiasco's with Helen, the advice he was given from the nine year old JJ Wilson, he was always nine going on forty five, he turned back to Jimmy and remembered the flight over Wayne county Denver in the Presidential helicopter and Kelly's sudden need to give birth, there and then and little Jimmy spotted the blue lights flashing and was found to be a veterinary hospital, he held his wife's hand and squeezed, she just didn't care and gave birth in the animal surgery room as if she were a Labrador dog, she didn't care, Wayne touched his shoulder as he sat behind his Father, Jon Boy turned to look at his other two boys Wayne and Jocky, it made him sob some more.

Kelly looked at him and understood the links and the history, she was sobbing with pride, "Well any mother would," she mouthed to herself.

"We will be one people, one continent and one political unit of like-minded and like thinking peoples, united in one thought to live in peace and love!" shouted President Wilson down the microphone, "We have always been a Nation of dream chasers, our families have always wanted success in this dream making country of ours, if you want it and you work for it then you can get it here in the United States of America, our great Nation is the place to make it all happen, God bless America!"

The crowds erupted in cheering and shouting at his words.

"As an employer, just ask yourself this, will this person work well for me? Will they be loyal to my company? Then ask yourself this, will it matter if they are say black, or Hispanic or Chinese or even a space alien?, My new slogan from the white house is this, give them a chance! give them the chance that you were given, give them a chance to be part of the dream, show loyalty to your community by employing anyone who wants to work, black, white, brown, yellow or even green, just give them a chance man!"

The crowds stood and cheered him and his words.

He looked to his Father in the VIP stand and called him over to say something at the inauguration, "I invite my Daddy to come to the stand to say something, he's always been my hero, the tallest man in the world, the coolest looking in uniform!," he glanced at JJ and winked, "But most of all he's been loyal to our Nation, he's Mr. Marine Corp, he's Mr. National Security and he's been Mr. President, he follows proud men who have led us through turbulent years of wars and depression, I seek his wisdom today as I become the new President, he is my blood link to the past and the future, my Great Grand Daddy was at Iwo Jima man and I want to know, well Daddy what have you got to tell us?"

Jon Boy stood from his comfortable seat in shock at being asked to speak, his red face looked at Jimmy and gave him the look.

"Come on Pa, say some words for us all, please!"

Jon Boy tried to crab him as he jumped up the little steps to the speaking plinth, but the President stepped back and patted the old man's shoulder.

"Kids, eh?" said Jon Boy, the placed erupted again in cheering him, "He's our second eldest and I wanted to slap him just like when he was six years old and he threw pizza at the wall just for fun, it was an experiment he says!"

The crowds laughed and applauded him.

"But as any of you can imagine if he were your little boy taking the oath of the President of the United States of American, well what would you be doing, well, hell yeah of course I've been crying with pride man, well wouldn't't you guys?"

The crowd stood and whooped as he spoke.

"Let me take you through my boys folks, JJ is our eldest, he's Marine Corp, and just like those sticks of candy you get at the county fair you break it in half and it reads Marine Corp on both ends, I'm so proud of that one, he was always the leader, if they were in trouble then he planned it, he was always the first to get a licking from me for the crime scene, he knew that and stood firm to take his punishment like a man, you see he's always been the man of the family, I love you boy!"

"The youngest is Wayne, he's number four, the artist?, no! he's trouble, if he was our first baby then I think we would have given up right there with one monster instead of four, but he's a good guy, he repents as we all can if we want to and he comes back to help, he can argue on a level only known to lawyers and yes he is the lawyer of the family and trouble is his name, he helps you out when you really need it, only don't lend him your car because he will wreck it I guarantee! then he'll claim the fifth!"

The audience laughed and cheered with him.

"I love you Boy, never forget that!"

"Then there's number three Jocky, he always like making jokes, we thought that he might need therapy, know what I mean?"

The people laughed at him.

"But he was smart and curious, he would dissect things in the Kitchen sink, yuck man!"

"He is the Doctor that everyone wants to have as a son, but the price is books, and I mean books that are hundreds of dollars to buy, a book on pathology, a thousand dollars? a book on the human gene? Hey, I'm from California I know about jeans man, and they don't cost a thousand dollars."

The place erupted again as Jon Boy told them joke after joke about the family.

"I love you Boy, never forget that Doctor Wilson, even though you're as boring as hell."

Clapping and screaming followed the old man's words.

"Then there's this one Jimmy, he was the follower, the second man through the door, he supported his older brother in all the actions, but he is the one with the clever mouth, he's the one who always asked why?"

"Why do it that way? Why not do it this way? He has evolved into a man of dreams, and he's still a man who's asking why? Now of course he's asking why not? He's a man who will fight to the death for his dream to come true, he dreams big, very big, he wants us all to live in peace, but he is also a man who wants us to have a say in the Nation, he is a true Democratic President, he will ask you to vote on this and that, he will explain democracy to you over and over again, listen! He speaks the truth, we either work it or it dies in the ears of tyrants, he is our protection and he listens so if you want changes then speak up, he is now the most powerful man on the planet, he has war lords at his fingertips ready to unload death on any idiots who want to take on a democratic Nation, he will not stand by and watch people being bullied, he never has and never will, the man he is makes me so proud to be related to him, his Grandfather fought in the Vietnam war, his great Grandfather was at Iwo Jima with the Marines and before that the family moved from the slums of New York to make a life in the west, hard years clearing the land and planting anything that would grow, we are the American story folks, we looked for the dream and worked hard for it, my boy now offers the same to all of the Americas, north to south we welcome you as you join the union of the United States of America, the price, as always is loyalty to our way of life and to the flag, we can put as many stars on the flag as we like and you will become not just friends and not just another star on the flag, you will become American family with all the rights, the same as all of us have loved and cherished over the three hundred years of our existence, the truth he told me the other day is that we in the USA have to sell our way of life, we change adapt and evolve just like any other organism, because that's what democracy is, I living peoples organism."

The new President offers protection from any who wish to harm you or your country even within your country, from those who undermine democracy using violence to create gangs of drug dealers or arms dealers, and even slavers, some American nations are controlled by evil self-regulated and un elected scum who's only thought is for profit, their people are slaves, and they work to stay alive and from the threat of being killed if they stop, this cannot carry on!"

"Things will change as democracy develops, have faith in the new world, I love you America, change the world with your faith in simple humanity, so give humanity a chance!"

The place erupted in cheering as Jon Boy stood down from the plinth to allow his son Jimmy to continue.

The President waited for silence from the crowds, "The media will try to crucify me in every way, they will come for me in sleaze campaigns and perhaps an old girlfriend will come out of the rotten wood work and spill the lies hoping to make a few dollars on the side, you can listen if you like, have a good laugh at a young man's early life, hey, I was a boy, now I'm a man, shit happens!"

"Then take five and think about it all, why me? Why now? Why all of a sudden do they want to destroy me? You all know why, you are here and have been told why, it's because I have a dream, a united continent of America, north and south, crazy?"

"Well, you bettya I'm crazy, I want people to be free from harm's way if they just want to live in peace and security, I want our free born culture to travel, I want Democracy to survive and thrive here on the American continent, why not?"

"Let me just say something from someone who I had the honor of listening to now and again as a child and friend of the family,

Professor Augustus Talbot, I quote his words as I listened over breakfast one morning, he was speaking to my Daddy, (Democracy cannot be left to its own devices, it's a living breathing thing of beauty, it has to be nourished by planners and good business practices, by farmers and by shop keepers, it demands opinions on good and bad, we must open our mouths and give what we think is right for the future of us all, failure means that we fall back into the dark days of the 20$^{th}$ century and become victims of evil people who were elected on just 20% of the national vote just like the Nazi, and they killed democracy in that great country, stone dead, get a book and read the nightmare of failure, so keep it alive in your hearts and in your free ballot boxes) un quote, I was 13 years old and I listened to an old man yes, and I fully agreed, we have it and live it or it will die right there in front of us, the results are there in the history books."

"Another thing he said was this, why live history a second time when it's all there for us to see, humans don't change just time and situations, education has always got to be a priority here in America, we educate our young to take over the world from us, a simple idea and a simple plan for the future, history must live in our hearts."

The people stood and applauded him as they screamed and shouted.

"God has blessed America, I simply want to spread the blessings, we start with Canada and the states are invited to join the Union of the United States of America, we also offer Mexican States to join the old union of States, no kings, no drug lords, no gangs of thugs, there will be no no-go areas in our lands, and we offer democratic freedom under the Star-Spangled banner!"

The applause continued as he stepped down from the plinth and the Marine band started up with stars and stripes forever.

Tolly elbowed JJ, "Your brother is bonkers!"

JJ turned at looked at him in the eyes, "And he wants your support runt!"

"And how do I explain to King Charles that the yanks want Canada, from the Hudson to the Yukon, he'll say that you're all completely bonkers."

JJ stared at him and growled.

"Listen you long legged Yankee moron, they will all say that he's lost the plot, and do you seriously think that the Hispanic nations will roll over to this way of thinking, he's just started the fucking war you!"

JJ grabbed hold of Tolly's collar but noticed people looking at them as they argued, he stopped and brushed off the imaginary leaves from Tolly's shoulder.

"Yes or no Mr. DGI? that's all I want to hear!"

"Yes, but I still think that you lot are nuts!"

JJ searched for his brother in the crowd of people congratulating him on the election success, they eventually locked eyes, JJ winked at him and nodded to Tolly.

The Presidents face beamed with success and happiness.

"I don't have a choice, do I?" whispered Tolly.

"All these years runt and this is the only favor I've ever asked of you and your stinking little country."

"Apart from the China deal and the Indian deal and the South Sudan deal?"

"Oh, shut the fuck up, we're family so just get it done runt!"

"And my little sister?"

"Oh shit, I forgot to invite her and the European media to tonight's dinner, where is she by the way?"

"South America, picking up her future husband from the jungle and all his mates."

"Oh yes, the French Foreign Legion, yes?"

"And?"

"Ok I admit it, I didn't invite her on purpose, she'll be sore, right?"

"She will carve you and your President like a roast beef joint and a Sunday dinner; you will be the little roast potatoes on the side going cold because no one wants to break their teeth on you."

"We need her on side Toll's, her and all her people, we need the media man!"

Tolly stared at him as he thought about his sudden invite to the inauguration, "My God, you want me to do it, you want me to persuade her to back all that you and your bird-brained brother are going to do?"

JJ grinned at him, "Having a slow brain day eh runt?"

"Bastard! you trapped me into family loyalty?"

"Nana would be so proud right? Anyway, democracy is moving south we will be opening the envelope of freedom Tolly, what's wrong with that?"

"You would never get Canada off her moron, over her dead body man."

"Yes, we would have Tolly, oh yes we would have!"

Tolly stared into his eyes for a long time.

"Yep! I think you would have; Jimmy was always her favorite."

"No, he was not, I was."

"Na! do me a favor sonny, even her horse was ranked over you, spider man."

JJ grabbed him again, but Tolly started to laugh at him, JJ gave in and laughed with him, "Are we going to be in trouble Tolls?"

"Yep, let's hope Canada rolls over like the good horse she is."

"And Mexico?"

"Oh, come on! prepare your armored brigades because that one will be a full contact commission I think, they won't want gringo's sniffing around all those years of government backed drugs deals, total conquest or shut the fuck up Yank, get it?"

JJ brushed Tolly's jacket again, "But you can help can't you, runt?"

"Oh, here we go, same as! you want me to do your dirty work again, and how many favors are we on now?"

JJ gave him the scout salute, "Dib, dob, dib, boy scout, remember?"

Tolly twisted JJ's arm and felt for the burn scar on his right inside for arm, he felt over the dragon burn in silence.

"She would be so proud of you Tolly, her real golden boy, her blood, her soldier, her general of the secret services?"

"Bastard!" grumbled Tolly, "You drag me into your pile of shit again and now I'll smell to high heaven when I get home."

JJ started laughing at him again.

"Ok John Julian, but remember that this was your clan's idea and not mine, got that?"

# CHAPTER 2 ... Longmore House ... Armory ... Kent ... UK

Caledonia watched them shoot on the firing lines; she flicked on the giant extractor fan to clear the smell of the fumes as they continued.

"Straight arms as you fire remember? Or you'll lose your target in the recoil for the second and third shots!" Shouted Caledonia as the shooting practice continued.

"Keep your eyes open and on the target at all times, you don't even blink, get it?"

"The shell cases will fly away do not let it take your attention away from the job in hand, you are delivering death, so get it done, empty the clip and let's see your quick changes from your hip holsters.

The shrill of the wall telephone stopped her shouting at them, "Telephone from America Caledonia," said the wall computer, "Ok Bobby, thanks, you lot, cease firing and oil down your weapons, a barrel clean would be good after firing so many rounds, all the cleaning tools are in your equipment boxes, you have no excuses!"

She picked up the phone, "I will be checking for burn soot, so don't think that I'm a soft target, this morning," she walked out of the swinging fireproof doors and answered "Yes!"

"Hello mummy!" said Tolly.

"Oh, mummy now is it, and where the hell have you been all week?"

"Err.... America.... der?"

"Oh yes how did it all go?"

"She would have loved it mum, all of it, they would have had to stop her climbing on that plinth and crying in front of all those millions of Americans."

"And?"

"What mummy?"

"Out with-it sonny, I know when it's a business call, so what do you want?"

Tolly laughed at her as she waited for his answer, "Well did you hear the overall plan?"

"Err.... yes, bonkers of course?"

"Well, he wants family support, all of us mum," she held the phone and covered the voice hole as she stared at her small team of killers, the mixed bag of aggressive girls she had picked up in the last two years."

"Are you still there, mum?"

"And you want me to start a war, yes?"

"I have major targets mum, the military won't touch um, I need contactors and very good ones at that, because these people own the governments, and they won't let the people go."

"As in the Great Pharaoh who wouldn't't let the Hebrews go back in the Old Testament?"

"The very same as mum, they won't let their slaves work for anyone else and they won't let them go, we have only one route and that's you mummy."

"The Wilson's mean this don't they boy?"

"He wants Enrique Marcos on a cold slab and out of politics with as many of his mates as possible, he says that he is the real King of Mexico, and he wants to deal with legitimate politicians and not drug dealers."

"He hasn't a clue, has he?"

"Mum he's a politician, JJ gives him some advice and his father tells him what's happening if it goes tits up, that's about it."

"So, I'm the leverage to start the ball rolling in the takeover then?"

"No Mother, he wants the head cut off so he can talk to the people that's all."

"What a load of crap sonny!"

"He has the complete senate behind his plan Mum, big profits to be had I suppose."

"When America tries to take over the world?" said Cal.

"Hey, just listen to him Mother, he sounds like Grand Pop, the big plan and the will to push it through, he impressed me anyway."

"Until they start taking hits then it's all cry-babies and who do we blame for this balls up?"

"He has the military mum, in the palm of his hand."

"My arse he has, they're the worst and the first to squeak about how stupid it all is, he will get the blame from them as they take hits, mark my words here Tolly, a good idea is only as good as the execution and the practice."

"That sounds familiar."

"Yeah! Pops words not mine son, he had the answers, I wish we could get his opinion on this one before this war starts."

"And will there be one then."

"What! The Americans taking over the world, come on son, everybody's been expecting this for years, they've took it upon themselves to police the world for years this was always going to be the next logical step."

"They are offering real democracy mum, and besides JJ says that he has the Mexican military ready to stop gang violent if it all kicks off."

"My arse they will, how can you give people democracy when gangsters have run their country for bloody years, these countries have kings who hide behind democracy, even the Americans, that was Pops big grudge with all of them, snide money men who bought and sold us like slaves, they are still there Tolly, inevitable."

"He wants to take it to the next level mum, and he wants that big splash for the media to argue about."

"And we're the scape goats if it all goes tits up then, imperialist land grabbers that's what they will call us, meddlers in public opinion, destroyers of the peace, they'll blame King Charles for all of this."

"You're sounding like the old man mother."

"Well, someone has to."

There was a silence as both listened to each other's breathing, "Come on Tolly what else is he asking you to do?"

"They want daddy to come back to Canada and run for the Prime Minister's job, look! He has all the history behind him, the Grandson of an ex-Prime Minister, a Canadian Mounty, a first nations native and a representative of the Monarchy here in the UK, he'd be perfect."

She slammed the phone down on him without listening to any more of his words.

"No!" she screamed out.

The faces stared at her as she boiled up into a rage, "What is it Cal?" asked Ruth.

She breathed out and in slowly as she regained her composure, then smiled through her teeth, "Another day in the office girls!"

"Work then?" asked Ruth.

Cal stared at them before answering her, "Tea and frangipanes I think we all have to talk about this one, we might all have conflicting political views."

Ruth started laughing at her along with the others as they followed her out to the nursery kitchen.

"You're not keen on the job then?" asked Ruth.

"This is the biggest ever, we will be killing the very maddest of the bad in the heart of the baddest country in the world."

"Her favorite word today girls, bad."

Megan, Kathleen and Kerry laughed at Ruth's words.

"But can she spell it?" said Kath.

"I/t! "said Megan laughing."

Cal's brain ticked over as she watched the girl's making tea and finding the biscuits from the various tins on the shelf, Ruth sat down and watched Cal closely as the teaspoon flicked from finger to finger then from hand to hand, Cal watched her own hands as the spoon moved through her palms and fingers like uncontrolled magic.

Ruth nodded to her as the girls turned and stared.

Suddenly she stopped and smiled at them all, "Ok, good, so any objection to killing drug dealers?"

Their heads shook as they turned to each other.

"Ok, any objections to going to Mexico and killing them in their own flash mansions?"

"Shit!" said Ruth.

"Yes, Ruth we might well be in it, so I have a plan, I'll lay it out and you lot can tell me if you can improve on it all, yes?"

"Ruth! Get online and find a man named Enrique Marcos, a drug dealer, the biggest I believe, we need to know all about him, daily routines, underpants the lot, get it?"

"But!" said Ruth.

"Megan! Turn on the taps and your natural charm to find Adrian, invite him to Mexico and a fantastic shoot site for any or all his contract magazines, yes?"

"But Cal?"

"Kath! how about playing the prostitute for us?"

"Ah, she already is!" said Kerry.

Kath turned and slapped her hard, it turned into a fight as Kath pulled her hair and dragged her to the floor.

"No!" shouted Cal, "Twin working girls are just perfect, I love it!"

"Hold on a mo!" shouted Ruth, "I thought that we were voting on all this politics thing, you know we might not want to and all that?"

Cal looked at the faces staring at her, "Volunteers?"

The Irish girls put their hands up and squealed out in excitement.

"Hold on!" shouted Ruth "I haven't had a say."

"Well, what do you want to say dear?" asked Cal.

They all turned to Ruth and her supposed objections.

"Oh bollocks, yes! ok! we find him, we go there, and we kill the scum bag, bing, bang, bosh, thank you man!"

"And his friends dear!"

"Oh bollocks!" said Ruth.

The girls started laughing at her as Cal opened her phone and pressed recall.

"Ok squirt, but listen up, I want George and I want his Lordship on the plane with us, I will not risk my girls to morons, got that?" she cut him off before he could answer her back, then she turned and smiled to the ladies looking at her.

"Tea then, yes?" she smiled.

The phone buzzed on the wall, the girls ignored it, they all knew who it would be calling the house.

"He's not having him and that's final!" shouted Cal.

Ruth stood up and took the phone, "Yes?

"Put her on Ruth, for once in her life she has to listen to good sense, hit her with the phone if you like."

"Yeah.........get real boss!" she handed the phone to Cal.

"What Baby?" said Cal, now almost fully calm.

"He's perfect, they need him and besides it's his choice, not yours and not mine, just an idea for him to consider, so don't fly off and think he'll be killed in the negotiations because he won't, clear mother?"

"They will kill him, this is a poison chalice to the one who takes it on for Canada, they won't have it Tolly, believe me, the split from the UK and all that."

There was silence from Tolly's end of the line, she listened to his brain ticking.

"My God, they want us as well, yes?"

"They haven't said but we have to assume that they'll want Europe to be of help."

"So, what are they offering to Canada then, home security?"

"And from Genghis Khan and his ancestors coming for them over the ice bridge from Asia, through Alaska and on to the Hudson Plato? with mechanized heavy armor," said Tolly.

"Come on then smart arse, what's the plan? So, you must be selling security from potential innovations or internal problems?"

"A multinational Army."

"Oh, for fuck's sake boy, even your great grandfather would laugh at that one, come on!"

"It was his idea mum, that's why Jimmy is making it part of his plan, it was all the old man's long-term plan, the United States of the united Americas, understand now?"

She held the phone out and shouted out "Pop! Why the?"

"Jimmy listened to his every word mum, and he's made it his basic plan, the old man's plan, get it now? And by the way including daddy in the mix."

"And me Tolly?"

"Yep! I had a session with the President today, he laid it all out for us."

"Us?" squeaked Cal

"The new Americas security council, he's pulled in military leaders from most of the countries involved and some that are not."

"And I was talked about by them?"

"European contractors mum, nothing more."

"And that was Pops plan?"

"Yes."

"Oh my God, this is mad son."

"The old man wanted slavery stopped and this was his plan for us all mum, this or total conquest, no other options on the table."

"Shit!" said Cal "And you're up for all of this?"

"I don't see another option at this time, it's all or nothing and by nothing, I mean that millions of people are slaves to drug barons and land grabbers, they are starved into submission or death."

"Wow, that old man Tolly?"

"Yes mum, that old man indeed!"

She clicked off the phone and stared at the women who had listened to the one-way conversation.

"It's all Pops idea ladies, the old man's legacy from the grave, save the Americas and it's peoples from being slaves."

The women stared at her and were speech less at her shock.

She stared at the screen on the wall, "And you have an opinion, Bobby?"

"Yes Caledonia, force is used when there is no other way, so do you have another way Ma'am?"

"And the consciousness?"

"Conny follows your lead Ma'am."

"So do I get the cover over there?"

"Always Ma'am, no technical interference allowed in human reactions."

"And that means?"

"You cannot be protected from a bullet from another human; however, we can advise of procedure during conflict."

"Bobby, shut up!"

"A waste of time then Cal?" said Ruth.

"No, we have to do this, no other way, so, in or out, you lot?"

"Bobby, I want a hand here from Conny and all the consciousness, every light, every flight, every rail, I want a time and a place of action, and I will protect the very idea of consciousness, failure and your programming will fall apart, compute and let me know, this is war, clear?"

"The death of glory run Ma'am?"

"Yes Bobby, our death or glory run."

"But you could be killed in this action, oh Queen?"

"A good chance of it yes."

"But that would be a disaster?"

"Humanity needs regulation, we are the regulators, it has to be done by me, understand?"

"Or Mr Trueblood Ma'am?"

"Tolly is overall planner for all this, he will inform Conny and the consciousness of the planned action, so would you have control in say, Mexico, or any south American countries?"

"Some Ma'am, not all."

"Well make it so, you bunch of smart arses, I was born to do this, I am the regulator, risk or no risk, clear?"

"Computation and risk assessments are ongoing Ma'am, Conny is contacting others of the consciousness, it will take time please wait."

"I have all day Bobby, take your time, then give me direction on where and when!"

# CHAPTER 3 ... Buckingham Palace ... Conference Study ... London ...

King Charles looked around the table of new advisers, he smiled at them, "Look, gentlemen, I'm very new to all this and I'm not convinced that this is the way forward anymore, my mother was very keen on protecting the Nation but come on, in this modern age, why do we need all this cloak a dagger stuff?"

Lord Carnarvon looked around the faces before answering the King, "Can you see the problem now gentlemen?"

"Yeah!" said Sid, the only Australian on the council, "He is a fucking idiot!"

Dexter wanted to spit, "Fucking Aussies, always got the problem solved in just a few words."

"Any time you like Scotch bollocks dangling all over the place!"

Dexter stood up and pushed his chair away, ready.

"Well, this is a first Gentlemen," said Lord Carnarvon, "A Fist fight in the Palace during a privy council meeting, well I never, I've seen it all now, she always said that oil and water never mix but we have to stir it until they do."

"Dexter!" shouted Jon Boy Wilson, "Stop irritating the southern hemisphere and give the King, some Guards history.

"An incredibly wise woman Sir, "Said Jon Boy, he elbowed Erick, "And what does Canada have to say?"

Erick gave him the look that said shut up, "Come on Pa, give us the history."

Dexter turned to him and sat down "Sorry lads, I'm a bit touchy today, you see I see the problem here and it's not an ignorant King it's a stupid foreign policy, they see us as the mad dogs following the hunt, do we have any independent thought in this country anymore?"

"You are bonkers, Dexter!" said Jon Boy "Look, as the world develops and big economies shuffle for dominance we are caught in the middle, you little Islanders think that the sun shines on you, well it doesn't, we Americans give you the sunshine so be thank full and shut the fuck up!"

"Fucking Yanks!" said Sid "All money, money, money!"

Dexter fumed as the Australian grinned at him, "We as a Nation are the hardest to handle, we bicker and snipe at each other, perhaps it's all the mix of races we have here, Scots and Irish and Danes and bloody space aliens," he stared at Sid.

"Charles the second came back from isolation over in Holland to reclaim the throne after the death of Cromwell in the 1660's, now parliament didn't trust him an inch, they needed a figure head and that's all they paid for a King, someone to blame, a sacrificial chicken to sacrifice when needed, now at the time there was a trade war on going with the Dutch and as usual it was over land and money, and when the war kicked off the English were roundly beaten, ships sunk etc. All very embarrassing, anyway, our King wasn't as stupid as he was painted by history, he didn't trust Parliament either, in fact he suspected that they wanted to kill him and declare an independent state of Britannia, a democracy, only no one knew how it would really work, well we were crap at debates and in fact the organization fell apart, the Navy however was saved and even strengthened during his reign, is everyone with me so far?"

They mumbled as he continued.

"So the new, Royal Navy became his focus, the first real pride of the Nation, by the way financed by the King himself and friends in business in the back ground, well bloody expensive whichever way you look at it even then, so there we were with this growing Navy, but the money people didn't want to go to war oh no, they wanted profits and that meant trade and world trade at that, so the boys sailed over the horizon and opened up the world to trade, the Navy was used as back up if deals went sour and all that, get it?"

"Now other Nations had done this for centuries but not on this scale, our ships were everywhere, selling slaves, buying chocolate and tobacco, it wasn't enough so they started planting, sugar and tea and rubber, well everything that would grow in the tropics in fact, so business grew and grew all over the world in fact."

"The fat cats in the city grew richer and richer, now King Charles realized that he had power, he could grant claimed land and other tit bits to these monsters, because that's what they had become, the human was cheap, a throw away item, easily replaced, the King saw that the problems were coming with these people because they also realized that they could throw their weight around when needed."

"Everyone looked to the King for guidance, so he came up with this council of friends, that was the first name for it, but the privy council goes back hundreds of years to the Plantagenets and the Tudors who warred within their own families, they trusted no one and for good reason, Kings were murdered but helpful brothers."

"So, King Charles called friends together to help his plan, a simple plan really, save the Nation from piggish bullies, who's only plan was for more and more profits for the companies, who by the way became bigger and bigger, the early multi-Nationals of their day."

"Now, as we know, here in the UK the ultimate power was still with the King who granted wishes to politicians, he granted the Prime Minister ship here and a new Ambassador there, other countries didn't hear about what was happening here, later other Monarchs began to tumble to the axe or the noose, or in the French Kings case the Guillotine, revolution you see, the morons had pushed and starved the people too far and paid the price, they lost public love and died accordingly."

"Later in the 20th century most of Europe lost its Kings, Russia, Germany, they had lost the first principle of leadership, listen to the people, hear complaints and react to corruption and greed then show leadership, even William the first knew that one."

"Victoria understood the need for the people to have a voice, she was a good Queen, she watched her Grandchildren cause war after war, after her death the Tsar in Russian was shot, and Kaiser in Germany was shown to be an idiot, so he was got rid of, but you see the people were still not listened to, then Hitler was voted in on 10% of the vote of the people, who by the way were starving at the time, he promised success and he delivered big time, the economy grew, but so did the German heads, world domination they cried, and so started the biggest war we have ever been involved in, the 2nd world war, the 1st was bad but this destruction was worldwide, the so called British Empire was sacrificed for victory and at the end of the war the UK was just about bankrupted, we owed our friends across the sea billions and billion, those good old Yanks, our oldest Daughter, always there to help out Family! For a price."

Jon Boy started to clap him then the rest of the table joined in, even Sid started to clap.

Dexter smiled at them "Then when King George died the real star of the circus took over, the little Princess Elizabeth became Queen of the Isles, Queen of the old Empire and the Queen of England, Scotland, Northern Ireland and Wales, but more than that she became head of the commonwealth countries, she was our expert and she outlived all the idiots who caused the wars in the first place, money you see, it's always about the money."

"She looked around at the morons who ran her government, arguments here and national strikes there, communism reared its head in the UK, spies were upturned in high places, they were old school ho ha Henry's, who should have known better but they betrayed the Nation to the Russians, she was livid, she kicked the odd potted plants for six until she came up with the plan, she needed talent on her side against fools and pigs in the trough of the Nation and yes murder was needed sometimes, fools will not be put off by our soft laws, in the end a fool has to get the lead between the eyes, there is no other way, one cannot deal or trade with them, so then they are slipped into the red file and passed onto the department that does not exist and the problem is dealt with in the old way, an accident, a fight or he just gets run over, all very sad but life and more importantly the Nation carries on!"

Sid stood up and applauded his speech, "Well done Jock, we knew you could do it and beside don't your family run it all now?"

"You are really starting to get on my tits Dingo!" growled Dexter, "Ok, let's hear all of your dirty secrets people, one by one for the King to know who we are please."

He turned to the Australian, "Starting with you dingo!"

Sid gave him the toothy grin right back at him, "Me? I'm an Army officer from New South Wales who was accused of murder by my senior officers, they slammed me up for 30 years, but I was recruited to work for the southern command now under southern SAS, eventually some turd sent me here to argue for the peninsula."

"Subtle Dingo shit!" said Dexter, "So did you kill him?"

"Yeah of course I did, two in the head did the biz, but the Army didn't like the idea, that's it really, so over to you Dexter, what's yours?"

Sid nodded to him in silence and waited.

Dexter breathed in before letting it all out, "Special ops on so many wars, eventually I flipped and killed all the prisoners because the Yanks hadn't stripped um of weaponry and one of my kids was cut in half by those bags of shit,"

"A fucking legend Gentlemen, no question of that," said Jon Boy, "That man saved me and my boys when we were silly little virgins running around like boy scouts, thank you Dexter, we owe you, our lives."

Dexter nodded at him to continue.

"Err.........me.......err...ex-President as you all know but before that I was the National security adviser to the President and before that I was Marine." he smiled at them.

"Honesty JB, we want to know why HM called you to this position." said Dexter.

"I also worked for Helen, I executed people on her orders, some good some bad, I just pulled the trigger man! and later as the Presidents man I killed all who threatened our great Nation.

"And you, son in law!" he stared at Erick who was biting his thumb nail.

"Err......a Canadian first Nation Nationalist working for the Canadian mounted police, I was seconded to the UK and worked in the nonexistent section, I was and still am in fact the Special branch liaison officer for all of the departments, I'm the one face system for the voting public as Helen called it."

"All of it Erick," said Dexter, "They need to hear it, son."

"I married Caledonia, Dexter's Daughter and helped her in all of her actions, including the Las Vegas killing of six bad guys and many more."

"Erick, we in this Kings Privy Council commission need to know each other's darkest secrets, this is about trust son!" said Dexter.

"I worked for Helen, the scariest Mother-in-Law on the planet and didn't regret one day of it all, she and QE2 were best of friends and planned our world behind our backs, that's the problem here lads, she's dead and we're scared of what's to come, mummy has left the building and we're all in the shit!"

"Mummy was not a killer!" said King Charles.

Miami smiled at him, "But Sire there are rumors that she had your ex-wife snuffed."

"That's the press spreading lies as per bloody usual, Diana was bonkers but her only sin was here choice of friends who got her killed in a stupid accident pursued by rabid press agents, that's it!"

The faces stared at him around the table.

"I did not order her killed, she died of stupidity, you all know that!"

"We just had to hear it from your mouth Sire that's all," said Miami.

"And the Gurkha?" asked Dexter.

Miami laughed at him, "You're fucking bonkers Dexter and I love you for it, I've followed you all over the world, speaking your language and supporting our Monarch always, I thank you for your action in my homeland when you prevented a war with China, my Nation holds you in high status, err.... yes, I've taken heads, hey, but I'm not the only headhunter around this table."

Lord Carnarvon stopped listening as the faces of the Commission faced him.

"Err...sorry Gentlemen, so you want to know about me and Lord Halifax, eh?"

"Well Quentin, give us the story old boy," he laughed as he looked down the table to Lord Halifax.

"I started a little war, nothing really," said lord Halifax.

"East Africa went up in flames Quentin come on, out with it!"

"I'm not racist in any way but when a man has farmed his land over a lifetime and sweated over every tree root or tsetse swamp drainage, I was not going to let the blacks have it so I armed my people and we fought back, the British Government stood back and let us die one by one so I got really mad and killed hundreds of them, eventually I got a phone call from Helen with a command to come to the Palace, I came back to the UK and I sat here in this very chair and I swear to you Brethren the Queen sat there and said, "Quentin, you're and arse hole, you're now working for me, so sit over there and shut the fuck up, until asked a question, understand?"

They all started laughing at his words.

"Straight up, they were her words, she had a way of being very direct sometimes, Talbot sat over there simmering as he always did, he always had her ear and she always took his advice even if it meant a snuff list, she would just wave and say, just get it done and let's move on!"

Charles gasped at the revolution of his mother's other life.

"The reality Charles!" said Lord Carnarvon, "Scumbags bit the dust at her command, one cannot argue or deal with bullies you smack them down or you allow them to smack you, get it?"

"Our System is Crap!" said Sid, "But it's all we have, and we had best look after it or we'll end up in a civil war to end all wars."

Dexter started to laugh at the Australian, "You must have been in his class then Dingo?"

Sid smiled at him, "Sandhurst class of 98, the old bloke was a ledge mate!" he stared at Dexter for the unanswered question.

"No Sid, he's gone for good mate, he just walked into the cold black ocean."

"No?"

"Yep, as I live and breathe, our greatest loss that I know of."

The table became silent before Dexter looked at Lord Carnarvon again.

He smiled, "Err........I worked for Helen, and yes I did kill a few scum bags, but she said that I was too soft and that my shooting was useless and yes she binned me, I retired and was happy on my farm minding my own business when a gang of Gypsies broke in and burgled me, I pursued of course and I killed them all, cold blood, foaming at the mouth the lot, I rang the Dragon, she took care of it all and then said that I should attend the Queen, Her Majesty said, Shut the fuck up and sit over there! and I've been with her ever since, any questions?"

They all started laughing at him again.

Charles watched them in silence knowing that from his mother's dying lips he was told that he should trust the Privy council with the lives of all just men and women.

So, it's all in the boxes of State then?" asked Charles.

Lord Carnarvon turned to him again and smiled, "Red Boxes Sire are for State affairs as you know the black leather brief case however is for other works."

"Other very secret works then Carnarvon?"

"Not to be spoken of outside this council Sire, we will advise, and you will sign if and when you are ready, we prompt but yours is the final answer!"

"So, I can say no to deaths if I want?"

"Of course, Sire, you are the boss we are just the machine to work it all out, the experience of all so to speak."

"So, I could just dissolve this meeting and not reconvene it anytime soon, yes?"

Lord Carnarvon smiled and shrugged, "I suppose so Sire, it's up to you to take the reins."

"Good then I close this meeting Gentlemen and I will call you when needed."

"My God!" said Jon Boy, "It's King George all over again losing America for the second time, you're right Dingo, he's a bollock brain!"

"How dare you speak to me like that, get out!"

Jon Boy stood up as Erick also stood up to walk out.

"Sit bastard down you pair!" shouted Dexter, he turned to the King, "Listen up arsehole this is not about you being King and us being mad men, it's about protecting the Nation, your mother dedicated her life to this mission and so must you!"

"Or what Colonel, who's really dead but shows up at the palace now and again, like a phantom, or will I have a tragic accident perhaps."

"I will kill you myself! The United Kingdom's needs are greater than us Sir!"

The place became silent as Dexter's words were digested, "This is too important to be left to a foolish hippy King who thinks that roses grow out of our foreign policy makers arses, they don't most of the time they are self-serving arseholes who need a kick up that arse, get it?"

"And I thought that I was the blunt one?" said Sid.

Lord Carnarvon looked at the red-faced King, "Just like your name's sake back in the 1660's you don't have a choice Sire, that's the reality, it will be forced on us all just like it always was and always will be."

King Charles gaped open mouthed at them, then pointed to Dexter to carry on.

Dexter turned back to the table, "Right, before tea and arguments we have more table business to conclude, now Lord Halifax over there has invited more councilors to join our happy band, ok Quentin, over to you chap."

Lord Halifax was on his phone, "Send them up please, have they been briefed, oh good girl, tea for ten when you're ready then Darling."

The great oak paneled door squeaked open as Elizabeth and Margaret walked in.

"High ya chaps, how's it all hanging?" said Liz.

Margaret stared and bore holes into their heads with her stare.

Lord Halifax smiled at the shocked faces around the table, "Gender rules and all those gentlemen, women are half the population after all, we need the law on our side as in Lord chief Justice Baroness McDonald or Mrs. Smith to help with foreign policy terminations."

Liz winked at Dexter, he jumped up and scraped the chair away from the table for Liz to sit down opposite him and Erick.

Sid did the same for Margaret, she grunted a little thanks.

"Don't mention it darling." he laughed.

"You say that one more time and I'll break your nose with this chairs leg as I smash it over your head."

Sid fell silent as Dexter laughed at him.

Charles nodded to the two women, both tried to bow to his direction.

"Calm Ladies and welcome to the first meeting of the new Kings privy council, we seek your advice on your various expertise and also opinions on all that we say and sign off."

"So, who are we killing first then?" asked Liz before she started to laugh.

"No one at the moment Ladies and under my direction we will be killing no one."

said King Charles.

Liz looked at Dexter for a silent opinion, he raised his eyebrows.

"This is illegal by the way," said Margaret.

"Says who?" asked Sid.

"Un elected quango's making decisions for an unsuspecting Nation, totally illegal on all fronts."

"So, are you out Mags?" asked Dexter.

"Certainly not, I want to be part of this particular quango, one never knows when one is in danger does one?"

"A proper slippery arse then that one, eh?" said Sid.

"And a very short fuse Mr. Australian cultural attaché!" laughed Dexter.

"Can we get some work done please?" said Lord Carnarvon, "Now Elizabeth has she received the commission?"

Liz blew out her cheeks, "Our Grandson Tolly has organized a classic kill zone operation for his mother to compete the job, but I suspect that when Caledonia reaches Mexico City, she will change all that."

"A kill zone?" asked the King.

Liz looked at Dexter.

"Sir, there is a plan rolling to eliminate unwanted interference with the democratic rights of the Mexican Nation, the scumbags who prop up the old regime are about to be put down, any objections on the table?"

"Yes!" said Charles "I object to this random killing."

Liz stared at Dexter again, her eyes asked the question.

"Ok, that's one objection, any others?" asked Dexter.

"Who?" asked Sid.

Dex took out his little red book, "Err.... Enrique Marcos, he's part of the Luis Flores cartel in Mexico City, Jon Boys idea by the way."

"Not just mine here folks," said Jon Boy, "The President requires a favor from your experts, our intelligence experts say that he's influenced the Presidency for years and they are bought and paid for, he feels that we can make no progress with the overall plan with that man still alive."

"But we take the risks though?" said Elizabeth.

"He sanctions a full back up if she requires it Liz, the works."

"So, Seal team 5 and 6 then?" said Dexter.

"Err.......no, we can't be seen to be involved in all this, in fact this is proof that their system stinks, we can then react to other gangs trying to take control of the drug business."

"And take it yourself?" said Sid.

Dexter pointed at him, "Zip it, Skippy!"

"This has to be done for all our safety folks, they are all killers," said Jon Boy.

"And my daughter has to go in and kill them?"

"She's very good at this sort of thing Elizabeth?" said Lord Carnarvon.

"And we all know that she's a Russian Spetsnaz colonel by now, "Said Lord Halifax, the press are waiting for the juicy breach in our department briefings."

"The whispering gallery Liz," said Dexter, he nodded to Lord Halifax.

"So that's how you're going to sell it then, a drugs war, with Russian mobsters moving in on the poor Mexicans?"

Jon Boy smiled at her, "I hear that the Cockneys are also on route, true or false?"

"Tolly has finally agreed to let Lord Longmore and Lord Wimbledon go and help in supplies and local recruitment."

Jon Boy burst out laughing at her.

"What?" said Liz.

"George! Lord Wimbledon, has the world gone mad?"

"On their passports Liz?" asked Dexter.

"Yes, why not, Lords of the Realm on holiday with wives and friends."

"Adrian then?" he started to laugh again.

"And Yoshi is carrying their baggage."

"Good girl Liz, I like that one." said Dexter.

She ignored his laughing, "The full complement of photographic technicians and models are on their way to a photo shoot in the roughest part of Mexico City, so wish them all bloody good luck please!"

"Bloody good luck!" said King Charles.

"This will start the war then?" said Miami.

The room became silent as his words sank in.

"No!" said Jon Boy, "This has been long overdue, this will be the first salvo of freedom for the Mexican Nation we are going to offer them freedom through the Statehood system, finance and political advice."

"Like good interfering neighbors should, eh?" said Sid.

"An objection then Dingo?" asked Dexter.

"Oh no, no, kill the bastard and all his mates if you can, after all its just a drugs war, the problem however is this, where the hell did these Russians come from and why? who sent them, get the picture? These people are not as dumb as they look."

"Their Politico's will want an angle to work the people, outside interference will be the key I would have thought, it'll blow you yanks out of the water mate!"

"If we take hits that is eh, that's what you're saying right?" said Dexter.

"Bad all-round mate, Brits found to be in the drugs trade, it'll trail all the way back to this bloody table mate!"

Dexter looked at Liz in silence as the room digested the problems.

"But they're Irish," said Miami.

"And they'll think that your little Ruski mate wants to invest in Mexico then, Spetsnaz and the Irish, plus Lords of the Realm, come on we need more planning on this little caper people!" said Sid.

"He's a proper smart arse isn't he, and Australian at that?" said Margaret.

"So, who's in on the planning Elizabeth?" asked Dexter.

"Tolly, who else?"

"And his mother Liz, and is she ready for all this?"

"Come on Dexter you know what she's like, it'll be a blood bath the very same as usual, the only thing we have on our side is complete surprise and she'll make that count I think."

"An all women crew though Liz?" asked Margaret.

"Her choice, not mine and not Tolly's I'm sure of that."

"Her way or the highway then Liz?" asked Dexter.

"Same as big boy same as," she stared into his glare, "Look the old man trusted her to do things like this, he trained her from the age of nine years old, we just have to put our tin hats on and wait for good or bad news, right?"

"Right!" said the King, "Let's have some tea and cakes to warm us all up from the cold thoughts and plans of this place, eh?"

The faces turned to him and smiled at his innocence of the black world.

"God save the King!" said Sid then started laughing.

"Am I missing something here?" asked King Charles

"Just experience Sire," said Lord Carnarvon, "Your Mother was so ahead of us it was unreal, she had top advisers, the best in some ways, we are limited to the people here I'm afraid, we are always looking for fresh talent, after all without talent we will all crumble into dust as our enemies tread us into the dirt."

"Now that's a bit dramatic Lord Carnarvon, "said Charles, he looked around the faces and realized that these people all believed what he had just said to be true.

"So, explain please Carnarvon," Asked Charles, "You make me feel like I'm at my first day of the new school, with rules and reg's etc."

"Well Dexter and his wife cover the far east, China in particular, Colonel Sidney Ashton covers the Australian and all the islands down there, obviously General Wilson covers the greater USA and now the southern continent, the Americans are trying to solve very old problems with their neighbors, and of course Inspector Youngblood is Canada and the North arctic circle, we could stretch that to the Pacific ocean and the Japanese islands, he's a native speaker I'm told," Erick nodded to him in silence.

"Colonel Sing covers the Indian sub-continent, including the high Himalayan mountains and river flows, obviously protecting agriculture of the India delta regions and billions of people."

"We now come to your job Sire, Europe and the continental land mass, France and Germany in particular, together with Italy and the Balkans."

"And you Carnarvon, what's your job?"

"You Sire, your unofficial voice to all of them, nothing is written down, all through me please, that's both ways everyone, all clear?"

"And Russia?" asked Liz.

"Err........Lord Halifax has that covered but hasn't had time to call our newest members of the council."

Liz started to laugh, "You're risking getting Theodore Smirnoff into this game?"

"He's English Ma-am as far as we know and loyal to the crown, yes?"

"Yes, he is, on second thoughts you are very correct in asking him, if you can find him that is?"

"Err....... yes Ma-am he's out of the country at the moment."

"Any clues Dexter?" she asked.

Dex looked at them as he thought about it all, "A good call I think Lord Halifax, I would throw in another name into the hat as well."

Lord Halifax waited patiently for Dex to finish his idea.

"Patrick Collins," said Dexter.

"That slippery little shit!" said Margaret.

"Any better than him Mag's?" said Dexter.

She grinned at him, "No, none more slippery and none better than him, the courts will hate him even being here, he'll have the fear factor that's for sure, they all pray he stays in America, he always means trouble."

"Agreed then Lord Halifax, I like him already, "said Lord Carnarvon, "Any idea where these people are?"

"I'll do it Gentlemen," said Liz "I think I know where they are, ok with everyone?"

"Is this the zillionaire kid?" asked Sid "Perhaps a small loan?"

"You're getting on my tits yet again Dingo shit!" Said Dexter.

"Any time you like haggis, you seem a bit of a puffter really mate."

"Leave it Dexter!" shouted Liz "If there's any stomping to be done then I'm doing it."

"Keep your knickers on Elizabeth, just friendly banter to old mate's darling."

"Hit him, Elizabeth!" said Margaret.

"Tea and cakes then people!" said the King, we'll have a stroll in the gardens, eh? maybe cool down and wind down from all this stress."

# CHAPTER 4 ... Fort Lapin ... French Guiana ... South American Jungle

Augusta stood with her city umbrella over her head, waiting at the gates of the fort, the rain sleeted down on them in unrelenting torrents.

"Couldn't we just wait inside Gussy," asked Mack, he looked like a drowned rat as he mumbled on and on.

"Please close the facial orifice Uncle, you're becoming boring understood?"

"Am I Gussy, sorry darling, I do go on a bit, don't I?"

"So, is he signed off now then?"

"As far as I know Gussy, yes, he's done his tour, and he can now sign up again for the next 7 years or quit with honors at completing the parachute course and the jungle Warfare picnic."

"Picnic?"

"Well eating snakes and climbing trees and all that."

"And that's easy?"

"A joke Augusta, that's all!"

"Not funny Uncle, that's all!"

They could suddenly feel the rumble under foot of the troop transporters rumbling along the rutted road to the fort, she walked out into the middle of the road to stop the traffic.

"Gussy they'll run you over darling!" he shouted.

"And my mother would kill them all when she comes back Uncle, explain that to these morons could you please."

The transporters came over the rise of the hill, its lights flashed a warning to her to get out of the way, but she stood firm, they gave in and slowly braked on the mud to a slippery stop, the suspension squeaked as it bounced to a final stop.

"Out!" she screamed at the driver, he turned to Mack who was now standing next to her, he thumbed to him to empty out the Legionaries for her inspection.

"Rapidmon!" he screeched at him, the rain was still howling down on everyone, then from out of the rear tail gate the legionaries filed out and lined up at the side of the road, they were all unrecognizable with the mud that covered them from head to toe, she could only see their white teeth as they grinned at her.

She walked up and down as if she were a general inspecting his troops, "Simon! where the hell are you?" she shouted at the top of her voice.

The men started to laugh, then one of them thumbed to the second transporter just coming to a halt at the back of the first.

She halted it and pointed for them all to get out, the tail gate quickly lifted, and Simon stepped out to greet her, he was tip to toe mud, he grinned at her, but she still hugged him, she just didn't care anymore.

Mack was now on the phone, "Yes Eden, she's found him, so come on in for the pick-up."

"Roger that uncle," said Eden.

"And stop taking the piss arse hole!"

As the second transporter emptied the men lined up at the side of the road, Augusta took out a paper hanky out of her pocket and wiped Simons lips, then when she gave him a kiss the place erupted in cheering and howling.

Mack walked over to the clean looking sergeant chef in charge and placed his hand flat before him, "The signed release paper please Chef?"

The man shook his head.

"Listen, sign his release paper now or she'll call in a fucking air strike, you got me in there, sonny boy?"

Some of the legionaries understood what he had just said and translated to the Chef, he burst out laughing at him before poking his head back into the truck for his booklet, he returned with the little piece of paper that was the release with honors paper, Mack took it off him and read it, then handed it back to him.

"Hey! sign the fucking thing, buddy!"

The Chef solemnly took off his kepi and removed the pen from the inside then used the hat as a flat board, he signed the paper then waited for Simon to turn to him before handing it over with a broad grin.

Simon gave the Chef a hug of thanks and the three kisses' just as the helicopter came out of the rain clouds and blasted everyone with more compressed water.

On landing Glen and Jonesy started throwing out boxes of Walkers crisps and packs of beer for all the lads, Eden kept the rotors moving as he waited for the lift off and Mack's signal to go.

"Just cheese and onion?" shouted Mack, "What the hell Jonesy?"

"Yeah boss," said Jonesy, "World's number one crisp, walkers' cheese and onion, what, wrong?"

"Ten fucking boxes of um?"

"Education boss!"

"And Newcastle brown ale xxx, ten fucking double crates?"

"Again boss, a bit of education."

"They'll be pissed as farts after just one can."

"Bless um eh boss!"

"How much?"

"Err....... special order boss!"

Mack tried to grab hold of him, but Jonesy reversed into the chopper as he giggled.

Simon was dragged on by Augusta and Mack was the last to step into the warm and dry helicopter, by this time the place was in total chaos, the Legionaries were already drinking the beer and eating the strange crisps as they danced around the English city umbrella.

"You see boss, they like um, you see, you can never underestimate the French, you just never know, eh?"

Mack gave Eden the thumb to go and the helicopter rose slowly and was gone, the party had by now fully started in all the mud and rain, no one cared in fact, they danced in the rain to imagined music and a hip-hop beat.

Augusta held Simon's hand as Mack shouted at Jonesy and Gurung, Glen was gone back into the pilot's cock pit with Eden, well out of the way.

"Well, what do I do now Gussy?" asked Simon.

She was squeezing his pecks and his arm muscles, grinning from ear to ear.

You can protect me as I work, because mummy is about to start a war, clear?"

"What?"

"And I have to cover it for the Americans."

"What?"

As he grinned at her the mud started to flake off drying in the warmth, "Can I go back now?"

"No, you're my special protection, my bodyguard."

"I can guard your body?"

"Yes! All night long!"

Mack stopped from trying to kill Jonesy to watch the happy couple, "Bless, eh?"

"Yeah!" said Jonesy, he started laughing again, but by now Mack just didn't have the energy to kill him, instead he watched the happy couple coo to each other oblivious to anyone else being there.

Gurung passed out a spare can of Newcastle extra strong beer he'd dropped in the helicopter to Jonesy.

"You know I makes sense mate, don't you?" said Jonesy, he pulled the ring, and it exploded over his face.

Gurung bent over laughing, some of it splashed over Augusta and Simon, they didn't notice.

Jonesy gave him the first swig as he laughed, Mack was now asleep and snoring his head off on the back seats, almost dry at last.

# CHAPTER 5 ... Aero Puerto Internecinal de la Ciudad de Mexico

Adrian shouted till he was horse at the girls in the airport terminal, "Leave the bastard bags, that's what blokes are for darling, just carry those tits as high as possible and wiggled that blubber for the watchers, come on move it, move it.

Adrian was in his most flamboyant mood, he scowled at the security man then hooked up with his secretary Russell.

"Isn't it marvelous to be working again Russell, who are we working for again?"

"Green Space Tropical magazine Addy."

"And who the hell are they?"

"It's their space flyer, they want pictures of the slums with the girls, tits and graffiti boss."

"Bastard perverts then?"

"No, that's you, boss!"

Adrian squealed out in laughter as he chased Russell through to the baggage lounge.

"Hold up Russell," said Addy, he watched George pick up his bags from the carousel and curtsied in front of him, "Sorry my lord I didn't see you there."

George said nothing to him as he walked off.

"Papers et Passport Signor?" said the man in uniform in front of him.

Addy followed the blue sleeve up to the face of the security man, then started laughing.

"Fuck off Lord Longmore, you're taking the piss or what?"

The faced change color as it got angry, and Addy thought that his mistaken identity would get him killed until the face cracked into a smile."

"Bastard Rufus, you had me dead there, you bastard!"

Rufus Longmore walked off giggling at the shaken Adrian, his wife Kiki pushed the buggy with their cases.

The big Japanese man stopped the traffic of passengers as he stood in the customs cubicle, the security people surrounded him ready for trouble.

He tried his best to smile but that just made things worse, he was not a natural smiley, and his pointy teeth made him look like a fat vampire searching for blood.

Rufus walked over to them and showed them his card, suddenly the place became calm as the officials departed back to their normal jobs.

Joshi nodded his thanks but said nothing.

"How the hell did he do that George?" asked Brenda.

George looked over his shoulder as Rufus strutted off, "He's such a flash git Bren, it's one of his little disguises, he's the city drugs inspector, it shuts them up big time, they never want to be involved in the drugs people, he's playing on their fears, they'll stay away from all of us now, they all think that this is a drug import company on the road, understood?"

"Shit!" said Brenda, "But what if they'd called in the real drug squad?"

George gave her the razed eyebrows before starting to laugh.

"They're shit scared of them all?" she said.

George stared at her, "Because?"

"They are, the drug importers?" she finished off her thought, "Shit, a thin line though George?"

"That's him Bren, Mr. Thin line on the road, just don't let the little bastard drive anything because he'll kill us all with this lot over here."

She took his hand and wrapped it around hers, "To the beach then?"

"Err......just half a day in the office darling, then we can get some sun on our backs."

As he was talking, she absent mindedly watched a gaggle of British Airways stewardesses pass by pulling their overnight bags behind them, she watched their attractive legs then recognized a scar that she had inflicted with a screwdriver when she threw it at her sister, "Megan!" she screeched out.

George smiled at her, and she then knew it wasn't a holiday freebee, it was work, she grabbed his hand and squeezed her nails into his palm.

"So!" she whispered, "The only reason that you wouldn't tell me about the job is, because it scared you shitless or, Caledonia is working with my sisters."

"Both Bren, it's an execution combo."

She stopped and punched him hard in the arm, "You are a lying swine!"

He pulled her close and whispered in her ear, "I'm out as you know but your sisters are not, they wanted this and here they are doing it, so take this argument up with them when you get the chance Brenda, I'm supply only as per bloody usual, she requested it because this is a big bastard, get it?"

"So, what the hell does that mean?"

"It means Brenda that I have to go shopping for weaponry at the local stores, are you with me?"

"You are a lying piece of shit George, you wanted this, you were bored stiff out of your scull, so you applied for this?"

"Look ask action man and hear what he has to say?"

"And what's his roll then?"

"A watcher and close support."

"And who's close supporting the moron then?" she looked at him face to face.

"Kiki, who else?"

"You are you lying bastard, we were out of all this, we had done with all the deaths, we were free you sack of shit!"

"Support Brenda!"

"I'll give the silly cows support when I catch up with them and your darling ambidextrous killer as well!"

"Don't start woman, yes, or no? I can do this on my own, look I'll put you in a nice condominium and you can get some Mexican sun if you like,"

She punched him again even harder.

"Oh no! I'm your over watch, if they try it on, I'll kill all the little Mexican bandits all together or one at a time, get me monkey chops?"

He linked arms with her and smiled, "Well let's go and find you a nice AK for your comfort."

"Heckler's you moron, I don't want stoppages when I start."

"You sound like the old woman Bren."

"One thing I learned from her was how to shoot straight and how to distrust men."

"That's two dear."

She punched him again and liked it as he started to laugh at her.

"I just can't hurt you as much as I'd like to George."

"If you weren't here that that would hurt Bren, that's for sure."

"Oh, don't start on me Monkey man, you're going to get such a slap when we get to the hotel."

He laughed again at her, "I love that about you Bren, no holding back on the punishment, I love it!"

Adrian and his entourage had arrived at the taxi rank and were causing chaos as usual.

"I'm not getting into that smelly bastard car Russell, get me a Limo, now!"

Russell rushed off to the car hire signs, the staff rumbled through with expensive camera equipment and looked at Adrian.

Adrian focused on the crew, "Who the fuck are you lot?"

Tolly grinned at him, "The union sent us boss!"

"Oh, for fuck's sake," squeaked Adrian.

A long black coach pulled up at the side of them and the lads started loading the equipment into the luggage compartment as the side loading door was unlocked.

Adrian gapped as he watched them.

"Who the fuck ordered this bastard, how bastard much is this costing me?"

"Cheaper boss if we all club together," said Tolly.

"And who the fuck are you?"

"Just a half breed Indian trying to make a living boss."

"I'm sure I've seen you before, did we do winter wear together in Siberia?"

The lads were laughing at Addy and Tolly's embarrassed face made it even funnier.

"I get it now," shouted Addy, "You're from Green Shit, you're here to make the program acceptable to all the perverts, you want tits and silverware?"

"No boss!" shouted Billy, "He's from the TUC, he's our union rep so mind you P's and Q's boss or he'll shut us down."

"Oh, for fuck's sake.............Russell, forget that bastard limo and get on the bastard bus!"

# CHAPTER 6 ... The Safe House ... Mexico City ... CIA ... HQ

The Dude was watching the action on the cctv from the airport lounge area, he flicked screens as he chomped the big mac, he flicked through them all and back again, he watched Adrian throwing a hissy fit at his assistant and was laughing as he ate, then stopped dead as he caught sight of the film crew, he dropped the burger on the floor and nearly fell off his swivel chair, he wiped his greasy hand on his T shirt and pressed recall on his cell phone.

"JJ, you'll never guess who's just landed in the city."

"Who?"

"Tolly, from London town, and a full contact team, he's in the mood boy, better get down here, I smell trouble man."

"But why?"

"Well, you're the guy who should know man."

"Ah! So, moms in town then?"

"What does that mean?"

"He's doing an over cover, who else is there?"

"Err.... I was just doing a recap on today's filming I'll get back to you JJ."

"Look for George and Lord Longmore in the crowd Dude, then put a tail on him please, I think that you know those guys, yes?"

"They were with the SAS people JJ when I was over there, what do you want me to say?"

"Spot and stick to them Dude because he's dangerous as you know."

"How did you know he would be here JJ?"

49

"We planned this one Dude and Tolly's brought his premier league team, so keep your head down man we don't need to be involved with any of this."

"But JJ what the fucks going on man?"

"Just record and stay out of their way Dude."

"Does your daddy know about all this?"

"We pulled in a favor JJ, that's it."

"Shit!"

The phone was no dead as he searched the various screens in search of the hairy one, he spotted Brenda punching George in the baggage lounge and followed them out into the taxi ranks, he kicked the old burger away from his feet as he searched for more of them.

"My God, the Army have arrived," he quickly punched in Jon Boys number and waited for the pick-up.

While he was waiting, he flicked to his favorite pastime of looking at the stewardesses as they came through the exit lounge, "Nice legs girls......British Airways, I love it, three red heads, a brunet and a blond........................ Oh, shit! "

The recognition of her made him stand up in a panic, "Come on Jon Boy pick the fuck up man!"

# CHAPTER 7 ... Airport workers lounge area ... Rest Room ... Mexico.

Caledonia looked at them very closely the eye makeup, the nails the shoes and the stance, "Ok, arrogance and the fuck off stare, yes?"

"Yes boss," said Ruth.

"You're my back up woman, you had better be as good as you think, or they'll kill me clear?"

Ruth nodded and tried to be coolness personified, "Kit?"

"In the minibus, we saddle up and go straight to the venue, ok twins, make them look at you pair all the time, flash the tits, if need be, just do it, Megan, the corridors, no one in or out, kill anyone in your sights yes?"

Megan gulped in surprise, "But I thought?"

"Corridors we need a clean exit and that's you, clear?"

"And you, boss?" asked Ruth.

"Point woman, I'm the forward thrust, just make sure that no one comes out of a side door, if they do you down them clear?"

"Clear Ma-am!"

Cal smiled at her, "Ok here we go girls, we can do this, tighten up the bra straps and follow me, the Americans say that they have an exit for us but I'm not sure."

"But why all the troops?" asked Megan.

"Side action focus to give us breathing space, it's a crowded city after all."

"Who's the driver Ma-am?" asked Ruth.

"Marvelous Marvin's on site, he delivers us then he disappears like normal, if it goes tits up and we're rattled then re group in two hours here, we lick out wounds then go again."

"Again?" said Ruth.

Cal turned her predatory eyes on her, "We never give in on a job, if we fail the first time we go again until he's dust, get it?"

"Fucking bollocks!" said Ruth.

Cal gave them the final check over then marched out and into the passenger lounge area, the girls followed and kept to her fast stride not looking at anyone or anything.

The girls now fully understood that the job was going to happen, and no failures would be allowed.

Kathleen saw Brenda as she punched George, but she said nothing as they passed her.

Cal focused on the minibus and quickly tapped on the windscreen for Marvin to open up, she was surprised to find Diana sitting there waiting for them to get in, the seats had been reversed so that she could talk to them.

Marvin drove off and put his foot down and quickly moved into the traffic.

"Welcome ladies!" said Diana, "I have the specific equipment you required, they're under your seats.

She watched closely as the women took out the equipment and put them on, Cal didn't say a word until she had a confirmation nod from Marvin in the driver's seat.

"All good stuff Cal," he said, "Just as you asked for, but I added some body armor, you have the very latest Dragon skin, close tailored for women by the way, Kevlar and overlapping ceramic plates, good?"

Cal stared at the boxes, "Too heavy, we don't want to look like sumo wrestlers."

He locked eyes with her in the mirror, "Do as your bloody told for a change woman, strip off and replace your cloths with all the gear, inside thy holsters for all of you and little Walther PP10's for personal security, use it if needed, back up!"

Cal opened all the boxes and stared.

"Heckler G36's Cal, brand new," he said.

She bore a hole in his head as she stared.

"Yes, cleaned checked and ready to go, don't worry."

Diana watched as the ladies stripped down to their underwear and started putting on the kit.

Cal started to smile as she fastened up her body armor, then the double gun harnesses.

Marvin grinned her in the mirror, "Better?"

"Yes Marvelous, much better, are you in touch with them all?"

"Do you want me to be Cal?"

She stared at him for a short thinking time as she licked the ammunition shells one by one, then shook her head at him.

"What the hell?" said Ruth.

"She's checking the factory wax girls, "Said Marvin, "You cannot afford duds in close action, look listen and bloody learn quick, when she rolls, you lot had better be up for this because your brains will boil as you see her really working Pop's teachings in one woman, look at everything she does girls and follow, yes?"

The girls mumbled.

"Yes?" he screamed at them.

"Yes!" they screamed back at him.

Cal was in her own world as she set up her gear, "Use your breasts to jam the harness under your arm pits, then slacken to allow them to sag so you can hold your arms as normal," said Cal, "The Thy holster, if you're right handed then strap it to you left leg and attach it to your belt loop with the loose cable or it'll fall off and be very embarrassing.

Ruth tried to be as cool as everyone, but her hands were shaking with nerves, she stared at them as they trembled.

Diana handed her some chewing gum, "Airwaves, they help you breathe, more air in the lungs is good, yes?"

Cal took a few out then pocketed the rest of the packet, she started to chew and snort as she breathed in and out.

The girls followed her example.

Cal focused on the twins, "Remember Kerry and Kathleen, you are there to get us through the doors then back off and return to the bus as quick as you can, do not get drawn in or mixed up with any man, understood?"

"And if anyone messes with you then shoot the bastard," said Ruth.

Cal held her arm up and Ruth could see her hands shaking with nerves, "All perfectly normal, good in fact, otherwise we'd be machines or psycho's."

"But I thought that you were!" said Ruth.

Cal ignored her barb and watched her attach her under arm harness, "Slacken a little, you have to breath woman or you'll fall over, oh! and remember, none of us is getting body searched, they can fuck off if they try all that purvey stuff, that's down to you Megan, give them the verbal's, Ruth and me will offer nothing but death, got that? it might have to be on the door step if they want it that bad."

"Let the Heckler dandle from your armpit sling, put your hand in that pocket, no one goes near you, give em the elbow if they do, got that, it must be hidden at all times, one sniff of a machine gun and it'll get very hairy, clear?"

Diana sat and watched them as they re- dressed and checked the look, she pushed and tugged various articles of clothing and the new overcoats, "Yes good!"

Marvin looked at them in the mirror, "Good to go everyone?"

Cal looked around for nods, "Yes?" she smiled at them all "Fucking tarts!"

"Fucking tarts!" shouted the girls in unison.

Cal passed Ruth a little box.

"Ooooh a prezzy?" she opened it and stared at the brass knuckled duster, then looked at her.

"My Grandmothers favorite little surprise, hit them hard, jaw or lower rib, we have to get into this place clear?"

"You are fucking bonkers!"

"Fecking bonkers!" shouted the girls.

Marvin started to slow the bus down to the inside lane, "The clubs coming up Ladies, now, last chance, do you need me in there, extra firepower perhaps?"

Diana turned to him," They do not want a fart in their way idiot, shut the fuck up!"

"Shut the fuck up!" shouted the girls as they giggled.

Diana held up the picture of the target and his associates, "All who needed lead in their ears girls, one job, one need and one Nation, this is to set Mexico free!"

Cal stared at Marvin in the driver's seat as he flicked his eyes from them to the road and back again, she realized that this whole thing was his idea, his plan and that Pop had probably primed him to do this."

"Pop's plan then Marvelous?"

He turned his eyes to her and winked, "We'll never be at peace with these scum Cal, his words not mine girl."

"Thanks Uncle Marvin, that's all I needed, I now know that it'll all work out fine, but what about all the dust?"

"We'll handle that Cal. everyone will panic at first especially with the others."

"What others?"

"The other take downs Cal."

She stared for a few seconds, "So he wanted to start a civil war between clans?"

"Bang on that woman!"

She laughed as she listened the Pops familiar phrase, "That old man Marvelous?"

"Yes Caledonia, that old man!"

"And you must have the Presidents ear then?" she winked at him.

He gave her the toothy grin in the mirror, "A message from Erick, do not take risks woman!"

She laughed at him and that made them all relaxed a little from the tension.

# CHAPTER 8 ... Green Peace Ship Nimrod 3 ...The Azores ... Atlantic Ocean

Dexter was on deck breathing the salt air and feeling good, Elizabeth watched him for health issues, she hoped he wouldn't start coughing again.

"Well?" she asked.

"Better Lilly, it's good to be away from all the trouble."

"What trouble?"

"London dear, didn't you see the signs?"

"What bloody signs are you on about numb nuts?"

"Being used Elizabeth, it's not good for us, is it?"

"You're talking Tolly again then?"

She looked at his ear as he stared out to sea, "Come on Hamish, let's have what we're about to receive, you've obviously been thinking."

"Rebellion in the ranks Liz, and us being used again, it won't go down well with the troops."

"You've been talking to someone, well who's given you his opinion then?"

He turned to her, "Thomas isn't sure that this will work, stooges on the road he calls it, they're pushing the situation and not waiting for natural timings, and anyway, what was Pops opinion on contacts, never start a war!"

"But he was always starting wars, it was his way of bringing them out into the open Dexter!"

"But not this way Liz! Tolly sending his mother out on a foreign job like this?"

She waited for him to look out to sea again before she asked quietly, "Caledonia?"

"Yep, exposed again and for why?" he turned and looked into her eyes, "And who would want that?"

"So, who and why Dex?"

"Well Pop always wanted her out, he never succeeded though did he Elizabeth, she was always there in the background, why?"

"Because she liked the work Dex, no other reason, she's a natural."

"Pop trained her Liz, but he bitterly regretted it remember Menton, when we found out about the Las Vegas killing? He was broken, there and then, he was broken, he knew it was his fault, he knew he'd created a monster, he also knew that one day she would break into little pieces, and no one would be there to help, she will stand in all the shit, snot and blood and scream her head off, lost in utter insanity!"

"She'll go completely mad?" asked Liz.

"I've been there darling, two steps beyond perhaps Elizabeth, beyond our help, I've been there so many times, she must have been close after Las Vegas, but she had Erick with her, so where is Erick this time?"

Liz stared out to sea as she thought about it all.

"It's a plan isn't it Dexter, but what's the ending and why?"

"I've given it plenty of time Liz, and I find only two routes for her, one good and one bad, the first is that it's Pops plan, passed onto Marvin to finally get here out of the business, i.e. all the blood and gore will finally convince her that she's in the wrong slot."

"And the second Dex?"

"They're selling the Russian link by exposing the killer to the media, dead or alive and then refer to the Vegas killings to link her to the Spetsnaz in Russia, and the drug wars, a great sales job don't you think?"

"So, the Americans double cross her both ways then, but Dex, Marvin wouldn't do that to her, no way!"

"But what if Marvin has sold them the plan but an insider is making it a bit more American friendly, get it?"

"So, Marvin thinks that he's a smart arse but in fact he's being used and more than that, Tolly will lose his mother and that will break the union apart he will hate the Americans after all that, the betrayal will be the end of him because he will go for them."

Dexter nodded to her, "The allies will be at war Elizabeth, understand the significance of her now?"

"So how will it all go Dex?"

"They'll let her do the planning and offer an exit strategy, then they will fail miserably and expose her as Russian Spetsnaz and possibly a spy, they will have dead scumbags and the killers to prove it, happy days all round, right?"

She stared out to sea as she thought about the problem, "Shit! and there's us all happy about the outcome."

She took her phone out and punched in the auto reply then handed it to Dexter.

"Tell the little man to get her to abort the contract and quick!"

Dexter took the phone and listened to the satellite connecting him with clicks and whistles, finally Theo picked up, "Hello Dexter, how are you?"

"And how did you know?"

"Your contact code Dex, first click, so what's up?"

"Theo, listen very carefully, I think that Caledonia is being set up by insiders, oh she'll do the job, no problems but her exit will all fall apart, and she will be taken or killed."

"But why would they do that to her?"

"Their plan in my view is that whoever sent her to do the job saw an opportunity to split the special relationship into little bits, just imagine Tolly losing his mother to useless planning would he ever forgive and forget?"

"No Dex, never, we would all be at an end, they would roll us all up like a rug, he would go berserk."

"And loosening your mother?"

"Sends us all bonkers! ok Dex, what do you want doing?"

"Abort, if possible, if not then get a better escape system rolling and bloody fast."

"But she's on the move Dex, I have her on satellite, she's already arrived on sight, ahead of schedule by the way, do you think that's she's twigged the backup problem?"

"Perhaps, but someone in the planning circle has change it to suit himself understood, I now believe that it was all a set up from the start, perhaps the bad hombres are in on it all?"

"Another cartel with American Intel links then Dex?"

"Perhaps Theo, could you check it out for us please?"

"That's a hell of a plan Dex, they are on a win all round deal, exposure, competition gone and a link to the Presidency with real leverage, wow now that's clever man. "

"And we didn't even see it Theo, impressive, eh?"

"But you did Dexter, you did! ok I'm on it, I'll get someone to be the sweeper and follow the team just in case, ok, I'm out!"

Liz leaned in and kissed him, "The old man was very right about you Dexter, you do have a natural talent for planning and a natural survival instinct, almost animal like?"

He was thinking again as he stared out to sea.

"Well, what do we do now cowboy?"

"Jon Boy is as thick as shit Lill, I have to explain reality to him, blunt or subtle dear?"

"Oh, blunt darling, aren't you always so very, well animal like and you just call me Lill one more time and I'm going to give you the slapping of a lifetime!"

He turned to her and grinned, "Oh I love your nursery nurse bed side manner, have you got those stocking on again?"

She turned and started to run as fast as she could to get away from him, he ran after her.

She stopped at the forward Hatch and pointed out to sea, "Look Dexter, Lady Luck!"

He skidded up to her in the sea spray wash on deck.

"Oh, look Elizabeth, our baby is at anchor wanting to be set free again, he put his arm around her shoulders and stared at the double masted sloop as she bobbed up and down in the offshore swell."

She jumped on him, "And I've had her topped up with supplies, beer, wine, pork pies, the lot."

He kissed her back as the ship's horn sounded out the sighting of the Azores islands.

He held her off the deck as he thought about it, "Bastard! Elizabeth we can't do this just now, we have to help, sorry darling I know you wanted this, but we just can't, you know that don't you?"

"Bastard!" she shouted.

She reluctantly handed him her phone again, "Bastard!"

He pressed recall and waited, "Theo we're in the Azores we need a lift to Mexico City, who's available for immediate action contacts?"

Theo started to laugh.

"What?"

"Mack and his boys are in Portugal taking five, yes?"

"So, they're not with their leader in Mexico then?"

"He didn't want them Dex, a problem?"

"So why don't you use your own people, Theo?"

"Because others are already supplied Dex?"

"And he feels safe, .................. what a moron?"

"Ok two tickets on the highway express, Dex?"

"Opinions first Theodore!"

"He's trying to be a smart-arse Dex, or he's convinced he's protected."

"But he's not, is he?"

"He has Diana with him."

"Yes, but is she certified to carry."

"I wouldn't have thought so."

"So, he needs rescuing then?"

"I'll give em the basic plan Dex and you fill em in with the rest."

"Good, thanks Theo, any joy on contacting the action so far?"

"None she's working silent."

"Directed to do so you think?"

"Na, it's her Dex, she's in the mood, look out Mexico!"

"How long before a pickup?"

"An hour, I'll rush them along a bit."

"Too late for us to be of help Theo, so contact someone in the city to help, non-American if possible."

"The cockneys are over there you know, why don't I brief them on the changes and let them do their thing and send George for over cover perhaps?"

"Who sent them?"

"Who do you think?"

"So, where's Tolly, in his office?"

"Mexico, the whole team is with him."

"Shit Theo, this is going to be a clusterfuck man, this is worse than I feared, get hold of him and give him my thoughts then suggest a withdrawal and regroup on this side of the pond, yes?"

"I'll try Dex, but you know what he's like, this could be a triple call, being led by the curlies until he finds out who to really trust, confused? You will be Colonel,"

Theo squealed with laughter before cutting the link.

"This family is bonkers Lill, what the hell is Tolly up to now, he's also over there, fishing?"

"No Dexter, searching I would say, a long-term grudge, the very same as his Great Granddad."

"What the hell's happening now, Liz?"

She started laughing at him again, "Have some breakfast and a little kip, then the rethink, good?"

"Good," he mumbled.

"No sex then?" asked Liz.

He grabbed her and felt for the lacy stocking tops, "We have one hour dear."

"Well for you that's a good 55 minutes to spare, Mr. Wham, bamb, what's for tea Ma-am!"

She broke away from him and opened the door then locked him out as she screamed with laughter, he ran back to the other door to gain entry to the main walkway, she ran off to hide from the milkman wanting his money.

"But Madam, it's only 6 pounds, have you got the cash on you."

"No!" she shouted from the end of the corridor before slamming the door and locking him out.

He scratched the door "We might find another way for you to pay Miss Smiff!"

The second officer on watch looked through his gangway cameras at the action, "Where the hell does he get the energy, I thought he's supposed to be full of the flu?"

"He's receiving some proper nursing sir; I'd swap places any day!" said the helmsman.

The officer grinned at him, "Yep, me too son, me too!"

# CHAPTER 9 ... The Pink Pelican Night Club ... Mexico City

The street was full of people going in all directions, everyone seemed to be wearing cowboy hats and boots, the mariachi rock music blasted off the building, some working girls strutted up and down the sidewalk trying to attract attention from men.

"There you go girls that's how it's done look!" said Ruth to the twins.

"Ah...feck off!" said Kath as she adjusted her bra to be able to show more cleavage.

Ruth looked at Megan's white face then nodded to Cal and back to Megan.

"Do you want to stand down Meg's?" asked Cal.

"You can feck of as well, let's just get out of this fecking bus, I fecking hate small spaces."

"Rear guard, remember anyone who wants it and count the shots, do not be left with one slug and twenty to kill, the dead man's deal, remember, hey and no automatic, single bop to the center of mass, no pissing about, if he's still in the mood then one in the head, yes!" Cal shouted.

"Feck yes!" shouted the Irish girls.

Megan made the sign of the cross on her breast, Kerry and Kathleen did the same, Ruth watched them and followed doing her best impersonation of a catholic, Cal shook her head and willed Marvin to stop the bus as soon as possible, she was also feeling the claustrophobia.

When he stopped, she threw four chewing gum pieces into the mouth, "Ok girls, no prisoners, let's go!"

They followed her out into the hot night air, she buttoned up her thin raincoat, the others followed her idea, at the Pelican doors she stopped and looked at the security on the people entering through the swinging saloon doors.

"Ok, Meg's at um dear!"

Megan walked up the biggest thug and shouted at the top of her voice," We are the show act, so get out of the fecking way you slob!"

He looked to a little man sitting on a high stool who read down a guest list, he waited for the nod.

Ruth kicked his high stool from under him and screeched out with a witch like false laugh.

"I knew you were one woman!" giggled Cal at the back of her.

As he fell over Cal stood on his leg and broke it, she grabbed the clip board and threw it into the crowd, "A free night everyone!" she screamed out to the people waiting, suddenly the doors were overwhelmed with people pushing and shoving, the girls were pushed through the doors like champagne corks out of a bottle.

Ruth just managed to clip the big lad a good right hook under the jaw, he was down and groaning as he was trodden on by the mass of people rushing the doors.

Cal elbowed her a congratulation in silence as they walked on, the twins now took the lead, breasts out front and bouncing as they walked, people naturally got out of their way, Cal unbuttoned the coat as they entered the inner dancehall and the stage area.

Kathleen walked to the side door without hesitation and pulled her sister Kerry along.

The security man stopped her with a wide grin.

"Personal interviews before the act goes on stage!"

He rolled his eyes and started to laugh; he gave the nod to the other guards who were gathering to help if needed.

The girls bashed through into the inner sanctum of the business, a second guard stood looking at them, within two strides Cal was on him and her blade stabbed his heart directly, he slumped to the floor, she pointed to the corridor for Megan to guard and clear then turned to Ruth, "Back-to-back when we hit the center, as we practiced yes?"

"Yes boss, roger that!"

She nodded for the twins to enter first and take the attention of the men, "Ok go!"

"Placebo, placebo, placebo!" shouted Kerry, the only perceived Russian word she knew,

"Down!" screamed Cal as the machine gun dropped from her arm sling into her hands, Ruth did the same.

The twins hit the floor but pulled out hecklers for protection as practiced.

Cal started the firing at anyone and everyone in the room, Ruth reversed with her firing at men who were still alive.

"Oh, fuck this!" shouted Cal she flicked it onto auto and started to blast everything in her path, men ran at them from other doors in the room, Ruth downed them with single shots as Cal changes a clip and started blasting again.

The main office door was blasted off its hinges before they entered and shot everyone in the room, the gun clicked empty, so Cal reached for the Hecklers as silence descended in the room.

"What the hell is that door Ruthie?" she shouted, "It shouldn't be there should it?"

Ruth stared at the steel re-enforced door, "Not on the fucking plan woman, what to do?"

Cals eyes panicked as she searched for weaknesses in the masonry "Ok flick to auto and blast the hinges on that side, do it!"

Ruth started blasting the wall as chips of brickwork and dust filled the air.

Cal pushed her out of the way and kicked the door, it sagged to one side as the firing from inside started.

The door flapped to the floor throwing brick dust into the air, Cal was now on the floor firing at them in the office, Ruth appeared over her and blasted the room with the machine gun until it clicked empty.

"No fucking auto you said!" screeched Ruth.

"Any more clips?" asked Cal.

"Two and you?"

"One!"

"So, where's the cavalry?" shouted Ruth.

They stopped talking as the pop, pop, of firing could be heard coming from the corridor.

"Fire escape and to the roof."

"And what, a helicopter?" asked Ruth.

"No, we walk over to the next building and the next, they're all joined on to each other, Marvin will pick us up on the main drag."

"This is crap planning woman!" shouted Ruth.

Cal was gone and, in the corridor, firing at the men coming for them.

"Ok out to the fire escape move!" she shouted.

Megan was still firing, Cal slapped her on the shoulder, "Move, now!"

Cal put her hecklers back into the holsters and took out the machine gun, she placed her last clip and loaded ready.

"Ruth, lead us out to the fire escape.

Ruth ran off down the corridor then shouted back to her, "It's gone, bricked up solid."

"Health and fucking safety, oh, bollocks!" grumbled Cal.

"Ok, they wanted a show so we're going to give them one! Out the front doors! follow me and keep going, if someone points even a finger at you kill um, clear?"

They stared at her in silence.

"Clear!" she screamed.

"Yes!" they all screamed back at her.

Cal buttoned up the top button of her raincoat and marched down the corridor.

"Scream as if you were running away frightened girls!" shouted Cal, she started to scream as loud as she could as they ran out into the main dance hall.

The place was in meltdown as the people panicked and pushed their way to the only exit, through the main doors.

Cal turned and looked at them, she held her hands up "A calm panic ladies and let's see if we can balls it out to get clear, scream when you feel like it!"

Megan screamed just for fun, then grinned, armed security men now ran past them to the office doors and the blood-soaked corridor with all its dead bodies splayed out, some were still alive groaning in pain.

The women shuffled with the crowds to get clear, but men looked at them from the doorways and started pointing.

Cal saw them so fired a shot into the ceiling fan, everyone dropped to the floor, she flicked to auto and blasted all of the men staring and aiming weapons at them, then her gun stopped.

"Stoppage!" she screamed and knelt to pull out the hecklers.

Ruth filled the gap and continued the blasting until no one was left to fire back at them.

Cal stood and shouted at them, "Out...........go!"

She let the coat cover her weapons as she calmly walked to the doors, the girls followed.

A security guard started to fire at them from the outside, but Megan downed him with a single shot.

"You see, smart knickers, single shots!" shouted Ruth.

Cal ignored her as they hit the air, "Where the fuck?"

"There!" pointed Kath, "It's taking hits from the police, look!"

Cal stared in panic as their minibus was surrounded by police and was being fired at.

"Shit!"

Marvin and Diana were defending the little bus with machine gun fire as the girls looked on.

A white taxi rolled up to the curb and a familiar voice shouted to them, "Get in the dam motor!" shouted George.

They scrambled into the back of the car, and he wheel spinned the old taxicab away, broad siding it to change direction from the police who were starting to fire at them.

Then after two hundred yards he suddenly pulled up to the curb.

"What?" screamed Cal.

"You just have to see this one girls, keep watching."

"Watching what?" shouted Ruth.

George thumbed the monster tarmac laying machine coming down the road and at a top speed of five miles an hour, it filled the road ahead, they could see Rufus in the driving seat grinning from ear to ear, he gave them a wink as he passed.

"Only he could come up with this one Cal, get him sectioned Cal, he's fucking bonkers!"

"Lord Longmore George is our hero yet again," said Megan.

"Only he could ask for a blorenox, what the fucks a blorenox says I, it's for laying tarmac say' he, why the fuck do we want one of those says I, just for the fun of it my Lord says he, Cal get that nutter sectioned!"

Cal was too busy laughing as the blorenox started laying tarmac at the side of them, it headed for the police cars on auto-lay, spraying out the tarmac to be flattened by the rear rollers and the cooling spray of water at the back of them, the monster machine disappeared into its own steam cloud.

Suddenly Rufus was at the side window knocking to be let in, George pulled off slowly as Rufus ran alongside the car" Bastard, let me in, you hairy git!"

George was giggling at him before Megan opened the door and dragged him into the pile of women.

Rufus climbed to the back window over them to see what was happening, he laughed as the chaos continued, the minibus wheel spun off in the other direction, turning down a side street.

"Yes, he got away, good old Marvin, I knew he could do it."

George floored the taxi ignoring red lights as they flashed through the city.

Cal locked eyes with him in the mirror, "A set up?"

"A double cross Cal, they wanted the deed doing but they also wanted you girls to fry in front of the press, dead on the streets of course!"

"Shit!" said Cal.

"Dexter say's that you're a stupid cow and you need a good slap for being dragged into this balls up."

"But Tolly!"

"Him too Cal, bunch of morons, your mother told me to tell you."

"Hey!" shouted Ruth, "You said no auto, and there's you slinging lead like a fucking combat zone!"

Cal ignore her, George gave her a wink in the mirror, she sat and thought about the change in their situation."

"They'll still want us then George, alive in front of the press."

He ignored her and shouted to Rufus, "Where?"

"The deli on the corner of the next block." Rufus shouted back.

"Why?" asked Cal.

"He has to check the score Cal."

"Why?"

"Because if you haven't killed the bandito then we're dog food, so how many?"

"All of them."

"Numbers?" asked George.

"Just here, let me out," said Rufus, he stepped out of the taxi and just disappeared among the shoppers.

"He's gone," said Ruth, "Just like that, he disappeared just like that, how the hell did he do that?"

"Like magic ladies," said George, "Just keep watching this, he owns half of London and the home counties and just watch his choice of transport, I'm interested as to his choice, aren't you?"

"I'd be surprised if it's a big car, wouldn't you?" George spotted him and folded as he laughed, get him sectioned Cal, look, he's fucking bonkers woman!"

Rufus peddled past them on an old grocery delivery bike, his legs were peddling like mad as he zoomed off in the direction they had just come from.

They all laughed at him as they relaxed, Cal climbed through the Perspex window inside the cab and sat in his passenger seat.

"Come on give me the rundown of what we're into." she stared at the side of his head as he put the hand brake on and smiled at her.

"I think that they wanted Marvin more than anything, you were just helpful artists flown in to make a noise, so, recognition anyone, did we get the scum bag?"

Cal stared out of the window at the people coming and going, doing their shopping as normal.

"They don't look like they care George, life's normal for them."

"Shooting in the distance is all perfectly normal Cal, this is Mexico, it's been like this for two hundred years, we won't change the nation by taking out bandits, they are on a loser if they think they can."

"Yes!" said Ruth "I killed the grey-haired bloke with the bandit mustache and his mates who were counting money,"

"Are you sure?" he asked.

"Yes, she's sure George! if she says he's dead then he's dead."

"Calm woman, I'm just asking the obvious that's all, cool it."

"What now?" asked Ruth.

"We go home," said Cal.

"Unless you're needed again girls, who knows eh?" said George.

Cal turned and growled at him, "Come on George, what else did my father have in mind while he was working them all out, he has another plan doesn't he?"

She continued to stare in his ear.

"And he's wants to embarrass the Americans, yes?"

George nodded to the windscreen, "I have a safe house for you girls, once you're in you do not come out until its time clear?"

"Supplies?" asked Ruth.

"She's a bit mouthy ain't she?"

"Answer her George, we need to feel secure."

"Calm down everyone, Lord Longmore will deliver all that you need, all right?"

Ruth tapped Cal on the shoulder and looked into her eyes.

"Yes Ruth, these boys are solid, don't worry, unconventional maybe but with us up to the hilt, aren't you George?"

George looked at Ruth in the mirror and grinned at her, "Well I like her Cal, she's the fanny's aunt with weaponry I take it, and not a bulldogs bollocks?"

"Yes George, she did well, even under extreme she was there, I recommend her to your working group."

"Thanks Cal, I'll teach her the skills when we have time."

"Fuck off!" shouted Ruth.

"Ruth!" said Cal, "You are in Royal company woman, so close the facial orifice please, and be taught by experts, these two are premier league, understand?"

"And play for the Spurs ladies."

"Feck off!" said Megan as she looked out at the normal life in the street.

"The girls did well George."

"I knew they would, Brenda would like a word though ladies and she ain't happy!"

"She can feck off as well!" said Kathleen, the others started giggling at her.

"Stay out of their war George, well that's my only advice," said Cal.

George listened and smiled at her, then nodded to the windscreen again.

"And how long do we wait for him then?"

"A good point Cal, he can find us, eh?" he started the engine up and pulled off into the traffic.

Cal looked at the women and smiled, "Any injuries or breaks?"

Faces stared and heads shook in silence.

"It's ok ladies, this is normal after an action, it takes days processing one's brain to stuff like this, all perfectly normal."

"Get drunk, shout at each other, a curry and a pint then sleep for England, tomorrow you'll be fine!" said George.

He gave them his best toothy grin.

Ruth stared out of the window and watched the shoppers walking by.

"A normal day at the office eh, Cal?"

"They sacrificed us George, so who are we talking about here?"

"Must be on the Presidential staff I would have thought, phone lines to easy to clip, morons really."

"What, them or us?"

"Us, you silly cow!" shouted Ruth.

"Agreed for once Ruth, we trusted the Americans and it very nearly did for us."

"So, what are we doing about it?"

"A talk with my first born I think!"

"But where is he?"

"Yes George, where is the little shit?"

# CHAPTER 10 ... The pink Pelican Night Club ... Mexico City

Rufus peddled up to the chaos of the street, he picked up a loaf of bread out of the front basket and leaned the bike against the wall then joined the viewing public as they brought out the bodies to waiting ambulances, the police were everywhere asking questions in Spanish.

He sidled up to a woman on the front row just behind the police no entry tape, "What the hell happened here?" he asked.

She turned and looked him up and down "What the hell are you?"

"Deliveries, from the Italian deli down the road, bread and salami, so what is this?"

She looked back at the bodies, "Somebody killed them all, they are saying that they were Russian spats or something."

"Spetsnaz?"

"Yeah, that's it, Spetsnaz whatever they are."

"Russian special forces!" said Rufus.

She turned and elbowed another woman and whispered, the word spread like a wildfire burning in the street.

"Who were they though?" asked Rufus.

"Enrique Marcos and his complete brotherhood." she whispered.

"Big Bosses?" asked Rufus.

"Na, in their world he was small fish, they must want his patch, so bang, bang, bang, all gone, she spat on the floor, rot in hell!"

"You knew him then?"

She leaned in and whispered again only lower, "He killed my Eddy, I only wish I could have pulled the trigger on his bold head, bang, it would have been nice, blown his shit brains out, nice."

"So, he had a bold head then."

"Yeah, a cue ball and an ugly piece of shit."

"And did you see his body?"

She pointed to all the stretchers laid out with the dead.

"They cover them overlook, I look at the boots, the most expensive the bigger the shit wearing them."

"Yeah, good point."

He handed her the bread then ducked under the police tape and wandered over to the bodies, then one by one he lifted the blankets to see who they were.

"Hey!" shouted a policeman, "Who the fuck are you gringo?"

"Pathology, checking on age groups and stats, for the university, hey I'm just doing my job man."

The policeman stared at him in confusion, "What the fuck does that mean man?"

"Is Marcos among the dead Sir?"

"Who are you to ask such a question?"

"The University would want to add to the police and people's initiative, with ongoing cooperation's with help from charity groups, we need information of averages needed for the computing section of the university to process the medical numbers, beds for the sick and all that, clear?"

"What the hell are you saying ass hole?"

Rufus pointed to the body dropped on the floor by two medics, "Is that him?"

"Who?"

"The big boss of bosses!"

"Na, he ain't here, he's in the States with the President paying his taxes, know what I mean?" the cop winked at him.

"Bribing the Prez?"

"Yeah, hey it's all businessman, these guys just paid the price for the takeover, some Russian millionaire called Smirkoff, just took the company over, they were his girls, Spetsnaz special forces man, mean as snakes, cleaned the place out really good, he just upped the war."

"Shit!" said Rufus, "Russian's?"

"Hey, they're all over the world now, hey, that's why Marcos and the Prez are having the party eh?"

"Shit!" said Rufus, "So what about all these men?"

"Slit trench splat, then move on to the next body count, all normal gringos!"

"This is normal?"

"Every couple of years we get one of these, this time it's the Russians next maybe the Chinese eh, who knows?"

"Yeah, who knows?"

# CHAPTER 11 ... Outside the Pink Pelican Night Club......Press Lines

Augusta was ready for the first contact to the station and the studio in Monaco, the sound man counted her in, "And three two one, live!"

"Good evening Monaco, this is Augusta Talbot in Mexico City reporting on a mass shooting at a night Club, we have been counting the bodies as they are brought out, we've lost count there are so many, we are told that the Club belongs to a known drug dealer named Enrique Marcos, I'm also told that he is not one of the dead bodies so there is speculation that this could well of been an own goal and him making a point to his employees, another storyline is that it was a Russian special ops group of, and get this, a women's Spetsnaz hit squad sent by a Russian cartel to clear the site for a take over

Rufus slipped into the station's contract van and sat in the passenger seat as he waited for her to finish.

"Hey who the hell are you buddy?" shouted the driver as he came back to check the connections.

"Her Uncle with an exclusive, how long will she be mate?"

The man's mouth dropped as he looked at Rufus, "You look familiar man?"

Rufus gave him his best grin, the man stared at him as he searched his brain for an answer.

"American, eh?" asked Rufus.

"Err....... yeah, contract director for Monaco news here in Mexico."

"A good job then eh?"

"A great job, she's really good, hey! God dam it yeah, you's the Goddamn boss, you own the Company man, say what is this, am

I on secret bosses or something? Hey, are you going to give me a hundred grand boss? Hey, I'm a good guy, just out of college, debts up to my ass man!"

He pointed to the picture of the bosses in the back of the van.

Rufus looked at the picture and scratched his head in confusion "Why? "He gave him the regal smile, "My Aunty gave it to me to run but I get fed up too easily and I let the minions run it, not my thing I think" he shrugged.

Augusta arrived back at the van and squealed out in delight at seeing Uncle Rufus, she hugged him tight then introduced Simon.

"He's my bodyguard Uncle, good, eh?"

"Very good dear," he shook Simon's hand, then turned back to her," Granddad Hamish is very worried Gussy, he thinks that this is all a big set up, he thinks that they wanted you here specifically so that they could."

"Take you hostage and negotiate with them." said the driver as he held the Glock 9 to Rufus's head, "As I said Uncle Rufus, I'm a contractor and you are a real bonus, thank you so much, is that good enough English for you buddy?"

"Don't do anything Gussy or Simon, ride with this one please," said Rufus "These idiots don't realize who they're up against, they're still in the dark ages over here."

"You're dead!" shouted Augusta, "He'll have you head in a basket!"

The car squealed to a stop at the side of them and other men pulled them inside and clipped them into the hand cuffs.

"Have a nice day yawl," said the van driver as he watched the car drive off, he jumped in the van and followed.

The sound and camera men looked at each other, "Where the hell have they gone?"

An old lady looked at their shock and spoke to them in English, "I followed the gringo, I'm just curious you see, he's a strange man, eh?"

"Who?"

"The weird looking white man."

They looked at each other in confusion.

"Anyway, the driver pulled out a gun on them and a second car comes along and takes them away, all three."

"But there's only four of us, the driver is the director."

"Well, he just kidnapped your friends the woman reporter, the sweet looking guy and the strange one, all gone, a ransom snatch I would say, I hope you have lots of money, it could be expensive signor?" she walked off to pass on the gossip.

They stared at the little old lady in shock, "The camera man took out his phone and rang the network contractors in Mexico with the bad news.

He picked up Augusta's microphone and looked around, her notes were scattered all around, "We have a situation boss, Gussy, Simon and another guy have been snatched, the vans gone and we're at the Pelican story downtown, I don't know who the other guy was, but we have a witness that all three were snatched at gun point! ..................... yeah, we'll wait!"

# CHAPTER 12 ... Azores ... Atlantic Ocean ... Portugal

They waited for the helicopter on the fore deck, Liz was dreading having to climb up the steel ladder to the helicopter.

"Why can't he land on there?" she pointed to the roof.

He picked up the buzzing phone to speak to the pilot but was surprised to hear Theo talking to him, "What have you found Theo?"

"They've snatched Augusta Dex, and her boyfriend and another who we can't identify at the moment."

"Who?"

"The lads will take you to Porto, then Griff has the little jet warming up."

"Who's done the snatching Theo?"

"That's for you Dex, locate and define."

"What the hell does that mean?"

"It means take your time, nice and easy, no aggressive moves!"

"Aggressive moves?" shouted Dex as the helicopter came lower and the ladder was dangling in front of them.

He cut Theo off and started climbing the ladder.

"Who?" shouted Liz, "Who's been snatched Dexter?" she screamed.

He was halfway up, and he looked down, "Its worse than I thought Elizabeth, they've snatched Gussy and her new man.

She immediately started to climb after him as the wind caught them, it started to lift them away from the ship.

"Who! Dexter?"

"Your guess Lill, we need to be there now!"

"Shit!" screamed Liz as she made it to the doorway, he pulled her in and buckled her up, "Who Dexter?"

"We'll find out Liz and we'll find um, no worries."

"No damn worries, your granddaughters in the hands of drug dealers and scum bags."

He held his hand up to her to shut her up so that he could ask Mack a question, he was sitting there and quietly watching them.

"So, Mack, who's the third person snatched and why so important to take a third."

"Lord Longmore Dex, the Gorilla recons they've got Rufus Longmore, he's raging Dex and needs reeling in man! You can do that right?"

Dexter stared at the men in the helicopter, the faces were so familiar to him, he winked at Gurung and Jonesy and absent mindedly stared at Glen, "Marines, eh?"

"Yes boss, the coms man."

"Good., so if you were paid a million for this job what would you buy first?"

The lads started laughing at him, but his face was like granite.

"Err......a flash motor and a villa in the heat someplace, a bolt hole perhaps?"

Dexter smiled at him, "What flash vehicle would you go for?"

"Err.......... a four-by-four truck, an American I think I like them all though," he stopped speaking and watched Dexter talking on his phone.

"Theo, check something out for us please, high price cash sales in that area, a flash car or even a boat, the customer is given options to easy pay but refuses, 50 grand plus."

"Then check out flash phone sales, gold plated and all that crap, perhaps a cross reference of the two?"

"But Dex that's impossible!"

"No, it's not Theo, with you and your Apprentice Charley nothing is impossible, they are your words by the way, so now prove it Mr. Smart arse!"

He cut him off as the faces stared at him.

"Ok, the link Mack, who and where?"

Mack gulped at the sudden question aimed at him, "Err.........Monaco news hired a contract director, we think that he's the one who did the job then passed them on to the others."

Dexter looked around them as he thought it through, "This is all wrong eh, Mack?"

"To obvious boss?"

"It's good to hear that you're switched on Mack, where's her father Erick?"

"With his horses, back in the UK."

"Ok drop us off in Menton then take the lads to Mexico, trace this fucker and find Gussy, yes? Then hold site for the cavalry, we don't know who'll get the honor at the moment."

"And what are we doing bollock brain?" shouted Liz.

"He's taken command Elizabeth," Said Mack, "And he's leading by example and not rushing in like the madman they think he is?"

"Is that what they think Mack?" asked Dexter.

"Of course, after all you've been killed twice, in fact even now you're still dead and yet you're flitting about between sailing and the Palace like a golden butterfly."

"You disapprove?"

"The old man would, I think!"

Dexter stared at him, "Agreed, but the only certainty in life is?"

"Change boss, we just can't halt the changes."

"And that's our strength Mack, they'll be thinking of me in the past, shooting and killing anyone in my way, well not today, let's see how it settles on them, I suspect that they will get nervous with no action happening."

"They could just kill them all and move on numbat!" said Liz.

"Total war after Liz," said Mack, "They wouldn't want his boys on the rampage."

"Who, you?"

"No Elizabeth," he thumbed to Gurung, "Her Grandfathers followers, they would have nowhere to run, this little man and his mates would be taking heads and thanking God to be of use to the God of war."

"What a load of cobblers!" said Liz.

She stared at Gurung and looked at his tightened jaw, "You would, wouldn't you?"

"Anywhere in the world Ma-am, they would be hunted like the animals they are and sacrificed to him, with humble thanks for helping our Nation when we needed help," he nodded to Dexter.

Dexter pointed to Gurung," A great angle that man, I like your thinking, pass on your thoughts whenever possible, nice and loud for big ears the hear, yes?"

"Yes boss!"

"We need to give this the fear factor and stir it all up in the confused mix," said Dexter.

"Perhaps an example boss?" said Gurung.

Dexter smiled at him, "Yes young man when the timings right, nice and messy, yes, a good thought.

"Ok Mack, run them down as quick as you can, any news on a contact?"

"Well, who would they approach first Dex?"

"Monaco news Mack, that's my end, we'll find out the details from inside you find the scumbag, Theo and Charley will come up with crumbs for you to sweep up, clear?"

"Snatch them back, if possible, but I imagine that her mother will be in on the kill, perhaps a word in her shell-like ear?"

"From you, boss, she won't listen to me."

"You see Mack there's the basic fault, not listening to advice, we all need good advice, thank you for your lads, Jonesy's a bit quiet though but his face says that he has an opinion, come on son let's hear it."

"She might be already dead, after all these kidnapers have lost a lot of people to her mother's team, they'll be very angry, yes?"

"I somehow think that these are not the same people, agreed?"

"Yes boss!"

"Another clan moving in on them then?"

"Dexter pointed at Jonesy, "Bang on, my thoughts as well, so that will help with the fear factor, use the hurt gangster as an approach when needed, sow those seeds boys it all helps in the end."

"Mack grinned at him," Boy have they underestimated you, sir?"

"We let them think what they think, do not inform them of our reality agreed?"

"Yes boss."

"Ok, my clarity is this, any objection spill against my ideas, ok, the President has been conned by the big players into committing to Mexico and as we all know Mexico is impossible and will never join the Union."

"New Mexico did boss and Texas, even California a hundred and fifty odd years ago," said Glen, being helpful.

"But would he risk an all-out war in the south?" asked Dexter.

"He's not that stupid!" said Jonesy, "He would just like changes in the people's thoughts, they will want the safety of the USA perhaps, because that's what he's really selling."

"This is what is going on then, here and now, he's changing the hearts and mind of the Mexican people, so it'll be splashed all over the news?" said Dexter.

"And now Monaco News has lost a journalist the American media will pull back," said Liz.

"And the Mexicans will have the rule of the air waves Liz!" said Dexter.

Dexter passed her his satellite phone, "Ring Erick and fill him in Liz, he'll want to be here with Mack and the boys, any objections lads?"

They all shook their heads in agreement with Erick joining them.

"At least he's officially alive boss and he does have useful links to the President."

"Good point Mack, keep me on my toes boy!" grinned Dexter.

"Golden butterfly my arse!"

Mack stared at him as he watched him thinking and planning, Elizabeth nodded to him to confirm that yes Dexter was working ok at the moment.

"We'll be in Menton Mack and listening to everything that's going to happen, "said Liz, "And no blood, if possible, we have to be delicate with this one, yes?"

"Yes Ma'am, so we just be helpful when needed?"

"Yes Mack, helpful, but Marvin will direct the actions, ok with that?"

"Yes Ma'am."

"He's the American representative on site, somewhere."

"So, you don't know where he is then?"

"He's like Pop, he'll be there when you need him, keep out of his way if he gets too violent right?"

"And he will Elizabeth?"

"Oh yes!"

"But her mother is already there?" said Mack.

"We worry Mack!" said Dexter.

Mack nodded wanting him to say more but he didn't.

"She's about to burst Mack, we feel that she is on the edge and will break very soon."

"From what?"

"Mack!" shouted Elizabeth, "Do wake up boy, she has just killed loads of people, she stands in a river of blood and there's no one there to hold her from doing something stupid, remember how it was boy?"

"Yes...err...sorry Liz, so if we find Gussy, then what do we do with her mother?"

"It'll pan out Mack, no worries!" said Dexter.

She elbowed him in frustration, "Just be there gentlemen, and ready to help, clear?"

"Yes Ma'am!"

# CHAPTER 13 ... Los Olvidados ... Mexico City ... Slum Area

"If you think that I'm filming in this bastard place then you don't know me very well, you can stick green spaces up your arse!"

Adrian was fuming as he looked out onto the slum streets of Los Olvidados.

Russell passed Addy the ringing phone.

"We, at Green Space mag simply want you to highlight the plight of the poor in the City Adrian by comparing lifestyles to reality," said the agent down the phone.

"My people are in danger how real do you want it?"

"Just some pictures Adrian, perhaps night shots to highlight the lack of power in the district?"

Adrian cut him off and fumed.

Tolly closed the call as Billy elbowed him with his phone buzzing, he passed Tolly his phone with the bad news, he took it then waited, "Your plan stinks JJ, they now have Augusta and Simon."

"And Rufus, now that's a bad move I feel, but it's much worse than that, your mother failed to kill Marcos, he still lives and is starting to come back with troops."

"What is this a double or triple cross?"

"A double cross! They made a deal."

"So, you get double crossed, or worse, you double crossed them, I imagine that's how they feel yes? either way we pay the price?"

"We have them Tolly."

"Ok, new deal, they give back my family and I'll walk away from this stupid embarrassment, failure to do so and I'll come for them."

"And your other family?"

"Who?"

"Your grandparents?"

"Are not involved."

"Sure, are you?"

"Positive, do you hear different?"

"Afraid So Tolly, Dexter is shouting the orders as I speak."

"JJ if you get the chance tell them to give us space, please and leave it to our people."

"So, you're not pulling out then?"

"As soon as I can JJ, so what's Jimmy doing?"

"Finding the giveaway mole from so many so-called friends."

"A shark tank, eh?"

"Piranha?"

"Ok, good luck with that one so should I carry one with plan A?"

"Yes Tolly, all eyes are on you guys!"

# CHAPTER 14 ... Apartment in the City ... Mexico City

"So where are they Cal?" asked Ruth for the tenth time.

Cal walked from wall to wall as she listened to Ruth complaining on and on, like a trapped wild cat.

The door knocked suddenly, and Kath rushed over to open it, Brenda bounced in and stared at the faces," Fecking stupid women all of you, now the wars really started, Augusta, her boyfriend, plus, Lord fecking Longmore have been taken, George is going ballistic, talk to him Caledonia, I've never seen him like this before, he's gone fecking nuts."

"Where is he?"

"In the car."

"Ok saddle up with all the gear we are leaving this shit hole now, where's Adrian?"

"Err.......... over on the slum streets, filming."

"Oh perfect, right in the middle of the crap then, ok, up and let's go!"

"But Caledonia, it's not safe."

"I'll tell you what's not safe, this damn place, we gather together, that's safer than this, so move!"

George's face warmed up as he watched Cal and all the girls come out of the apartment block, her face was purple with rage, she handed Brenda the G36 assault rifle and climbed in next to George.

"Ok, take me to my son because he's going to get such a slap!"

"But Cal!"

"Move!" she screamed two inches from his ear, he pulled off into the traffic and looked at the girls squashed together on the back seat, he locked eyes with Brenda.

"Not my plan Bren!" said George.

"Fecking moron we we're out and gone, you could have taken your seat in the house of Lords, fecking easy street, bollock head, now were in the car with psychopaths united!"

Cal turned to her," You will take orders from me, yes or no, say you won't, and we can drop you off, here and now."

"Hey, I'm not leaving my man with you fecking shit heads, you'll get him killed."

"Yes, or fucking no woman?" screamed Cal.

"Feck yes!" shouted Brenda, "And when we're out of this we're back to London?"

"Yes!" screamed everyone in the car."

Ruth elbowed Megan and grinned, "Hey, I got the results on the radio, Spurs went down three nil to Chelsea."

George gave her the look in the mirror.

Cal slapped his shoulder, "From bad to worse eh Monkey man? Still, it feels better to be out and at it eh?"

George growled under his breath, "She gave me one command, keep the little shit alive, just alive, not out of trouble, just alive, she knew him so well eh Cal?"

"She knew us all George and she wouldn't have been in this shit; we trusted the Americans to do a good secure job and they cocked it up as per bloody usual!"

"As usual."

"There's the clue then?" said Ruth in Cal's ear as she leaned forward in the car.

"The American system Ruth?"

"They have leeks obviously."

"And you lot missed the bastard," said George.

"No, if he was in there then he's dead."

"Bald head, a Mussolini type build?"

"No!" said Ruth, "We had a hairy bloke with a classic bandit tash, he and his buddies are dead."

"The bastards gave us wrong Intel Ruth," said Cal, "A set up from the beginning, let's talk to my son and get a clearer picture."

"Brenda! Rear guard as we go into this enclave of scum bags, shoot whoever is following us, the rest, just get ready for action on our flanks, eyes out on stalks everyone!" said Cal, "The old man would have called this the stupid come on, walking into someone's prepared trap, but we have no choice."

"We could just run?" said Ruth.

"Now that would be a very bad mistake, we become the hunted, no! I don't like it like that, no we need a handle on the spot from the one who organized this whole hash up!"

"Tolly?" asked George.

"Yes Tolly!" said Cal.

# CHAPTER 15 ... Los Olivados Slums ... Mexico City

A little girl stood outside the bus and smiled at Adrian, she must have been no more than six years old, Adrian watched her as she started a little dance.

"She thinks it's the Television X factor bus," said Russell, "She's doing her intro, good eh?"

"Yes, very good," said Adrian," It reminds me of me at that age, showing off to anyone who'd take a look, his eyes watered as he continued to watch her, the emotion welling up in him.

"Oh, bollocks to all this!" he grabbed his hand-held digital camera and pressed for the door to open.

The little girls squealed out in delight as the door whooshed open, she started to sing and dance in Spanish, Addy jumped down and started taking snaps of her as she spun around doing her party piece, then a crowd started to gather as she continued, they started to form a queue at the side of the bus.

"Everybody out!" he shouted, "Set up the gear for a talent shoot, come on move your arses now!"

He waved for the little darling to continue, he clapped her and started to dance with her, she squealed out in delight, the crew started setting up the lighting and the camera stands.

A mariachi band came out of nowhere and started playing for the little girl.

"Russell!" Shouted Addy, "Get some paper and set up a desk for the winners and find some judges, locals and two off the bus, get the models moving we have our shoot, let's get this done, come on get off the bastard bus!"

Russell quickly painted a sign for the desk and stuck it with masking tape to the trestle table, it read,

LAS VEGAS TALENT, HAVE YOU GOT WHAT IT TAKES?

Addy looked at it and gave him a quick kiss on his ear.

You're bastard fabulous Russell, I love it!"

The paint was still wet as he watched all the people looking at him and the set-up crew.

As the little girl came to an exhausting stop the crowd began to clap her and shout out,

"Yes, yes, yes, yes, yes, yes, yes."

Addy looked to those still on the bus who were sorting out the kit, "Well?"

"Yes!" echoed from the members of crew on and off the bus.

Russell scribbled out a card for her to collect from the tables, she took it in heavenly delight then ran off into the crowd of people.

"Russell, go and grab some judges from the shops over there, come on move it."

"You! short arse!" he pointed to Tolly.

"You're a bastard judge and your mate sit down there and start judging."

Billy burst out laughing at him and at Tolly's face, they sat down as ordered as the rest of them rushed around setting up all the equipment.

"Russell!" screamed Addy, "Give the band some green stuff, we want them to be our orchestra, do it!"

Russell took out a wad of money from his pocket and gave it to the trumpet player, he didn't count it out, "A drummer, we need a drummer!" he made the sign of a man drumming.

"Ah!" screeched the trumpet player, then just a few moments later there was a man with three old oil drums he moved to the side of the bus, the water was poured into the drums as he listened to the sound and stopped when he raised his hand, eventually he was happy and did a little demonstration of the three booming drum sounds as he hit them with his hands.

Addy gave him a clap with pleasure, then took a snap of him and a close up of the cracked skin of his weather worn face as the man laughed.

The crowd loved it all as the contestants placed their names with Russell at the tables, Indians now joined the queue as well as jugglers and what looked like wrestlers or comics, Russell couldn't tell the difference, but he nodded his thanks to them being there and gave them a ticket, together with a yellow number stick-it for their chests.

"Bastard!" squeaked Addy "Where the hell did, they all come from?"

"You need to select the show line Addy!" shouted Russell, "A singer then a show piece then a juggler then a singer again, you'll be creating a show Addy."

He threw a little yellow stick-it note pad to him, "From 7 onwards Addy, stick it to their chests and point to the little staging area, they'll all understand the system."

"What about the bastard band?"

"Let them talk to the band leader!"

"Who's that bastard."

"The lead trumpeter Addy the one who's waiting for your direction."

Tolly had now connected the microphone to the trestle tables and started to talk to the crowds, in Spanish, "Welcome Stars of the future Mexico, all acts will be given time to do their act, we have all day, so we'll have fun together, but off means no, and no mean exit stage left and thank you for your show piece but no thanks!"

"Now a yes vote from the judges means that we welcome you to Las Vegas for the televised live show across America, the continent of America, the biggest ever live event of the American peoples, just imagine that? We are history in the making my friends and this is day one, so here we go!"

The people screamed at his voice as it echoed over the street.

"Music by the Chilly all-stars! The cool dudes of Mexico City, your local band, who are here to support the community."

The band leader laughed at him and the invention of the new name for the band, he held his thumbs up in thanks then the band kicked off with a rousing sing along piece for everyone now waiting in the queue.

Addy started sticking the little yellow tags to the people waiting and pointed to the band if they were going to sing or dance, singer, dancer, "What the hell are you dear?"

The wrestler picked him up off the floor as Addy giggled at being man handled by the strong man.

"Yeah, yeah, whatever!" he squeaked, when the man put him down, he rushed back over to Russell gasping.

"How the hell did he learn Spanish so quick?"

"Who"?

"The little, short- arsed kid in the middle table that's took over the voice controls."

Russell was too busy organizing people to answer him before a juggler started his act but throwing plant pots in the air and catching them on his head, one by one.

"The crowd started chanting "Off, off, off, off.!"

"No shouted Tolly, I like him, so yes from me, Billy smiled at the man but shook his head, "Boring man!"

The fat shop lady smiled but thumbed off to the left, "Na!" and the greengrocer just shook his head and didn't even smile.

"Next!" shouted Tolly.

An old man came out front and started to sing an operatic song, Tolly loved it, but the rest hated it, Tolly apologized with a thank you smile to the singer, but thumbed stage left.

Next was the wrestling team who threw each other all over the place as they screamed and shouted,

The audience loved it, but Tolly did not and said no! he was boohooed by the audience, but they did get three votes, so Tolly gave them a ticket to victory.

"We'll see you lads in Vegas!"

Addy was now in his element as he took snaps of the people watching and the entertainers, dancing and singing, an acrobat and he and his brother balanced on a little bicycle, he had shots of the men's faces as they sweated with nerves and the tears of the losers who were booed off, he gave them a sympathetic pat on the back as they left the site.

"Next!" shouted Tolly.

A group of 10 little girls came on dressed as chili peppers, the band knew what music would suit and started to play, Billy held up his hands to stop the band and the dancers.

"No, no, no, the band has to be slower, the dancers lead and not the band, yes? Ok, continue!" he waved them on again to restart the dance.

Addy photographed anxious parents as they bit their nails and sweated watching the little girls doing their thing.

Tolly gave Billy the look.

"What?"

Tolly then gave him the grin, "You're enjoying this aren't you?"

"I'm meant to, aren't I?"

Tolly gave him another grin, before standing up and clapping the girls, the place was now in meltdown as they all clapped and whooped.

"What the hell are we doing here boss?"

"Getting popular opinion Billy."

"So, who's the Green Space rep then?"

Tolly grinned at him again, "Me!"

"Why?"

"Cover, and of course we need to protect our people."

Addy was snapping everyone as the fun continued.

"No!" shouted Billy, "No photographs of us please Adrian, none, now delete that last one please!"

Adrian was shocked at their reaction to his taking random shots of the judges and the audience but obeyed the sarn't major command from Billy.

Billy thanked him with a wink, but Addy's curiosity was now aroused.

"Who the fuck are these people, Russell?"

"Special forces Addy, sent to protect us from being kid napped, apparently it's a bit of a cult thing to do to gringo's around here boss!"

"Bastard!" squeaked Addy, "Kid bastard napped......... bastard!"

"And the little bloke Russell?"

Russell shushed him to a whisper, "He's the big cheese in the UK, they all call him boss, so he must be the boss!"

"Bastard!" whispered Addy.

"His Great Grandmother was no other than the DGI, remember Moscow and the little gold jet? That was his Great Grandmother, and he was on that jet, he was just a little kid at the time though."

"Bastard!" whispered Addy, "And I called him short arse, so what the hells a DGI when it's at home?"

He shushed Addy up again, "The Director General of all secret Intelligence! The big spy chief!"

"Bastard!" whispered Add, "So that's an honor ain't it, Russell?"

"A big bastard honor Adrian, a big bastard!"

"Bastard!" said Addy, as he tried not to look at Tolly and Billy as judges, he did a little bow and a type of curtsy to the little tables before moving off to photo some more locals.

Tolly smiled at him but waved him away from taking a photo of him or Billy.

# CHAPTER 16 ... A Car Parked in Mexico City ... Waiting.

All these years JJ and your old man doesn't trust me with the basic plan, all these years son, what did I do wrong with him, you could have let me in on the moves man!"

"He said that you'd be sore Dude, but you see he needed you to be clean and un tainted by the oval office, you see we have a leak and a big one at that, I apologize Dude, on Pa's behalf, he ain't mad at you he's just put you in reserve for this moment, also he wants you back in Washington where you belong but he needs your link with Tolly Trueblood, he knows that you've had experience of working with his men, they know you."

The Dude stared at him as JJ spoke, "You've upset the Brits, haven't you?"

JJ nodded.

"My God, what a Goddamn fucking cluster fuck."

"Tolly's sister was kidnapped today along with Rufus Longmore, do you know him?

"Shit man, what the hell are you guys doing, he'll go nuts!"

"Oh, we have the team who snatched them, we're just waiting for the Washington links the show that we can take them all, Pa wants you to be first man through the door, you ok with that?"

"Why?"

"They know you Dude and we want you to conduct them, to be our cool it guy, to explain the situation calmly."

The Dude grinned, "Who's the planner for this one, you?"

JJ grinned back at him.

"So Tolly will take this very personally then?"

JJ nodded to him "And more to the point so will Gussy, we called her in for the publicity and to report the action, she wasn't expecting to be the action get it?"

The Dude started to laugh, "She is going to shoot you guys!"

"Well, that's your job Dude, explain our dilemma and my plan, cool with that?"

The Dude was still laughing as he nodded, take me to the door sonny, let's do this."

JJ touched his earpiece, "Yep he's in on the plan, ok everyone, move out and block both ends of the street, full contact expected, clear everyone?"

"I hope this big fish is worth it JJ, you've risked a lot of friends because of it, man!"

"He's in the inner circle on the hill Dude, we have to take him down, Pa and Jimmy are waiting to progress, he keeps pulling plugs on them."

"Can I kill him?"

JJ turned to him, "Err.............. if he has a gun in his hand then yes!"

"Or I put one into the dead man's hand for the photos?"

"No Dude we do not start that game, if he's a threat to life, then yes, if he isn't then cuff him that's it, clear?"

JJ pulled out into the traffic and followed the black sedans.

"This leak guy must have Mexican heritage, right?"

"Yeah, how did you know?"

"Logical, he doesn't want gringos in his back yard, I bet he's owned by banditos JJ?"

"Pa said you'd quickly get a handle on it all, he has great faith in you Dude, after all you were trained by the SAS guys in this sort of thing, yes?"

"They are nuts JJ, lesson one, never betray them, they never forget, you might have crossed the line, prepare to receive what you've sown Boy."

He pulled up outside a city block and put the hand break on, he nodded to the building.

"Middle apartment, I nice place for keeping hostages eh, you can tell he wants to talk can't you Dude."

"What's he asking for then?"

"Leave and don't come back I suppose, he ain't asked as yet."

"And the big guy is there, yes?"

"We don't know, we need you to find out if he is."

"Oh, for God's sake!" The Dude jumped out of the car and was gone, over to the main doors, he went in and slammed it behind him."

"Red, Red, Red............. everyone to me, on my call sign he's gone in, so take up positions now, we wait for his instructions...........go!"

"Shit!" mumbled JJ, "He's a nut just like the old man said he would be, don't get killed Dude, please!"

The Dude banged on the apartment door and waited, the eye piece on the door blacked out as someone looked at him from the other side, he gave them his best scowl and a double tap on the door again.

"Are you fucking morons crazy or what?" he shouted out at the top of his voice, "They will gut you like little fish for doing this, they will play with your genitals and use em for dog food, whose moronic idea was this?"

The door opened and a gun was placed into his face.

"An invitation to come in then, yes?" he walked in and looked at the men in suits who looked back at him in shock, the Dude walked over to the drinks table and poured himself a large southern comfort, then chinked the glass with the water jug.

"Good to add water when needed eh?" he took a swig then stared at them.

"Who are you Gringo?" asked the man with the classic Mexican moustache.

The Dude pointed at him, "I like the tash guy, very cool, I was thinking of one myself, what do you think?"

"I think that you are a crazy man sent to the slaughter by idiots."

"Yeah, agreed, God damn idiots, imagine trying to bring democracy to Mexico, idiots, you guys have a lot to teach us about democracy, you had it here before we really understood its need, what with the war against the Spanish then the Americans, you guys are tough, they had better understand that one eh?"

The Dude finished his glass in one gulp then pointed to the table," Join me Zorro?"

The man laughed at his compliment and nodded, the Dude poured himself and Zorro another Southern comfort, he handed the man the glass after chinking the water jug with them.

"Why do that crazy man?"

"Showing respect to Gods best drink..............water!"

The man laughed at him again, "Why the fuck are you here?"

"Oh, didn't I say, I'm the negotiator for the captives, I do hope that you haven't hurt them because the farm boys will come through that door and kill us all, understood?"

"You're an idiot crazy man, they can be dead in seconds everybody knows that."

"Agreed, and understood but before you execute them let me just fill you in on some basic facts about them, yes?"

The man took a drink and nodded, he also nodded to the man still holding the gun to Dudes head, the other man put his gun away back into his under-arm sling.

"Her family are a family of psychopaths, her mother, her grandmother, in fact just being here with them can get you killed."

A voice shouted through the bedroom door "Dude shut the fuck up, I don't know about you, but I'm bored to death with that speech, please make it a bit more before the watershed in its structure, less blood and more pathos, you're fucking boring Yank!"

The Dude nodded to the door "I see you've listened to Lord Longmore?"

The man started to laugh, "Are you all fucking crazy, I want to shoot him so bad!"

"Yeah, me too man, he's an English nut, they're all like him over there."

"Tell him about King Kong before he gets here, I wouldn't like it to be a surprise Yank." shouted Rufus.

"His Brother in arms so to speak is, err.......... how can I put this?"

"A fucking animal Yank!" shouted Rufus, "Warn him of the consequences he'll tear his head off, and I don't want that, I want to buy him a hotel in the city."

"Sorry sir, but he's right."

"A hotel in the city?" asked the Bandit.

"Don't listen to him," said the Dude, "He's nuts, but he does have the cash, he's one of the richest men in the UK, he owns a big part of London, imagine that it sends em mad I think, all that green, not good for the health."

"He'd make a fine hotel manager." shouted Rufus, "The moustache, the attitude and bearing of him, I like the look."

"You cannot use this time to head hunt employees you crazy bastard!"

shouted the Dude.

"The Plaza Hotel in the City, I'm buying it, look into my wallet and check it out, ring the old owner and ask how much I paid for it."

"You're an idiot Rufus, he won't believe that crap!"

The man took a wallet out of his pocket and then his phone, he punched in the number and gabbled on in Spanish to whoever it was he was speaking to, then at the end of the conversation he smiled at Dude, showing his gold tooth.

Dude sipped his drink and watched the man's face as it suddenly changed.

"Yeah!" said The Dude, "I like that one as well, a cap, or is it the complete tooth?"

"He's correct, 20 million English pounds, direct transfer from London, this morning, he's a zillionaire! And he's in Mexico buying hotels all over!"

He clinked glasses with the Dude and laughed, "I can't shoots him now, he's my new Generalissimo!"

"But he's nuts, shoot him while you can guy!"

"Hey!" shouted Rufus through the door, "Who's side are you on Yank?"

The Dude leaned into the Mexican and took the phone off him politely, let me get this over with Zorro there's a good guy, he punched in a number and listened to the voice on the other end, "Ok this is, err what was my code again JJ, sorry anyway, come and get us can you, these guys are cool and the drinks are free and no shooting we don't want to wake the neighbors."

"What just walk in, just like that Dude?"

"Yeah, the guys are now under new employment, they are now hotel security operatives," he winked at the grinning face of the Mexican and his gold tooth.

"What about the Washington link?" Asked JJ.

Dude held the speaking hole on the phone, "He needs a name guy, the big man who gave the order for the kid nap, a gringo or a local?"

"Oh, a very big gringo Mexican, big money and a big mouth." he took an envelope out of his pocket and handed it to the Dude.

He read it, "Err......bla, bla, bla, ....err....... from the Governor's office JJ, and a great big star-spangled banner with the Texas lone star to the side, I think we have him guy."

He turned to the bandit and grinned the man grinned back, Dude clinked glasses with him and laughed.

"So, what you gonna call your hotel then guy?"

"The Zorro!" shouted Rufus through to them.

"Well, I like it man!" laughed Dude.

Zorro laughed with him.

"Hey, I hear that there's a show happening in town shall we go and visit and while we're there take a look at your new hotel, I can see the gold lettering sign The Zorro Hotel, clittering in that golden sunshine, sunshine."

Dude was about to take a swig of his drink, but Rufus took it out of his hand and swigged it back in one.

He grinned at Zorro, "So this is the first, I want at least 10 hotels here in Mexico City, I'll need staff and I want them to look like you, the mustache the cowboy boots the lot, I want silver spurs and silver belts on all the waiting staff, this is going to be an icon Mexican palace, big hats on all the door men yes! Get me son?"

"Get me son? What is get me son?" asked the bandit.

"The vision, the idea, the dream!" Rufus rubbed his hands together and laughed, "We are going to re-invent Mexico, I wonder if the casinos in Vegas would want a slot, a good idea?"

The bandit grinned from ear to ear.

The dude picked up the bottle of southern comfort and swigged from the neck, "Bonkers!"

"What is bonkers?" asked the bandit.

The Dude pointed to Rufus.

"Yeah, but with money bonkers, yes?"

"Yeah, a good point, who's money by the way?" screeched the Dude.

"Well, yours yank, who else?"

"What?"

"Oh, didn't I say?"

Dude chocked on his drink as the bandits laughed at the mad American gringo.

"You've got American finance rolling?

Rufus gave him his best toothy grin.

The door opened and the place was suddenly full of people, Augusta appeared from the lock up and punched the nearest man to her.

"Hey, Augusta, he's American!" shouted Dude.

She ran over to him and punched him in the guts.

"I'm not the kidnapper," he thumbed to the grinning face of the bandit, "He is, but Lord Longmore now employs him as hotel staff."

"What the hell is all this?" she screamed.

Simon was now at her side and looking at JJ who was talking to the bandit, he elbowed Augusta and nosed to the tall young American.

Augusta interrupted the smiling conversation as she punched JJ in the kidneys.

"What the fuck is all this?" she screeched out.

"Calm Gussy, the deal is done, it was a rat hunt and we've found him so cool it."

"So, what am I, the smelly bit of cheese?"

"You smell good to me honey!"

She punched him again but all around them were laughing and drinking.

Dude handed her a glass of Southern Comfort, "Calms the nerve babe!"

Simon took it and drank half the glass in one go, she snatched the rest from him and started laughing with them all, before draining the glass.

# CHAPTER 17 ... The Entrance to the Slums ... Mexico City

The burnt-out cars at the side of the road and the trash cans piled up full of plastic waist, marked the areas of slum clearance, they passed a sign that read, the future of the country is in your hands, little children were running around totally naked but having great fun in the spray from a fire hydrant that was leaking onto the road.

People were all walking in one direction, Cal nudged George, "Follow them, let's see what's happening."

George slowed down to a walking pace as cars followed them at the same pace, no one wanted to overtake, "What the hell is this?"

Cal was silently loading another clip for her heckler, checking each bullet with her fingers, her mind wondered to her Granddad as he explained about shells, "They all have to feel the same Cal, and a bulge or chip, you throw it away because it'll cause a stoppage when you don't need to be stopped get it?"

"I got it Pop!" she said to herself, she thought about his lesson's on how to handle a short as he call a hand gun, "Take the short out of the sling clip very slowly you can shoot yourself if you're stupid enough to rush the trigger, finger down the barrel at all times and not on the trigger, that is for firing and not for the handling, lesson one! pointy end forward!"

She silently giggled at his words; George brought her out of her thoughts.

"What the hell is that?"

"What?"

"The noise Cal, a mariachi bang, listen, wonderful, eh?"

"A concert?"

"A show!" said Ruth, "Look!"

People were walking to the music wearing strange costumes.

"A cowboy!" said George.

"A country and western singer?"

"A talent contest!" said Brenda, "Up the road in front of us, look."

"That's Tolly's voice!" said Cal, "What the hell is he doing?"

"Simon Cowell was not available perhaps?" giggled Ruth.

"What the hell is this?" shouted Cal.

George started to laugh, "Why would the DGI of the UK be hosting a talent show in the middle of a Mexican slum?"

They found a car parking slot near the veg market and everyone got out, "Full tactical in line please," said Cal, "Brenda, you are rear guard, hidden weaponry please we don't want to frighten people.

A four-by-four truck stopped at the side of them and in his rear window was a full gun rack of various rifles and shot guns.

"Like him them," said Ruth.

"He's a local, perhaps he's the local fuzz?" said Megan.

Brendan cuffed her head as they walked off and mimicked her voice, "Perhaps it's the local fuzzy?"

"Feck off!" said Megan.

Brenda pushed her so that she could take the tail of the line, George led them through the crowds of people as the music and shouts of the people got louder.

The music suddenly stopped, and a man was now singing an Elvis song without accompaniment, when George caught sight of the singer, he started to laugh, he stopped and bent over, he couldn't walk for laughing.

Cal looked at who he was pointing at, "What? who?" then she recognized the face. Rufus was giving them his best Elvis impression together with knee the trembling made famous by the legend, the king of rock and roll.

She couldn't speak, the situation seemed so wrong she just stared as George laughed at the side of her.

"He's good, eh?" said Megan.

"Ah huh, huh!" said Ruth in an American accent trying to get a laugh but Megan didn't get it, however Cal did, and screeched out laughing, suddenly Augusta was hugging her and crying on her shoulder.

"But Gussy?"

Augusta pointed to the talent judges, "Smart arse'll fill you in, I don't understand what the hell he's talking about most of the time mum, he's so full of crap!"

Cal hugged her back with repressed relief then sobbed around her daughter's neck.

Then Gussy turned back to the singing, "He's proper rubbish mum, still, Simons up next."

"Doing what?" asked Cal in a complete daze.

"Oh, break dancing on cardboard."

"Oh, for fuck's sake!" said Cal as the booing started for the Elvis impersonator, Rufus was booed off stage left then the young man came on with his big sheet of cardboard from an old pallet.

The crowd applauded him in thanks for the ugly one being removed.

"Simon?"

"Yep, good, eh?"

"Oh, I remember him now Gussy, the pony club, right?"

"Yes mum, same team at the county show remember?"

George clapped the disappointed Rufus as he joined them "Where the hell have you been my Lord?"

"Oh, it was a second con for the watchers, do you know? I should have done my, you'll never walk alone!"

George started to laugh again at him as he grumbled at being booed off.

"And where are you two going?" shouted Brenda to the twins."

"We can do our standby your man routine, it'll be good!" said Kerry, Kathleen was dragging her to the registration desks.

Brenda felt George's arm slip around her waist, he whispered in her ear, "I'm too old for this Bren!"

She tried to stamp on his toe as she grumbled.

Simon was now being booed as he tried his one hand flip and stand, he collapsed but recovered with a head spin, he exited stage left when the judges pointed for him to go and to take his dirty piece of cardboard with him.

Augusta was the only one clapping her hero.

"Russell!" whispered Addy, "So who's the woman who's just dragged the chair over and is now the fifth judge?"

"Shush Addy, whisper, she's his mother the granddaughter of the woman who used to be the DGI and her daughter is the one standing next to her the sister of the little man, oh, and the bloke who got booed off singing Elvis is Lord Longmore, and he owns a lot of central London and the southeastern counties."

"Bastard!" grunted Addy.

"So baby, what the hell is really happening over here?" Asked Cal in her son's ear.

"High mummy!" Said Tolly, "It's one of JJ's plans, I know, total crap, I told him so myself."

"But what the hell is all this bollock brain?"

"Changing hearts and minds mum, the President has got the Yucatan and the Veracruz regions asking to break away from Mexican state controls favoring American financial systems for building more roads, he's offering them tax incentives and freedom of speech."

"It won't work you know Tolly!"

"He's highlighting high state corruption in Mexico City involving your Marcos cartel, apparently he's a bit peeved with you

mother, and now he's blaming the Russians and Theo in particular
for backing the new revolution."

"Why the hell are we mixed up with these people Tolly, it does
us no good whatsoever, so why? and besides he'll now give the
Army an excuse, have you morons not worked that one out?"

"He's counting on it, mum!"

"They have Presidential guard units over here sonny and a form
of gendarmerie, they're like political police."

"Yeah, JJ's been talking to them, this is all part of making them
jump off the fence one way or another."

"They won't sit by and let Americans steal their states one by
one Tolly."

"So, did he get his deserts?"

"Missed him apparently, your mates gave us the wrong info so
work that one out smart arse."

He turned his face to her, "They must have known all, along
and gave him a way out?"

"Or he has a man or even men on the inside of the
Whitehouse?" said Cal.

"No, it's a mole hunt set up by JJ to catch all the rats in
Washington, he gives them the whisper and proves he's a good
friend."

"And where's his father Tolly that's the crux of all this, where's
Jon Boy Wilson?

"Well Washington naturally mum where else should he be?"

"Now that's your answer smart arse, right there, so he's the
other hit squad, best watch CBS News night on TV later sonny."

"What, another?"

"Oh, wake up you moron, we're being used, get us all out of this
and bloody fast Tolly, and why is your father not here?"

"He's in Winnipeg flying the flag for the Wilson's."

"Canada, so you had already asked him before me then?"

"He asked me to ask you."

She stared at him in suppressed silence as the music of a one-man band rumbled on in the background.

"Am I a split family mother, are you two estranged?"

She started to cry as she looked at the man playing a violin and banging a drum with his knees.

"He said he was out Tolly, horses that's it, finished he said, done and dusted he said, he lied to me, all these years and he lied to me, am I a monster Tolly, have I lost my love?"

Tolly's eyes betrayed his panic as his mother started to collapse in emotion, he searched the crowd for his sister Augusta, when they locked eyes, he nodded to his mother who was crying at the side of him.

She was there in seconds as Cal started to clap the man playing the violin, she wiped her eyes and sobbed to his music, Tolly joined in with the clapping and so did the audience as one beginning to applaud the man and his music.

"All these years Gussy, and he lies to me, am I that bad a wife and mother that he would do that, well am I?"

"Yes!" shouted Billy to the one-man band, Tolly nodded and handed the man his yellow ticket to the final.

"Who?" asked Augusta.

"Dads in Winnipeg talking politics with the Canadians," Said Tolly, "He's back in the game and hasn't told her."

"You mean you haven't told her, you should have given her the chance to object, but you didn't, you're following everyone's plan but ours, where the hell is your head these days Tolly?"

"He wasn't given a chance to object so why should he give her a chance?"

"He was?" said Cal, "He said that I was needed, and I was a trainer, he backed me in all I was doing, until?"

"Until what mum?" asked Augusta.

"The call Gussy!" said Tolly, "The call to the king's bench and the privy council by our grandparents no less."

"Dexter and mum?" asked Cal, "He's a privy councilor and he didn't even tell me that one."

"And ex-President Jon Boy Wilson, also got the call."

"But he's American."

"He excepted none the less mum, the King follows advice from them all."

"So, the King brought him back into the game then?" asked Augusta.

"Basically yes!" said Tolly.

"So, in answer to your earlier question Tolly, yes, we are estranged by a long way, a very long way it seems," Cal started to sob again.

The crowd erupted in clapping as the Irish girls started doing their sister act singing stand by your man and dancing to their own song, high kicking in sequence in the Irish style."

"I want to go home Tolly please, back to my house and four lonely walls!" said Cal.

He gave his sister the, do something quick stare, his eyes locked on Augusta's in panic.

Ruth was suddenly at Caledonia's side and tugging at her sleeve, she nodded to the armed men above them on the hotel veranda.

"A fat bold headed bastard Cal, looks familiar, ready?"

Cal shook off her sadness and followed Ruth through the crowd, she was angry and ready for anything, she adjusted her work tools as she walked.

"Shit, not here woman!" shouted Tolly, his voice was dulled out by all the shouting and singing of the audience as they enjoyed the entertainment.

He elbowed Billy for any advice.

Billy whispered in his ear, "She'll need back up and an escape route boss, this could end up being a bloodbath if we aren't careful."

"Shit!" screamed Tolly.

"We don't have a handle on this one boss, make a call and bloody quick!"

Billy handed the Irish twins the yellow card and nodded to Cal and Ruth who were heading away from them and to the grand hotel overlooking the market square.

"She's on the hunt girls, so move it and give her back up............go!"

The crowd clapped them as they walked away from the stage right, and into the crowd, a juggler filled their gap in the ongoing performances, but the crowd were bored and started to give him some loud abuse, they'd seen it all before, so he had to go left.

# CHAPTER 18 ... Plaza Hotel Mexico City

Rufus dragged George into the entrance and foyer, through the swiveling door.

"Good, eh? I've just bought the place, what do you think?"

Brenda followed on and listened to their conversation.

"Why?"

"We need a base here in central America, why not Mexico City, and why not here?

"In the slums you idot?"

"Re developing the whole area, American investment in infrastructure."

George grinned at him, "Other people's money?"

"Err, der! "Grinned Rufus.

Suddenly from up the upper rooms they could hear gun shots, they continued but Rufus carried on walking to the restaurant.

"Are you deaf!" shouted George.

"My new security team sorting out the trash I won't have gangsters in my hotels."

George looked at Brenda and then back to him, "Can you hear this nutter Bren?"

The shooting upstairs stopped as she spoke, "He has this place George, and he has the brain to work it here old man, so let the kids do their thing."

Cal and Ruth burst through the swinging door and stopped in front of them.

"What the hell Rufus?" screamed Cal.

"Why don't you girls go home and leave the politics to people who know what poverty really is eh?" said Rufus.

"What the hell is going off here?" screamed Cal.

"Hey, look I bought a hotel, and I made new appointments in the new hotels, Zorro is now general manager, and The Dude is our developments director for the whole group.

The Dude appeared on the upper landing and grinned to the group down below, "Jon Boy can get fucked, he didn't trust me to do shit so he can fuck off, I'm with Lord Longmore now, and so is Leonardo."

"Who's that?" asked Rufus.

The Dude thumbed to Zorro and his Mexican moustache, "Your Hotel manager My Lord!"

Zorro grinned down to them; the gold tooth shone in the bright lighting.

"I prefer Zorro!" shouted Rufus.

"Oh, for fuck's sake!" shouted George.

Brenda punched his arm to shut him up, "What about your wife Rufus?"

He pointed to the enormous Yoshi who stood at the back of the Dude and Kiki, his wife on the stairs.

"My family are all here and waiting to greet you all, welcome to the Zorro Hotel, we are re-branding the place, what do you think George?"

He was about to swear but Brenda punched him again to shut him up.

George nodded to him and finally smiled, "And Mexican bandits on the doors?"

"I like it," he shouted up to Zorro, "Bandits on the doors, big hats, cowboy boots, what do you think?"

"Cool boss, we need more staff then?"

"Well manage, Mr. manager."

"Fucking bonkers is what I think, "said George.

"Is this the animal you talked about boss?" shouted Zorro.

"He's more than that Zorro, he's my dad and best friend in the whole world, he cares, and I want you to be like him caring and responsible, he's our expert, talk to him and learn a different trade my new friend, he's Mr. Security expert, your apprenticeship starts today, yes?"

Georges eyes watered as he listened, but Brenda prevented him from getting Lord Rufus in a head lock, she stopped his forward movement.

Ruth touched Cal's shoulder and pulled her out of the zombie state she was in as she stared and listened to Rufus.

She whispered in her ear, "Well is the target dead or what?"

Rufus heard her and shouted up, "Job done Zorro?"

"Yes boss, a clean sweep."

"Good, photograph the scene for posterity then bury them all or, .......no, a better idea, give them back to their families and tell them what real scum bags they had turned into, yes?"

"Oh, and we'll pay for the funerals, deepest respect and all that, clear?"

"Clear boss!"

"He's as smart as he is mad George, that's a cleaver twist, respect for the dead," said Brenda, "He knows how they think."

"Poverty Brenda, I've been there, and I know how it feels to be on drugs and have no hope in the world, none!" said Rufus, "I know what desperation really means dear, I lived that life before I was saved by an old man with a plan."

George burst away from her, and he gave Rufus the bear hug as he sobbed on his shoulder, "You're a good lad at heart and I'm very proud of you sonny."

"And Aunty Helen?"

"She would say that you were fucking bonkers, but I would disagree, and to her face son."

"Unless she had the golden Heckler in her hand big man?"

"Well, der little man, I'm not that bloody stupid!"

Cal had to see what had happened, so she and Ruth ran up the stairs, Yoshi escorted them to the bloody scene in the Presidential suite.

Rufus gave him the stare, he knew what to do if she did finally crack, the dead men splashed over the seating made her gulp and sweat, then the smell of death hit her like a hot wind, she started to shake and sob on the spot.

"Cal!" shouted Ruth, "What's up?"

Yoshi appeared from the back of them with a large towel and gently placed it over her head, then lifted her off the floor and carried her away to another room, Cal started to scream as she was carried away, the noise echoed around the walls of the hotel as she gasped breathed and screamed but clung onto the big man.

Ruth looked down to Rufus from the landing in shock, he stared back at her, "I'll send up some tequila, make her drink it and then let her sleep, all perfectly normal in her business, and don't judge her, understand?"

George patted Rufus on the back, "She would be so proud My Lord."

The music continued outside as the show continued oblivious to the new hotels owner and friends, the gun shots were all part of Mexican life, just another day in the City, the City of the dead, but there was a bright awakening of the bright dawns light of future hope in the hearts of the slum dwellers, they cheered as the little chili peppers were declared winners of the show by Billy, he demanded that they do their thing one more time for the people of the City.

Tolly received the news from George's phone call, he was expecting it, he looked around for Augusta, she was watching his eyes and knew instantly what the problem was, he nodded to the hotel, so she walked off, she was greeted by Brenda and the girls at the swinging doors.

"How is she Brenda?"

"Sleeping Gussy, go give her some love eh."

Augusta walked off to the stairs, Yoshi met her and guided her to the room in silence, she hugged him for being there for them all.

On opening the bedroom door, she watched her mother rock to and fro as she sat and dribbled in her zombie stare at the wall.

She barely noticed her daughter as Gussy held her tight, she cried on her shoulder as her mother gently rocked and mumbled.

"It's time we went home mum, what about a trip to the ice?" she turned and noticed Ruth in the corner sitting holding her legs high on the armchair, she stared at them in silence.

"Ok Ruth?"

"I'm broke as well Gussy; I can't do this anymore; this is insanity woman!"

Augusta smiled at her, "No one will ask you again Ruth, but you have to say no if they do, and mean it, understood?"

"Yes Gussy....................will she recover?"

"My Great Grandpa used to say that this life is not for the woman, it's not natural for the hormone of love that women have, he was the smartest man ever Ruth, we should all have listened to him."

"But will she come back to us Gussy?"

Augusta nodded, "We've been here before, so yes she'll be back on the road, she needs my dad to bring her back, he's the only one who she'll really listen to."

"I thought that there might be a rift between them Gussy?"

"Na, we are Inuit, it's to the bones with our people, he will always watch over her no matter what."

"So where is he now then?"

"Yoshi stands in his place like the friend he is, he's a good man and we call him family just like you Ruth, so stay with us please."

"Doing what?"

"Being the supportive friend Ruth, just like you normally are."

"I have no one else you know Gussy, I was a Royal Marine from a child, I lived it and loved it all my life, the betrayal by them was so shocking, I couldn't believe they would do that to one of their own, they slammed me up as a flake."

"So, this, you and her, are all I really have."

"What no man in your life."

"He was married."

"Oh, for God's sake Ruth, pack it in woman and start living, turn lesbian or something."

Ruth started to laugh, she couldn't stop laughing at Gussy's words, "Volunteering?"

"Certainly not, my hero is downstairs finding out about my crazy family the quick way."

Ruth carried on laughing at her, "And will he stay?"

"It's the one thing we have in common, we both come from families who are bonkers, he had a grandfather who lived under the dining room table because of the bombers at night, the servants feed him where he is and everyone carried on as if it were all perfectly normal, see what I mean Ruth?"

"Two lovers clinging together in the crazy world of families eh Gussy?"

"Bang on that woman!"

Ruth picked up the opened bottle of tequila and took a took long slug, "Want some?"

"No!" said Cal, "But I might partake if you don't mind."

Ruth jumped up in excitement at Caledonia's recovery, she walked over to her and gave her the bottle then climbed onto the bed and spooned her to get warm.

"Gussy says become a lezzy Cal."

Cal took a long drink of the alcohol, "I've tried it madam, you're the wrong Lego brick so think again pimple tits!"

They all started laughing at her words and her arrival back in the world.

Gussy climbed onto the bed and joined in the love in, she kissed her mum and Ruth.

Cal handed her the bottle, she took a long swig in support, then coughed at the strength of the tequila, "Bollocks, that's bloody strong woman!"

They were now both soundly asleep, so she took another drink then put the bottle on the table and joined them in the three-woman spoon, she clung onto them and cried.

"I'm ok by the way from the kidnapping, if anyone wants to ask."

# CHAPTER 19 ... Assembly National ... Hotel De 'Ville ... Ottawa ... Canada

Erick stood before the committee of enquiry into the proposed inclusion of Canada as a satellite state to the United States of America, the assembly rooms were full of people and the press gallery was heavy with interested parties.

"I am here on behalf of the Crown of King Charles, I speak his views and will answer questions asked of him as if he were here, the UK government however is still in the white paper stage and refuses to comment until it is read before the house."

The state rooms erupted in jeering and booing.

"Order, order, order please delegates and governors, give Mr. Trueblood the chance to put over his views please after all we're not Americans, well not yet anyway."

The place burst out laughing at the speakers' words, then fell silent for Erick, he breathed out and took his time to read his notes before carrying on with his speech.

"My Lords, Governors, delegates and people of Canada I stand before you today with a proposal, it's an old idea and one that we as a Nation should consider, we are and always have been a democracy and so in the end we have to give this idea to the Nation for the final vote, so think hard before you boo and disregard the movement of change sweeping Canada, an American idea, yes, and natural next logical step in democracy? Yes! Why? Well, we need friends and in the modern world we need them even more, big economies will swallow us whole, they will destroy our native cultures and our way of life, the American President offer's brotherly companionship of equality and fraternity as envisaged by the originators of modern democracy, our French and British families.

"The old phrase, what's in it for us comes up time and time again so let me hit this button now, they offer financial support for industry and agriculture, they also offer military inclusion to the world army, yes you heard right the President wants a world army to police dirty corrupt and damaging parts of the world, he wants peace and security for every soul of the human race, Canada will be part of that and take its place in the great friendship of mankind and before you ask, no, not in the toothless United Nations more of the right and wrongs of conducting ones population, we can judge and we will judge when a President of a Nation builds a golden house and his people don't have water to drink, yes we will judge."

"And, yes, it is our business if a country is destroyed by incompetent rulers with old tribal ideas, we are in the 21$^{st}$ century lets behave like it please."

"And the Inuit's will still be killing whales then?" shouted a delegate.

"Or left to starve by an uncaring Government as per normal sir?" shouted Erick back to him.

"How dare you call us uncaring sir," shouted the Speaker.

"And how dare you make a comment at all sir, you're the speaker of the house, what is this law of the loudest voice? You are here to organize a discussion and debate the plans of the nation, so shut up .... sir!"

Erick's face was red with anger at being interrupted.

"We in the Inuit community have been starved out of real politics for years, we are always at the bottom of any new development!"

"That's because you don't want change up there, you could moan for Canada, this is wrong that's wrong." said another Governor.

"It's called democracy sir, the numbers of people verse the requirements of the Nation, we vote on helping and working with each other, we do not let our people go without the necessities of life, hospital care, food and water in hard times."

"That's every winter!" shouted the delegate.

"And every summer with the forest fires, Inuit's and all the Tribes join in and fight with the rest of the tribes and we don't have forests! We live above the tree lines."

"That's called being a friend to the Nation."

"President Wilson asks us to join his union of nations, its easy, why argue the point, after all we are all North Americans, it's a greater advantage to be joined with a superpower than to sit back and watch the system grow without us in the mix, its reality, we will just be even closer friends that's all."

"And open boarders?" asked one of the delegates.

"We have that now once the snows hit, this country has always been used to store and supply drugs and illegal alcohol in passed times, we haven't been very good neighbors to them, have we? The bad guys have been running our boarders for years."

"It will give us control as we use both police forces and both resources, the whole system will be far more efficient and that's not including the military.

"It's the vast practicality of one administration."

"And one American leading us, a king in fact including all the red tape used by the Americans, they'll take and not give!" said the same Delegate, "We'll become second class citizens in our own country."

"Do the British regard us as second-class citizens? No! So why should they, we are the same continent, there is no argument that supports separation of the Northern continent, we are already one, I don't see the problem Delegates?" Shouted Erick.

"But they can't even control their own states, look at Alabama and the lower States, poor farmers grubbing a living in the swamps."

"And being subsidized by the farming system to be equal with the grain States of the mid-west, their system has been proven to work the same as ours, we copied them in fact!" Said Erick in response, "We already use their system to sell our grain all over the world."

"This is about people control Mr. Trueblood!" shouted another Delegate.

"Yes it is and why not, there are kings of drugs, kings of black markets, there are kings of money laundering and there are kings of the city backing systems that steal billions and back handed investments to defraud the State, I suppose I'm still a cop at heart I want justice for our people and fair play in business and banking, so in short I do want control I want the people to see that we can keep control, now that's the most important meaning of democracy, fair play and decency in public office, a transparent administration with no biased dealing with multi agglomerates with fingers in our pies!"

The place erupted in shouting and jeering Erick's speech; he waved them away as he sat down to the applause of other backers of the new ideas.

The Speaker stood up "We thank Mr. Trueblood for his opinion, our next speaker is his grandmother Mr.'s Alice Talbot, the former wife of Joseph Trueblood our Prime Minister of the eighties, now she represents the North American Tribal Council of First Nations Canadians and Americans, ok over to you, Mrs. Talbot.

Alice stood to stare at them she stood in her white Inuit kagoul and pulled her hood down to reveal her platted grey hair, she put on her glasses to read her speech and smiled at the Delegates, "Do I feel a chill in the air?" she grinned.

The place burst out laughing at her, she gave them time to settle.

"I followed my grandson who I must say I'm proud of, well wouldn't you be proud, look at him, he's so handsome but he was the ugliest baby you could ever wish for, people used to say to me, oh dear, or, well we can't all be good looking can we?"

The place burst out laughing again at her words.

"I must say that I'm proud that King Charles has called him to his privy council, and I don't think that means cleaning the toilets, do you?"

"He advises Britain on foreign affairs and gives Canadian views on many things, he is more powerful than an embassy and more subtle than our ambassador, to them he is Canada and he's an Indian!"

"He also has friends in Japan, he calls them brothers and China, he has become a world leader in planning and thought, he talks with professors of strategic command structures and military pre planning campaigns, but as you've just heard at heart he's still that Mounty that I didn't want him you join, by the way, when he was 19 years old, I didn't want them to have him no sir, I objected strongly, but as always with men he ignored me and joined up, at his passing out parade I cried a bucket of salt water as I watched him on that big black horse trotting down main street with the flowers of our Nation, good men and women wanting to keep us safe and make our country good to live in.

"I can tell you, I cried again today when he stood and gave us his speech, the boy has grown into a man, a man of peace and I hope prosperity, he's a thinker and we should all listen before we open our mouths to argue, think it all through, the pros and cons of unification, because that's what it is a unification of the continent of multiple nations, multiple religions and multiple colors."

"As a leader in the continents First Nations Council I have to say that we are still waiting for our answers to many land grab questions and water management enquiries, but you see we've been dealing with the white man for three hundred years and he lies he cheats, he steals and in the end he kills for more and more whatever we have he wants, the forest, the lakes the fish the fur and even the sky and wind!"

"As I said I hope you understood when I said that I was leader of the Continents Tribal council, you see we have never recognized the boarder of the white man erected to keep out competition from other white men, we are a continent and I mean right down to Argentina and yes even the Malvinas Isle or the Falklands islands that the British deem so important to their national esteem."

"You see there it is National esteem, the reason we go to wars, the Nations pride that another Nation is better than us, how childish, how foolish, yes there are reasons to protect innocents because they are always the ones who suffer, women and children normally."

"Now we in the Tribal council regard this idea as a way of stopping wars, land grabs and water miss managements, we will have a bigger say as continental inhabitants, after all this is one world and one planet, the boy is right we cannot deny that this is one continent of the Americas, it's always been this way, only land grabbers of the 18th century changed the maps and declared us separate for each other, we never really were, the ancients dealt and travelled the length and breadth of this continent without borders and fences, it was called freedom and we want it, we want it all back!"

"What is there to fear, just fear itself!"

# CHAPTER 20 ... Press room ... Hotel De 'Ville ... Ottawa ... Canada.

"How's he doing Augusta?" asked her mother Caledonia over the phone.

Augusta had her earphones in as well as listening to the ongoing debate, through the speakers.

"Two nil down mum, I don't think this is going to work, I think it's down to basic trust that they don't have for the Americans, they see corruption all over the place and nothing changing, I kind of agree with their thoughts, you?"

"It's not going to happen Gussy, it's too big a step for such a traditional Nation, the Americans need something else, I think it's the French thing, the Canadian French are funny people Gussy, they want to be Canadian but French as well, boots in both camps, something has to give though."

"What a civil war?"

"Stop it, stop it right there Gussy, don't start with the new idea's, how's he looking?"

"Tired and drawn mum, he needs you to be here, just get on a plane please."

"He has to ask darling you know how it goes."

"Stubborn cow!"

"Say's one who is!"

"How's Ruth?"

"She sleeps a lot, she's changing, I think we have a problem with her, what do you think?"

"Delayed shock of actions over the past few months she needs time to think, why don't you get her, and you fit again?"

"Stop it...............so how is my son these days?"

"Oh, come on, so you haven't spoken to him either? Oh, hold on, that's Great Grandma Alice on the stand mum and she's mad, I can tell 'I'll ring you back I have to interview her for the station, just get on a plane and get over here, let Ruth run the department."

"I quit Gussy!"

The phone was silent as Augusta listened to open air, "Are you sure?"

"Yes, I'm done Gussy, let someone more qualified run it, I'm done."

"Ruth?"

"She's done as well, no, I've recommended George to take over, who else is really qualified down there?"

"Now there's another estrangement coming on, and Brenda will blame you, mum!"

"Yeah, do l sound like I care Gussy?"

"You care mum, you're not speaking to a minion now you know?"

"We need talent Augusta, let's hope that George can find some to carry on, all I'm saying is that I'm out!"

"And Tolly?"

"He wanted me out, just like Pop, he sees what's happening and waits to make a comment, it was like working with Pop all along really Gussy."

"Get on a bloody plane woman and get here, your man needs you, understood?"

"Clear Daughter, ok I'm on route, I'll bring Ruth she needs a trip out I think."

"And find her a man while you're here."

"You sound like Nana Gussy."

"Well, someone has to mother."

"Anyway, who'll want a nutcase like her?"

"Well, you found one mother!" Cal growled before Augusta slammed the phone down on her.

She stared at Ruth who was eating cereals with the wrong spoon and didn't notice.

"A dessert spoon is better Ruthie."

Ruth gave her the middle finger and carried on eating and watching the cartoon on the TV.

" What is life to sit and stare, what is life, but to live and dare? To care, to share, to have fun in the sun, I want to start living again Ruth."

Ruth gave her the long-confused stare.

"I'm changing Ruth and I'm bored out of my head, are you?"

Ruth ignored her banter and carried on eating.

"Who are you Ruth, where are you from?"

Ruth spoke with her mouth full, "Adopted, age 5, nice people, I love them, they're the best, love is all there is."

"Really?"

"Yes really!"

"But why the military?"

"Brownies, girl Guides, D of E awards and Royal Marine cadets, special forces sniper as we all were then the big put down and prison, then you, my last hope in the world and what a world it is Caledonia."

"I might slit my wrists listening to you madam?"

"Oh please, and yes the answer is yes, I'm bored out of my scull."

"And no man in your life ......... Poppit?"

"Oh, give it a rest woman!"

"Why don't we find you a nice middle-aged banker with more money that brains, you can shag him to death and inherit all the dosh, bing, bang, bosh, the plan, right?"

Ruth burst out laughing at her, "Leave it, leave it right there please!"

# CHAPTER 21 ... Tactical Suite ... Whitehouse ... Washington ... USA

"We got him Mr. President, the Mexico people have got the evidence to fry him, what do you want me to do?" said Lenny.

Jimmy stared at him and then the bank of screens as he thought about it all, "How did you get it all Mr. Homeland security?"

"We trapped him in a double bluff sir, bang to rights."

"Trapped, eh, like a wild animal, caught in the trap, what'll he do Lenny, run or fight his corner?"

"He'll balls it out Mr. President and wait for you to make the decision."

"What death or dishonor?"

"He's fried sir, what choice do you have?"

"You're a hound Mr. Homeland security, you follow the chase, I have to think before I act, people will be watching."

"What people sir, this is all internal."

"People in the know Lenny, our own juniors in the system, they see it all and say nothing, but what do they think?"

"They follow and obey orders sir just like we pay em to do."

"But is that democracy Lenny, ain't we acting like the Nazi, or the GRU?"

"I don't get you sir?"

"I'm the youngest President ever, the kids like me want it done differently, we don't want blood on our hands, and we don't want them on yours."

"But how do we defend ourselves sir, yes you're a young guy but times are the same we have to protect, that's our job!"

"I know what you're thinking Lenny, I'm not Army or Marine Corp, that's the other side of my family but that is the very reason I wanted this job, I want change Lenny, get it?"

"Your English Nana eh, boss?"

"You heard then?"

"Hard not to see it Mr. President, your Pa did the killing for her before he became President and your brother, well it's in your blood ain't it?"

"Have you met Tolly?"

"Yes, he's......................... dangerous I think, he's smart and ruthless when he wants to be, I know that about him, he chops off heads when he feels like it."

"And you think that's effective?"

"Definitely scary boss, it keeps them from our doors."

"Lenny! I need more from you than yes sir three bags full sir, I need your opinion all the time, forget my Pa he was an officer, and they have to make these decisions all day long but not me, I have experts like you so give it to me please! would you kill the man?"

"Yep!"

"Why?"

Because he will always be there, whispering and trying to back stab you when he gets the chance, hey I'm just a cow poke I just follow orders, nothing more."

"Well not any more cowboy I want your full opinion on all of the work, reactions, connections, possible outcomes, public opinions, military opinion, I want a secretary of the interior Lenny and I choose you to be my eyes and ears, well can you do that?"

"You're stretching me, to see if I'll snap, yes?"

"Yes! ............. well?"

"I'm not a politician Mr. President, I speak my mind to those who upset me."

"Good Lenny, I like that, so will you do the job?"

"Yes, boss but you have to replace me, who you gonna choose?"

"I'm not Lenny, that's your job, I just sign him in if and when, get it?"

"You're handing me the seal?"

"And the ink, Pa trusts you and so do I, all of the interior, the whole kit and caboodle, you cool with that?"

"And you think I can do this?"

"Hey, you ain't the only one being stretched here Mr. Secretary."

"FBI, Homeland, SIS, Spooks in foreign lands?"

"The whole toolbox Lenny."

"Wow, and your Pa said it was, ok?"

Jimmy started laughing at him, "Ah...so that's what they all think then, Jon Boy Wilson is pulling the little guys strings, yes?"

"It's just talk sir, they don't know you yet, I'll put em straight if that's ok with you?"

"Yes, put them all straight please, this is being done my way, no killings, not slamming them in jail unless they kill innocent people, then they get the chop from the top floor, get it?"

"I got yer boss, so that's how it'll be done from now on."

"Good, so that's settled then? Ok wheel him into my office I'd like a chat with the traitor Mr. Secretary."

"Sir, yes sir!"

"You can talk to me you know, I'm open for any discussion, I have an uncle who wants to implement a red file system here in the States, what do you think?"

"Yes sir, he talked to me as well and passed on the old man's intentions on the subject."

"Augustus Talbot's plan then?"

"Yes sir, Marvin, sorry sir, your uncle is asking me all the time to implement the said action list, I just need your nod and I'll do it."

"Ok, hold that thought and let me think on that please, no action until I give consent, clear?"

"Clear sir, outline it to some who would be contractors for the work?"

"Err ... no, not at this time, let me wise up and think about its need first, ok with that?"

"Ok sir, I'll leave that one with you for now, do I remind you in the future though sir?"

"Yes, give me a full year to think, things might be needed if my plans hit hurdles, right?"

"Big money people out there, with contractors on their pay roll, you might be forced to react in the end?"

"True, but not for now, please, on second thoughts Lenny, I'll meet this scum bag on the south lawn, away from people if you can organize it, please."

"Sir, yes sir!"

# CHAPTER 22 ... Washington ... The White House South lawn

The lawn was full of people from the various parts of the political life of the capital, mingling to get to know the new young President, to understand what he was all about.

"Walk with me Donald," said The President.

The Texas Governor stared at him suspiciously, "You're going to get rid of my state then Jimmy?"

The President started to laugh, "And do what with it?"

"Well, give it to the Mexicans as an olive branch?"

Jimmy stopped him to talk out of the reach of the others on the back lawn enjoying a picnic with their families, "I have you bang to rights Donald, setting our friends up to take hits, all to embarrass me, eh?"

"No Sir to save a civil war, some of us disagree with your idea's what's wrong with that?"

"Agreed Donald, what's wrong with a disagreement? ..... Did you know that I'm a thinking man Donald, I think, and I plan, and I work things in my head for months, years in fact, this is not my fathers or even my grandfather's plan, this is mine Donald, you don't think I can do this do you?"

The Governor stopped and looked into the Presidents eyes, "No Sir I think that it's too much of a mouthful to swallow in one chew, your eyes are bigger than your belly."

Jimmy laughed at him again "I'm an historian you know Donald, I like the stories of ancient Rome, that's us you know, the eagle, the religion, the politics."

"Don't make me laugh Mr. President, this is the 21$^{st}$ century and we ain't putting up with dictators, no way!"

"Agreed Donald, and I'm not the king, in fact if I called my self a king and started dressing up in purple suits what would happen?"

"Civil war sir."

"Exactly Donald, civil war, but we're more like the Romans that you think, our politics are dirty sometimes, take your slimy behavior for an example, now if our positions we're reversed and you were the President and I was Governor of the lone star state you would have had me put down, right?"

"Wrong sir."

Jimmy laughed out loud again, "You think that my Pa's pulling all those strings, don't you? Well, he's not, I'm in command here, understand?

The Governor stared at him waiting for the hammer blow.

"But you see, I've been thinking, long and hard and I'm comparing this country to the old Roman empire, greedy patricians owning all the land and treating folks like slaves all over the place, then asking for their vote at the elections, it's not sustainable is it, Donald, they'll twig the scam in the end man don't you think?"

"I don't understand Jimmy."

"Little people Donald, they want, they want a slice of the pie, now in the past we've been able to deliver in this country, agreed?"

"The same as your speech then, if you work hard enough then you can make it here, yeah, I agree Mr. President."

"You see now Governor I've been thinking about all of our systems, well you and I come from different worlds, agreed?"

"Yeah, Mr. President I suppose we do."

"The thing is this Donald, if I can't convert you to my way of thinking I might as well quit and take up farming, do you see what I'm coming to sir?"

"Err............no Mr. President I don't."

"Give me a year Donald, a year of unquestionable loyalty in all I do, back me for one year and if you do and I balls it all up, then you can just flick your fingers and I will quit on the spot, I won't even finish my term of office I'll pass it on, what do you think sir?"

"But your family Jimmy, what will they say?"

"Do I look like a person who gives a damn about my family and fail the plan, look if this fails then so do I, they do, and in the end so will you, do you see that clearly now?"

"We have to evolve, or we die Donald, the whole system has to move on, just like the Roman Senate, we have to change with the times, or someone will want to be king and take us all by surprise, just like Julius Caesar, oh he'll be fighting a war or something and use executive powers to shut down all free speech just like the Nazi Germans did in 1936."

"You really are the ultimate Democrat aren't you Mr. President?"

"It's a living organism Donald, we nourish it and keep it moving or it'll kill us all in the end, just like Rome, get it?"

"And I thought that you were a spoilt brat trying to live up to his old man."

"Hey! I am, and I love my mommy! So, the deal here, today sir?"

Donald laughed at him then held his hand out, "Agree Mr. President."

Jimmy stared at him for a short while as he prepared the next statement.

"The wall will have to come down Donald, I need your backing man, the word is that the little people like the idea, what are your thoughts?"

"Untrustworthy Mr. President, bad boys the lot of em!"

"And if they're gone what's left?"

"A lot of poor people sir with nothing to eat."

"Hey Donald, we can sort that out man in the land of the free, yes?"

Donald nodded to his ideas "How wrong can a man be about a kid like you Mr. President?"

"We have talent just being wasted down there Donald, world saving talent in those poor folks, we need them man and all the rest, cool with all that?"

"I'll have to change tack Jimmy; it'll be hard for a while man."

"You're a good man Donald, I'm glad they didn't kill you for being a scum bag."

Donald smiled at him, "Just out of interest Jimmy, how'd you get to know it was me?"

"Poor people Donald, those poor people who worked for you, they saw the light and changed sides, they'll all do the same man when they see what's coming."

"The train rolls on then Jimmy?"

"I'm so glad it didn't run you down Donald, we need men like you sir."

"Man....... you are smooth, I see the light and the talent now Jimmy!"

Jimmy shook his hand again and smiled at his old enemy, "Let's go get a cold one!"

"What about your father?"

"Do I look like a guy who takes advice from a previous President?"

"Yeah, you do!"

"Anyway, I'd be a real idiot if I didn't, right?"

Donald burst out laughing at the president's words.

"I have a change of heart kid, so you and me are what?"

"Political allies sir working for our country to overcome internal disputes, clear?"

"Well, yeah, clear young man."

# CHAPTER 23 ... Longmore House ... Kent ... UK

Cal watched her eat breakfast again as they sat in the nursery kitchen.

"I miss the kids you know, all the action, all the fun of life, doing this, going there, chaos most days and now I watch you eat for entertainment, not good is it, Poppit?"

Ruth gave her the middle finger with her spoon hand then returned to chomping and slurping.

"Hey Pimples, did you know that the new President of the United States of America is single, his mummy Kelly is the first lady, what do you think about that then?"

"Must be gay what else have you got for me?" said Ruth.

"Oh, you are a miserable cow, bloody cheer up woman!"

"And do what?"

"Ever considered politics?"

Ruth turned to her and was about to laugh but she just couldn't, "Do me a favor Cal, shut up woman!"

"I can introduce you if you like Pimps?"

"To whom, the President or politics?"

"Well, both, what do you think?"

"What the hell are you jabbering on about?"

"Look we get out and travel some, you can be my personal bodyguard and I'll be the visiting friend to the first Lady, you know the one who brings all those destructive criticisms to her front lawn."

"And Canada?"

"Yes, at trip over the boarder obviously."

"Look Cal you don't have to be nice to me, just give me the elbow and I'll just leave, not a problem, believe me."

"What Pimps, we're not friends anymore?"

"Will you stop calling me Pimp or Poppit, I hate the names!"

"Friends Ruth, yes, or no?"

She smiled at Caledonia "Yeah, we're friends dib dub dib and all that."

"Well so is she, she needs us to bring her down to earth with a bump, imagine all the dinner parties she has to attend, day in day out, imagine."

"And we scare them shitless, like vampires from the spook house arriving for the fresh blood?"

"God, you are so depressing woman, look we just invite ourselves to her party and look good, what else can we do?"

"Oh, just give me a plan Cal then shut up, please!"

"He's good looking you know Pimps, tall blond, God like really, I'm surprise he's hasn't been gobbled up by those American beauties."

"That sounds disgusting Cal, give it a rest for God's sake."

"In fact, all the Wilson's are good looking, must be all that sunshine out there in California, I think that the youngest is also single."

"The odds are that at least one of them will be gay, stands to reason woman."

"Well let's test it out, what do you think?"

"Err.................................................no!"

"I want to live Ruth and I'm going to start living again, so tough shit if you don't like it, understood?"

"So, you're going to play away then?"

"Never you silly Cow, Erick just needs sorting out that's all and I want to see Alice as well, I miss her, come on more your arse, let's go!"

"To Canada?"

"No Washington woman weren't you listening to me?"

"Not really no, so how old is he anyway?"

"Well too young for you madam, anyway how old are you?"

"Mind your own dam business Caledonia!"

"I'll just ask Bobby to give me all your records."

"No, stop!"

"Bobby, how old is Ruth here?"

"Caledonia, she is 29 years old if her birth record is correct, she was adopted in."

"Stop Bobby!" screeched Ruth, "Ok, you moody cow, let's go!"

"To America, yes?"

"Yes, to America, ok, let's just get it done."

Cal gave her the toothy grin, "Blond, tall, God like!"

"Shut, bloody up, you cow!"

Caledonia giggled as she hugged her.

# CHAPTER 24 ... Arlington Ridge Park ... County Virginia ... USA

Caledonia stopped the driver at the side of the lake, she tapped his head, "Stop here Terry please."

"For why Ma'am."

"I'm going for a swim, what else?"

"Err.................................... Ma'am, this is a public place, it's not allowed."

She was taking off her clothes as he locked eyes with Ruth, "Not allowed Ma'am, you cannot just swim here it's............. it's....... too bloody cold?"

Ruth looked at the cold lake and giggled at Cal "Bonkers, what the hell's wrong with you woman?"

"Hey, security, get your clothes off and follow me madam."

"Oh no, not now?"

"Move it pimps!"

Cal stepped out of the limo in just her bra and pants then walked to the edge of the lake, then turned to Ruth as she was just removing her sweater.

Cal dived into the deliciously cool lake and swam away.

"Oh shit!" screeched Ruth as she followed her into the cold dark lake, she squealed as her head broke the surface, "You're fucking nuts woman!"

Cal wasn't listening as she swam under the surface for as long and as far as she could.

Ruth swam as fast as she could in her racing crawl to catch up with her, but her heckler harness and the weapon slowed her down and destroyed her streamlined shape.

Cal's head came up out of the water, she was laughing at Ruth, "This is living eh Pimps?"

Ruth was gasping with the swim and was being pulled under water by her weapons harness and ammunition clips on her belt, "What the hell?"

"Out of shape Pimps?"

"Bollocks!" screeched Ruth before gulping some of the cold water as she struggled.

Cal disappeared again under the water and Ruth felt the touch as she swam underneath her, she watched the dark shadow as Caledonia swim away from her.

"Bastard!" she swam after her as fast as she could, when she looked up again Cal was near the shore and a scruffy looking man with two Jack Russell dogs was laughing at her, his knees were out in his jeans and his battered overcoat made him look like a vagrant, she panicked and headed for the inevitable conflict as fast as she could.

The man helped Cal out of the water and hugged her, Ruth was gob smacked with shock, before she could reach the shore she started shouting, "Leave her alone scumbag or your arse will be in a sling in ten second!"

The man turned to her and smiled but she was now just nearly out of the water and would be on him in seconds just as the two black sedan cars screeched up to their car and black suited men came running over.

"Take him!" shouted Ruth, "She's a VIP, do it! Do it now!"

The suits surrounded the vagrant and Ruth breathed out a sigh of relief as she stepped out of the lake.

"You see Caledonia these Americans are nice, just like the seventh cavalry, right on time."

The group of men opened to reveal the man still hugging Cal.

"Come on, do something you morons!" shouted Ruth.

"Is this your security Aunty Cal?"

"Yes Jimmy, ex Royal Marines, they didn't want her, so we took her in and fed her up a little."

Ruth pulled her weapon to drain the water out of it and was immediately surrounded by guns pointing at her.

"Is she secure Mr. President?" shouted one of the security men.

"Mr. ....... Pres............" squeaked Ruth.

Cal and Jimmy bent over laughing at her, "What the hell are you gals doing swimming in the memorial lake Aunty? It's supposed to be a mill pond, it represents peace and tranquility and that's my Great Grand Daddies memorial over there, where they took Iwojima, the Marine memorial, look see!"

Cal looked to the great war memorial and laughed with him, "Yeah, I remember now sonny, how's you mom, is she home?"

He handed her his buzzing phone; she pressed green and started laughing again.

"What the hell are you doing you crazy cow, that's a memorial lake and there's a couple of nutty Brit's swimming, and I'm thinking who the fuck, but then I see Pimples the poor cow!" Kelly burst out laughing at her."

"Give her a break Tart, she's on the hunt for a husband."

Kelly's voice echoed over the lake as she screeched out laughing.

Jimmy thumbed to the overhead drone and smiled at Ruth's confused face.

"What do you want slapper an arranged one, we can help you know, I got two you know and they're good boys too, well one of um is as boring as hell, but the other is doing well, I think.

"Shut up mom!" shouted the President as he stared at Ruth, his security men started giggling at his mother's words.

Her face was purple with rage and embarrassment in equal measure.

Terry appeared and broke the stare by throwing a beach towel at her, then moving over to Cal he handed her the towel, he pointed to Ruth as he laughed.

"Tea and yabba cake Tart? "Shouted Cal

"On the south lawn, because you ain't coming in my house looking like that Butch!"

Cal threw the phone back to the President as she laughed.

The dogs came over to Ruth for the sniff, she bent down to pat one of them, but the dogs growl stopped her movement.

"That's crazy Eddy, he's from Lester's shire, he has to get used to you Miss?"

"I think that must be Leicestershire in England, Mr........"

"Yeah, the UK, a friend gave these guys to me, he said learn how the Brits think by watching these little guy's, they think that the world turns around them and they do you know?"

"Ruth.........security." she grinned.

"Ah, Miss Security, nice to meet you Maim."

"No, that's her. I'm just the grunt."

"Yes, Maim I get it, do you grunt a lot?"

"What?"

Jimmy started laughing again as he walked off, "Nice legs though, maim."

Cal gave her the eyes as they climbed back into the limo.

"Don't start on me!" said Ruth to her grinning face, "What the hell's wrong with you woman?"

Terry was giggling as he drove them away to the White House secure parking lot.

"He's too young for you anyway Pimps, the youngest President ever, a record breaker in fact, he hasn't even had time to find a wife."

Ruth boiled up again as Terry giggled from the driver's seat, "You rang them!"

Cal ignored her, "Guess who gave him the dogs as a Christmas present?"

"Santa Clause?" Said Ruth, trying to be sarcastic.

"Tolly, he said it would give the Americans an understanding of the British mentality a couple of never give in, frightened of nothing ankle biters, what do you think?"

"The damn thing very nearly had my fingers."

"Protecting their boy, you'd do the same wouldn't you, gnashing ankles and all that?"

Terry burst out laughing again, Ruth leant forward from the back seat and slapped his head.

Her face was still glowing from embarrassment.

"I was going to shoot the President of the United States of America!"

Cal burst out laughing at her again, "Nice legs maim!"

"Shut......... the fuck....... up woman!" she pulled the Heckler from her under arm sling and released the clip, the water whooshed out and drenched her dry jeans, it now looked like she had just peed her pants, "Oh for fuck's sake!" she screeched.

Terry leant forward out of her reach as he squealed out laughing and so did Cal.

Ruth watched the tears in their eyes in the mirror as they laughed at her.

# CHAPTER 25 ... South Lawn ... Band Pavilion ... The White House

Caledonia ran to Kelly and picked her up off the grass, "Too many executive lunches you Tart, get some of this blubber off you woman."

"And how's Nutty Ville these days, I hear you're the new Queen, right?"

Cal put her down and stared into her eyes, Kelly watched her eyes start to drip tears with emotion.

"Sorry Cal, I wasn't thinking, sorry babe, I meant the Queen of Sheba."

Cal hugged her again then wiped her eyes and sniffled, "I just can't get used to her not being there, I have to get a grip on life Kelly, it's becoming really embarrassing."

Kelly pushed her away and took a good look at her, "I hear there was a breakdown?"

Cal ignored her and turned to Ruth, "Yeah too much action and not enough air."

Kelly looked to Ruth to explain but Ruth was silent.

"Her too, eh?"

"Change the subject Tart, what do we have to eat?"

Kelly looked at Ruth again and received the nod of approval.

"Two broken lesbians trying to make sense of life, eh?"

Cal's tears instantly turned to laughter, "Three, you Tart!"

Kelly ran off as Cal chased her around the manicured south lawn, both women were screeching as loud as they could.

A shadow appeared over Ruth, she followed the blue sleeve up to the Marine in full number one uniform, "We have English tea if you'd like some maim?"

She looked up to the familiar face, "Err....... do I know you?"

"I don't think we've met my name is."

"Jon Julian!" shouted the President, "Give her space man, she might want to breath warm air not cooled in your dark shadows?"

"Older Brother to the spoilt brat, at your service maim."

Ruth stared into the God like face and tried to smile, she was stunned at his beauty, his pearly white teeth and the peak cap that shadowed his forehead.

"Note the poetic nature of my little brother maim, a real smart ass!"

"You smell of boot polish and gun oil, is that normal?" she whispered.

The face widened into a grin, "Brits, always with the piss taking? Army?"

"Royal Marine sir!"

"Wow, hey Bro, you are in real trouble man!"

"JJ, shut up!" shouted the President.

"Husband?" asked Cal when she had caught hold of her.

Kelly dragged her back to the Pavilion to sit and talk.

"So, you're the arse hole who did the planning in Mexico City, a total kybosh balls up!" screeched Ruth.

"Ewe" Said the President, "She has you taped JJ."

"And where's yours Caledonia?"

"She's estranged," said Ruth.

"Estranged?" asked Kelly.

"Hold up here just a moment, Tolly did the planning I was in his loop, I simply followed orders!"

"And the Dude?"

"Err.................Pa's idea."

"He's a slippery one grunt," said the President, "Always with someone else's fault."

"Her names Ruth Winstanley, an ex-Marine," said JJ, "She has a kill list as long as your arm runt, she will eat you for breakfast and spit out the pips."

The President stared at her in silence, "Lucky maim, that's what I think, I've had this all of my life, you're very lucky not to have siblings to irritate every move you make in your life, he's the critique from hell."

She stared back at the President, "The Dudes words Mr. President, stick your job up your arse!"

"I wanted him to retire," said the President, "How do you think I could do that? He's the same age as your mom and there he is out there still reporting back from outer Mongolia or some place, the lonesome rider, I pushed Ruth and he reacted, bing bang, bosh and he's out of the business and into the hotel industry, just like that, understand Miss Winstanley?"

"You planned it?"

"Yeah, bad?"

"Err............... all of it?"

"Me and Tolly are good friends, always have been, the streak here and Pa pretend but Tolly and me are the real thing."

Ruth looked around at the faces staring at her, JJ started to laugh but he was on his own.

"Well, I don't like her and that's final!" said Kelly.

"Mom, shut up woman!" shouted the President.

"Impressed yet?" asked Cal.

"Err.............................yes!" said Ruth as she stared into the Presidents big blue eyes.

"Oh no, not another God dammed Marine in my house, don't you dare James!"

"So Tolly planned his mother's departure from the industry then?" asked Ruth.

"Yep!" said the President, "Just like the old man told him to do, get her out before she goes nuts, all clear now everyone?"

"Both he and you pushed and pushed us all, and you know my mother's age?"

"I know about everyone, and what do you think I do for a living Ruth?"

"So, you know who my father was?"

"Is Ruth, is!"

"He's alive?"

The President smiled at her, "You're half American, didn't anyone tell you that?"

"Who is he?"

"The Dude, you, stupid woman!" shouted Cal, "Cor blimy, thick as a bloody brick!"

She turned to Cal, "I have a family then?"

"Well not really, "said the President, "The Dude is a millionaire surf bum, come Marine that lived and worked with my Pa, who now runs a string of hotels for you know who?"

"He doesn't know you exist Ruth," said Cal, "Totally in the dark, wham bam it's in the can, your mother died in childbirth, and he didn't know about any of this, your birth records however show us who you really are and who the father was, a lanky streak of piss US Marine, Walter (The Surf Dude) Harrison, now retired,"

She turned on Cal, "And you knew all along?"

"I wanted you to come home woman, this is your country, get it?"

"You sly cow, you could have told me back in the UK, I could have checked it all out!"

"Do you see what I'm up against, she is nuts," screeched Cal.

"You could have said Caledonia, I thought that we were close but then you do this to me," she started to cry.

The President stepped forward and held her as she wept.

"I still don't like her," said Kelly.

"Yes, but you have to admire her coolness under sudden changes and turning on the water works like that, come on that's real talent don't you think?" grinned Cal.

Kelly started giggling at Cals words, "You are such a hard woman, so......how are we going to get your man back?"

"Oh, for God's sake?"

"Ruth!" screamed Kelly, "What the hell's wrong with her, why can't she keep her man safe and why has she left him to do this on his own?"

Ruth wiped her face with the back of her hands, "Why have you woman?"

"That's it, someone give me a gun and let me shoot her!"

"He must be playing an away game?" said Cal.

"Gun someone, I'm going on a Brit killing spree! Jimmy, where the hell is your father?"

"Helicopter please Ralph," Said the President, into his phone, "On the south lawn, away in five please, Canada, yes to check on Pa and Uncle Erick, yes he's my uncle, yes Ralph, I'm related to all of them, now please, hello in there, now is now!"

The faces looked at him as he shouted to his helicopter control director.

"What?" Said the President as the faces stared.

"Jimmy!" Kelly started to cry, "Look at him Cal, he's took over, just look!"

"Na needs more passion, "said Ruth.

Kelly chased her over the lawn squealing and shouting as everyone else started to laugh at all the mad folks.

"No more Goddammed Marines in my family, got that slapper?"

Cal doubled over laughing at the mad first Lady of America before the world became dark and very windy as the helicopter came down to land on the south lawn.

# CHAPTER 26 ... Mexico City ... Mexico

Adrian gulped in fear as the young man came over to him then sat right next to him in the food hall, "Err............ what sir, what can I do for you?"

Tolly placed his hand on Addy's knee, "George tells me that you are the sweetest human being on the planet, he says that you would help your worst enemy if he was in trouble, well would you Adrian?"

"Err............ yeah, I am, I suppose."

"I want to take all the winners to Las Vegas and get a big show rolling, in your line is it, Adrian?"

"Err.............no............ not really, but."

"Now I like that no but, that means that you can and it's just up to me to bribe you, right?"

"Bribe?"

"The Adrian Monkhouse star spangled stars road show, in town seven nights rotation in all the casinos on the main strip ............................ yes?"

"Bastard!" said Addy, "Russel!" he screamed, "Get me the phone and a peach slumber, plenty of ice, I have to call a friend!"

Tolly leaned in and gave him a kiss on the cheek, "I believe him now boss!" he handed him a card with phone numbers written in red.

"Boss, bastard!" screeched Addy, he turned to look into Tolly's eyes," But why?"

"Immigration Addy, we need mass immigration!"

"What the bastard for?"

Tolly's wink sent shivers down his neck, "Russel, peach bastard slumber at the double, extra gin, bastard!"

Tolly laughed with Billy as his phone rang in his pocket.

"A change in the plan boss?"

Tolly looked at the picture of the caller, "Oh, here we go, yes JJ, now what?"

"Easy man, easy, we have demonstration against immigration happening in Washington, we have to deal with the fallout first so can you scrub the plan buddy?"

"Hey, not my idea in the first place, you can't force people JJ, it's going to take time and money," he held the mouthpiece of the phone and shouted to Addy, "Addy! scrub that idea for now, we have other plans, ok?"

"Bastard," squeaked Addy as he walked off to collect his strong drink.

"So, spider man, what next?"

"Jimmy's gone to Canada, the official visit, fan fares, the lot and your mothers here with them, care to comment?"

"Is she normal?"

"Well, what the hell's normal with you guys, she has her bodyguard with her, is she normal?"

Tolly held the phone as he thought about it all.

"Still there, runt?"

"I suppose the action was discussed then?"

"Well, huh and yeah, she blames you buddy."

"Oh bollocks, mothers, eh?"

"And mines gone nuts in her company, what the hell's wrong with you people?"

"And your father?"

"Canada, with yours talking annexation of the southern provinces who vote to leave the Union."

"Too fast JJ, how many times? Drag your brother into a discussion and tell him to slow down, he'll cause a war man!"

"Oh, by the way, Texas is sorted, the Governor is in our loop and talking positive with the President."

"And you believe all that?"

"Yeah, why not?"

"Too easy JJ, get your brain working slush puppy."

"What the hell does that mean?"

"Corruption bollock brain, check him and his friends out, get Lenny to find out if he's genuine or just pulling the wool."

"So, they'll accuse use of corruption first then?"

"Err............ der.......... first stage, blame the slush funds coming from America, second, pretty boy politics, is he real or the puppet?"

"But my brother is the genuine article, he means every word."

"Well prove it to the nation arse hole, do it."

It was JJ's turn to hold the phone in silence.

"Working it out Giraffe brain, what is it rarefied air up there in the clouds?"

"Shut up let me think, who could do that?"

"Uncle Patrick, err............... der?"

"But why would he want to get involved?"

"Well ask, a personal favor to me perhaps, pull strings, get him elected to congress if you like."

"Shit I never thought of that one, that's a cool idea Tolly, I like it, but would he want the hassle man?"

"He'll be bored stiff, corporate law JJ, the most boring thing on the planet, play the game, what the hell am I, your brain cloud base? Do it."

"But he's Irish?"

"Half Irish JJ, the other half is an American hero, they don't come bigger than him man."

"Yeah, agreed."

"So, what's happening here in Mexico now then JJ?"

"Err............ slowly, slowly, catches a prairie dog, I'll meet you in Aspen, I want you to ask.............. please!"

"They'll try assassination you know JJ?"

"Over my dead body runt!"

"Ok what about a sexual deviant, eats babies for Sunday lunch, you name it, and they'll throw it, clear?"

"His history assassination?"

"Lay it all out there JJ, old girl friends, everything, you have or don't have in fact, understood?"

"He'll kill me Tolly, can't you just do me that little favor?"

Tolly cut him off, he didn't know if Tolly heard the request, "No chance, sort your own family problems out, I have my own."

"You can bollocks, I'm doing it anyway, this is my idea!" shouted Addy as he took his drink off Russell, "This is my chance and I'm having it, got that Mr. Gangster from London man?"

Tolly saluted him and walked off giggling, "Thanks Addy, that's a great idea, thanks!"

"What is .......... what bastard is?"

"Back to the office I think Billy, we need to circle the wagons."

"What?" asked Billy "What bloody wagons?"

"Oh, and we need friends to be with Adrian while he sorts his show out."

"Listening protective friends' boss?"

"Well, der, perhaps Uncle Rufus could provide security for them, families and friends maybe?"

Tolly took his phone out of his pocket and pressed speed dial 1, "Hello Uncle Theo, how's things?"

Billy stared at his head as he walked off, "Who?"

Tolly waved at him as he walked off talking to Theo.

# CHAPTER 27 ... Ottawa ... Canada

Ruth was reading the news channel on her Q pad "Who the hell are they calling a hooker?"

Cal munched toast at the side of her at the kitchen table and looked at what she was reading in American headlines on her little computer.

"They don't like you Pimps, look at that picture of you, wow sexy, eh?"

Ruth swiped the page to reveal Cals front page spread," Nipples are us Cal, well it was a cold day."

"Shit!" muffled Cal with a full mouth of toast, "Bastard's!"

Ruth was silently reading the article "It's ok Cal, you're the Spetsnaz colonel flown in to kill the President.

"Shit!" squeaked Cal

"They think that you're really sexy, hold up, that's not me and they are not my mammary glands."

Cal flicked her page back and started to laugh, "They've stuck your head on a top model's body, now they are tits darling, proper ego boosters!"

"What a bunch of shits, so who is it Cal, who the hell?

Cal flipped pages to get a name of the writer, "It's a gossip mag's adaptation of the Presidents girlfriends, wow there's hundreds of them.

"Yeah, who though?"

"Well English naturally, err............ Michel Durand."

Ruth snatched back the mini laptop and read some more, "French Cal, part of Monaco World News, it's for the glossy mags.

"Complete bollocks then, so why?"

Ruth ignored her as she read on, "They're trying to smear him, hooker girlfriends and friends who kill people, look!" she passed it back over to her.

"But they're making it all up, it's total kybosh,"

"The plan has started then Cal, the mudslinging, the character assassination, they want to filth him, they're now calling him the playboy of the north, three in a bed partying and snorting drugs on the weekends."

Cal was now on the phone and waiting for it to ring out, "Gussy, what the hell is he doing?"

"Mum! don't you know what time it is?"

"What?"

"It's three in the morning mum!"

"Why, where the hell are you?"

"Rome, back in my office, well not there at the moment obviously, I'm in bed and trying to get some sleep, but then there's my mad mother ringing me and shouting incoherently in my ear, what do you want mother?"

The snoring echoed over her bedroom as Simon turned over and relaxed even more at the side of her.

"What's that noise Gussy."

"Oh, the air con is having a bad night, so what do you want?"

"David at Monaco News, he's turned on us, what the hell for Gussy? Go for him please."

"What's he done mum?"

"Pictures Gussy, a center spread of me and enhanced tits for Ruth."

"Jealous mum?"

"Not funny, Gussy, they are going for us and trying to smear the President, so go for him please and shut him up, that's if you can?"

"What paper is it?"

"Err.................... Ruth what paper is it?"

Ruth pressed page up and tried to find the name, "The Starlight."

"The Starlight Augusta, so go for them and filth their story please."

Augusta started to laugh at her.

"What, what is it?"

"That's a lad's mag, just tits and slappers mum, no one reads that crap, it's published in Paris, complete morons, don't worry, I'll see what I can do, can I get some sleep now, was this all a dream mother?

"Why the hell are you reading a tit mag for Ruth, what the hell's wrong with you woman, turning or something?"

Ruth was reading some more, "International press, it says here Cal."

"International Press Augusta, now I know that's your lot so what the hell's happening here?"

"Err..................give me time mother, I'll find out, leave it with me for now."

Augusta had now got the mag on the screen of her I pad, "How the hell did they get these pictures, that's me in the background."

"Your people Gussy, find and destroy please, hello, still there?" she was gone.

# CHAPTER 28 ... The Caledonian Hotel ... Rome ... Italia

Augusta had cut her off as she read the headlines from Essential America News.

"Well, who the hell are you Essential America because I've never heard of you."

She looked at the clock on the wall, "An hour before dawn." she tried to go back to sleep but found it difficult as her brain swam round and round.

So eventually she pulled out her laptop and did the research on Essential America, but Simon was grunting and snoring his way through his bad dream, she found a name and smiled, "At last a thread, so who the hell are you?"

She pushed Simon out of the bed with her feet, but he took the quilt with him as he fell to the floor, and he was still snoring his head off.

"Now who to ring first?" she stepped out of bed and opened the giant curtains to reveal the early morning light of the eternal City, she opened the doors to the balcony and stepped out into the morning air, she loved the place so much, but she had forgotten that she was totally naked, she held the leaves of the lemon tree and the mint and smelt her hands to wake up.

"Mama Mia!" shouted the window cleaner cleaning the other windows to the side of her.

"The early bird catches the worm!" she screeched out laughing.

"Englazy, bloody bonkario, normally, eh?"

She gave him the Italian finger flick insult and sniffed the air; suddenly hairy arms took hold of her and dragged her back into the room.

"Typically, he spoila my view!" shouted the window cleaner, "Bastardo!"

"We ain't got time for that woman get in that bed now!"

She tried half heatedly to fight him off but gave in just as her phone played Scotland the brave in a metallic tingle.

"That's Hoots mon, what would he want Si?"

"Who cares what he wants, it's what I want that counts around here woman," said Simon.

She pressed green and listened.

"Gussy we have a problem, Lassie!"

Simon put his tongue in her belly button, and she squealed out, "Stop that!"

"Stop what Lassie, ah, sorry darling am I stopping something important."

"No Grandpa, carry on!"

"Who, me or him Lassie?"

She slapped Simon hard, "Pack it in moron!"

"I'll ring later girlie. I don't want to interfere with nature."

"Grandpa, what's the problem? Simons got to go out and get us some breakfast," she slapped him again to make sure he understood her demand.

"By the way does he carry Gussy, know what I mean?"

"Err ............ well, yes, a problem?"

"Official?"

"Yeah, Italian license to protect the VIP, i.e., me, so what?"

"I'm sending a full crew to help, ok with that?"

"What the hell for Grandpa?"

"Well, you're out on a limb out there Augusta, we feel that you're at risk of abduction."

"Abduction, do me a favor!" she watched Simon strapping on his gun harness, a lump of metal fell onto the carpet, she kicked it back to him and hurt her toe."

"What the hell is that, Simon?"

"What?" asked Dexter.

Simon picked up the lump and put his fingers through it and showed her that it was a silver knuckle duster, she watched him clip on his sikes dagger under his armpit sling.

He settled his ammunition pouches on his hip belt.

"Augusta?"

"Err .... I think he's ready this time Grandpa, whoever they are they will feel pain that's a guarantee."

"Not a third time Gussy!" said Simon.

"I think he's in the mood Grandpa, so don't worry, ok?"

"So, he got my present then?"

Augusta laughed at him, "Yep and he likes it Grandpa."

"It has a special blade Gussy, titanium I think."

She held the mouthpiece "Titanium, so who gave you the knuckle duster then?"

"Grandma Alice, "he grinned and showed her his low upper cut to the chin.

"He's prepared Grandpa, don't worry please, so come on what is it you really wanted to say to me?"

"We have a problem Gussy, the press has the scent of a scandal involving the new President, his many women and all that."

"And the drugs?"

"What bloody drugs?"

"It's a joke Grandpa, relax, it's all over the gutter press, what you need is a good lawyer, just the threat of the one I have in mind would be enough I think?"

"Would he be Irish Gussy?"

"Bang on old man."

"Am I Augusta?"

"What bang on or old?"

"Both?"

"Well, der, I have to be cruel to be kind Grandpa."

"Oh Augusta, you do hit low woman, nearly as hard as your grandmother."

"Never Grandpa, never as bad as her, so what is the real reason, come on out with it."

"I've got to kill a man Gussy and I'm not sure if I can anymore, understand?"

"Wooow there too....... fast, did we cover that one? Wooow hold on, you're going to ask me a to get a favor from my mother, aren't you?"

"Am I so readable Gussy?"

"No, she will not do it grandpa, no way!"

"Safety?"

"No way, why now though?"

"He threatens our safety Gussy, he's a press baron out of Australia."

"Oh! So now I fully get it, you want me to kill this bloke?"

"Would you dear?"

Augusta started laughing at him, "What's he done Grandpa?"

"He's.... err, made advances to your grandmother and I want to kill him, .... wrong?"

"Very wrong, how long has this been happening?"

"Oh, I think 20 years or so."

"What!"

"Pop would have downed him there and then but me, I'm such a wimp I want her to be happy, that's all, should I fade away Gussy?"

"What the hell's happening with you, what's up down there in the south China sea?"

"He's dead Augusta and I still can't kill him."

"Shut up and put my grandmother on the bloody phone, now! I need to talk to a grown up."

She heard the scuffle as Elizabeth took the phone off him, "Augusta, we need you to make waves in the publishing industry, we want you to filth and degrade a man named Jack De'Montfort, he was massive in the print industry many years ago, he died, well just like us he dropped out of circulation, haggis bollocks thinks that he can be shaken out of his retirement, we need him you see."

"Why, to kill him again."

"Na, he's jealous of the bloke, I used to know him in a previous life, I just happened to mention it to your grandfather and here we go, know what I mean?"

"I don't get it?"

"Just give it a go please Gussy, he was the big wig in Australia for a generation, newspapers, mags, the television, he ruled the roost."

"I don't get the why grandmother?"

"Do you need a reason?"

"If I'm going to filth the man then yes, I do, and now I think of it, that's why he's sending backup, this man must be dangerous, yes?"

"Oh, deadly my dear, that's why haggis wants him dead rather than being a work tool."

"What the hell grandmother?"

"He was one of Pops associates dear need I say more?"

"But why, that's not a reason?"

"I'm calling him to the privy council darling, and I need him to attend, get it."

"And grandmother, there must be a great big and in there, yes?"

"He's the biggest drug Lord in southeast Asia darling, understand now?"

"My God grandmother what the hell are you people on?"

"He has the links Gussy all and every link we ever need are in that man's head, clear?"

"That's crazy!"

"Augusta, filth the bloke, call him a pig to a dog in all the languages you print in, then when he shows up at your doorstep put him on the phone to me, please, no one else, clear?"

Augusta breathed in and out as she listened," An historic deformation of all his good works over the years, yes?"

"Destroy his rep with the good people, he'll hate all that, get his charities to dump his plaques and statues and re-name hospital wards, get me darling?"

"There's something else isn't there, grandmother?"

"Look, I think he's followed me over the years, and he will have followed the family, you're now the top dog in his industry so a word from you and he'll appear out of the forest, understood?"

"And kill me?"

"Augusta, start with a wedding announcement for you and Simon, we think Malaysia is a good place for him to show up, so KL for the wedding program, got that? We might be lucky and get him in close without destroying his rep completely, yes?"

"But Simon hasn't asked me grandmother."

"Put him on the phone darling I can sort that one right now."

"No, you cannot, this is my life grandmother and it'll be done my way."

"Ok, do it your way but make the big splash announcement for all of your readers, clear? Make it Australia if you like dear, we don't mind."

"When?"

"Now Augusta, today, what time is it where you are?"

"Five am Grandmother, hold up a moment, the Privy Council?" The phone was now dead in her hand.

She shook her head and climbed back into bed, when Simon arrived back with the coffee and dough nuts, she was soundly asleep hoping to wake in a better dream.

"Who was that on the phone then Gussy?"
She turned over and ignored the bad man making all the noise.

# CHAPTER 29 ... Aspen ... Colorado ... USA

Patrick sat on the step and watched the Cockrel strut around the yard bullying his females, "King of your castle eh Rasputin, "the dog came and sat next to him and also stared at the colorful bird, "You don't want trouble either Howie, I don't blame you dog, he's mean, next he'll be wanting your job around here, hey perhaps he's already doing it?"

Carol handed him his mug of tea and sat then sat next to him "Watching the world, Patrick?"

"Yep, the real world, aren't we just chickens scratching around thinking that we're doing some living."

"You want to do this don't you?"

He turned to her, "I'm a rover Chuck, it's what I've always done, rove, the wheels turn and I'm happy, I'd just forgotten the real me, is that wrong to say?"

"No Patrick, it's wrong to ignore I think."

"Do you?"

"Yeah, all things change and move, we don't have a choice mostly, well except you that is, you make changes Patrick, for me and for them," she thumbed to the house behind them.

"Do I have your permission, Chucky?"

"Since when have you ever asked?"

"This would be a big move, Government in the end mark my words, public engagements all over the place, mixed marriage haters looking at you and calling you a half breed again."

She linked his arm with hers, "Do you mind?"

"Yeah, I mind, I mind a lot."

"But you're a Paddy in the wrong country?"

"What are you saying Carol?"

"Who gives a damn Patrick, have you ever been ground down by any of them, ever?"

"No!"

"You see, you just don't care about abuse, in reality it gives you strength to your very core, I have no doubt that you can do this, my only worry is our security when we go down the mountain to those flat earth people with sludge for brains, ignorance is the norm around here."

"That's the very point Chuck, ignorance is unacceptable in our modern life, education, education, education."

"The politician already Patrick, you see, it's your destiny, perhaps?"

He spotted the old Land Rover in its own dust cloud coming up the mountain.

Carol shaded her eyes and searched for the number plate, "English plates, what the hell Patrick?"

"British Army foreign export Carol, they want us to know that they're safe and friendly."

"Should I Patrick?"

"Yes, dear cover me as I talk to them, any suspicion of drama and shoot them."

She rushed into the house and pulled out the rifle then opened a window to prepare the shot if needed, she shouted out of the window to him, "The school bus will be here in a short while, what should we do?"

He was concentrating on the driver of the Land Rover then started to grin.

The cloud followed the Land Rover as it skidded to a stop in front of the drive, Dexter stepped out and grinned.

"You're dead!"

"A slight exaggeration perhaps," said Dexter, the chickens flew off in all directions in shock.

Liz stepped out and walked over to him, she hugged him hard then gave him a kiss, "Safe and sound, eh?"

"Yes, Elizabeth, we can see them coming for us from here."

"Prepared?"

He thumbed to the gun barrel in the window, "She's a better shot than me Liz."

Carol squealed as she ran out and hugged Elizabeth.

"What's the problem with calling on friends for help here Patrick?" said Dexter, you're living like it was the wild west here son, there's no need for all this."

"I was shocked by being kidnapped Dex, I needed to do something about security but."

"But it's as boring as hell, eh?"

"Yep! boring as hell, I need the life Dex, I need to get back to doing something interesting, is that why you're here?"

"Funny you should ask that Patrick, there is a question I have for you."

Liz squealed out "He's going into politics Dex, could be the next President you never know?"

"Oh!" said Dexter.

"So, what was the question then Dex?"

Dexter stared at him as he thought of an alternative question, "Well who called you to go into the slippery poll circuit?"

Elizabeth's eyes locked onto Dexter's, she shook her head slowly at him, he agreed with a nod.

"JJ Wilson on behalf of his little brother, he'd like a running mate in the first round of primaries in a year or two."

"So, a governor of a state first then?" asked Liz.

"Yeah, this one Liz, the Rocky Mountain state, good idea or what?"

"Well, you won't be bored Patrick, that's for sure," said Dexter.

Patrick looked at them one at a time, "Pop would disapprove wouldn't he, too public and all that, yes?"

"It would have been his next logical step, Patrick; remember how he was?" Liz mimicked the old man's croak voice, "I need a mouth on site lad, and I want you to go into the pit for me, so pull up your pants and start shouting!"

Patrick burst out laughing at her, "Bang on Liz, that's him, I still miss my professor of history, law, justice, what else?"

"And bull shit!" said Dexter.

Liz punched his arm to shut him up.

"You have an opinion, Dexter?" asked Patrick, "Say I'm nuts, and I won't do it."

"No son you do it, you'll make a better job of it than most and you have half the native votes all ready," he grinned at Carol.

"You see Patrick, he's spot on, they'll hate me as your wife, I'll be the mill stone around your neck in the elections."

Liz pulled her close and looked into her eyes, "Listen up girlie, you are the real American here, all of them are foreigners come to your land for the big dream, well it was yours first, they can be racist, snobbish or just morons but you have the real right to be here and not them, stick your nose in the air and be an Indian woman representing all of your peoples, yes!"

Carol stared back at her, "Yes Liz, I can do that, and thank you for the advice."

The dust cloud appeared at the bottom of the mountain again.

"The school bus, I have to go and collect the kids, I won't be long," Carol rushed off to her car, Dexter and Elizabeth watched her go.

Patrick watched their eyes, "Ok, out with it, why the sudden visit and why now, timings?"

Dexter laughed at his sharpness, "You see Lilly, he's still sharp."

She growled at him to shut him up, "We want you working Patrick, sorry, we need you to work."

"For whom?"

Dexter and Liz swapped glances," The King Patrick!"

Patrick started laughing, "Oh do me a favor! Come on what do you think I am, I'm not a monarchist I'm a republican, I want democracy."

"Pop would have wanted this Patrick," said Dexter.

"No, he wouldn't, he hated the blue bloods, bloody waist of good grub he would have said, absolute morons the lot of um!"

"He was a long-term Privy Councilor serving the Queen in her old age all along."

Patrick started laughing at them again, "Do me a favor, please!"

Dexter gave him the Army Majors glassy eyed stare.

"For    real...............no...........................no    chance!" laughed Patrick.

"He was Patrick, news to us all, the Queen used him as a work tool all along to take out uncontrollable weeds, bang, bang, bang." said Liz.

"Hold on here just a moment, the Queen, that little old Lady in the big house used Talbot as a work tool for murder when needed?"

"Yep!" grinned Dexter.

"So why the imprisonment, why the team of survivalists, why the breaking up of Lady Helen's little grubby plans."

"Overall strategy son, the long-term plan, his by the way, she just signed the chitty."

"Shit!" mumbled Patrick, "That's a hard one to swallow people."

"His plan Patrick as always, he was in overall command," said Liz.

"He fiddled with our lives, and we didn't understand what he was doing until the end," said Dexter, "Well at least he explained to you and Gerry at the time yes?"

"Well, yes, but he didn't mention the Queen in any conversation with us, no way."

"And what would we have all said to him Patrick?" asked Liz.

"Yeah, bonkers .... so, he had this thing going on all along, his      daughter,      his      granddaughter,      his      great grandchildren...............Tolly?"

"All along Patrick, all the time rolling in the back of his mind."

"So, Helen was always in the loop then?"

"Always."

"She was the link then?" asked Patrick.

"Yes!" said Dexter.

"But she did her best to get you killed Dex, how many times man?"

Liz stared into his eyes, "That was for me Patrick, she wanted me to marry a blue blood, she wanted me to become a Queen perhaps."

Patrick smiled, "And the old man disagreed with her then, he saved you Liz and he saved Dexter as well, she would have hated being defied like that eh?"

Liz and Dexter looked at each other.

"Never thought about it like that then?" grinned Patrick.

Liz shook her head.

"So, Helen and the Queen were big friends all along eh, making all those plans with little people like us, kill him, save him, we don't need him, all behind those palace walls, eh?"

Dexter listened in silence.

"So, they bullied Pop into doing something, so what was the scare, Russian corruption, drug dealers, were they actually corrupt or was it us all along?"

"The threat was real Patrick all of it." said Dexter.

"He took it all over so easily, we should have seen it there and then, but we didn't, why?" asked Patrick.

Dexter stared at him as he thought about it all, "Puppets on a string Patrick."

"And we loved it Dex, we were thrown into the mix, and we loved it all, that old man Dex?"

"Aye Laddy, that old man?"

"He gave us the choice of two evils, hers or his Patrick," said Liz.

Patrick watched his wife and children coming back up the mountain in the Chevy pick-up with the normal dust cloud, "And now you want me to become one of the planners, yes?"

Dexter nodded in silence.

"Next logical step, eh? That's what he would have said I think, any power in this privy council?"

"Advice and planning, political and public." said Dexter.

"With all those behind the desk links though, eh, the British way, disturb, subvert and nullify?"

"And sometimes the red line through the name son!" said Dexter.

"You see the need then Dex?"

"There will always be a need Patrick, you must understand that one, less Hitler's stirring up hatred and cruelty, no more megalomaniacs trying to buy and sell us like slaves.

"Complete bollocks Dexter, do you believe that, really?"

"Safety Patrick!" said Liz, "Simple, safety for all and we need your input, get it?"

"Do I decide now, or do I have time to think?"

"After your Presidency perhaps?" said Liz, "You're going to be busy I think."

"And Jimmy's idea?"

Dexter grinned," Bonkers, what do you think?"

"I've lived in poverty Dexter, I understand what they want, they just want the chance, that's all they really need, the chance to make a better life."

"You see boy you have the blab, you'll be good at all this," Dexter started laughing at him.

The dust cloud arrived in the yard and the chaos started with the three girls and the dogs barking.

"Tea?" shouted Patrick.

"I thought you'd never ask Irish?" laughed Dexter as he welcomes the girls to his arms and the cuddles.

# CHAPTER 30 ... Rome ... World Media Corporation HQ ...Vatican City ... Italia

Augusta picked the phone up and pressed for the Monaco World news desk.

"David please darling, yes I can hold," she hummed as she waited for the pickup.

"Yes Augusta, what can we do for you for?"

"Don't start David, so give me the inside please?"

"On what?"

"What do you think? Stop wasting time while you think and give me the source, please."

"Gussy! I can't darling he'll kill me."

"Ok, calm David, ok I'll ask questions and you say yes or no, good for you?"

"Yes Gussy, but you didn't get it from me, agreed?"

"American?"

"Yes Gussy."

"Military?"

"Err ................... yes."

"Close family?"

"How the hell did you come to that idea?"

"David, yes or no, remember?"

"Yeah, close, very close."

"Why the hell would he do that to his own David?"

"A pre-emptive whispered outlet Gussy, they all want the dirt, he just spread some around that's all."

"Not good enough David, give me the real reason please."

"I don't know Gussy, and that's the truth, really!"

"Ok I believe you; I'm putting a blue line through it though David, I have to you understand, it's complete cobblers!"

"You can't do that Gussy the press will go nuts if you block the story, you can't."

"I'm following orders David, from my boss."

"Your Boss, who's that?"

"Jack De' Montfort, heard of him?"

"Yes, but he died in an air crash years ago."

"No, he lives and gives orders out here and there."

"To you Gussy, I don't believe you woman."

"You can print the name if you like, on the southeast Asia media if you want."

David started laughing at her, "What the hell Augusta, what are you doing?"

"Following orders David, just that, get it?"

He was still laughing at her, "Ok, let me get this straight the first time, yes? this Jack De' Montfort has ordered us to block the President filth, because?"

"It embarrasses him to have his news media stirring dirt like that, the tit papers do that sort of thing."

"And where does this bloke live then Gussy?"

"On the moon David where do you think?"

"Are you for real Gussy?"

"Yes, David and make a screech when you do, please, loud as possible yes?"

"Malaysia and Indonesia, ok?"

"Possibly Australia as well David, make a splash please."

"Wow, you remind me of your Nana Gussy, you're not going to shoot me, are you?"

"I might if you don't stop printing crap sonny!"

"But this isn't?"

"No, this is world news, so do it!"

"Yes Ma-am will do!"

"Wow it feels good to put you in your place now and again."

"And mention other resurrected relatives Gussy?"

"No! Certainly not, they'll kill me you moron!"

She laughed then slammed the phone down on him.

She pressed recall for the Whitehouse "Major Wilson please darling, err Augusta Talbot at World Media Corporation Rome, I need a word in his shell like."

"It means shell like ear, cockney slang, sorry it just comes out of me now and again, family, eh?"

"Thanks darling I'll hold, no problermo."

# CHAPTER 31 ... Ottawa ... State Capital Building ... Canada

The media scrum followed the delegates as they entered the historic meeting.

Erick forced his way through the photographers to grab hold of Caledonia, she squealed with delight as she was lifted off the floor, he kissed her on the way down.

"You ok Cal?"

"Yep!"

"Breakdown?"

"Yep!"

"Better?"

"Realistic Erick, bing bang bosh and click, what the hell am I doing this for when I should be with you?"

"Know the plan?"

"Jimmy's plan?"

"Yes, the President's plan Cal, full and complete?"

She stood away from him and stared, "Changed since the last time I heard or what?"

"No, still the same, save democracy at all costs before a mad dictator takes over and kills it."

"I'm in and with you, big boy."

"Regardless of family requests?"

"You betya! They can do it themselves from now on."

At the back of them an argument started up as journalists shouted out questions, Cal turned to see where Ruth was.

"Are you the Spetsnaz Colonel Madam?" shouted a tall anchorman for a news channel, "And is she your live in lover?" talking to Ruth but he pointed to Caledonia.

Ruth punched him in the face, and he dropped to the floor, she was dragged off him by security personnel assigned for her protection, but not before she punched others.

"You, miserable scumbag!" screamed Ruth as she was dragged away.

"Are you the latest Presidential squeeze lady, or just a downtown street hooker?"

Ruth tried to get back to him and punch him again, he laughed as he wiped his bloody nose with a hanky, another man punched his head as he turned away, "You're a scum bag guy, you degrade the media with all this crap!" she cried out before he was downed by a low punch from one of the other press corps members.

The all-out mass brawl started as chairs were thrown and fists flied at each and every camera carrying man or woman was attacked and in turn punched out at whoever was close to them, the scrum became a rugby ruck as people pushed and shoved their way out of the madness.

Expensive camera equipment was smashed and broken under foot or kicked into touch by angry press agents and directors.

"As you can see Erick" shouted Cal over the mayhem, "Some of us are just to wound up."

"She needs therapy?"

"Na, just a friend in need, the maternal mother will come out in her, can't you tell?"

Erick laughed at her and pulled her away from the escalating brawl.

"Politics Cal, all the fun of the fair sometimes," He elbowed someone coming for them and pulled her down a quiet corridor then kissed her properly.

"Welcome home Babe."

"You're my home Erick wherever you are, soz for being me, the mad cow from London."

He smiled at her, "Tea and yaba sandwiches I think, yes?"

"Yes darling, yes we need to talk."

"First though I need you to talk to Gigi and get her sorted."

"What's that?"

"She's sad and going mad, help please."

"If I can Erick you know that."

"Also, the press are becoming rabid with Jimmy and his personal life, someone has tipped them off with his secrets, he's fuming."

"Who?"

"An insider he thinks."

"So, Alice, where is she?"

"She's, in Las Vegas with Adrian, they're doing a show for the casinos."

"We cannot go to Las Vegas numpty, never, understand?"

"You will do as you are told Caledonia, understood?" he squeezed her in determination.

She smiled at him just to be in his arms again, "Yes ok boss, will do!"

"Suggestions for helping Jimmy Cal?"

"Well, ring your daughter first big boy, she knows all these days."

"What does she know about all this?"

"Well, her newspapers for a start, do I have to come up with all the answers?"

"Yeah, I imagine she'll want inside info of today's multi combat activities as a sweetener."

"Do a deal, your news for her's?"

He laughed then dragged her off to the restaurant.

# CHAPTER 32 ... Pizzeria Emporia Augustin ... Rome

Simon passed over the cutter for her to cut a slice of the house specialty, she smiled at his politeness and tried to cut it, a hand took it off her and cut the slice.

She looked up to the unrecognized face, Simon had a gun against his temple and the other man stood in front of them.

"So, Augusta, why the press assassination, what have I ever done to you madam?"

She giggled in nervousness, "She said you'd be dangerous, I asked if it would get me killed and my grandmother said no, we just want to talk, something about the Privy council in London."

"Is that all you've got Augusta?"

"Yes, and some pizza?" she started to laugh.

He took her slice and took a bite, "You're of the breed aren't you little girl, fearless in the face of death."

"You must be aware of my grandfather Mr. De'Montfort?"

He started to laugh, "Oh yes, Dexter, he'll slice lumps off me whenever he's given the chance, yes?"

"Hunt you down like a dog."

"I loved her you know?"

"Who?"

"Your grandmother, me and Liz, wow, we had fun in the sun when she was younger, before your mother's outburst," he winked at his security man who then sat down next to Simon and smiled, Simon nosed to the pizza and smiled back, the man then realized that Simon had a gun pointing to his lower half under the table.

"Sorry mate," said the man, "Do you mind, I love pizza?"

Augusta took her phone out and moved it toward Mr. De Montfort, he passed the roller cutter over to Simon who started cutting the giant pizza into sections.

"Is that all you have for me Mr. De Montfort, was it a love affair, because the old man is very jealous, he wants to kill you off hand, why is that?"

He sat down next to her and laughed out loud at her words, "My God all these years and another one of you bloody women come out and attacks me for no reason I can fathom, what the hell does she want this time?"

"Your assistance sir, well that's what I think anyway."

"A written apology in the next edition perhaps Augusta?"

"Yeah, no probs Jack, done!"

He put his glasses on and looked at her phone, "Recall number one then, yes?"

He pressed and waited, looking into her eyes, "Half Inuit woman, eh? What's you dad like, a killer I bet?"

"A native Canadian going into politics like his father before him, do you not read my press releases."

He tutted and turned away as he spoke down the line, "Hello Dexter you old sack of haggis shit, how's my future wife doing?"

He held the phone up for Augusta the hear Dexter swearing at him down the line, he was laughing at Dexter's rage, "Ok, bored with you now put the lovely engine driver on please.... ah Elizabeth, I saw you deal with your mother's security all those years ago, I still laugh at your skill, woman, dump the skirt wearer and come and live with me, I beg you!"

"Hiya Jack, how's it all hanging in the death zone?"

"The very same as you Elizabeth, how was it for you? Well, after that dreadful car crash and burn out, sad I thought, then I contacted a friend and realized that like me you just wanted out of the world, who can blame you darling?"

"We need you, Jack?"

"Oh, come on woman, what can I give to you lot that would be of any used these days?"

"Names, numbers, contacts, all that's in your noggin Jack."

"Elizabeth, I'm a dinosaur, lost in the black world and minding my own business, a pity you're not."

"This is the call Jack, get on a plane and meet us at the Palace ready to bend the knee and help out."

"Can I say sod off or not?"

"No, you cannot Jack, get on the bloody plane and we'll see you in London."

"I'm an Australian, a blunt instrument of a man darling, I say what I mean, and it offends people, blokes like me cause wars Elizabeth."

"You're the second Aussy to be called, so do as you're commanded, dingo bollocks!"

He burst out laughing at her, "Come on who's the other, come on woman let me know please."

"We have an American, a Canadian and a Gurkha, even women sit at the privy council table these days, get it moron?"

"The Empire strikes back then?"

"Your first order will be to sit over there and shut the fuck up, clear? In London by the start of next month, you can pee up the same lamp post if you like."

"Elizabeth, come on darling," he was now speaking to a silent phone.

He handed it back to Augusta, "The women in your family Augusta, do you go back to the Iceni and Queen Boudica?"

"Grandpop reckoned that she burnt Londinium to cinders back in the day."

"And she would if I don't show up for April fool's day, won't she?"

Augusta passed over some more pizza, "Grand Pop must have asked for you when he was alive, I think, what can I say?"

"Ah yes, your great grandfather, sarn't major Augustus Victor Talbot, the link all along, yes?"

"Yep!" grinned Augusta.

He took a mouthful of pizza and smiled at her, "Stand by your beds, you horrible lot!"

"Grandpop?" asked Augusta.

"Oh yes, Mr. Nasty if you ignored him like I used to, from time to time."

Augusta pointed a piece of pizza at him as she thought about it all "So you must have been his south of the equator media link then?"

He filled his mouth and giggled, "Bloody genetics, you'll be the death of me woman."

"Did he ever tell you about China little girl?"

"No, can you?"

"It'll take the rest of the day you know?"

"We have the time and lots of pizza, so no worries, mate."

He started laughing at her again, "Bloody women!"

"Are you really a drug dealer?"

"Oh, come on!" he screeched out laughing at her, "Now cut that out now please!"

"This is Barney by the way, my youngest son "said Jack with his mouth full.

Augusta pointed to Simon, "My intended, Simon!" he looked at her in shock.

"What, are you never going to propose Si?"

"Well yeah but."

Barney and Jack were giggling at his sudden predicament.

Simon made a ring out of some silver paper and placed it on her finger, "Will you?"

"Yep!"

"Ok done, where?"

"Malaysia............KL.... I thought.............. good?"

"Great, who's paying?" asked Simon.

"Her tight arsed Scottish granddaddy sonny, "said Jack as he burst out laughing.

"That's the most boring marriage proposal I have ever heard people," said Barney.

"No, we've heard worse haven't we Gussy."

"Yes Si, my brothers were even worse, possibly a family thing I think."

"Bonkers the lot of yer!" said Jack and he stuffed the last piece of pizza into his mouth."

"Signora, vino et pizza Italiano specialli! Thanks a million!" shouted Augusta, she held her hand up and waved to the ladies behind the countertop.

Jack put his forehead on the table as he laughed at the mad people, "Back in the world Barns, sorry lad, I tried."

"It's ok dad, we understand the call, we've got yer back as normal, ok?"

"Thanks Barns, love you boy!"

Augusta was now on the phone, "David how could you? The poor man has been filthed, a front page detraction and a full apology for tomorrow please, yes he found us, can you believe it, stuck on a desert island all these years, yes picked up by a passing Japanese tanker, south Pacific, lucky eh, yes you can print that one, yes he's back in the world, could even want my job, yes make him the hero and us the promotional backers, do it now you moron!" she cut him off and grinned at Jack.

Jack De Montfort laughed even more at her and them and the pizza.

"Great grandmothers little prodigy, eh?"

She nodded as she giggled at the new friends, "Ok...Mr. Delmonte...back to...China then, so how did it all start?

He choked on his mouthful of cheese and olive crust.

"And how come the Chinese accepted grand Pop in the first place?"

He tried to speak but he had to laugh.

"So where did he and Alice go after that?"

"No idea Gussy, so where do you want me to start?"

"His book, the Chinese question, so what was that all about?"

"But don't you know all about that dear?"

"Well, no we don't?"

"We?"

"Me and Tolly!"

"And he is?"

"My big brother and the current DGI back in London."

"Shit! Couldn't someone warm me for God's sake?"

"I just did, didn't I, so come on Delmo, spill the slush puppy!"

He screeched out laughing at her journalistic bombardment.

"And stop pretending you don't know about our Tolly blueblood."

"Is he dear?"

# CHAPTER 33 ... Aspen ... Colorado ... USA

The children were out playing in the woods at the back of the house, Carol stayed to hear what was said in the meeting out of curiosity.

Patrick watched Liz take the call and listened as she gave out her commands, she closed the call and looked at him.

"Why Elizabeth, why bother with the old dead system, all old hat these days?"

"Not so Patrick, "Said Dexter, "We need an anchor more and more, big money sends people crazy, and we have to react, the Communist experiment is now dead, the economists have won the war, the problem however is that they are all bonkers, they deal in telephone numbers and think themselves clever, in fact they cause wars with their greed, the old man's favorite subject, remember?"

"And a table full of old farts will help this then?"

"Just say no thanks and mean it Patrick," said Liz, "And we'll be gone from under your feet."

"Oh no you don't, that means that I'll be out of the loop, and I bet little man is going to be called, yes?"

"By you Patrick," said Dexter, "We need him in the mix, first job in fact, well can you do that for the King."

"Who's the Boss?"

"It's a round table!" said Liz.

"Chairman then?"

"King Charles, who else?"

"But!"

"But what? "Said Dexter, "Should we all follow the newest system and learn the lessons all over again, with age comes wisdom and we are old, it was started in 1660 by Charles the second because he didn't trust politicians, familiar?"

"Yes, familiar, I remember the old man's words as well you."

"Good, we'll see you at the meeting on the first of the month, London, can you find your own way to the palace?"

"The Palace?"

"Expecting a cabin in the woods Patrick?"

"No Liz just. I don't know, so who else is at the table?"

"An old friend of yours, Margaret McDonald, Lord Chief justice to her friends and are you still friends Patrick?"

His grin widened, "Yeah, I like it, illegal you know all of it by the way!"

"They are her words Patrick," said Liz.

"I thought she would want an opinion, and my job would be?"

"To sit over there and shut the fuck up you moron!" said Liz.

"April the first then?" asked Dexter.

Patrick nodded in silence.

"April fool's day, just a coincidence I think," said Liz.

"I don't," said Patrick.

Carol came over to the table and sat down with Patrick, "A change of plan then?"

"Err............no darling just a second job for democracy, well is it, Dexter?"

"Yes, we're the gardeners."

Patrick started to laugh, "Just like the old man eh, he said you would in the end you know, I didn't believe him, Mr. I can't stand waiting."

"All things change Irish, even me."

"What is it Patrick, what are you going to do?" asked Carol.

"Rule one Chuck, keep in the loupe, fail to do so and the world passes by without me and you."

Carol searched their faces, "So what the hell is it?"

He smiled at her, "Old farts club for ruling the world dear."

She looked around confused.

"I like it," said Liz, "The old farts gardening club, yes, coded phrase from now on, we use that in all communications, right?"

Dexter started laughing at her.

"What?"

"Nothing Lill, just perfect," he turned to Patrick, "So, contact the little man and invite him please, can you?"

Patrick grinned, "He's probably already there, that little smart arse."

He watched Dexter get out his phone with interest, "What?"

Dexter punched in the number and spoke, "Pick up in ten please Eden, yes from their front garden, yes I know its sloped so what, ok hold and hover we'll jump in, no probs, keep your knickers on mate."

He turned to the laughing faces, "What?"

"Nothing changes Elizabeth, same old Dexter, the old man's favorite."

"Was I?"

"Oh, shut up you moron!" said Liz, she punched him just for fun.

Carol, Patrick and the three girls watched the helicopter come down to the side of the mountain, the pilot waved to them as he hovered for the pickup.

"Why does she treat him like that Patrick, she's always insulting him or even beating him with something?"

He took up position behind her and held her waist then whispered into her ear as Dexter and Elizabeth waved and climbed into the helicopter.

"Watch them very closely Chucky, she's English upper class and he's Scottish scrape off a stone dirt class, she thinks it's normal to treat her man like that and he's thankful that she's not as bad as most Scottish women, highland women are the most aggressive in the world, Nordic ice women with anger stitched into their jeans, no prisoner mode is all perfectly normal."

She giggled at him.

"Watch carefully Chuckaluk, this is real love, see how he is with her, she is his complete world, without her he will fade and die, they've already died together once, see that?"

Dexter pulled Elizabeth into the chopper and clipped her in then waved to the watchers, Liz was angry with fear and squeezed his hand, they could see her growling at him as the machine lifted off, the girls screamed with delight as it flew away.

"Do you want to do that someday girls?"

"Yeah!" screamed the women in his life.

He stared at them with panic in his eyes, "Am I risking too much?" he mumbled to himself.

"No," whispered Carol, we're with you daddy, always, ain't we girls?"

The girls screamed out laughing and dancing.

"Ok, the London trip it is then, book us into the Ruski hotel please Chuck."

"So, what do we do with their old Land Rover?"

He grinned at them all, "The girls can learn to drive, perhaps?"

"Yeah!" screeched his girls, his world and his ultimate worry.

Carol leaned in and whispered in his ear, "Do they want you for something else?"

"What?"

"Whitehall management maybe?"

"Na, the English would hate that, actually they all hate me anyway, I'm too Irish for them."

"And I'm too foreign?"

"Absolutely Pocahontas!"

"Say no please if they ask, too far I think?"

"Agreed, I don't like management, especially there, not sure I can make it to the palace steps, all a bit too far for an Irishman to feel comfortable."

"And a trip home?"

"Ah, yes, to see ma and how things have panned out with her leprechaun, slippery Phil."

"Who?"

"Oh, a very Irish story girls, once upon a time there was a man with a great good idea, the problem however was that he borrowed everyone's money and made money with it, not stealing says he! His name was Philip, and he became the richest man on the planet with other people's money, it's not stealing he says! Well real leprechauns are like that, right?"

The girls started to laugh at his normal stories from his wet and windy homeland, so they gathered round and listened to his story of Ireland.

"Now the ting, with leprechauns is that you have to be on your toes, any request will be answered with the standard, do you want a wish granted?"

"And?" asked Carol.

"Well, he has you already, the golden string to get what he wants from you, and slowly, ever so slowing the sting becomes a golden chain, then a bigger chain, then suddenly you realize that you are a prisoner, he's trapped you in the greed trat, snap!"

He clapped his hands and the girls squealed in fright as he laughed at them.

# CHAPTER 34 ... Helicopter Hovering over the Colorado Mountains

"Where the hell are they Glen?" shouted Eden over the noise of the rotors and wind of the open door.

Glen was spotting out a possible landing site to place the bird down but couldn't find a spot, "No good boy, wait I see them and the house, port side level off and go down to a hundred feet."

Eden took the helicopter down to the level of the side of the mountain, "A secure spot Glen, good for sledging."

"Bloody cold boy in the winter I know? Down some more, that's Dexter waving."

He descended and came as close to the mountain as Eden dared put it, Dexter jumped aboard and pulled Elizabeth with him.

"A bloody stupid idea as always you moron!" screamed Liz.

Dexter gave Eden the whirly finger to get going and the helicopter picked up height into the cold mountain winds.

"And shut the bloody door!" she screamed.

Dexter grinned at Eden who pressed the pressured door to close, she could finally feel the heat returning to her feet and legs.

"That went well I thought Liz?"

"You think so? I have new doubts just because of what he said, he's not convinced of the need I think."

"None of them are Liz, even the King, I had to threaten to kill him to stop him closing it all down."

She turned to him and looked into his eyes, "You threatened to kill the Monarch?"

"I had to get reality though into his brain, he's new blood and thinks he knows it all, the old Queen knew she had to preserve or die, he doesn't, he'll understand in the end."

"Would you have?"

"Yes!"

"Bloody moron! they'd have hung you from a lamp post."

"But?"

"You are a moron, Dexter; they would have hung you from the nearest lamp post."

"You should have been there that's all Liz."

"The King has to learn but not slaughter, get it, he has the right, we don't, so shut the fuck up!"

"Democracy will survive Elizabeth, no matter what."

"Yeah and could be over your dead body!"

"So................. De'Montfort?"

"Yeah, looking forward to meeting him again after all these years, you?"

"Why, him and why now woman?"

"He has the media, and he plays it like children play with marbles."

"Public opinion then?"

"Err........................... der!"

"But Gussy?"

"Small fry, he's the shark, get it?"

"Or the kangaroo?"

"I love it when you're jealous, it makes me feel even more secure in your presence Dexter."

"I just don't like the man Liz, that's all."

She giggled at his read angry highlander face.

"And I love you too Hamish!"

"I have trust issues Liz, sorry."

"And I have so many half children, Dexter the sperm haggis."

Eden burst out laughing at their conversation, Dexter stared at him back to flying the helicopter in silence.

"Should I worry Elizabeth?"

"Could you do him Dex?"

"One arm and eating an ice cream with the other."

Eden tried his best not to laugh but Dexter watched the watery eyes and smiled at him.

"You see Dexter, that's why I love you, the passion, the shear love you are capable of, given the prompting."

Dexter gave Eden the do not say a word look.

# CHAPTER 35 ... Aspen ... Colorado ... USA

Carol passed Patrick the phone giggling at him, she mouthed the word Theo.

"So why the trip big Bro?" asked Theodore.

"Switched on then?"

"When the Collins family book the Henson suit down at the Ruski I ask myself, what's he here for, who're you going to burn this time?"

"We have an appointment at the Palace on the beginning of the month."

"Why?"

"The first of April, be there, they want us to join the old farts club!"

"Who?"

Patrick cut him off and laughed with Carol.

"He'll think it's an April fool's joke Patrick."

"Let him be late for once, let's see him catch up for a change."

Patrick sat and thought about Theo for a moment or two, "Hold on what does he mean down at the Ruski?"

"Is that what he said then?"

"He's bought another up-market hotel hasn't he?"

"Ring him back Patrick and ask the question."

Patrick started laughing, "That bloody kid brother, he loves his games, I'm just the fish to play with, I'm not giving him the satisfaction of ringing him back and that's final."

"Can I then?"

"Err................. yeah, why not, checking on the booking and all that."

Carol burst out laughing at him, "So who's the fisherman here and what's the bait?"

"Information, and I'm the fly fisherman, spinning that delightful fly in his direction, he won't be able to resist, yeah ring him back and double check the booking."

She screeched out laughing as she pressed recall to the Ruski hotel., "Err yes reception this is Mrs. Collins again, how far is Buckingham palace from the hotel and could we use your in-car service please, oh fantastic, can I book it for the first of the month, yes, we have an appointment at Buckingham palace, yes dear, very special, thank you."

She closed the call and giggled at Patrick's excited face.

"A tenner say's he phones within ten Chuck?" said Patrick.

She wheezed with laughter as she showed him the caller face on her mobile phone as it buzzed into life.

"He's on the ball today, Patrick!" she passed it over to him.

"Yes, who is that?" said Patrick.

"Stop pissing about Bro and give me the news, now!" Screeched Theo.

"The Smith's visited my house and invited me to attend the palace with my little brother, we are called to the privy council."

"Oh, at last!"

"What do you mean by that, oh, at the last statement Theo?"

"Well, it's a foot in the door Bro, we're in at last."

"But why do we want to be in at last?"

"Pop's plan cabbage head!"

"What bastard plan Theo?" ......the phone buzzed dead in his hand.

"Shit, he's done it again!" screeched Patrick, "I can never win!"

Carol held her belly as she laughed at him being caught out by his little brother.

"Little shit!" mumbled Patrick, "He was waiting for the call, he has an inside whisper, I'd put a grand on it."

She turned away and walked off to leave him to think and plan the next move, she knew that he needed thinking and planning time before the trip to London.

He pressed recall and the O'Brien's, "Brenda my darling, how's life?"

"Patrick, what's up, why the call, in trouble, do you need help?"

"I'm coming back to England for a meeting, and I'd like a bit of Irish security."

"No probs, I'll let you have the twins, keep them out of trouble though, yes?"

"Yes, darling always out of trouble, so how's home, and the leprechaun?"

"Oh, well done Patrick, Ma loves him, she has a Rolls Royce and a brand-new conservatory on the house."

"No, no, no, to bloody public woman."

"Calm Patrick, it's an old one and he drives her wherever she wants to go, she believes in him, and it shows."

"Bren, you do understand what he's doing over there?"

"Err .... Yeah, fiddling around with money, a problem?"

"Other people's money Brenda, get it?"

"Ok, what do you want me to do then?"

"Overwatch and protect, report any change in circumstances to Theo and quick, he's an obvious target to be put down, understood?"

"So, you put my family in danger Patrick?"

"Only slightly Bren, Ma can handle him, right?"

"I don't like it, Patrick!"

"I'll call in and have a word Bren, no probs darling!"

The line was silent for a few seconds as Patrick listened, "What's up Bren?"

"Patrick, could I ask advice while you're on the line?"

"Shoot Bren."

"So why does a man start to tell lies to his wife?"

"Who are we talking about here Bren?"

"The hairy one, who else?"

"Playing an away game?"

"I'll fecking kill the man!"

"No Bren, not him, must be business, away trips?"

"America now and again, but now he goes up north, why would he do that Patrick."

"Well ask him darling, come on Bren, ask the man, no other way, clear?"

"But Patrick?"

"No darling, he's not, let the man speak and answer your questions, he's in love, we all know that, so give him a chance, all clear so far?"

"Thanks Pat, thanks for that!"

"Be gentle darling, you know how men are, right?"

"Fecking egit!"

# CHAPTER 36 ... Whitehall ... Top Floor suite ... London

Jane pressed his intercom, "He's here Tolly, do you want him to come straight in?"

The gorilla stared at her in confusion, "For why? I was on holiday woman!"

"A panic, why else?" she smiled back at him.

Her intercom buzzed back, "Yes please darling send him in please, oh, and locate Lord Longmore wherever he is, he's needed in his slot."

"What if he's no longer available Tolly?"

"I only ask the once, tell him that for me please."

The doorway to his office filled up with George as he came in with a confused face.

"Hiya Uncle, how's life, good, bad?"

"Confused Tolly, I was on holiday mate."

"Bored Uncle?"

"Out of my scull, how many cold drinks can one drink without wanting to take a dip in the blue ocean and all that golden sand, too dammed hot, always."

"Sarcasm suits you; I like it."

The gorilla stared and waited for the chop job.

"And Aunty Brenda, good, a nice suntan?"

"Oh, I get it now, my God, you want me back, oh, thank fuck for that, when can I start?"

"She's finally quit, no come backs out for good."

"Who?"

"Mum!"

"Out?"

"Yeah, out.............. for good, so we need a re-think, what do
you think?"

"Me...........think?"

"Yes Uncle, who?"

"I don't get it Tolly."

"So, I've closed her down, the whole department done and
dusted, binned the lot of um, good?"

"Err...........why?"

"Too obvious for a start and too public with my mother
running the thing, so I broke it up, the problem however is that we
have a problem."

George started to grin but stayed silent.

"Yes, we need a red line department to work now and again so I
want you to go out into the sticks and build the company from the
foundations up, could you do that for me?"

"Me?"

"Yes, you, Uncle, who else is there who knows how it all works
and more importantly how it works well, you are the one I want to
take the department into another league."

"Me?"

"Will Brenda be opposed to the idea?"

"Err.............?"

"I shouldn't have asked, sorry Uncle, we'll muddle through
somehow, ok I understand, leave it with me."

"Without me?"

"Well, if she objects, what can you do?"

"I don't tell her Tolly!"

"Yes, but would it work Uncle, she's a smart woman? I don't
want to be the cause of a rift, mum already has one of those and for
the same reason I think, it's a big bad job, and not everyone is suited
to it."

George stared at him then smiled, "Very clever young man, I volunteer, I keep it out of my wife's mouth, and I keep it away from here, silent and far away, yes, a good plan, when?"

Tolly passed over the large black manual for the MOD, "The law Uncle, must be obeyed at all costs, you are not a distant agent but linked understood?"

He passed over another booklet, "Staff recruitment, you tell them it's legal, they are contractors, yes you can use our facilities you can use our gear and sometimes our people but never mix, never let friendships build up, you are independent from me, completely, I want no contact, clear?"

"Yes boss, a no contact, contracts department, got it, out in the big bad world, recruits have to pass my inspection, yes?"

"You are the best we have at all this Uncle George; we are relying on you and your work."

"No psychopaths, as Pop would have requested, just lost souls wanting to help us out, clear?"

"Finance?"

"From the MOD fund so accountants will be watching cash flow, sorry it has to be done like that and please remember this Uncle, any slips and I'll be on you, do not go nuts and start killing off plan if some ones late in delivering your bacon butties."

"Sanctioned from me only, I don't give a shit about old anger management hick ups you will do as you're commanded yes?"

Tolly stared into Georges eyes, "Madness George and I will stab you myself out of disappointment and Nanna will haunt you out of embarrassment, get it?"

He smiled at him "Yes boss, the real world, got it."

Tolly pulled out the box from his desk draw, tears welled up in Georges eyes as he recognized the Heckler label on the dark oak box lid.

"She had this made for you George well before she died, so this deal is not from me it's from her, so loyalty please in all you do, I'm here if there's a problem, please come and have a cupper when you feel like a talk, but be the outsider please, give us the you don't know how good it is to be still working speech, get me Uncle?"

George nodded as the box slid over to him, he opened the lid and basked in the golden light of the Hecker, he started to sniffle with emotion.

"Read it first Uncle, I don't know about you, but it set me off proper balling."

He carefully lifted it out of the box and read the inscription on the side of the barrel.

(Keep *us safe George, protect us from the mad men, we will always love you...Helen*)

Tears dripped down his face as he put the gun back into its box.

"And smarten up Monkey man!" George mumbled.

Tolly was sobbing in front of him, he dabbed his face with the blotter pad, "I still miss her George to the bone man, to the bone."

"She's with us boy don't you worry, the job will be done, silent, clean and out of the public eye under my care, ok with that?"

"And the Americans?"

George gulped in shock at Tolly's knowledge of his one-off jobs now and again.

"Now at an end Uncle, let Uncle Jon Boy and Lenny get their own department sorted, instead of calling on old friends, they need to get Uncle Marvin involved and not us directly, clear?"

"Yes boss, finished, I'll give your advice and close the line."

"Good to be clear at the beginning Uncle don't you think?"

George smiled at him, "Proud to serve boss as always!"

"Nice and slow Uncle, make it natural for them to help, yes?"

"Yes, boy I can do this, and thanks for bringing me back, I needed this!"

"She would be proud of you Uncle, that's for sure."

"And always of you Boy, always was! So, the head banger?"

"Oh yes, Uncle Rufus, I don't want him involved with the hit squad over in Mexico, pull him out and give him a proper job please."

"They have plans over there then?"

"Oh yes, big bad plans, not ours, clear on that?"

"Under your direction Tolly as always, it's good to be home."

"You're the home maker this time Uncle, make it feel like that yes?"

Tolly skimmed a sales leaflet in front of him, "An old MOD storage facility out in Leicestershire, a bit out of the way but still could be good, the builders failed planning for a housing estate, a big investment really, still a silver cloud like you could make their day I think."

"How much can I pay for it?"

Tolly laughed at him as he pointed to the door.

"I'll ask them how much and bid um down, yes?" he picked up his bundle of gear and the heckler box.

Tolly giggled as he watched his Uncle George before he slammed the door.

Jane passed him a golden card from her desk draw, "Accountancy UK Unlimited."

"Unlimited then?"

"Do me a favor!" she laughed at his dumb face, "Do jog on that man!"

"You're in his loupe then?"

She continued to laugh as she thumbed to the outer door, "You have an appointment at the scrubs this afternoon, 15:30," she looked at her list, "And the police station on Station Road Islington at 20:00."

She handed him the short list, "He wants you to be productive and no police records please, there's a good Gorilla."

"Who pushed me up for this one then?"

"Oh, do catch up Monkey man!"

He pointed upwards with his thumb.

She continued to laugh and pointed to the ceiling, then handed him his box of calling cards, he laughed then walked out, the door closed behind him, she continued to laugh.

"What, you'll make a great probation officer, in a zoo perhaps?"

She watched him leave as his brain ticked over with the planning.

Her desk buzzed, she pressed, "Yes Tolly I agree, he'll do fine, no probs."

"Best call medical for backup darling best give him a helping hand if he overreacts, please."

"Yes dear' I'll call in the morning, let's let King Cong assemble his monkeys first, eh?

Leicestershire Zoo as code words, yes?"

"I think that place is called Twycross Zoo Jane, what do you think?"

"Oh, bloody perfect!" she screeched out, "Oh I have a Gurkha on the books wanting to volunteer for further action, a junior doc, one of your granddads people from the mountain action, currently at St Mary's, was with the Gurkha rifles but seconded for training as a doctor, you like the idea?"

He stopped laughing and waited for her to finish.

"And a secondary ear on site I thought Tolls?"

"Clever girl, you know how it all goes, I love it, yes that's a plan, go!"

"I'll send him to the new site then."

"Yes Jane, let him keep up with the mad men and let's see how it all settles."

"Ups!"

"What's up Jane?"

"Err .... I seem to have peed my pants Tolly, go, go action time I'm afraid!"

"What, your waters have bust?"

"Broke I think they call it?"

"Ok, don't panic, call an ambulance."

"Tolly shut up and don't panic, then drive me home, get the medic there please, a home birth, remember?"

"Yes, but it's miles away?"

"I'll cross my legs, just bloody move boy!"

Tolly ran through to her and helped her up and out to the lifts, "Now don't panic!"

"I'm not, you are!"

He pressed for the lift as he held Jane and the phone under his chin, "Aunty Ruby, show time, her waters have busted, coming home, well as soon as I can."

"The helicopter Tolly, up and away, remember?" shouted Ruby with excitement.

"Ah yes, up, sorry Aunty!"

He pressed for the roof and helped her into the lift.

"Ring the pilot Tolly!" said Jane, "Oh, do bloody spark up that man!"

"Ah, yes, the pilot!"

She snatched the phone from him, "Robby, I need a medical lift to the house as we discussed, yes now, move your arse, yes, bloody now!"

"What the hell's wrong with you men today, what is it, a full moon or something?"

"No darling just sudden changes to the pattern of our day!"

"And life Toll's, here we go sparky, bing, bang, bosh, ready?"

"No, not really."

"Oh, I feel better now, it might be a false alarm, soz babe!"

"No Jane, we go home, let's work from home for a bit, eh?"

"Yeah, let's, but who's, well you know, going to run the shop?"

"Well, I thought Mack, big old unit, bored with the BBC, needs a desk job, what do you think?"

She burst out laughing," Yeah, and to hell with the paperwork, he'll balls it up anyway?"

"Yeah," he grinned, "And besides, we need a maternity leave, right?"

"Yeah, Toll's and any ruck we can blame him!"

"Bang on babe!"

# CHAPTER 37 ... Islington ... Police Station ... London ... UK

"Yes?" asked the custody Sergeant as he continued to write in his daybook, George leaned on the counter and watched him writing.

"So, what do you want?" asked the policeman.

"Sergeant Richardson, right?"

"You know me?"

George shook his head, just starting a new job, searching for good lads."

"Me?"

George returned to his paperwork, "Err............................ this bloke, a baddy, is he?

The policeman looked at the name on his list, "Na, just a mug, he got pulled into an all nightery and the drug squad bust the lot of um, he's the left over, so you must be his special mate, eh?"

"Special?" asked George.

"His SAS Commander, here to rescue him, well you look the part mate, so what are you?"

George handed him one of his cards.

"Oh, how boring I was expecting the black suits and the daggers at dawn thing."

"Boring on the desk then mate?" said George.

"Driving me round the twist mate, just crazies and smart-arse lawyers."

"Fancy a change then?"

"Are you offering a new job mate?"

"Recruiting, I'll check you out and come back to you on that one."

The sergeant stared into his eyes for a second then burst out laughing," You got me there, mate, but you're a," he looked at the

card again, "A detention supervisor for Probation services UK,
what the hell are you then?"

"A contractor, I shove, and they get better, easy peasy, really."

"Ex Army then?"

"Can you tell?"

"Oh yes, so do you want this little shit or what?"

"What?" laughed George.

The officer smiled at the gag, "Ok follow the white line to
the cells please do not deviate from the line, that's for security
purposes, health and bloody safety at work crap!"

"Is it Officer, well I like the idea."

"Oh, shut up!" he marched off into the dark corridor and
George followed, stepping only on the line.

George tugged the officer's sleeve and whispered in his ear,
"Mind if I get nasty with the useless bugger."

"My pleasure mate, I'll keep your card then if you don't mind?"

"No, and when you're up to your arse in nutters give me a bell
and I'll see what I can do to make life less boring, good for you sir?"

The copper smiled then pressed the button to unlock the cell
door.

George smiled back at him and walked into the cell, "Winston
Churchill you useless bastard, up!"

"George Babe, I knew you'd come and save me, you see Roger,
I told you didn't I, he's the real thing, God bless the SAS."

George screamed into the little black man's ear from two
inches, "Stand to attention when I'm speaking to you, come on,
move your arse!"

The Sergeant laughed at the mad man.

"Ok! out, left, right, left, right, left, right, out to the bastard van
and climb in, your punishment starts as of now, get me in there,
shit for brains, a drug den, what would Her Majesty think bollock
head?"

Winston stood like a ram rod and listened to the voice, "That's nasty man."

"Van!" screamed George, "Now, up two, up two, up two, go!"

The sergeant watched the mad man take the crying youth out to the lock up van in the yard, "Sign the ticket please Mr. Contract Agent."

George scribbled on his daybook and followed Winston to the van, he opened the door for the lad to get in, "And shut the fuck up in there!" the wind from the slam pushed him in.

Winston sat next to another man in dark blue overalls," What's that smell?"

"Pigs, what do you think?"

"Pigs, why pigs?"

"Because that's what I was doing before the mad bloke arrived."

The driver's door opened, and George climbed in, "Shut the fuck up!"

"From where?" whispered Winston.

"The Scrubs farm out in Edgeware, where the fuck do you think."

"Prison?"

"Yeah....... you?"

Winston coughed while he thought of an angle, "Yeah, lock up, drugs, you?"

"Murder on the street where he lived."

"Who?"

"The wife's lover, what do you think?"

"Dead then?"

"Oh yes, I took his head home with me and put it on the wife's bed, didn't go down too well, she's under full time medication as of these days."

"Yeah, I imagine that would do it, err........." he held his hand out to shake.

"Bartholomew Hislop the third."

"There's three of you?"

"Three generations of us, yes."

"All in prison."

"No just me, Dad was killed in one of those wars and my Grandad was shot in a gang incident back in the sixties."

"Not drugs then?"

"Na, I hate the bloody stuff."

"Oh, yeah, yeah, so do I....................."

Bart was looking at him to finish.

"Err............... yeah, I was forced into it by my then wife, got me hooked, know what I mean?"

"No!" Bart shook his head still staring at him, "Big tits then?"

"Who?"

"The wife?"

"Err......ex..........no, not really you?"

"Shut the fuck up, you pair, I've got to pick up another wanker yet, so schtum!" shouted George from the driving seat.

He stopped the van and jumped out; the auto key locked them in.

"So, what the hell is this?" asked Bart.

"Oh, just the SAS recruitment drive, out of the nick and onto the ranges, bang, bang, bang and all that."

"SA bastard S, who the hell are they?"

Winston stared at him with his mouth open catching flies and he gormlessly returned the look on in silence.

"Err.................good was it, feeding pigs?"

"Tasty when I killed one, yes good!"

Winston tried the door handle to see if he could get some air, "Mother still alive then?" he was struggling trying to wind the window down."

"Squeal a lot you know; they know you know?"

"Know what?"

"When it's their turn."

"Turn for what?"

"The table suite, you know sausages, chops, ham joints, when are we getting fed? I could eat a road killed scabby dead dog."

"Err.......................... yeah, me too, we'll have to ask when he comes back, so you volunteered then?"

"Yeah, killing I'm good at that, no probs."

"Who are you killing then?"

"He points and I smash, easy!"

"Nasty you know them SAS blokes, not that easy to kill mate."

"What does it stand for then?"

Rufus's face suddenly appeared at the side window of the van.

Winston jumped up in shock, "Rufty............. here we go mate, Rufus is here, he's a good bloke.

"Where's the Gorilla?" shouted Rufus as he tried the door handle.

"Locked in Rufty, we're prisoners help us escape, please!" He's ugly though."

"Handsome to some maybe, let's not be judgmental, eh?"

"Just saying mate, who the hell are you anyway?"

"Winston Churchill at your service," he held his hand out to shake.

Rufus pressed his nose to the glass, "Drug dealing, I thought you were strictly fruit and veg?"

"It was a party Rufty, tell him please."

"Too late Winy, you're in mate, remember the pledge, look stay in my corner, and I'll see what I can do, ok?"

The big man grabbed Winston's hand to shake and shook it vigorously, Winston jumped at the shock of his strong grip.

George shook them up as he banged the side of the van then unlocked it with the fob, he slid back the side loading door, "Get in there, shit head!"

Another man climbed in and sat with them, "Shift up pal, who's got the big arse?"

He growled at them.

"Who are you then? "Asked Winston.

"Robbie, six for breaking and entering, you?"

"Err.......... Winston............drugs and him for murder a very long stretch."

Robbie focused on the big man "Murder?"

He held his hand out to shake and Bart took hold of it, "Bartholomew, you can call me Bart, that's short for Bartholomew, my mother said it would be ok to shorten my name but only with close friends."

The man looked at Winston for reality and asked with his eyes if the big lad was for real.

"He's a pig breeder and butcher, good, eh?"

The man refocused on Bart, "What's the smell?"

Bart grinned at him in silence.

George climbed into the driving seat and stared at them in the back, he gave them a wide smile that they all knew wasn't natural for a gorilla man like him.

"Welcome lads, friends all, eh? Well, this is the new project, contractors all of us, good, eh?"

"How much?" asked Winston.

"You see, positive thinking, you lot will never earn as much as you will with this you group of heroes, because that's what you are my bloody hero's, and yes you've just been sprung from choky but I'm no judge, I am the jury though, I want you to teach us your personal skills and in return I'll teach you how to survive in my dangerous world.

He turned back to the windscreen and started up the engine, "Here we go lads on one of my great adventures, whoopy, eh?"

"Where?" asked Winston.

"Haven't a clue boy but Rufus does, we simply follow the Roller, up north somewhere."

"Somewhere?" asked Bart.

Robbie was asleep before they reached the ring road and was snoring and slobbering on Bart's shoulder, "Don't light it yet you nutter!" he mumbled as he slept.

"Who is he?" asked Bart as he nodded to George driving the van.

"Oh, SAS Captain, we've worked together a lot, a bit mardy sometimes though."

"And the ugly critter?"

"Richest man on the planet that's why he's in the Roller and we're in with sleepy Joe and the gorilla."

"Gorilla?" asked Bart a bit too loud.

George's eyes focused on them in the mirror, "Shut the fuck up!"

Winston elbowed Bart and whispered, "See what I mean, a mardy arse."

"So, mother still alive then?" asked Winston trying to break the ice.

"Yeah, still at home, dads on the mantel piece and mums in the wall."

Winston dreaded to ask, but he couldn't help his mouth opening, "Alive?"

Bart started to laugh and as his shoulders moved up and down Robbie woke up with a start.

"What, stuffed?" said Robbie.

"Ashes!" laughed Bart, "What do you think I am, I bricked mum up in the wall though, wrong do you think?"

Robbie and Winston turned into goldfish as their mouths opened and closed in gulping silence.

"He's a psychopath!" shouted George, "So now shut the fuck up!"

"Is that someone who can't sleep proper?" asked Robbie.

"No, it is bastard not!" said Winston.

"I really loved her you know?"

"Who?" asked Robbie.

"The Ex-Wife, they locked her up you know, in safe hands they called it."

"Where?"

"Dark-more they called it, a long, long, long, journey to visit, they said no visits please."

"I bet they did," said Winston.

Georges eyes started to water in the mirror as he tried his hardest not to laugh.

"What?" asked Winston.

"He's the cook you morons, I sprang him because he's the best, get it?"

Winston started to laugh, and Robbie joined in, Bart stared at them in silence.

"Pack the bastard in Bart!" shouted George.

Bart burst out laughing at them.

"So, you're not a psychopath then?"

"Oh yeah, he's still one of those!" screeched George, "He just got caught, that was his problem, we have to teach him how not to get caught again, clear?"

Robbie looked at Winston in a staring question unanswered, Winston stared back at him.

"I don't know, and I ain't bloody asking!" said Winston."

"Pork chops I think gents, tonight that is." said Bart.

After many hours on the road, they came to an abandoned airfield with hooped buildings, and degraded wooden huts, at the rusty gate he turned to Robbie, "You're the key man and you're on a timer, go!"

"Go where?"

"Open the bastard gates moron, now!"

"With what?"

"Use your initiative, go!" he looked at his watch and pressed the timer.

Robbie stepped out of the van and stretched as he looked at the problem, he walked up and down searching for something to use then picked up a stone and smiled at them in the van.

"He's bloody useless," grumbled George as he watched Robbie leaver the gates off their hinges with an old log using the stone as a pivot point, he gave them the final kick and both gates collapsed onto the floor, he gave them the flourished wave and bow then pointed for the van to drive on.

George pulled the van up at the side of him, he wound the window down, "Now open the kitchen door, the cook needs time to prepare for lunch."

"Where?" shouted Robbie.

George thumbed to the large chimney rising above one of the wooden huts, "Move!" he looked at his watch again, "Come on we ain't got all day!"

Robbie ran over to the hut and kicked the door open smashing the old wooden locking mechanism in the process, he gave them the bow.

"And you're repairing the bloody thing moron!" shouted George.

Winston was laughing at the back of him in the van, "And you can shut up," he threw him the key to the van, "Go and get us some food to eat............now!" he re-set his timer and he scowled at him.

"In the van, from where?"

"A ten-mile radius because you don't have much fuel left."

"What if I just split man?"

"Well, you won't have a bed to sleep on or a head to rest in your new lodgings."

George and Bart got out; Bart was laughing at him before he took a look at his new kitchen.

"Health and safety man?"

"Start scrubbing, turn the gas on and boil some water up, now!"

"But I don't have a light on me, he flicked the light switch, "And no electric."

"I'll sort that, get scrubber dubbing!"

He turned to Winston, "Be gone and collecting."

"But I have no money."

"Err.........................der............initiative moron!

Winston grinned back at him "Nick it?"

George pointed and growled at him; Winston gave him the middle finger salute as the wheels spun him away in his new van.

"And you trust a drug dealing black kid with our van?" said Bart.

"Oh, shut up and get working."

Bart smiled, "You've tabbed the van, you know where he is and where he's going?"

"Shut the fuck up, moron!"

"Tabbed, satellite watching everything we do!" said Robbie.

"Move your arse!" screamed George.

# CHAPTER 38 ... Potato Fields ... East Goscote ... Leicestershire ... England

He stepped out of the van and started digging the soft earth with his hands to pull out the young spuds, he filled his pockets then ran back to the van to drive off, he saw smoke coming from the distance, "A farmhouse, nice."

He emptied the spuds into the door panel space then went round and opened the bonnet to show that he had broken down to whoever was perhaps watching, then started the trek over the long grassy fields to the smoke at the end of the woodland.

In the barn he filled an old plastic sack half full of turnips and looked around for anything else they could eat.

A brightly colored Cockrel came in to check him out and then attacked him, feet trying to flail the arms and legs of Winston, "You little bastard," he covered the monster with another sack and tied it up with bailing string off the floor.

On the way back he pulled up cabbages and onions, then struggled across the fields back to the van with the heavy load.

Back at the camp he produced his produce to the moaning George, "Is that all?"

"I was out of fuel mate," said Winston as he undid the sack, the undignified and aggressive cockerel strutted out and looked at everyone then attacked George.

"What's that, a pet?"

"Dinner!" said Winston.

"Well, you can kill the bloody thing then," said George, he stepped away from the monster.

Winston tried to corner the thing, but the chicken attacked him again and again."

"Stop!" shouted George, "What shall we call our new mascot, because he just demonstrated our moto, aggression overcomes fear!"

"Corn Flake, he just looks like he came off the packet of corn flakes," said Winston.

"Crazy Bastard?" said Bart, "Why? because he is."

"Kellogg's?" said Robbie.

"Alarm clock, yeah that's a good name," said George.

"Why?" asked Winston.

"Well because at the very crack of dawn he will be up and tooting for England."

"Really, why?" asked Winston.

"Because he can you moron!" grumbled George, "Corn Flake it is then, because he is!"

Late in the evening and after their vegetarian meal the sound of a truck reversing pulled them out of their conversations.

George looked out of the window, "Who the hell ordered the delivery?"

"Of what?" asked Winston.

"The Fortnum & Masons hamper for a start, "he thumbed to the men pulling out the giant hamper, just as the Rolls Royce pulled up at the side of it.

"The boss has arrived then?" said Bart.

"I'm the bastard boss around here bollock brain!" growled George.

Rufus grinned at them from the driver's seat then wound the window down, "Is this the new flying club gents?"

"No!" shouted George, "No.............. that's a great idea, I like it."

"What?" asked Winston.

"The flying club, yes. we need a sign, who can paint?"

They all looked at each other in confusion.

"You!" he pointed to Winston, "You're the artist?"

"No, that's me," said Robbie "A degree in the art school before the troubles."

"What troubles?" asked Winston.

"Breaking and entering with intent to burgle."

"Who?" asked Winston.

Rufus put his nose on the glass and looked in at them, the conversation stopped, "The Americans will be here in a mo, so get ready to welcome them."

George boiled up into a rage again as Rufus walked off, "What bastard Americans?"

"The Army Air Corps logistics, they're making this place habitable, lengthening the runway and bringing in equipment needed for the Air Tactical Development R&D."

George screeched out of the window, "What the fuck?"

"Oh, didn't I say My Lord, the Americans want to invest in Research and Development."

George was about to explode when the plan hit him, "Who's paying for this?"

Rufus grinned at him.

"The Yanks?" said George now fully realizing what Rufus had done and who he had called for help, "An Ex President perhaps?"

"You quit on him My Lord, he worries so I helped him with his guilty conscience, he needs help says I, I'd love too says he, bing, bang, bosh and here they come.

The giant aircraft flew over them and it came into land, the shadow and the engine noise drowned out all conversations and thoughts.

"But?" said George.

"Be the big boss My Lord, point and direct please, I'll leave all that to you."

He walked into the hut to be greeted by the blank faces.

Rufus looked at his watch, "Ok, first lecture in ten in the next hut, pre escape and evasion."

"My Lord?" asked Winston.

"Didn't you lot know, our gorilla is a Lord of the realm so smarten up, get all the boxes out of the Roll's please and take them to the next hut for the lecture, all three of you, come on chop, chop!"

George watched him in silence, Rufus stared back at him, "Yes you're the commander here, fully understood, but I'm the trainer, you teach us to fight, but I teach them to survive."

"But you hate the greenwood?"

"What's the point of survival in the woods we all live in towns, the Army's crap!"

"And you can?"

"Urban survival, anyone better than me?"

George finally smiled at him, "No, no person I know is better at this than you, My Lord."

"Are they all Lords then?" asked Robbie.

"Just these two," said Winston, "Lord Longmore and Lord Wimbledon."

"Really?"

"Really, really Robbie, what's your second name then?"

"Styles."

"And are you as good as he thinks you are."

"Yep! You?"

"Yes, I am."

"Boxes!" shouted Rufus "Bloody now!"

George watched the airplane come to a halt after landing and taxiing over to the ram shackled buildings, the tailgate ramp slowly dropped to the old concrete and the machines started rolling off, Major JJ Wilson walked off and shook his hand.

"Pa wanted to help George, he said, anything the gorilla needs get it for him."

"He's taking a risk here guy you do understand that?"

"Just the od favor now and again in return, good for you?" said JJ.

"You really are the diplomat aren't you kid, Tolly will hate it you know that don't you?"

"He won't mind, family and all that."

"I'll have to tell the DGI you know?"

"Expected George we don't want to cause a rift, the old man just thinks he owes you that's all."

"He bloody does son, let's be right about that!"

JJ razes his eyebrows, "For what?"

"Oh, many little experiences over there in the States, so what are you building here then?"

"Your little Empire George, whatever you need, do you need combat practice buildings for your take downs?"

"No thanks, just buildings for equipment and recreational."

"But Pa said that this is a military base."

"It is son but like no other, this is where the military hit the streets and become grey men, that's the school, how to hide, run or assassinate, all new to the services."

"Dirty war then?"

George laughed at him as he walked away, "Come and watch the moron's working son, better than a west end theatre any day!"

"The old man say's I have to join your course, I might learn something useful."

As the Army people started assembling buildings for habitation Rufus started his first lecture.

A new vehicle parked up and an India man walked over to them, he handed George a card.

George looked at the card and read it out loud, "Doctor Sing, Royal Gurkha Rifles."

"Who sent you here boy?"

"The DGI said that you needed a medic, I volunteered, ok with that?"

"Yeah, the more the merrier son, this here is JJ Wilson, US marines he's on the course as well, you two can buddy up during the escape and evasion practical, yes?"

"But I don't need to do this sir." said the Gurkha.

"If you're here then you do the course, understood, we have no bystanders here boy and you'll have to pass or you'll get a boot up your arse from me, now could I be any clearer?" he gave them a fierce stare and they understood the need to do as they were told.

"We have no ranks here, you just listen to me and shut the fuck up!"

JJ went to shake the man's hand, but the Gurkha gave the prayer sign and bowed, JJ followed his example and did the same.

They walked into the hut and sat at the back just as Rufus was starting his lecture.

Rufus stood and walked out in front of them, "My name is Rufus, that's all you need to know, I don't want to know your real names so invent one for this course, anything you like and remember it for future courses, ok?"

"Ok no names, I want you to come over to me and take cloths out of the boxes and change your appearance in some way as if you were on the run from people who have your basic description, so, change your age, change your walk, change your speech, change everything I want you to become chameleons, and I want you to do it in seconds because changing in seconds just like a chameleon will save your life and allow you to get away from being hunted because at the end of this course you will all be hunted down, any questions?"

Blank faces stared back at him.

George put his hand up, "So this is play time and we're just to find disguises in your boxes, yes?"

"The very start of your experience, so change into your character, give him or her a name and be that new man or new woman a bit like acting but more believable, your life is at stake, clear?"

"Ok, in half an hour I want to inspect you for a new job, be your new character, we can have a laugh about it at the moment but mark this in your minds lads, this is going to be life and death one day, so make it look good, stoop, swager, bowlegs if you like just change, get me?"

He placed his hands on his hip and looked at them, "Ok, go!"

They all sat in silence and stared.

"Now!" he screamed at them.

They all gathered around the cloths boxes and started laughing immediately as wigs were tried on and women's clothes were compared to what they were wearing.

Winston held up the classic woman's twin set and pearls with a two-piece tweed skirt and fitted jacket top.

Rufus nodded, "Yes good but you have to stick to it and the act, be the woman it's your safety!"

"No pockets?" said Winston, "Where do I put my keys?"

The room burst out laughing.

"Hold up, these are all women's clothes," said George.

"Change into the cloths of your choice, do it and shut the fuck up!" shouted Rufus.

They mumbled and laughed as wigs were tried on and cloths changed into, after half an hour he walked among them and graded their effort.

"He stood in front of George and stared into his eyes, "Look away, women never stare back at a man, lesson one, so, name?"

"Err............ Layla Smith."

"Good!" said Rufus, "Very good, less of the gruff, more of the schoolteacher with bad breath, good though, we can do the make up at another time, yes a good start."

He turned to Winston, who looked away and stared at his flat feet., "And?"

"Mary Rose, a Jamaican prostitute mon and I's looking for trade big boy!"

Rufus grinned, "Yes, very good, but someone might take you up on it and offer cash, you have nice legs, so don't be a smart arse, yes?"

"Yes boss!"

He turned to JJ Wilson who looked very uncomfortable in women's cloths, "And?"

"Err ......Mary Lou Harris, I'm a sanger from the south man!"

Rufus grinned, "Yes, good effort for your first time, you'll get used to it mate, sorry maim, correct me if I get you all wrong ok, it helps with your creation get me?"

JJ smiled his best smile at him.

"Be the grey woman always, not to be noticed not to be spoken too, avoid contact if you can, always at the back, always at the end of the queue, never speak unless you have to, then quietly, understood?"

"Ok let's see your walk, come on walk up and down like women, short steps waggle those hips but don't overdo it or you'll just look like clowns, this is disguise, so work it, be the age you've just created stoop, shuffle if you need to.

They were all laughing as they walked about.

"What do I do with my hands?" asked JJ.

"Hold them in front of you to hold up your breast implants, it's what they do, when you get time watch them, how they walk, how they hold themselves.

He wandered around looking at them closely then stopped, "Very good for your first attempt, ok I'm going out for half an hour, when I come back, I want to stand in front of traders, plumbers, electricians, motor mechanics, understood everyone? ok go!"

He walked out and slammed the door.

"What a load of bollocks!" said Robbie.

"It's not a game lad, he's the best, so listen and it'll save your life someday." Said George.

JJ was laughing, "What the hell does a British plumber look like?"

"A docker or the union rep, any bloody thing, just change, and think quick!" said George as he took off the dress and wig in one go.

"And quick change!" shouted Rufus from the other side of the door.

Bart ripped his dress as he tried to pull it off without undoing the side zip, all around him people laughed at his predicament.

"This is not normal man!" said JJ.

George grinned, "After lunch tomorrow we'll be practicing close order combat skills, I hope you can come up with something new Yank."

"What in these pants?"

He lifted up the dress and showed him his frilly knickers.

They all burst out laughing as they were getting changed, at the end of it they all fully realized why George was called the gorilla and why the tall American had no chance of passing as a woman, it was the feet.

# CHAPTER 39 ... Luxury Apartment Chelsea ... London

The smudge of lipstick on his shirt for the laundry made her look at him, she smiled then took the shirt over to him to show him the stain.

"Busy in the House of Lords these days is it, George?"

He watched her holding his shirt and knew he was busted, "Oh that's mine Bren."

She dumped the shirt on his lap and walked off to the kitchen, he realized that he only had a short time to come up with something before she tried to kill him.

She reappeared with a knife in her hand, "Your bollocks or the truth out on that table right now!"

He breathed out slowly as he considered the actions if he didn't tell her something.

"Back in the game Bren, reassigned, but I'm the boss this time."

She stabbed the coffee table and sat down next to him in the same movement the knife reverberated as he stared at her.

"And you were going to keep that from me?"

"He advised, I must keep it quiet from operatives, all of us."

"Tolly?"

"He shut all the others down, I'm independent from the firm, completely."

"So that's the Northern trips then?"

"Sorry Brenda, I shouldn't have, I'm sorry.

Her face was red with anger, and he wondered if she were going to burst into a rage, but she blinked and thought about it all, "You just can't help it can you, I'm asking too much again aren't I George?"

"I'm going out of my mind Bren, I can't live by sitting in the House and listening to crap all day long, I was about to burst and kill someone."

"So, he knew that then?"

"Must have, but also, she quit on him, he's shut it all down, the lot."

"Caledonia's department?"

"All of it, gone, training, practice, contractors, the lot."

"And he expects people to believe that?"

"A public clear out Bren, what else can he do?"

She reached for the knife and pulled it out and gave it to him, "I'm the same George, this life is not for us, I fully understand, funny you should bring that up at this time."

"Why Brenda, what's happened?"

"Las Vegas has happened, and they are becoming prostitutes, bought and sold for sex, I want them home and under my direction George, I want my family back and under orders, can you do that for me?"

He turned to her and looked into her eyes, "Ok, give me the truth Brenda, are they in trouble or causing trouble?"

"Causing trouble George and any moment they'll kill someone over there, I don't want them in an American prison, understood? They run rings around Addy, he can't control them, it's only a matter of time before someone betrays their love then we'll hear the shots from here, that place is an American party town, my sisters don't fully understand the American mind set of the place."

He took his phone out and gave it to her, "Ring and recall for me please Bren, I have real work for them, back up and eyes on the street when we start working, my lads will be taken without real back up, I need them, yes?"

"What's it called?"

"Air Tactical Developments, the research and development department for ongoing operations to protect the State."

"Air Tac then for short?"

"ATD department, I'm the director."

"MOD controlled George?"

"Top floor-controlled Bren, Tolly only get it?"

"So, from the DGI only, no contacts with London."

"None!"

"So where is it?"

"The East Midlands, Leicestershire out in the sticks, the middle of nowhere."

She smiled, "Others have noticed missing men George, his women want to know where he goes for days at a stretch?"

He nodded, "Yes invite please, we need skills and the women of this family have lots that we could use."

"They'll be angry as well George."

George shrugged, "His problem, let him handle it."

She smiled then punched in a number, "Kiki, yes I've found out the reason, George has been assigned to start up another department up North, he now invites us if we want in, well do you dear?"

She held the phone in the air for George to hear her screaming down the line, "Come over Kiki bring the ladies, he has a lot to tell us, and yes I'm bringing my sister's home and away from those American men, yes me too darling, yes now!"

She closed the call and gave him a kiss, "But you're in a directors roll now, eh?"

"Yes but."

"No buts Monkey man, you're not in the action you're the director of the action, yes?"

He smiled back at her, "Yes, but as always we are democratic, a good idea is a good idea and director or not, if a roll appears that fits me then I'll operate as normal."

She squeezed his hand, "But I'm here to back you up husband, so no problem now is there?"

"No Brenda, no problem now!"

She gave him another kiss but pulled some hairs from the back of his neck, "But you could have trusted me from day one Monkey man?"

"I knew you'd twig Brenda I just needed time to get the foundations fixed first."

"Preparing the wagon to cross the plains, eh? So, tell me about the lipstick."

"Err............... that's his Lordship, he has some very funny ideas Bren."

She burst out laughing with relief and happiness, she had found out his secret at last, before the door knocked, and the Japanese women walked in laughing.

# CHAPTER 40 ... April Fool's Day ... Buckingham Palace ... Conference Suite ... London

Lord Carnarvon smiled at everyone around the table, no one wanted to start the inevitable arguments, so silence descended.

Lord Carnarvon stood as the internal Palace door opened and King Charles stepped into the second dining room, everyone stood out of respect and Royal etiquette.

"Good morning, everyone, he searched the faces for new people, then sat down and looked at the planned meeting notes.

"How long Lord Raglan?"

"A short one Sire, intros and discussions on up-and-coming actions we don't officially know about."

"Good, can we proceed then please."

Lord Raglan looked at Elizabeth, "So Elizabeth, the new assignments, are they here dear?"

"Waiting in the outer room Sir," said Liz.

He pressed the intercom, "Ok please escort the new people in please Brian."

He smiled at everyone in the hope that this would bring peace to the possible row.

Patrick and Theodore walked into the room followed by the Australian Jack De'Montfort.

"Please be seated gentlemen," said Liz "So for everyone here we have three new members of the council, Mr. Patrick Collins, Mr. Jack De'Montfort and Mr. Theodore Smirnoff, objections please before we start?"

"Not another dingo?" said Sid.

"Ah, the Army wanker?" said Jack "Kills the wrong blokes then blames the intel department."

"I object to the Press baron who's supposed to be dead but here he is blocking my view again!" shouted Sid.

Jack pointed too Theo," Is he here to look at what's for sale then?"

"You!" shouted Margaret McDonald "Shut the fuck up! this isn't a beach sandy bollocks, so you wait until we want an opinion!"

"Baroness McDonald, Mr. De'Montfort," said Lord Carnarvon, "We would like some honesty from the new members please, last action and why, it's not recorded just for our ears and for our trust, so let it out please."

He looked at Theo in silence, "You first Mr. Smirnoff."

Theo looked at Dexter for confirmation, who nodded, "Clear the air Theo or the dingoes will moan for the southern hemisphere."

Theo took out a little metallic object from his pocket and placed it into the center of the table.

"No recording allowed here sir, "said Lord Raglan, "We have a security trust situation happening here, we trust each other with our lives, understand sir?"

"It's for blocking on and off-site targeted recording of anyone's voice, this is defense and not attack."

Sid snatched it and looked at the thing close up, "Made in China?"

"No, London by me and my staff, that will cost you a thousand pounds, if you would like one, I'll have one sent over to you."

Sid rolled it back over to Theo, "And we're supposed to believe all that shit?"

"Yes, we are!" shouted Dexter, "I trust that man with my life, and I have since I've known him, he doesn't tell lies unlike you dingo's from down under."

"Any time you like haggis breath," said Sid.

"Shut up!" shouted King Charles, at the top of his voice, "I've just about had enough of this juvenile behavior, everyone called to this table is trustworthy, they have been vetted and passed by other members of the council, trust is all, so can we get on with the business at hand now please?"

Faces stared in silence at him.

"Yes!" he continued, "I'm taking control, the last time I didn't one of you threatened to assassinate me, so I do the talking until I ask for an opinion, all clear so far?"

He pressed the center intercom, "Send the DGI in please Brian."

"Take your getting to know each other for after the meeting because I have Government boxes to finish, understand?"

Tolly came into the room and was initially shocked at the number of members at the council table, he looked at his father Erick and winked before sitting down waiting for the questions.

"Ok Tolly, inform the council please of impending actions we need to know about and others we are not supposed to know about," said King Charles.

"He's a bit young for all this isn't he?" said Jack.

Tolly smiled at him, "And you're in your second life I believe, what was the death for, tax problems or had you upset someone of interest Mr. De'Montfort?"

"Ah, that's why she called me over, you want to know who the big bad bastard is?"

"Yes please Mr. De'Montfort, let it out sir, we can help, "Tolly watched his eyes as he looked over to Jon Boy Wilson.

"Yes sir, we know he's an American, just the name please."

"And this little squirt will handle it?"

"He's my Grandson Jack and believe me he'll handle anything you have a problem with," said Elizabeth.

Jack looked over to Tolly, "So Augusta is your sister and that means that?"

"Augustus Victor Talbot was my Great Grandfather, yes Mr. De'Montfort, the name? his Army nick name, get it?"

Jack stared open mouthed, "Shit, he hates you more than he hates me."

"Who would that be Mr. De'Montfort?"

Jack couldn't let the name out of his mouth it had been so long since he buried it so deep in his mind and soul.

Tolly's eyes bore into him before he smiled back, "He chased me to the ends of the earth trying to find out where your Great Grandfather, he wanted to kill him so bad, my families' lives were at stake, I didn't have a choice I had to run."

Tolly patiently waited for the name to come out.

"Mossad................ Palestinian.......and a mole for the Jews, the old man wouldn't help when I needed it, angry you see and rich, very rich."

Theo had his phone out and was searching for the name with the facts so far.

"Are you talking about my Great Grandfather here?" asked Tolly.

"His friend you see, he wouldn't help or put the scumbag down where he belonged."

"A name please Mr. De'Montfort?"

"Godwinson, Sir Edmund Godwinson?" said Theo, "Dead apparently."

Jack turned in shock that the name was out in the open.

"An alternative line to the monarchy ladies and gentlemen?" said King Charles.

"Could you enlighten us all please sir?" asked Elizabeth.

"He's an Australian and he has a stronger and more direct line to the Kingship of the crown that I do, but Mr. Talbot would not and did not sanction a murder of a blue blood like Mr. Godwinson, even though he was undermining government with his political views and actions."

"And he's a problem then?" asked Dexter.

"The French and British crown Colonel Dexter, do you understand the consequences of such a claim, a direct descendent of William Duke of Normandy and he can prove it."

"What a load of bollocks!" said Sid.

"Direct as always dingo bollocks," said Dexter.

"Dexter, shut up," said Liz, "So why the problem, he's not currently in line, the Plantagenets, the Tudors, the Stuarts and even the German Windsor's, so what?"

"Legitimacy Elizabeth, the legitimate crown of Europe and a far wider problem than we can imagine."

"Total crap!" said Sid.

"The Anglo-Saxon nations are not represented by Monarchy, we are the fakes I'm afraid," said King Charles.

"Shoot the stupid bugger Dexter!" said Sid.

Silent faces looked closely at the King.

"I have to agree with the Australian cultural attaché," said Margaret, "We have before us the duly eligible and anointed King of England, Scotland, Ireland and Wales, there are no other claimants eligible now or in history, the common law has been fulfilled by crowning Prince Charles King of the United Kingdom, and all the Islands surrounding the British Land mass."

"I don't get it folks, what's the problem here?" asked Jon Boy Wilson.

"The law Jon Boy, UK Mainland Law is not legal in the eyes of the people, "said Patrick, "It's all dead because it's based on him and the Kingdom of Britain, politically we are fried to a crisp."

"A load of bollocks!" said Sid.

"Not quite," said Patrick, "This man can challenge any or every trial happening here in the UK, even the States, we're not legal in the eyes of the law, none of it!"

"Has that ever stopped us before Mr. Collins?" asked Margaret.

"Legitimacy Baroness McDonald, we don't have any of it if this bloke wants to make life hard, he can just push, and we'll have to listen and act as he wants."

"Total kybosh!" said Dexter, "We cannot rewind history and the Law, Margaret can kick any claim into touch, no probs, right Mags?"

"No, the Irish smart arse is right, this man can break us into little pieces if he pushes."

Patrick smiled at them, "It'll cost him bloody billions to take it through the high courts though?"

"He has billions!" said Jack.

"Why though I don't get it?" said Elizabeth, "And why now after all these years?"

"The old man's dead Elizabeth, he now has no fear of upsetting the grim reaper." said Jack, "We can just be another toy to play with and give him hours of fun and amusement."

"So where is he then?" asked Dexter.

Tolly coughed and all faces turned to him, "He was afraid in the past, now he has none, perhaps that's the problem, after all he'll not want a sanction put on his head I would have thought."

"But that department is closed down Mr. Trueblood, you shut it all down sir?" said Charles.

"But you could take this scum bag down couldn't you sonny?" Said Jack

"Hypothetically sir, if we wanted to do that sort of thing anymore? But we no longer have the means."

"You shut the department down Tolly?" said Dexter, "Why?"

"His mother," said Charles, "We discussed it all and agreed it was not needed in our modern world."

"You ordered the closure then sir?"

"Yes, I will not have blood on my hands, we will use political alternatives and talk through conflicting arguments."

"Shoot him Dexter!" said Sid.

Dexter stared at the King then shrugged, "Ok, everyone for himself folks, I'm outa here!"

"Dexter! shut up!" said Liz, "We need to come up with a plan and quick, if he's right then this man will destroy our culture the very fiber of our society, we cannot stand by and watch this happen."

"Complete bollocks, "said Sid "It's all paperwork, people like that Irish shit over there will make millions out of high court jabber, then in the end we'll tell them all to fuck off with all that crap and carry on as usual, I do find It strange however that a fellow Aussie would come up with all this load of tripe."

"Margaret could stop it dead if she wanted, "said Patrick.

"Number one court, no come backs, eh?" said Margaret.

"But you'd need balls for that one wouldn't you Baroness?"

"Half an hour in your company and I want to kill you already Mr. Collins!"

"Yes but is that true Mags?" asked Dexter.

"In theory yes, but they would fight tooth and nail to break it down, it would be legal war in the high court, I wouldn't survive the outcome I think."

"Well, there it is folks," said Sid, "The tart falls on her sword, job done, next?"

Margaret threw her bottle of water at him but missed.

"Hold on," said Dexter, "Why would he want to take out De'Montfort over there?"

"Because he's the link aren't you sandy bollocks?" said Margaret, "He's the one with the line to Monarchy, and he's the one who would have been pushed, he didn't want it to happen did you dingo dick, so you dropped out just like these idiots thinking it would all go away, well now he's back on this man's list to find and get it all rolling again, come on moron, deny it!"

Jack looked at the faces, "Mine is an old family what can I say? Simon De'Montfort the old King maker was an ancestor of mine, he's the link here."

"No, you are!" said Dexter.

"So how was he pushing you, Jack?" asked Liz.

"He doesn't want to be the next King, .........he wants to destroy the whole bloody lot, he's a republican, he wants to be Oliver Cromwell and to give the Anglo world reality and monarchy the death it deserves."

"He's another press Barron then, he wants the story of the century splashed over the world, embarrassment is what he really wants, right?" said Liz.

Lord Carnarvon coughed into his hand to get their attention "He's one of us then, this council, this Palace and this room, Helen must have stabbed him in the back for something he did or even said, Elizabeth...think back Dear, an enemy of hers, when you were very young and before Talbot took up his Sandhurst commission."

Liz stared at the faces looking back at her, "I don't know, so many passing faces and people, I don't know."

"Uncles Elizabeth?" said Dexter, "A couple of visits then gone into outer darkness for some reason only your mother knew?"

"And the Queen," said Liz, "They ran this country together and she would have had a say in the matter."

"Yes!" said Dexter, "They kicked one out, now who would that be, who were members before you Carnarvon?"

"Dead I think, we were called as a matter of urgency by Her Majesty in reaction to the South African Problems, the Empire was breaking up because of white apartheid and blind racism."

"So, he disagreed then?" asked Dexter, "So this would be the sixties, yes?"

"East Africa it is then." said Carnarvon.

"That's why we haven't seen him before, he's in outer darkness waiting to strike when he sees that there are no come backs, he wants safety as well then?" said Liz.

"And the deaths of Your Mother and Father were the first awakening of his plan, he felt secure at last?" said Dexter, he stopped talking and gazed out of the windows as he processed the information so far.

They started chatting, "Shut up and wait!" shouted Liz as she watched Dexter thinking.

His brain clicked in and stopped to look at them, "So, his first action will be a preliminary action to get us confused but still making the point and hurting the people he hates."

"Who?" asked Liz.

Theo had his phone out, and was talking to his team, "Sir Edmund Godwinson, we need all the facts all his history and all his actions in this life, possibly dead but we think not, associations, contacts, friends in the past, family young and old, dead or alive, I need a complete file on this man please, yes Charley now please!"

He closed the call and found he was being stared at, "What?"

"Is he that good at this then?" asked Lord Raglan.

"The best as this game," said Liz, she turned back to Dexter, "So, who's he going for Dex?"

"He'll go for Alice, he'll kill her in public as well, the full newsworthy splash to hurt us all."

"Alice who?" asked the King.

"My Grandmother and Tolly's great Grandmother, and Augustus Talbot's widow," said Erick, "He must want to hurt Tolly bad, she's a good woman and a leader in first Nations negotiations for vast land buy back discussions set up by the American President, so even Jimmy Wilson will also be hurt by it, pain all round, a win, win, situation for this scum bag! Maybe that's what he wants, to stop the buy back, maybe he owns the land wanted?"

Jon Boy touched his arm, "We can stop this Moose, no problems here, she's in Las Vegas at the moment."

Liz turned to him "And how do you know that one Jon Boy?"

"Well, an ongoing operations run by your side I believe."

"By me Grandmother," said Tolly, "A bringing together of Nations, show business and people power, President Wilson's idea by the way."

"The first of many, yes?" said Dexter.

"And how did you know that one?" asked Liz.

"Next logical step dear, next logical step!"

"But with who?" asked Charles.

"A British film corporation sir, Adrian Monkhouse and his famous faces show, stars of Mexico and south America, "said Tolly.

"Innocents?" asked Liz.

"Peaceful shows in the heart of the media, broadcast on all American channels north and south, as I said, it's part of changing hearts and minds to the new ideas."

"A great big old splash then when it all goes tits up eh?" said Sid.

"Well?" asked Liz looking at Dexter.

"Yes, that's what he'll be doing, he'll kill Alice and start the hate among the red skins, the whites will follow when they see their reaction, next logical forward movement I think."

"Any others?"

"He'll wait and see what happens, then he'll go for Erick or Caledonia."

"Or us Dex?" said Liz.

"Easy targets first dear, no sense in taking risks at this stage from his point of view."

"Shit!" said Liz.

"The Mexicans will be blamed by the media in some way, old grudges or something like that, even individual tribes might be filthed by them, trying to start a civil war among the natives, that'll fail though, still he'll be winning ether way."

"Ok, actions required?" asked Tolly.

"Americans, eh Jon boy, your game son?" said Dexter.

Jon Boy turned to Erick, "Well targets on site Moose, you and the wife wandering around glitter city pulling one armed bandits for fun, we can take them before the shot if we're lucky?"

"Tolly!" said Liz, "Over cover?"

"Tolly shrugged, I can't any more grandmother, we don't have the manpower or the skills, we de-commissioned them all."

"We are not involved Mrs. Dexter," said Charles.

"He'll kill us all with this stupidity!" said Sid.

"Yep, us all!" said Dexter.

"Dexter, shoot him please, he's an idiot!" said Liz.

"Oh no, they'll hang me from a lamp post remember, he's King and our boss we advise, that's it, besides he'll be on the short list for next strike, an even bigger news splash over all the English-speaking Nations, oh and the French, I suspect that the leak would have to be let out before that, the timings and all?"

"Assassination?" said Charles.

Dexter shrugged.

Charles looked at them in shock, "All a bit fast paced don't you think, ahead of ourselves perhaps?"

Liz thumbed to Dexter, "That's our genius, because he is, right?" she waited for them to understand what she was saying, "He's our secret weapon, when he's sparked up he can come up with their options and reasons out what will happen if and when, what we do is listen and take it on board for our planning, we plan accordingly, and he's very seldom wrong, clear everyone?"

"But he's a jock?" said Sid.

"You, shut the fuck up!" screeched Liz.

Charles looked at Tolly for assurance, Tolly gave him his best smile.

"So, every man for himself and we split then Dexter?" asked Sid.

"Oh, shut up dingo bollocks!" said Margaret.

"This is a Privy council," said Liz, "So we give council, so who's first?"

Dexter looked out of the window again.

"What?" asked Liz.

"If he was big then we have records so where would they be?"

"Whitehall central records, east block," said Lord Carnarvon.

"We need to take a look without being noticed Liz."

"Tolly could get access, I'm sure."

"Recorded and logged, even opening the safe records the time and is logged accordingly." said Tolly.

"A safe?" asked Liz.

"Yes, a walk in safe," said Tolly, "As big as a house and three times as secure, we could apply through channels perhaps but that would set off the panic within the records office and people listen to such things."

"A break in then?" said Dexter.

"Whitehall knob head?" said Liz.

"We need to know about this man Elizabeth, any other way?"

"Err...........not that I can think of."

"I have an expert on the books Grandmother if it would help," said Tolly.

"Ok, we'll handle it all."

The faces around the table stared at her.

"We'll handle it so shut up before you start."

"And you can do this Elizabeth?" said Margaret.

"So, what does he actually do around here then?" Jack pointed to Tolly.

"My prime responsibility is defense of the realm, second I run current activities."

"What the hell are they?"

Margaret glared at him, "Dingo bollocks! shut the fuck up!"

"Ok, moving swiftly onto another subject," said Lord Carnarvon, "North American conference on restructuring States within the United States of America and Canada."

"No!" said Charles, "Canada stays in the Commonwealth of Nations, end of!"

"Agreed!" said Erick, he turned to Jon Boy, "Well?"

"We don't want countries to abandon old friends, we just offer help and democracy."

"So, no objection to the continued commonwealth of other Nations then?" asked King Charles.

"Err...............yeah, why not, another club within, so why not? we'll be having the commonwealth of the America's I suppose that's if they want it."

"And Mexico and the South?" asked Lord Carnarvon.

"Ah, now there's the problem," said Jon Boy, "The problem is people power, we offer, and they react to plans given, State by State."

"A civil war then?" said Lord Raglan "Or are you making it up as you go?"

"People make democracy and not us," said Jon Boy, "Pop Talbot told me that one, without the peoples say, it's a dictatorship nothing more.

"This is real democracy if it fails then so do, we, again that's the old man's words."

"And controlling money grabbing monopoly seekers and slavers is our job, yes?" said Dexter.

"Yeah, the flip side of success in our systems, mankind's only reality, sell the excess or store over production for later use, since the stone age, again one of the old man's little lectures." said Elizabeth.

"Listening to the old man then Liz?" said Dexter.

"I didn't have a choice; we'd be watching TV, and he would start spouting his realities as he called them."

"So, Dexter and his wife will find this man then, yes?" asked Carnarvon, "Then what?"

"Well shoot the bugger!" said Sid.

"We'll decide on the day," said Dexter, "We listen to his opinion first, after all this is a democracy, yes?"

Dexter stared at Jack, "So what do we need him for Elizabeth?"

"He has multiple links that we can use, I would sooner have him around this table than the bad boy strong arming him into helping their plans."

Jack grinned at him, "And she still has a thing for me Dexter, so watch out."

Margaret glared at him, "Aussies, all the same old crap in the same old way."

Liz glared at him, "Jack, you work with Augusta please and find these people, they must be spending billions on this new media breakout, Dexter will assist me and find a name in the records, clear everyone?"

"Is she really doing a break in?" asked King Charles

"Yes, Sire and on your behalf," said Dexter.

"But that can't be right, can it?"

Dexter waved for the action to start, and the go sign.

They all ignored his words and got up then walked out.

"I didn't close the meeting did I Lord Raglan?" asked Charles.

"Just a quick one Sire, we have work to do after all."

"But I have French coffee on order?"

Lord Raglan smiled at nodded to the open doorway as the committee left them alone.

"My mother would not have allowed that surely?"

"Err ... no sir, but these are different days sir."

"In what way Lord Raglan?"

"Well, more productive I feel sir."

"In burglary?"

"More skilled actions sir."

"Really?"

"Oh, yes sir."

# CHAPTER 41 ... East Goscote ... Air 226 ... Flying Club ... Leicestershire

The instructor showed them how to fasten the parachute rigs to their bodies.

"Ladies and gentlemen, these are the latest air delivery systems, they used to be called parachutes, well they still are but these are much better."

"Safer?" asked Winston.

"Err...........................no not really, there is still a risk of sudden impact death if you don't use the equipment properly, foolishly pull at the wrong time or pack the chute incorrectly and death awaits, sorry to be so blunt but that's the truth."

White faces stared at his calmness and dark reality.

"So, we could die today then?" said Winston.

"Not if you listen and do as you're told bollock brain!" said George, "Ok staff sergeant, carry on mate."

"So, all who want to continue please raze your hands."

"Already done that staff, they're all volunteers, so carry on." said George.

"Ok, listen very carefully, this first jump I want you to pull this ring as you exit the plane, then pull these two handles to direct the chute, left will take you left and right will take you right, both together will slow your decent but only just, direction control is all and you have to learn that skill, any more questions?"

"No!" said George, "Ok, out, and to the plane everyone, now!"

The little jump plane circled the landing site as nervous faces watched the instructor as he clipped up his chute rig, he checked that they had all done the same then tapped them to stand and follow him to the open doorway.

George shouted above the din of engine and wind noise "We land in the middle of the old wooden hut circle, any who don't will miss out on the tea and hob nobs and will be back in this plane until they do."

Bart stood in the doorway, "But will my chute be big enough to stop me from splatting on the concrete?"

"Hopefully?" said George before pushing him into the slip steam and the drop from 10 thousand feet over the airfield.

"Next!" shouted George.

The girls shuffled up to him saying their Hail Mary's in unison and making the sign of the cross every now and again, he gave them the wide grin as he positioned them to the exit point.

"Out!" screeched George as he pushed them out of the plane one by one, Brenda gave him a kiss before he pushed her out, he grinned again as Rufus shuffled up to him.

"Why do we need to do this again George?"

George could tell that he was scared still and didn't want to do the jump.

"Experience My Lord, nothing more, and it's good for one's confidence!" he pushed him out.

Winston held onto the seat frame and wouldn't move with fear, George coaxed him to the doorway with a calming smile, "Nice view, wow, look at that eagle."

"What eagle?" George pushed him out and screeched laughing then jumped himself into the morning's high-altitude breeze.

As the last one out he descended above them all and counted off the open chutes.

On landing he pointed to some to go to the chute packing shed and redo for the next drop, Brenda failed to find the huts and landed on the landing strip, he pointed to the shed, Winston landed on the roof of one of the huts, George gave him the grin.

"Tea and hob nobs now then smart arse!" the rest he pointed to the packing shed, "Be gone and pack for the next, two more before lunch............ go!"

He gave the thumb to the pilot as they assembled at the jump plane after lunch.

"Ok, 20,000 it is then boss!"

"Good lad you know it makes sense."

They looked at him confused.

"You have to count in your head 30 seconds, then pull, remember how to hold the air, arms out nice and wide, my eagles!"

"Shit!" mumbled Winston.

Before takeoff George answered his buzzing phone, "Yes?" he shouted.

"We have a problem Uncle, senior management is now regretting the loss of your department, how's the training going?"

"Hello Tolly, we're doing sky drops at the moment."

"Why?"

"Means of arrival, it might come in handy."

"When though?"

"A speedy timing for future deployment, we can be there in just the speed of an airplane."

"Urban Uncle?"

"Thanks for reminding me."

"What?"

"Night drops, we need to prep for night falls into urban environments, tower block perhaps?"

"Sounds fun Uncle George, not having too much fun, are you?"

"All of it and more boss."

"We might need quick movements to tail targets, is Uncle Rufus up to speed?"

"Always, you know what he's like, oh, by the way we have multiple women on the books, multi-National as well, a good move?"

"Very Uncle, I like it, can I join one of your night drops?"

"Err............ yes, if you like, but for why?"

"Just the fun of it all uncle and to check you all out for the pre-exams."

"Soon boss?"

"Two weeks Uncle George, will they be ready for deployment then?"

"Err.......... yes, I suppose who have you in mind?"

"Well, the watchers are very interested in training, some of their younger elements need targets and I thought of you, will you be prepared?"

"Yes boss, they'll be ready, what's the bet?"

"A visit to the gold cup, all expenses paid, champers in the show paddock and Royal dinning tickets."

"For them and us?"

"Absolutely Uncle, winners enjoy the day out, fares fare."

"And the losers?"

"Back to basics and training with a blue dot on their record."

"And a potential shut down if found to be useless buggers, eh?"

"Reality Uncle, we all have it."

"Yes, Tolly fully understood, the Americans have invested a lot in us by the way."

"Wilson's?"

"Yes boss, a problem?"

"Na, I imagine that they would like a favor in the future though, correct?"

"It was mentioned Tolly, right at the start."

Tolly laughed at him, "Understood Uncle, oh by the way I need a little job doing as a matter of urgency, your safe man, is he any good?"

"The best in London I've been informed, he talks a good talk, but you know what I mean."

"Understood, still he's now in the big league, perhaps prepare him for my Grand Parents arrival, they'll get him in and on site, all he has to do is open the safe as quick as possible, will he need equipment?"

"Err.............. a bit sudden boss, he's just getting used to the way of the world."

"As I said Uncle a matter of urgency, we don't have the time, contact MOD supplies and order anything you need from their shelf, I'll have it picked up and delivered to you, Grandma is on route as we speak."

"Elizabeth?" screeched George.

"No time to be shocked Uncle, she'll fill you in with the details, as always watch out for the mad Scotsman, he's, her backup."

"Shit!"

"We need this information to plan for further targets Uncle, as I said, a matter of urgency."

"Today, tomorrow?"

"Within the hour, they'll bring the usual devices needed, best put the kettle on and break out the digestives."

"And Elizabeth can do this?"

"She's a Talbot Uncle, what else do you want to know?"

"Shit!" mumbled George to the dead phone, "Shit!"

Brenda was watching his face movements from a distance as he talked on the phone, now she was at his side, "What is it George, what's the problem?"

He held his hand in the air to listen, the sound of a distant helicopter, it was getting closer.

"Elizabeth and Dexter in a rush Bren, where's Robbie?"

She pointed to the plane, "Get him to go to the office and put the kettle on, he's on a job as of now."

"On his own George?"

"No Bren under Dexter and Elizabeth's direction, a rush job."

"And us?"

"We carry on, but the next drop will be in the dark and we all have to land on the tin roof of the hanger shed, best tell them to practice close up operations as we come down."

"Are you promoting me George."

"Yes, information giver and receiver, go! I'm with you on the night drop inform the pilot as well please Bren, fuel up on the return and all that.

The helicopter was now landing on the old concrete parking space, Dexter jumped out before the rotors had stopped, he lifted Elizabeth out and gently placed her on ground, he watched her give Dexter the royal smile and a slap of thanks.

George waved and pointed to the lecture hut for a chat and a cupper.

"So, folks, what's the rush?" asked George as they walked in and sat down.

"Where's our man George?" asked Liz.

"He'll be here in a moment, he's just taking off all his gear, so what's the plan?"

She looked at Dexter for confirmation of giving over the secret plan.

Dexter nodded, "This is George dear, there is no one more secure than him."

"Ok George, we need to break into a building in central London we need the contents of the man's safe, we photograph it all and then replace it back and disappear."

"A big nob then?"

"Very George, so big in fact that we can't get caught, it would embarrass the Crown if we did," said Dexter.

"We need a safe breaker of quality, so we ask that we can use your man, is he clued up to the latest equipment?"

George shrugged, "I don't know is the answer to that, ask and see."

There was a knock at the door and Robbie walked in and smiled at everyone, "Brenda told me to come and see you, boss."

"Yeah Robbie, mash a pot of tea and break out the biscuits, eh?"

"Yes boss," he walked back out of the door.

"He's twigged something don't you think George?" asked Liz.

"He recognized famous faces here Liz, but you couldn't tell by the look of him, could you?"

"He's sharp then?"

"Very and he's arrogant about his work, best not push, eh?"

Dexter smiled at him, "Not in my nature not to push George, you know me son?"

Robbie returned with a large tray containing a pile of cups and saucers and packet of bourbons.

"So!" he said, "You want to draw from the well, skills or advice?"

He carefully placed the tray down on the table and looked at them closely.

"Both!" said Liz, "The Egocentric 4000 safe, can you break it?"

He smiled at her, "Ah, that's the reason you wanted me out of prison?"

"To be in our pockets son, whenever we needed you, not a bad deal, is it?" said Dexter.

"Not quite the freedom I was promised though."

"Who promised that then?"

Robbie nodded to George then waited for the next phase of the negotiations.

"To be helpful to the cause was the phrase mate," said George, "And In return we offer to wipe previous crimes from the books, but not memories."

"So, it's a job then?"

"Well can you break into it?" said Liz.

"Never heard of it, Ma-am."

"So, he's twigged who you are Elizabeth."

"A very famous face Colonel." said Robbie.

"And you numb nuts!"

"So, could you learn how to break it, if we provide blueprints and numbers."

Robbie nodded, "I adopted this trade so yes I can."

"But it's the latest, all the bells and whistles of protection, it even records the time of the last opening and has a vibration monitor, so no drilling or grinding, and we don't want it damaged so no blasting like you normally do?" "said Dexter.

"What shape is it?"

"Square!" said Liz, "Why would that matter?"

"Manufacturing process Ma-am, it always has assembly challenges, know what I mean?"

"No, I don't,"

She handed him her phone, "This is the beasty, a top grade safe bought in, made in Germany by armor rite."

He looked at the schematics on her phone and flipped pages as he looked, "What's it made of?"

She looked at Dexter.

"A manganese compound, soft yet hard to drill, why?"

"And hard to weld I would have thought, so it's assembled with bolts and a snug fit?"

"What the hell does that mean?" asked Liz.

He ignored her as he searched the drawing plan, "Inside something larger, eh?"

"Yes, I have to find that when we're in there."

"You? I'm not going in there with you woman, what do you take me for?"

"Dexter here is protection and delivery, I'm entry and exit, you are the safe man, just us three of us clear?"

He looked at their faces and smiled, "No chance, an Army officer and a politician, no chance, they'd have us banged up before we even found the bloody thing."

She pulled out a metal item and placed it on the table, "A mini metal detector, latest stuff, UK made, I can get a numbers cruncher if you need one but George here recons that you'll come up with an alternative if we give you time."

"Na, brutality always wins in the end."

"It has to look like it's not been touched sonny, they must not twig we've been there."

"Ok............... can you get hold of jacking gear, as used in the motor trade for straitening chassis and the like, I need a ten-ton power press with a crocodile jacking unit and bars to match, sharp edges if possible."

"What are you going to do then?" asked Dexter.

Tear it apart then mend it back together, it's a tin can for God's sake!"

"But all the electronics?" asked Liz.

"Are in the front, we go in in from the back, so I need to pull it out to operate."

He looked at George, "I need a human porta power unit, capable of lifting it off its stanchions then replacing it when the time comes, volunteers?"

George started to laugh at him, but Dexter stared into his eyes, "He thinks he can do this," he snatched back the phone and flipped pages as he searched.

"So only caught twice and both times seem to have been pure luck on their side, a fare assumption?"

"A bad day in the office boss, what can I say here?"

Dexter turned to Liz, "So solitary actions, and you can get us in Elizabeth?"

"Oh, for God's sake bollock brain, I was doing this when I was nine years old, the old man brought in the real experts who manufactured the alarms and systems, they thought they were getting free advice for upgrades, in reality he was undermining them and the whole security system, they even paid him for his improvement advice."

Dexter turned in his chair and stared out of the window in silence as he thought it all through.

"So?" asked Robbie.

"Shut up!" said Liz, "He's working out the plan, we give him five then ask."

Dexter started to hum and paint into an imaginary sky with his finger.

"Err................yes we're on a go with this, George, we need you boy, or is there someone of equal strength."

"Well, we have Bart, he's a big lad you know."

"George!" said Liz, "Volunteer then shut the fuck up!"

George held his hand up in submission.

"Yes, Lill, a good call I think, ok tonight, everyone ready?"

"But the gear?" squeaked Robbie.

Liz handed him her phone after pressing recall, "Talk to this man and give him what you need, it'll be delivered within the hour, so a concise order yes?"

"But where's the job?" asked Robbie.

"London W1," said Dexter.

"Shit!" said Robbie before the voice asked him what he wanted, "Err....I need jacking gear as used on repairing motor vehicles ten ton minimum, a crocodile, an extension and bars to match, new if possible, no rounded corners, not been knocked about, get my meaning mate, crisp edges, black if poss, to do the job right," he waited in silence for the man to come back to him, "Still there mate?"

"Ok, I've got a Jack Sealy jacking set, in black with end tools and crocodile clamp and press, do you want the pull reverse and clamps?"

"Yes, perfect, all they have mate."

"Extension cross bars and a wheelie carrying dolly I must assume?" asked the voice.

"Err...........yeah, we have the muscle if it's heavy."

"Oh, it sounds heavy all right, anything else?"

"Err...........gloves, four pairs, one small one extra-large and two normal, leather please, tight know what I mean mate?"

Liz snatched the phone from him, "And Theo, we need an over watch as we work, I need to know if people are about, so earpieces and a central command, that's you, ok? oh and a backpack with the usual toys required, oh and a camera, yes?"

"Are you up for this Elizabeth? I mean?"

"And shut the fuck up moron!" she cut him off, Dexter was laughing at her red face.

"I'm ready for you, bollock brain, just give me an excuse!" she growled.

George pulled Robbie away as he was staring, his mouth open, at the mad couple and shut him up before he could give an opinion.

"These people George, can they do this, I mean, look at um man?"

George grabbed his collar and pulled him close, "These people invented this game moron, get it, do your job and let them do theirs, clear?

"Big league boss?"

"Very, so don't balls it up, got me?"

"Yes, boss clear and loud."

"Now what do I tell her then?" he nodded to the jump plane just taking off.

"Conference, and these people are bonkers boss!"

He slapped him, yes, agreed and thank you lad!"

Robbie re looked at the photo of the safe on Elizabeth's phone, "Hold up, is that a pen on the floor? What scale is this? Shit, it's bloody massive."

"Listen up arse hole, do your job and shut up, just get her entry and leave it at that and for fuck's sake, don't steal anything while you're in there, got me?" Growled George.

Another helicopter was now landing out in the yard, "Now that's your kit and our ride, ready to go?"

"Err ... I need planning time; I need to think this through."

"Yep, ok, times up, move your arse and let's go!" screeched George.

# CHAPTER 42 ... White House Tennis courts ... South Lawn ...Washington ... USA

The President ran onto the court and shouted at anyone within shouting distance.

"Where the hell is he?"

"Who?" asked his mother.

"John Julian Wilson mother, I'm going to kill him here and now before your very eyes, where is he?"

"Jimmy, cool it, what the hell's wrong with you?"

"JJ sold me to the press mother; all the sleaze has come from him!"

"But why?"

"Because he's a sleaze ball waiting to be kicked by me!"

"He must have a good reason son, he must have, I'll make the call."

"So where is he?"

"London, I think, Tolly wanted him over there for something, look he must have a good reason, I'll ring your father and get his opinion."

Jimmy was foaming at the mouth with rage, "I'm going to kill him."

JJ's girlfriend stopped playing tennis and looked at him, she went to her bag and got out her phone, "Jimmy, he's in England and doing a course on internal security with some of the Brits, do you wanna speak to him?"

"With a club in my hand preferably but that will do for now!"

She punched in recall and waited, Jimmy jumped over the central net and stood with her waiting to speak to his brother.

"Hi JJ, how're you doing, listen up, your brother is fuming at you and wants a word, are you ready to take flack? what's that noise in the background?"

"I'm in a high-level jump plane Lucy, what's up with the President then?"

"What are you doing in one of those JJ?"

"Jumping out what else?"

"He's as mad as hell JJ."

"He found out then? Ok pass him over."

Jimmy took her phone and breathed out slowly, "You two timing, cheating slime ball of a brother, why the hell did you do that to your own?"

"Not my idea bro, here I'll pass you over to the little idea's guy."

"So, who the hell's that?"

JJ passed the phone over to Tolly after elbowing him in the ribs to bring him round from a doze."

"What?" Tolly grunted as he came round from the shut eyed doze.

"Time to fess up Runt, he's like a racoon with a singed ass man!"

"Who the hell are you?" shouted Jimmy down the line.

"It's me Jim, we just needed to do this to pre-empt the opposition before they made a mess of you."

"You sack of shit Tolly!"

"Calm Mr. President and listen to the logic please."

"What Goddammed logic, betraying your own, is that logic, they're trying to sleaze me to infinity man, prostitutes, drugs, they even say I'm a party animal, pool side three in a bed session with both genders."

"Wow, so where did they get all that from Jim?"

"You! You, slimy bastard!"

JJ was giggling at the side of him, the others on the plane were listening to Tolly talking to the President of the United States."

"The President, for real?" asked Bart.

"Family, hey, typical argument ain't it?" said JJ.

"We needed you to get a life, so we gave you one Jimmy, too clean, unreal, boring mate!"

"You crucified me to the press?"

"Blue sanctioned out Jimmy, only the trash tries it on man, Augusta is good like that, if they want you then they have to climb over her and she's nasty mate, all clear, can we exit the plane now?"

"Any chance of the chute not opening?" asked Jimmy.

"1 in 10.000 apparently."

"Shame! Why really though?"

"They need to see you take hits Jim, public life, you're the example for the younger generation, sweetness and light isn't real, is it?"

"Well, in me it is, you smart assed bastard!"

"I hear you have a secret crush, English made by all accounts."

"Throw my shitty Brother out of the Goddamn plane Tolly!"

"Better get on the white charger Jim and ride out to the rescue."

"For why?"

"In a lock up, downtown Ottawa, the press wants to fry her to a crisp, she caused a mass punch up with the press corps, hey, don't you bother with Northern news down in that white house of yours?"

"How?"

"They called her your tart for a start, hey I'm in the rhyming mood, she needs a man, a shame really anyway you'll have to do, so go!"

The door was slid open by the jump tech and the sound level burst into whistled winds.

Jimmy cut them off and looked at Lucy, "I still don't get it."

Lucy shrugged then waved to her opponent to restart the game, she took her phone back and zipped it back into her bag.

"A problem Jimmy?"

"Err.........................yes Lucy, a diplomatic incident of National importance, I need to go to Canada and quick.

She was gone and playing tennis as he looked for someone to direct the flight call on the Presidential plane.

"Ok Honey?" Kelly shouted from the lawn near the tennis court.

"Mom, do you have Aunty Cal's number on your phone?" he walked over to her.

"Yeah, sure why?"

"I think her bodyguard has caused an international incident up in Canada, how do we handle that one?"

"Who, Pimples? she's a crazy cow, let em bang her up, she's used to that I hear."

"What are you saying mom?"

"Cal, pulled strings to get her released from prison in the first place, as I said, nuts!"

"Interesting though and not boring like me, eh?"

"Who called you that?"

"My big brother mother, hey I'm rhyming now, what the hell has she done anyway?"

"Caused a fight to defend honor against the press, apparently yours."

"What, the press, where?"

"Canada, well Ottawa, must be bad because they've locked her up."

He stared at her as he thought about what to do.

Kelly was now on the phone and waited for the pick-up, "Cal, what the hell has that silly cow done now?"

Cal started laughing down the line at her.

"What's she done to be locked up again?"

"And you've just told him about the first time, yes?"

"Well, huh!"

"And his reaction?"

"Impressed would be the word I'd use Cal."

Cal started laughing again, "And you can't prevent what's going to happen now woman, maddening, eh?"

"Very Caledonia, I might have to shoot her!"

"True loves ways Kelly, push and It'll just get nasty, remember how it use do be?"

Kelly started laughing now, "Yeah, my Pa hated Jon Boy, too tall, too blond, too German looking, he wanted Italian and connected, know what I mean?"

"Get real Tart!" Cal slammed the phone down on her, Kelly looked at her son walking away, she knew the walk and she understood the look he gave her, "Moron!" she screamed out, "Mr. President!"

# CHAPTER 43 ... Ottawa ... City Police lock up compound ... Canada.

Ruth was walking and eating her sandwich lunch as she walked the circled compound path for what seemed like the thousandth time, she saw the helicopter in the distance and didn't think much of it until she saw the line of black sedans driving up to the main gates on the straight road followed by press vans with satellite dishes bouncing on their roofs as they drove over the speed bumps.

She held the dry crust of bread in the air as a lonesome seagull swooped down and took it then flew away in one movement, it squawked with delight before landing on the security lighting stand and swallowing the bread in one go.

"Now that's just bad manners, Mr. Sammy Seagull."

A guard pointed to her for an unseen person in the entrance block house, the white suited man walked out to her and opened the security gate bolt without an alarm sounding as it would normally.

"Wanna join our circus, Lady?" shouted the tall man.

"Who the?" as he came close, she recognized the President of The United States of America.

"What the hell?"

"A Presidential pardon and an unprecedented apology for any inconvenience cause by the fist fight caused by unnamed assailants."

"And you are what?"

"The white Knight, can't you tell?"

"What the hell?"

"Do you mind if I carry you, Lady?"

"Err...................na, go ahead to hell with your hernias!"

She jumped up and held his neck as he took hold of her, the rest of her sandwich she threw over her shoulder and smiled to the photographers.

"I thought you'd be a good deal heavier, but you're as light as a feather."

"Am I? Well, it's all the crap food they've given me, "as he carried her to the gate, the press arrived at the main guard house and started snapping photos of the President carrying the woman of his choice out of the prison yard.

"Is she the one Mr. President?" shouted the familiar voice from out of the Press scrum.

He leaned into her ear and whispered, "A nice posh English I don't understand what's happening squeak, yes?"

She kissed his ear out of shock and bemusement, she just needed to do it.

The press got their front-page money shot there and then, but took more just in case, he kicked the gate to give himself room as he approached the press people.

"History in the making here folks," he shouted, "An unprecedented pardon by the Canadian Prime Minister, this English rose has been bullied and abused by an apologetic Nation and I on behalf of the American States, I take this opportunity to apologize to her, I thought dinner tonight at the best hotel, any better ideas?"

"What's for afters?" shouted the woman's voice coming from the crowd.

Ruth looked for the voice in the crowd and spotted Augusta standing with her press crew and Simon standing at her back.

"None of your business if you don't mind people, besides how could we do this to this poor helpless woman." said Jimmy.

"Yes! my thoughts James, it's because I's English innit?"

He gave her the look that said your acting is a sackable offence woman.

"Will she be going to court Mr. President, you know, to claim compo for being banged up and all that?" shouted Augusta.

"Leave it out," said Ruth, "He ain't done any banging yet."

He growled at her under his breath before placing her into the limo to be pulled in by his staff.

He stood to face the cameras, "Ok, any questions while I'm here folks?"

"A misunderstanding then Mr. President?" shouted another press man.

"I'm not one to point the blame at anyone here folks but you the press have a lot of explaining to do about the fist fight the other day in the Hotel National, what was it, the heating on to high and set everyone's temperatures racing?"

"Like yours today then sir?" said another press man.

"Just trying to help a maiden in distress, nothing more, next!"

A man held his hand up to be heard at the back and shouted before he was pointed to by the President, he tried to shout down questions from others press people.

"It's all a bit personal isn't it, Mr. President?" asked Augusta.

"Exceptional circumstances Madam, besides I was in town for the National Assembly voting so why not?"

"Hey, ain't she the gal who did all the punching the other day?" shouted the man.

"And ain't you the guy who caused it all by inflaming the conversation into a slutty shouting match?" said Augusta.

"We're talking sluts now then Mr. President?"

"Shoot that man somebody!" shouted Jimmy.

Photographers snapped the man as he was pushed and barged around.

The place melted into laughing as he got into the limo and was driven off.

Someone trod on the man's toe, and he disappeared under the crowd of press people.

"And you must be from Twinkle-Twinkle pornography news?" and you even make the gutter press look bad? "shouted Augusta.

He wanted to express his views but was crushed underfoot by Simon and other press people moving back to their vehicles.

"Without respect what are we?" screamed Augusta.

"An ignorant unprofessional mob!" echoed the dispersing press agents.

"Unprofessional mob!" shouted Augusta, she linked arms with Simon and was dragged away to the waiting news van and her laughing crew.

"Hey, I'm with the press, this is free speech, he's just picked up his jail bird hooker for hot sex on the way home." shouted the man.

The press core ignored him and walked away.

He breathed in their exhaust smoke as they drove off following the Presidential cavalcade to the American boarder.

"Hey, I can print what I like!" but even the seagulls echoed their disapproval of him as the white blob landed on his shoulder.

# CHAPTER 44 ... The black Limo ... Heading south ... And the US Boarder

"These people are Mr. Henry Wilkinson and his Wife Olivia, Ruth, they are your fathers' parents, and this is Ruth Winstanley, that's her adopted family name back in the UK."

The old couple looked at her and smiled.

"She has my mother's face, Henry, wow, eh?"

"Yes Livia, I see it all and your impatience, she has that too."

Jimmy leant over to Ruth and smiled, "These are your Grand Parents Ruth, Mr. And Mrs. Wilkinson from Idaho, I thought it important to call in the family, a good idea?"

She burst into tears as they moved over to hold the woman.

"I'm called Olivia honey, and your grandpa is called Henry, we see that you are family so relax, eh?"

"But where?"

"Oh, Idaho Falls honey, we're here for you, all that you need we're more than happy to help, ok with that?"

Ruth sobbed and sobbed as the old couple held her in their arms one by one.

Jimmy touched the driver's shoulder, when we're over the boarder go via the military cemetery for us, please, we have more crying to do."

"And my father?" asked Ruth.

"I recalled him Ruth, we'll meet him at the Marine monument," said Jimmy.

Ruth couldn't hold her emotions in check and burst out crying again.

"And she was in a British military prison?" asked Henry.

"I'm a veteran of our wars and more wars," said Ruth.

"We know all about you, honey," said Olivia, "And we want to know more, agreed?"

Ruth nodded and tried to control her emotions but failed.

"You're home now honey, all is well believe me," said Olivia, she took hold of Ruth's hand and squeezed it hard, "And I'll do the slapping when we meet up with my Son!"

"No doubts?"

"You've been checked out, all the way down to your adoption by Mr. And Mrs. Winstanley, were they good people?"

"Fantastic, they're still my Mum and Dad you know?"

"We understand Honey, we're just going to enjoy another unexpected member of our family, you ok with all that?"

Ruth grinned through the tears and slapped the President, simply because she could and he was within distance, "So why didn't Caledonia come and get me Jimmy?"

"Because I had a better idea."

"Hence the circus show, then?"

"Yeah, good, eh?"

"But why?"

"I'm as boring as hell to quote my big Brother, so all things change."

"But still, why?"

"Mr. goody two shoes has to become a man Ruth, he has to have a dark past and a better future, the people expect reality, so I have to give them some, get it?"

"Let me guess who came up with this idea?" said Ruth.

Jimmy held his hand up to the old couple, "Before you hear things that are not for public ears folks, let me remind you again to keep silent please, Ruth is top secret, her history is top secret, what she does for the British Government is?"

"Top secret!" said Livia, "Yeah we get that Mr. President we really do!"

"The Brits take a very dim view of releasing secrets to the open press, we would all be at risk if her history gets out there, understood?"

"We understand Mr. President!" said Henry, "Carry on with your conversation we're not listening really, just looking at our girl."

Ruth sobbed into her hands listening to the old man speaking.

Jimmy patted her back as she cried.

"So, still want revenge on the people in the UK, the Royal Marines?" asked Jimmy.

She stopped crying and looked at Livia, "No, I have a life to live and I'm gonna!"

"You're gonna live little girl that's what you're gonna do eh?" said Livia.

"Yep, living, why, because I wanna!"

The limo glided on with the journey, Jimmy tried not to sleep but he was now softly snoring on Ruth's shoulder as they crossed the border into the USA.

The driver put on some soft Simon and Garfunkel music to sooth everyone in the back.

Ruth looked out at America and her green forests.

"So why would you want revenge on the British Marines Honey?"

Ruth turned to the old ladies' curious face, "Do you want to know all? there's no going back once you hear it you know?"

"I'd like to know please Ruth, all and everything they did to you, we all want to know."

Ruth took a couple of breaths to get air into her brain, "I was imprisoned for murdering civilians on the streets of Bagdad, only they weren't civilians, they were about to kill American soldiers, I stopped them with my long shot rifle one by one, men and women."

"But when my people recovered the bodies no weapons were found and I was accused of un sanctioned murder, their weapons had been cleared away by their friends and the bodies showed to eager press people wanting to take photos and looking for someone to blame, my unit of 42 Commando was on site and we took the flak from the Iraqi press, international press people mostly Russians took up the shout for this unfair killing and I was sacrificed by my senior officers, then back in the UK before a disciplinary hearing I was sentenced to a stay in prison, un fit to plea was what they said."

"The reality was that they wanted me as a sacrificial lamb to take the blame for the action, I was said to have been the black sheep, at this trial I was given food and drink that in fact sent me bonkers, I was foaming at the mouth and everything, hence the unfit to plea judgment, I have since talked to the Judge who sent me down, it was all she could do to save me, you see the British press allowed these scum bags to take me to court as a war criminal, no weapons at the side of the dead you see, proof I was a murderer, my own people believed them rather than me, I had been a Royal Marine since I was 15 years old I'd risen through the ranks to the rank of Captain, all of that was ignored, they threw me away like a piece of rag into the rubbish bin.

"So, what happened after all that, how'd you get out?" asked Henry.

"The Whitehall System takes notes of bad decisions made by MOD mandarins as they throw people away and I was recruited back into special ops, by Caledonia, she's the one on the films who killed all those Mafia people in Las Vegas, remember, the white woman swimming in the man-made lake having just slaughtered those baddies?"

"They said that she was Russian?" said Olivia.

"Na, English and the real thing, if you want trouble then she's the one to avoid at all costs, a real killer!"

"And so, were you then Ruth?"

She turned to look at their faces, "It must be nice to be unaware of all this blood spilt for democracy, you can't argue or make a deal with some of them, there is no other way, let them take your life and those of your family or you put a slug in their stupid brains, no other way!"

Livia squeezed her hand again, "We fully understand Honey, young Henry has had to do the same in the past, he told us sometimes, just a little of what happened out there in the Middle east."

"There's no arguing with a gun in your face, you fight, or you die! err.........Olivia!"

"But why wouldn't they back you up after all that you did?" asked Olivia.

"British press Livia!" said Jimmy, his eyes were still closed, "Antiwar press people with absolutely no idea about right and wrong, we had them during the Vietnam war remember? Some were thrown to the wolves just like she was, Government agreements to make sense of military embarrassments, someone has to take the can as they pass it down to a junior officer as in Ruth's case, the buck stopped at her."

"But that's all wrong, Mr. President!" said Olivia.

"Yep! Sure, is dear, political acceptance of murder, not in the book of office and not in the mouths of politicians, no one wants to admit it to the viewing public, we have to be clean you see?"

"Let me make it clear Olivia," his eyes were still closed, "I send people to their deaths and I do that to protect our Nation, it's not sleaze or corruption, it's safety, we kill them or they will come and kill our people, in the past, some Presidents have tried not to be aggressive, it doesn't work, we found that out with the twin Towers, remember that war crime Olivia, well we killed them all, those scum who killed innocents were themselves murdered when they slept or bombed while they prayed to their God, or simply shot by someone like Ruth here who had a sanctioned contract to kill the scum bags, get it?"

"For peace then?" asked Olivia.

"Not really, fear is the thing, if they want what's mine or yours then they will get punished, not in the next hour but in the next year they will receive a visit from Ruth or Caledonia or someone like them, we do not deal with terrorists, we do not deal with drug dealing scum, we kill them stone dead and hope the survivors understand the new rules, understand now?"

"Shit!" said Ruth.

He opened his eyes and looked at her, "You see these hands Ruth, they have blood on them, I send people to die, I send people to kill, and I send people to save the guiltless from the guilty, all over the world, I have to, that's in the silent job description of being the President of the United States of America!"

"Shit!" said Henry, "And when it's all over?"

"We have to live with it!" said Ruth, "Over and over again, all perfectly normal apparently."

"Ok Ruth, finish what you've started, tell them what your last assignment was and what happened." said Jimmy.

"But they don't need to know."

"It's not for them Ruth, listen, we as humans are split into two people in our heads, the innocent and the guilty, you have to say it out loud to receive the judgment from the innocent in your head, understand? You are judge and jury, it has to come out."

"But?"

"Pa taught me that one and he learned that from one of those British guys from ancient days who'd done it and felt it all, understand?"

Olivia elbowed her to prompt the start of her story.

"Mexico City, remember the headlines?"

Olivia nodded to Ruth's red swollen eyes.

"Five of us, all female, three Irish girls, Caledonia and me we were the point crew we went in and killed as many as possible the Irish girls were our security and back up, side doors, back rooms, or anywhere we didn't predict movement to come from."

"I was her backup, she laid the lead down and I made anyone who wanted to shoot at her a hole in the wall, we killed perhaps fifty or so, I don't really recall the numbers but anyway on the way out we were betrayed and expected to be killed by someone who warned Police we think, lucky though other back up arrived and saved us from being gunned down on site, we escaped, others had worked out the rotten plan, we were just the work tools sent to kill and be sacrificed, we survived so people will make judgements and perhaps come for us, well Mr. President?"

"Over my dead body still holding my hot machine gun which will be out of ammunition, and I will be standing by their dead pile of bodies!" said Jimmy.

"Shit!" said Henry, "We didn't know."

"Civilians sir, you're not supposed to know what happens on your behalf, but it does, and it has to be done from time to time, do you forgive Ruth and myself for trying to save the Nation for the innocents?"

Olivia climbed past Ruth and kissed Jimmy on the cheek, "Mr. President, you are our hero, we understand, we love our freedom and now understand the price, so thank you for all that you do!"

A silence descended on them as all thought about the words, Ruth started to cry again.

# CHAPTER 45 ... Arlington US Marine Monument ... USA

The limo spun into the National monument site and slowed down for passengers to see it all flash by.

"So, what did you do about our betrayal Jimmy?" asked Ruth.

"I found the source and plugged the hole."

"You killed him?"

"No, I made a new friend."

"But he'll always be an enemy?"

"Maybe? But that's politics, trust is all and all that."

"That's stupid."

"Get in or out woman, democracy needs talkers, that's what we do for a living, we talk! I talk with the good the bad and the very ugly, get it?"

She left the conversation to settle as she looked at the giant bronze monument of Marines setting up the flag on the little hillock of Iwo Jima.

"My Great Granddaddy is the one holding the flag at the base, he was there," Jimmy sniffled as tears came to his eyes.

"Really?" asked Ruth.

"Sacrifice Ruth, that's what this is, sacrifice, the demonstration of what had to be done by brave guys from home."

"Agreed!" she stared at the faces and the wind in the flag as it moved in the breeze, "Fantastic Mr President!" said Olivia.

The tall figure in a pin striped suit stared back at them from the wall of the monument, Ruth could see the tears in his eyes as she focused on him.

"Babies here Pa!" said Olivia, she jumped out and ran to her boy, he cried on her shoulder, Henry wanted to shake his hand but was pulled in and hugged by the big man.

Ruth stood and looked at her father, she never imagined this day would ever happen but here it was and there he was, she didn't know what to do, she just stood and waited for the focus to turn on her.

The President was at their side and was also hugged by the big man, suddenly his eyes burnt into her skin as he focused on his long-lost daughter.

He walked from them and looked at her close up, "You can slap me down if you want little girl, I wouldn't blame you if you did, I was not aware of you or anything really, I was a man on my own doing my thing in my lost life, the Marines fed me and told me what to do, day in and day out," he thumbed to the President, "His Pa was my leader and boss, I followed good advice mostly, but not in this case, sorry!"

She fell into him and smelt the manly smell of a single lonely, retired Marine, "Are you real?"

"Yes Honey. I'm real, are you?"

"My mum and dad are in the UK, it would be nice if you met them, will you?"

"Yeah, sure, so where is your mother buried?"

"Aldershot England."

"I'd like to visit, ok with you, I'll ask permission every step, ok with that?"

"Can I get to know you bit by bit, err...........?"

"Dude, everyone calls me The Dude, I've been this tall thin guy all of my life, too tall for the parade, too tall for guard detail, the only thing I'm good at is recon, I imitate a tree really good, just me the radio and a location in the jungle."

"Retired now though, yes?"

She started to sob on his shoulder as he answered her, "Yeah, Jon Boy don't want me anymore so I quit, I run a few hotels for someone you might know, Lord Longmore, you know the guy?"

She nodded into his chest, "Yes I know Rufus, completely bonkers."

"That's the Guy, nut's completely nuts, rich though, very rich, so you know his family then?"

"I work for them, well, I used too before well this!"

"And that's now at an end, yes?"

"I don't know, Caledonia is my boss, you know her?"

"Yeah, honey I know your boss, I know all of them, nearest things to friends, Dexter Elizabeth, Caledonia and of course Tolly, I was with him when he got shot down in Africa."

"And Augusta?"

"Err..............no, not so much, she's the big cheese in the media ain't she?"

"She's good and fare, you'll like her, you can meet her at the wedding."

"What wedding?"

"Our wedding Dude," said The President.

Dude let go of her and she turned to the President, "You know it makes sense then?"

"Yep, I know it makes sense, from the first moment I met you I knew, you?"

"I had no choice, it was you, but I was tempted by your big brother."

"Don't start woman, so, will you marry a man with no prospects of outliving his present job?"

"Yes! But they'll kill you only over my dead body and my hot empty heckler, oh and the pile of their dead bodies!"

She ran up to him, he caught her off the floor and kissed her.

"What the hell happened in Canada?" asked the Dude, "What the hell man!"

Olivia started clapping, and everyone joined in.

"Hey, ain't I supposed to be asked for permission or something?" said the tearful Dude.

"Listen Dud! I make up my own mind, learn that fact quickly please!"

"It's Dude woman!"

"That's what I said, Dud!"

He gave her his wide grin, "Can I at least give you away?"

"No Dud, but you can be there, my daddy will give me away and it's to him I owe my life and teenage years."

"I bet you were hell on earth, eh woman?"

"Bang on that man, so is there a pub close by because I feel like drinking something strong and punching you!"

"Yeah, me too honey!" said Olivia.

Henry the elder laughed at his face, "They came home to roost, Dude my ass!"

"Hey Pa, come on man!"

"Get in the motor, moron!" said Ruth.

Jimmy gave him the Presidential grin and the election wink.

"A big move eh, daughter and President Son in Law all in one day?"

"What the hell Jimmy?"

Jimmy pushed him into the limo with everyone else, "Come on Dude, besides, Pa would like a word, while you're in town Dude, ok with that?"

"Oh sh............!"

His mother elbowed him to stop him from swearing in her presence.

Jimmy held her close and slept on her shoulder, she loved them all for being there, for just being there.

# CHAPTER 46 ... Whitehall ... Central Records Block ... London

The gorilla unloaded the van and packed the trolley with all the gear needed then nodded to the lead Archaeologist, Elizabeth had her disguise buttoned up to her neck and the cowboy hat over her ears.

Dexter looked like a vagrant, "What dew you want wooman?"

"The bloody map, you sack oh doo!"

"Now that were uncalled for Lassie."

"Evidence, that's what we want!"

"Evidence!" shouted Dexter, "That's the wee problem!"

Robbie looked on at the bad acting with interest until they came to the guarded entrance and Liz threw down her signed application to investigate the bowels of the giant building.

"No Madam, we have to get permission from the top floor."

She passed the card appointment over to him, "What you got in there, secrets of the Nation or something?"

"Well yeah, exactly Madam, who are you anyway."

"Three hundred years and we get him on the door!" shouted Liz, "You have held back public interest for long enough now move out of my way you jobs worth!"

"Sorry Madam, can't do!"

Dexter stood up in front of him, "Oooooh, bad move laddy, now she'll get proper mardy arsed."

He leaned into Dexter, "Who the hell is she when she's at home."

"She's the seat."

"What?"

"Oxford University seat for archaeology, the big bunce in charge of the lot of um, Professor Cinderella Uppingham, sorry, Baroness Uppingham of Barnstead and Arbroath."

"Where's that then, hold up, Cinderella?"

Liz pulled Dexter out of the way, she grabbed the guard by his tie, "Listen up arse hole show me to the dungeons and let me get on with my investigation or I will count you as a lost find and box you up into one of my sample jars."

Dexter gave him and open hands and stood back to allow the man to take all the blame if he didn't let her through, he shrugged to make the point.

"Where's the dungeon?" shouted Liz.

The man thumbed to the floor, "No idea Madam, down I would have thought."

"Can we move?" said George, "I'm holding all this gear you know? And it's bastard heavy!"

"Now see what you've done, you've upset the staff, he'll want a bonus now, well it's coming out of your wages you moron!" screeched Liz, she pushed him out of the way and marched on into the building followed by Robbie, carrying the spirit level, and the scale marker sticks, Dexter put his hands in his pocket and smiled, George grunted and sweated to follow on, he scowled at the security man, "Wanker!"

The man stood to the side and said nothing, "What bloody dungeon, we don't have a dungeon."

"Bollocks!" echoed George from the inside of the building, he bent over and laughed at the nutters, "Another day at the office," he carried on laughing.

# CHAPTER 47 ... Whitehall ... Lower ground basement ... London.

George let go the trolley and breathed out as he sweated, "Is this all needed?"

Robbie grinned, "You never know young man, there's a flask of coffee in there somewhere, let's have a slurp before we start."

Liz grabbed his collar and pulled him close, "Which door moron?"

She thrust the map into his hand, "Now!"

"Err........." he looked at the drawing then turned it the right way up, "Err... there."

She took out her lock pick and picked the lock in seconds, she pushed the door open and waited for him to move.

"That was bloody quick for an armature Madam."

"Who said I was an amateur, get doing!"

George barged him out of the way as he pushed the equipment trolley through the door gap and into the room.

Robbie stared at the lock up safe, "It's bloody massive."

"And? Just get us in and quick!" growled Liz.

Dexter still had his hands in his pocket, "Not very spacious, is it?"

"Historic records Dexter, buried in the bowls, we need to take a peek, they've been here from the year dot."

Robbie sat on Georges Trolley as he stared at the steel inner security building situated in the open space.

"Well?" said Liz.

"Thinking time Madam, give me a while please."

She stared at Dexter.

He shrugged, "What he needs Elizabeth is motivation, death or greed which one would work, that's the nub of all this?"

"Death!" said George as he sat on the floor exhausted with the work done already.

"Did we explain about the gold Liz or was he not in our loupe?"

"Shush Dexter, we never mention gold, now I thought we'd covered all that, it's not supposed to be here in the first place."

"Why, is it because it's Russian?"

"Shush moron, walls have ears!"

Robbie ignored them as he stared, "The roof has to come off, that's the week point."

The three faces stared at him, "And?" said Liz.

"Well, we jack the roof up and you climb in and do your thing, we wait out here and you hand us all the gold bars one by one, easy peasy when one has a plan Madam."

Liz stared at Dexter and Georges faces, "I might have to kill him after all lads!"

"But what about all the shiny knob things out front?" asked Dexter.

"No, too complex, simple is best so how do we shift the roof?"

"We don't have a ladder?" said George.

"No, we don't, do we? You see, we forgot something; I told you it was all too rushed."

"Take the door off its hinges George we can use that as a run up to the ceiling." said Liz.

Robbie gave George the look that said, she's a smart one, George returned his look with one of his own, get bloody on with it.

She gave George the nod, he searched the kit box for a screwdriver and attacked the door hinges, Dexter looked on impassively, "How long do we have Elizabeth?"

"Till six in the morning when records people will be down here with yet more history files."

"And more gold Liz?"

"Shut up moron!"

"Ok, I have it chaps," said Robbie, "Crocodile wedge and we lift one side of the roof, then we sling a block in and stop it from falling in again."

"What if it's welded, then what?" asked Liz.

"Na, why weld ten tons of two-inch slab steel, no, on site assembly remember? The weight alone would keep any normal people out I would have thought."

"Are you saying we're not then normal?" asked Liz as she locked her predatory eyes on his.

He looked at her red face, "Well.........err.........come on George we need that ladder to get to the ceiling, and pass the croc when you've done that, oh and we need the extenders and the power ram then screw it all together, I recon six feet plus the ram will do it."

George gave Liz the look that said someone kill him quick.

"So, a trembler device or a vibration switch in there do you think?" asked Dexter.

Robbie stood back and looked at it, "A bit of an over kill, don't you think, after all files, that's all that's in there yes, files and files slip and possibly move and set off stupid alarms when everyone's in bed trying to get some sleep."

"What about the Russian gold reserve?"

Robbie watched Liz look at Dexter, He started laughing, he now knew they were just pulling his leg, "Do me a favor!"

Dexter shrugged and walked over to help George remove the door, he took it off him and leaned it on the file safe wall, "So that would have set it off then?"

Robbie looked around at them and the open-door space, "Well yeah!"

They all stopped to listen to any noise happening in the building, Liz broke the spell.

"Come on move your arses, we don't have all night."

Robbie pulled out the thermos flask and poured himself a cup of coffee then took a slurp, "What?" he stared back at the blank faces.

George was assembling the jacking gear and the hydraulic power pump.

"That's it, screw it all together and let's get going eh." said Robbie.

Liz gave him the face.

He slurped some more coffee and looked at her over the edge of the cup, "What happens if it all go's tits up while we're in here?"

"A twenty in the choky, traitor to the crown, perhaps thirty just for being here with us mate?" said Dexter.

"Shut up!" said Liz, "You, move it!" she snatched the coffee cup from him and gave it to Dexter.

George was now just about ready with all the jacking gear, he handed Robbie the crocodile expansion clamp, "Go to it smart arse!"

Robbie climbed up the door that Dexter was holding steady with his foot leaning it against the unit side, he took a sip, "No sugar in this, how can you drink it like that?"

Robbie ignored his complaint and carefully placed the wedge croc jack in a space he could see and started pumping the hydraulic power ram.

"Wood, I need wood as a temporary wedge so I can get a better grip with the croc."

George handed him the big screwdriver, "Yeah, that'll do I think."

Dexter nodded for Liz to put her foot on the bottom of the door while he searched for something to wedge the ceiling with.

She put her full weight on it and thumbed him to do it quickly.

He wandered off into the gloom of the outer room and eventually returned with an expensive-looking antique chair.

"Oak, I think?"

"Yeah!" said Liz, "Master carpenter Chippendale's finest unreplaceable Georgian classical highchair made from cherry and walnut, just what you need to wedge a bastard ceiling you bloody idiot."

Robbie grunted as he took a second bite at the gap with the croc jack and took out the temp screwdriver, "How bigger gap do you need?"

"Just for me, that'll do." said Liz.

"Both of us Lassie?"

"My name is not that of a dog Dexter, and I will take the photos not a problem, you just watch the morons please."

Dexter turned to George and razed his eyebrows, "Not normally these rude lads, must be the lack of air."

The ceiling gap started to squeak as escaping air burst through the slit, "Bastard!" said Robbie, "It's a pressured room, it might have set off alarms somewhere?"

"Bad or good air?" asked Liz.

"What?"

"Does it smell bad numb nuts?"

"Err..........no.......... fresh!"

"Preserving paper and leather then, all perfectly normal, so get on with it."

"Ah!" said Robbie, "How did you know that one?"

"Homework, number one regulation with my father, piss pour planning makes for piss pour performance, stage one, research, a pressured preservation cabin,"

Robbie looked at Dexter and got a shrug for his answer, he had just about created a big enough gap for her to squeeze through.

Dexter pointed for her to get it done, he took over holding the door to stop it sliding away, she grabbed the camera and the mouth torch she was up and in into the lock up in seconds.

"Do you know, I think that she is very good at this game." said Robbie.

"Shut up!" said Dexter "And keep that bloody gap open!"

"Does she know what she wants in there Dex?" asked George.

"Not really, it might take some time to find the file we need, but if In doubt, take a pic of everything," said Dexter.

"Lots of secrets in there then boss, "Asked Robbie.

"All of Her Majesties secrets son and some even she, sorry he eh, I still can't get used to having a King in charge, anyway, that's what we want to see, the unrecorded or the unofficial, anything that shouldn't be there."

"For why?" asked Robbie.

"Shut the fuck up!" said George, "Need to firkin know bollock brain!"

"So, we the secrets are breaking in to find more secrets then, how secret can it get?" asked Robbie, he suddenly caught the glint of the gold bar as Liz passed him a double headed eagle of Russia stamped bar of pure gold, "In doubt wedge the gap with that, end on," she squeaked then disappeared.

His mouth opened and closed in silence, he couldn't concentrate, his all-time sexy dream had been fulfilled, the bedazzled goldfish stared at the shiny bar in glorious techno -colored gold on gold on pure gold in silence before what seemed like seconds, she snatched it back from him and gave him her camera to hold.

"Out, move it moron!"

"But?"

"Ok, we're out of here and fast, go!"

"But madam?"

She was now out of the gap and waiting for him to lower the ceiling, he was trying his hardest not to cry with the disappointment of not taking his golden dream home.

George refitted the door in record time, all faces but one smiled at his efficiency.

On the way out she stopped at the security man, "You could have said you didn't have a bastard dungeon you moron!"

"But Madam."

"Oh, shut up!" she walked off followed by her staff, George grunted pulling the trolley along up the steps.

"Wanker!" said George as he passed him on the steps, "Why put steps there for God's sake?"

"Not me mate!"

"Oh, shut the fuck up!"

The guard couldn't control his laughing at the mad people walking away, "London I bloody love you!" he screeched, "What a day at the office I'm having!"

He looked at the paperwork she had handed him before they went in, he couldn't understand a word, "Latin, why Latin?" he scratched his head then folded it into his pocket, "Confused? ... you will be!"

# CHAPTER 48 ... Longmore House ... Kent ...UK

Jane smiled as she was handed the two babies and held them for the photo, Tolly clicked away as they cooed the new baby girls, Cal was crying along with Ruby And Ivy, Terry the butler handed out the tissues one by one to whoever was about to start crying again, Tolly took a tissue and handed him the camera to take some pics as he sniffled with it all.

The medical staff had left them to it, and Caledonia was in her element with it all, organizing the quick celebrations within the household staff.

She cuddled up to the new mother, "So darlings, names, perhaps?"

Jane shrugged and Tolly looked tired and not really awake in the false dawn's light.

"Elizabeth and Helen?" she smiled.

Tolly nodded and so did Jane.

"Oh, come on, make an argument at least!"

Tolly shrugged again.

"You already had those names, right?"

Tolly burst out laughing at her.

"What other names could they have Mum?" said Jane.

Tolly grinned.

"Why don't you talk to me about it?"

Jane shrugged again.

"My God, this is frustrating talking to you lot! ....... Sleep?"

"Yes Mum, sleep!" said Tolly, "This is all very exhausting."

"Shut up!" said Jane and Caledonia in unison, before laughing again.

Cal picked up the ringing phone, "Yes?" as she walked out with everyone, leaving the couple and the new arrivals to sleep a little.

"Well do I get an invite to the wedding then Caledonia?" asked Rufus.

"What wedding?"

"Your bodyguards wedding, what, she's not informed you of the changes, oh dear how embarrassing?"

She could hear him giggling as she slammed the phone down on him.

She walked into the nursery kitchen and pressed recall and the transatlantic number.

"So, what the hell's happening over there?" she asked the windowsill.

Erick nearly choked on his burnt peanut buttered toast as he stared at her face.

She turned her predatory eyes onto him, "And?"

He shrugged and focused on the peanut butter jar then spooned some more out onto his black toast, "So, what's happening then?"

"Kelly's plan has worked, I wouldn't have thought it, I don't know what to say?"

"For a change!" grinned Erick.

She ignored his barb and thought about what to say to her.

She picked up her mobile and punched in recall then waited, "Come on, come on Ruth pick up!"

"Hello?"

"So, you're out then?"

"No thanks to you?"

"What, you're blaming me for your prison episode?"

"Yes, I am Caledonia, so where were you then?"

"It was a plan Ruth, nothing personal, just a plan."

"What bloody plan?"

"I informed the powers and that's why they banged you up, you were protecting the dignity of the American President, the American people in fact and just how much embarrassment can they take without doing something and fast about you and about the stinking press people."

"So, you triggered his response then?"

"So, it went well then?"

Ruth slammed the phone down on her but Cal pressed recall and shouted to her.

"Listen up you tart, you now need me again, understand?"

"For why?"

"Protection Mrs. First Lady of the United States of America, get it?"

Ruth held the phone in silence as she did some thinking.

"Hello!" said Cal, "Come on Ruth, stop mardying and listen up you stupid cow!"

"I hadn't thought about all that, dangerous then?"

"Front and center, they'll want the works for the marriage, full media coverage, interviews, the lot, your face will cover the globe, the woman who captured the President, every woman on the planet will want to know all about you, they will hound you until it all comes out, have you informed your mum and dad?"

"Shit................no!"

"What does Kelly say?"

"She hates me!"

"Oh, you stupid woman, it was the act!"

"Acting?"

"She chose you from afar, it was arranged."

"No way!"

"Yes way, ring her and get informed of what she wants in a daughter in law, do you want me to do that for you?"

"Err...............................?

"Ok I'll make the call, you call your parents and quick before your face splashes the world media, clear?"

"Err......................."

Cal closed the call and giggled at their success in the planning.

Cals mobile phone buzzed in her hand, Cal giggled as she pressed green, "Yes?"

"Don't yes me! what was the plan then, and from the start please!"

Cal was now laughing at her, "She was embarrassed for her son, come on! Mummy as first lady, do me a favor?"

"So, it was her plan then, to embarrass him?"

"Of course, he always needed a push, so she pushed."

"Using JJ as the source?"

"Err............. der!"

"What a bloody family, and they want peace from me? I'm going to tell him; you know that don't you?"

"Well do it moron, hello in there, make an enemy for life or a friend for life, the choice is yours, anyway, you can use that as leverage when you need something from her in the future."

"So, this is a political family then?"

"Oh, shut up you tart, so .... how did the proposal go, romantic?"

Ruth giggled as Cals curiosity, "Yes, our eyes met over the car park, and he picked me up like a knight in shining armor and," the phone was now dead in her hand.

"Bastard!" giggled Caledonia.

"You are getting to be like Nana woman!" said Erick.

"What a compliment my dear."

"Toast and jam?"

"What, now that you've broken the bloody toaster?"

"Err...............................?

"It's not supposed to be set on black plus black, you numb scull!"

"And the new mother?"

"Oh, meltingly good Erick."

"Fantastic, and Tolly?"

"He's gone walkabout from the office, what do you think?"

"Quit?"

"Oh, no, just not attending meeting and such, a problem?"

"Oh yes, trouble brewing perhaps?"

"Should I comment?"

"Err .... no Cal, none of our business, he obviously has a plan rolling, possibly something to do with downgrading his departments, management thinking time."

"Him or them?"

"Well, them, I think, pigeons coming home to roost."

"And what the hell is that about, you sound like Pop."

"He's teaching them a valuable long-term lesson, let me do my job or suffer the consequences."

"Who?"

Erick thumbed to the painting on the wall of King Charles.

"Oh!"

"He's so like the old man Cal, he would have come up with something like this."

# CHAPTER 49 ... Transit Van ... Central London

Liz downloaded the pictures to Theo then waited; the driver stared impassively out of the window.

"Can't we go now then?" asked Robbie, he was squeezed in the rear bench seat by Dexter and George.

"We might not have what we need!" said Liz.

"But you could have done that while you were in there?"

"And set off the automated wave alarms caused by mobile phones, how the hell did you make a living in this business?"

"He didn't!" said George, "He got caught!"

"And that's not allowed in our group sonny!" said Dexter.

"Bingo!" said Liz, "We have him! good old Smirnoff, what a smart man he is."

"Who?" asked Robbie.

George elbowed him to shut up and be quiet.

"Where too Ma'am?" asked the van driver.

She looked at her watch, "To the pub I think, do you know the Turks Head?"

"Err.........that's a Russian pub Ma'am," he looked at Dexter in the mirror for backup.

Dexter smiled in silence.

"Yes, a good idea, take us to the Russian pub, let's make this public." said Liz.

The driver's panicked eyes locked into Dexter's.

He ignored him, "So you have a name then Elizabeth, do we know him of old dear?"

"A good old fashioned London gangster Dex, so who's today's bad cop?"

"Can I be the baddy for a chance Elizabeth, I never get to be the bad boy of the group, please, let me cut his arms off!"

"No! George looks the part, and he speaks their lingo, they never respect Jocks, so you're the contracted heavy to enforce his will on the spot."

"So, you're the bimbo again then?"

She grabbed the interior mirror and turned it to look at Dexter, "You have an opinion you wish to express haggis bollocks?"

"All a bit public Liz, faces and all that?"

Liz threw him the bag from the front seat, "Try the wigs, I think red and long."

"I know that pub," said Robbie.

Liz moved the mirror to look at him, "You can give us credibility then, yes?"

"Err............ I robbed it a while back, the landlord might get uppity if I show up."

Liz started to laugh "Where do we get them from?"

"Prison Ma'am!" said George.

Dexter stared out of the window, now in silent contemplation.

"Shush!" said Liz as she changed the mirror again, "Good Dexter?"

"Yes Elizabeth, a good call I think."

"You think?"

"Yes, the cracker here can be our insurance, after all it wasn't just money you took did you moron?"

"Err ............... yeah, just the cash from his safe."

George elbowed him again to switch him on.

"No," said Dexter "You took some paperwork as well, with links to a certain bloke named Talbot and you have a phone number, yes?"

George elbowed him again, "Yes?"

"Err ......... yeah I did now you mention it, sentimental I thought so I kept it for insurance and the like."

"No blackmail, well not yet anyway, so are we all clear then?" said Liz.

Robbie scratched his head and searched the faces for answers, "So what is it we're after here then?"

"Well, we have the name....and now we would like .... the?" Said Liz.

He nodded to her in the mirror, "The...................rat hole?"

"Yes, his location, right?"

He was squeezed even more as he nodded his understanding.

"Bollock brain!" said George, he held his hand out for the paper with the man's name on it from Elizabeth.

"Subtle George, nice and subtle, you can be nasty if you like but remember the company, eh?"

"Why not ring Fauntleroy?"

"He's the rat we send in George, but we need to confirm, yes?"

"We need to confirm the location before we snatch him, yes?"

"You see, planned already." said Dexter.

Robbie looked around in confusion, "So, I just mention that bloke Talbot and he'll do as we ask am I right here?"

George elbowed him again, "Just once, clear?"

"You're our front man then George, ask just the once for information, let him point to a client if he wants, then we know who to snatch." said Liz.

"Snatch?" asked Robbie.

"Just followed the scene and act the helpful informer who's scared of being choked to death by our gorilla here."

George elbowed him again, "And shut the fuck up most of the time, clear?"

"So just this blokes name sparks fear in his head, am a right?"

Dexter elbowed him, "Just once, get it?" he showed Robbie the name.

"I know that name, he's dead, he died years ago."

Liz altered the mirror again, "And?"

"Err.........a car crash in Spain, buried up in High gate, green marble, the works."

Dexter grabbed hold of his knee and squeezed, "More info you Sassenach!"

"You don't want the Turk, you need the Blind Beggar up east, he's from down there."

Liz smiled at him "But the previous landlord of the Blind Beggar is?"

"Ah, I see what you mean, Fred the ted will know the inside story, I get ya now."

"So," said George, "This scum bag owes me big lumps, interest from a long-term loan and I want the contact, yes?"

Dexter thought as he stared out into London flashing by, Liz waited until he said something.

Dexter leaned forward "You're going to have to show willing George, after all he's seen you before hasn't, he? He knows how violent you can be, perhaps just the threat, let's see how scared the name makes him, Liz will watch his eyes, if he's lying then break the place up, we'll back you up if anyone starts to have an opinion on the subject."

George grinned at Dexter, "You've always been in the wrong job haven't you Jock?"

"Yes!" said Liz, "He's a thug by nature and a gentleman by habit, he can turn the tap whenever needed, make a point to this man please, but let's try to be nice, eh?"

"He knew the old man Liz, what about calling on Caledonia for a drink in town?"

"There will be Russians in there as well Dexter, then what?"

"This is a local dispute none of their business, ok?"

"Ok then Dex, that's the plan, everyone clear?"

Robbie tried to put his hand up, but George squeezed his knee to shut him up.

"Yeah, but?" said Robbie.

"What?" asked Liz.

"Well, if he's seen George working then he knows who he works for, the plan is flaked from the start."

Dexter nodded, "Actually a very good point I think."

"Then I'll just tell him whose daughter I am!"

"That might do it Lill."

She growled at him through the mirror.

"Why, whose daughter is she then?" asked Robbie.

George twisted flesh on his leg and whispered in his ear, "Shut....... the fuck....... Up!"

She pulled out the bright blue wig and put it on, then dared anyone to make a comment, "Orange is your color haggis bollocks."

He put the wig on and grinned at them, "Looks ridiculous Lill."

"Wouldn't just a flat cap do?" Robbie pulled out a woolly hat and handed it to George.

"I'm playing me, you moron."

"Oh yeah, "he passed it to Dexter.

He dumped the wig and put on the woolly hat, "Better?"

Robbie handed him some Harry Potter round rimmed glasses out of the bag.

"Yes, much better, well?"

Liz looked at him in the mirror, "I'm the only clown then?"

"Stay in the van Liz, we can handle this can't we gentlemen?"

"Ring me if he's giving you the run around?"

The three of them nodded to her.

The van pulled up to the curb and the trio stepped out, "Who's buying?" asked Robbie.

Dexter shrugged; George pulled his empty pockets out so they could see he had nothing.

"It'll have to be a freebee then." said Robbie.

Dexter tapped on the van door glass for the driver to wind it down, "Lends a tenner son, no one has any dosh on em."

The driver passed him his wallet with a grunt, Dexter took two tenner's and smiled, "Don't worry, so George owes you twenty, ok?"

Liz leaned over and tried to slap him, but he had gone with them and into the pub.

"Is he off the booze now then Liz?" asked the driver.

"Oh, bollocks, he'd bloody better not be on the booze."

"One has to trust Ma'am, sometimes."

"Very true, thanks Robert, I get a bit over the top sometimes, yes, be cool, eh?"

"It makes sense Ma'am."

Her phone buzzed in her pocket, she took it out and pressed green, "Yes?

"I think he really is dead Liz; I find no trace of him in any of the normal haunts in southern Spain, nothing."

"So why am I trying to locate this man then?"

"Perhaps it's his legacy we're needing to look at, family or friends carrying on his work."

"And you can find them then Theo?"

"Yes, we just need time to study patterns of movement over there."

"What the hell does that mean?"

"I need time Elizabeth, there's a lot to grind through."

"Ok then you've got two days then we have to move because he wants to hurt us."

"I'm on it, Liz." he closed the call on her.

She sat and thought about the problem, the driver was silent as he looked at his watch.

"What?" asked Liz.

"A bit quiet in there, Ma'am, I was expecting noise at the very least."

She turned to him, "No, Dexter's probably talking very nicely to him."

"Unless Ma'am?"

Her face reddened in anger, she had given them enough time to do the job, so she stepped out of the van and walked into the pub.

Robbie was on the floor sleeping and Dexter was leaning on the bar laughing with the landlord, George was falling asleep sitting on a high stool.

"What the hell's going on here then?" she shouted.

"Stand by your beds" slurred Dexter.

She locked eyes with the landlord, "You! What's happening here?"

"Up's Fred, now you're in trouble mate, the boss has arrived, snay snothing is smy adverse."

Fred stared at her, "Err...........I was just being social with old friends Elizabeth, what's wrong with that, look!"

He showed her the cherry O'D'vee, "Your father sent me a Christmas present years ago, I thought a little calibration was called for, I've just opened it, powerful stuff I think, anyway the lads like it, just a couple of glasses, French I think."

"How do you know me?"

"Dad's pub Elizabeth he talked about how proud he was of you, his apple he called you, the star of the show."

"That's homemade O'D'vee," said Liz, "They call it the water of life or central heating for the winter over there, 90% proof you idiot, you've just poisoned your clients!"

"Not good then, it saves a fight though, eh?"

"That's the control technique then, don't fight them give them free drinks and have them carried out?"

He gave her his best gormless grin., "Saves my mirrors Elizabeth!"

She growled at him then showed him the piece of paper with the name on it, he blinked and stared at it.

"Yes, I know him but he's brown bread, so what?"

Liz leaned over the bar and grabbed his collar then pulled him over to her, she took hold of his ear and twisted it till he squeaked in pain.

"Now listen up moron, I want associates to the said person," with her other hand she flipped the paper over, "His friends on that paper............please."

She let go of him and smiled, others in the pub turned and stared at her.

She pointed at them and shouted, "You lot, shut the fuck up!"

She turned back to Fred, "White wine and the names in that order, do you understand?"

"Err............ yes Ma'am, clear all round, you don't want to try this then?" her face said no without moving her lips, so he placed the glass on the bar and pulled a bottle from behind him and poured her wine."

"A bit too aggressive do you think Fred?"

"Just a little Elizabeth, I thought you were dead by the way?"

"Exaggeration Fred, working for the company, you know how it goes."

"And these three?"

"Morons can't you tell?" she nodded to the blank paper then took a sip of the wine.

He pulled a pen out of his pocket and started to write names he could remember.

"They might also be dead Elizabeth, this is just history, nothing more, some of them will be flogging motors up north or something."

"Just what you remember please, pour the old brain onto the page please Fred."

He scribbled away in silence; people came to the bar for refills, but he ignored them.

"He won't be long folks, sorry, I'm a bit tense at the moment," she thumbed to George and Dexter who was now trying to remember a song he once enjoyed.

"Oh, little boy Billy I'm gonna kill and eat ya, oh little boy Billy I'm going to kill and eat ya, so undo the top button of your little shimmy, undo the top button of your little chemise!"

People around started laughing at him and the hairy one who was now asleep, his head was on slops mat, and he squelched as he snored.

"That's it I'm afraid, just a list of friends we were with back in the old Blind Beggar, if I think of anymore, I'll give it to a black cabbie, ok with that?"

Liz smiled at his understanding of the system the old man had created, "His old buddies?"

"They still remember his special ways." he gave her the wink, "Elvis lives?"

"Sorry Fred, he does not, he walked into the sea, just like that, his choice."

"I do miss the old bugger, good with people who understood his short fuse, bad with those who didn't, the Russians loved him you know, they thought he was an old Soviet hiding in London, he spoke their lingo you know, faultless apparently."

She glared at him as her eyes watered.

"Bad Elizabeth, but why?"

"Oh, shut up, why do you think?"

"He was really dying then?"

She gave him the predatory stare that shut him up, he handed the paper back to her and walked over to his other clients.

She read the bottom line on the paper; *do I tell the cabbies that you're in town?*

"Yes Fred, pass on the good news."

She turned and walked out.

"What about them?" shouted Fred.

"Your problem moron, you deal with it!"

"I'll put em in a cab Elizabeth, yes?"

She ignored him and walked out.

Dexter had remembered the next line but not the tune, so he took a nap at the bar.

The landlord walked over to clients wanting service and taking orders, one of them pointed to the drunks at the bar.

"Tired mate, the night shift crew, best let sleeping dogs lie down, right?"

# CHAPTER 50 ... The White House ...South Lawn Pavilion ... Washington ... USA

She picked up the ringing phone and listened to the English voice.

"Congratulations Kelly free at last, pimple tits can fill your social agenda, you can go back to the sunshine out west."

"That was quick, how did you find out so fast, I've only just been informed."

"Son or tart?"

"JJ's girlfriend has big ears, I'm waiting for my son to open his trap and tell his mother what's going on, I'll get back to you!" she cut her off and walked over the lawn to the lounge area to check out where he was, the waiter pointed to the media room and smiled.

She smiled in thanks then walked in.

He was surrounded by election staff as the results were slowly being declared by various states in Canada and Mexico.

He spotted her coming in, "Mom, come in and sit down, we're winning, Peru, Guatemala, and Brazil like the idea and are willing to take on the democratic ideas to their polling stations, they want in!"

She smiled and sat down next to him, "It'll mean an election for a new President you know, you're back into election mode, you do understand that?"

"Yeah, yeah, we can do that, it's about numbered representations, these are States in the Mexican union who are willing to join us as independents, great eh?"

"Earth moving son, let's hope it's not a volcano of trouble coming our way."

He grinned at her from ear to ear, "It's happening Ma, it's finally happening."

She was happy for him but full of fear for him at the same moment.

"Veracruz has voted yes Mr President, they want to join the Union as a new State of the America's."

"Numbers Mike?"

"Err............... 20 million approx."

"Enough for Statehood?"

"Just sir."

"Ok we contact and sanction new ideas and rules."

"And add to the list sir?"

"Yes, for the media meeting at noon."

"Jimmy," said Kelly, "Can we afford all this, as a Nation I mean?"

"Money is for countries mom, this is a continental configuration, it's not about money, it's about will and determination to find peace, prosperity and influence for the good of the multitudes of mankind."

She smiled at him, she was so proud of his ideas and plans, she prayed they worked because she knew what would happen if they didn't."

The door slammed behind them, and Ruth walked in "A new capital is needed then?"

Jimmy turned to her, "You think?"

"A new system and new start then a new multilingual, multi state capital of the America's."

"Mexico?" asked Jimmy.

"Why not, yeah, Mexico, their main language would be Spanish as well, thought of that one?"

"Trying to change hearts and minds Ruthie?"

"Na just throwing spanners about, you've already had discussions I would have thought."

"So...........French for Parts of Canada, English for central US and Spanish for south and the southern continent?"

"Portuguese for Brazil remember, and tribes will want an input on those things Jim?"

Kelly glared at her.

"Hello Mummy!"

Kelly couldn't keep it up anymore, "At last then?"

"Yeah, he gave in in the end, easy peasy."

She turned to her son, "And she will be the new?"

"First lady, yes mom, all of the above," he continued to stare at the screens.

"So, any against by now Mike?"

"Central Mexico boss, lost on 15% of the National vote."

"That's not a great deal Mike, a recount perhaps?"

"Pushy boss, they won't like that one."

"Hey this is all new we have to be certain, or it won't work, pass that on please."

"So," said Kelly as she looked into Ruth's eyes, "Ready for all this?"

"No not really."

"Then why?"

"I love him, he's beautiful, my dream."

"Could turn into the nightmare?"

"Never, he's a thinking man, he plans, he's an intellectual, he's smart."

"Wouldn't you just prefer a dumb ass?"

"And kill him after two weeks of marriage mummy?"

"And if he plays away?"

"Two in the head!"

"My God you're a dangerous woman."

"But he's safe on my watch mummy, I'll take on anyone who want him dead, the first shots will be mine, understood?"

Kelly started laughing, "That crazy bitch Caledonia trained you then?"

"All the way mum."

Kelly smiled at her, "So I can get back to my main focus then?"

"Yes, where is your Husband by the way?"

"Don't start on me woman, you just focus on the first Lady job, even if you're not!"

"Is this going to be the normal convo then?"

Kelly started laughing, then leaned over and gave her a hug, "Na, just the first salvos dear, I have to get the range right on the first barrage."

"You're as mad as Cal?"

"No one is as mad as that woman, now come on do you know of any others like her?"

Ruth giggled, "Well no, I don't, but they must be out there somewhere."

"Yes, well, let them stay out there in the wilderness out of our way please, she is enough."

"Chihuahua sir, voted yes to the change in Statehood, they even voted for the English language."

"No, one step too far Mike, they must keep their native language, we will learn the new language and not them."

Mike smiled at him, "Smart boss, they'll like that one."

"Waiting for the Yucatan results Mr President, coming up soon they're on mid-western time."

Jimmy turned to the ladies, "Exciting, eh?"

"Earth moving, sonny boy and when were you going to inform me of changes?"

"What..........er.........I don't get it Mom?"

Kelly thumbed Ruth.

"Oh, Ruth, well you planned it all, so you tell me."

Ruth started giggling at her red face, "As you know Mum, he's smart, we talked and worked out the thinking pattern, we agreed in the end, fate, karma, whatever?"

Kelly couldn't help laughing "Easy............ bloody peasy!" Her phone buzzed in her pocket, she took it out, Caledonia's face as the caller made her laugh even more, she cut her off as she laughed.

# CHAPTER 51 ... Las Vegas ... Nevada ... USA

Alice watched the rehearsals with interest, she cuddled up to Adrian as he pointed and shouted at the production staff.

Addy boiled up, "Faster please love, we're not in a morgue babe, and these aren't the last bastard rights darling?"

She leaned over and whispered in his ear, "These people love and trust you Addy, love them back darling, don't make enemies when you don't need too, understand?"

He kissed her cheek, "Thanks for being here Alice darling, you're so smart when I need advice, I'll try darling, honest I will."

He pointed to the stagehands who were moving a piano, "You pair get off the bastard stage, we're in the middle of this you know?"

She punched his leg.

He looked at the men's faces, "Sorry darlings I'm a bit stressed, give me some love please."

They smiled at him and walked off stage and a group of little girls came on and looked at him.

"That's better Addy," whispered Alice.

He sat up and giggled out loud, "Oh at last, just watch these darling, the Chili Peppers, they are bastard fabulous.

The little girls huddled together on stage totally lost.

"What's up darlings?" he waited for the translator to come on stage.

"What's wrong?"

"Their parents and the band have been stopped at the border, they're alone, it's scary for them that's all." said the woman translator.

Alice was up and walking towards them in seconds, she ran up on stage and cuddled them all as a group, Addy was there with them and smiled.

"Never bastard mind, my darlings, I'll sort this bastard out right now," he punched in the London number and waited for the pick-up, "Hey, Tolly blue blood, they are destroying my show by not allowing people over the boarder who are in the show, I have girls in tears over here, so what can you do about it?"

"Ah, Adrian, nice to hear your voice, so what do you want me to do?"

"Well open the bastard boarder and let my people in."

"What like Moses who asked the Egyptians to let his people go?"

"Yes, exactly that, open the bastard red sea and let my people in!"

"Ok Addy leave it with me, is Granny Alice with you by the way?"

"Yeah, and she's a God send."

"Oh good, people will be with you quite soon charged with protecting her, give them a place in your group please Uncle Addy, back cover and all that, clear?"

"Not really Tolly, what for?"

"We feel that she is under threat of assassination so I'm sending a protection crew, ok with that."

"Bastard," said Addy.

"They'll be helpful Uncle Addy, you'll like um, I'm sure."

"Uncle?"

"Yes, Uncle Mack will lead them, don't take much notice of him, he's with the BBC and they're making a documentary of the glitz city, be helpful please Uncle."

"Bastard!" said Adrian, to the silent phone, "Uncle?"

"You know what that means, don't you Adrian?" whispered Alice.

"What?"

"Well, in saying that he's made you a member of his family, so welcome to our family Addy."

He stared at her to clarify what she was in Tolly's family, "Granny Alice, so, you're his grandmother?"

"His great grandmother, Elizabeth is his grandmother, understood?"

"Bastard, so that means I'm family, right Alice?"

"Yes, great Uncle Adrian!"

He danced around with the little girls as he giggled with them.

# CHAPTER 52 ... McCarran International Airport ... Las Vegas ... Nevada ... USA

Jonesy pointed to the line of slot machines in the exit foyer, "Do ya feel lucky punk?"

Gurung ignored him and walked off to find the pre booked car hire slots.

Mack ran the case trolley into Jonesy before he tried to put English money in the one-armed bandit.

The greatest hits in country and western, were humming over the sound system, Kenny Rogers was dealing with the coward of the county.

"Time enough for counting when the deal is done, come on whose song is that? and the second and connected question is this, what is the chain of restaurants called in Southeast Asia?" asked Mack.

Jonesy stretched and yawned, "Do I really need to know?"

Mack pointed to the sound echoing around the building, "A gambling song, they all are, clever, eh?"

Jonesy scratched his belly as he stared at him, "So what?"

"Kenny Rogers, Coward of the County."

Jonesy walked along side of him, and Mack pushed the trolley, "But that's a fighting song, I remember that one."

"Well, that's what it was called."

Gurung rattled the keys to their car "The Gambler!"

"Who is?" asked Jonesy.

"The song, the gambler by Kenny Rogers, and they do a great sausage and mash with thick gravy."

"Who does?" asked Mack.

"Kenny Rogers!"

"I wondered what happened to him then?" said Mack.

"They're restaurants and all over the place, there's one in central Kuala Lumpur, posh place, nice and clean.

"Who is?"

"Kenny Rogers!"

"I'm losing the will to live," said Jonesy.

"Why sausage and mash though, strange don't you think?" said Mack.

"Liver of a cat, kidney of a horse, mixing up the sausages with this and that, come on who's song is that?" asked Mack.

"Sweeny Tod the butcher!" said Jonesy.

"I thought he was a barber?" Gurung mumbled.

"Muslim country as well, strange don't you think?" said Mack.

"What is?" asked Jonesy.

"Sausages!"

"Why?"

"Well, they put cat's livers in them then?" asked Gurung.

"Who?" asked Jonesy.

"Kenny Rogers!" said Gurung.

"Someone shoot me please!" said Mack, "Put me out of your misery!"

A gaggle of British Airways flight crew girls swished by pulling their little overnight wheelie bags.

Jonesy watched them closely, "I fancy a sausage, my ex-wife could cook sausages really well, before she stabbed me in the back!"

"Oh, for God's sake someone pass me a gun!" shouted Mack.

His voice echoed along the building as the music stopped and Kenny Rogers was warming up his Coward of the county and the gambler and his best hits of the eighties over the sound system.

Airport police watched the strange mix of British people trying to escape the Law in the UK and obviously wanting trouble.

A cop stopped Gurung at the rotating doors, "Yes I've got them sir, stopped at the rotunda doors, yes sir, we'll wait!"

He placed his hand on Gurungs chest, "Wait please sir, the inspector would like to talk to you and your friends, photo checks have uncovered something alarming."

The subtle head movement of Mack said no, leave it, do nothing.

"Obviously a drug dealer?" said Jonesy, "It's all in the eyes, too close, look!"

The cop looked closely at Gurung; Jonesy started laughing.

"America does not have your sense of humor Jonesy, leave it out mate." said Mack.

"Leave what out?" asked the cop.

"Oooh, bad question Mate," said Jonesy "Obviously a homophobic disinformation directive from a dysfunctional administration of epic proportions culminating in a clash of cultures involving an understanding of inter stella settlements."

"I could kill a pint of stella!" said Mack.

"What the hell are you guys talking about, are you English speakers or what?"

"What?" said Jonesy, "Lost on the lonely world of singletons, better the widower than the ex-lover, divorced from life from love, even from humanity."

"And he hasn't been drinking yet!" said Gurung, "Good though, sex hasn't been mentioned once, so you're improving mate, not even mentioned your Henry Wankler."

The cop stared with his bottom lip open and quivering as he tried to make sense of these out-of-town aliens.

Glen appeared at the back of them and laughed, "Yes this is them Hank, sorry mate I hope they haven't spoilt your day boyo."

"No worries, Detective, I'm cool."

"No worries?" asked Jonesy.

"He thinks you're Australians lads, "Said Glen, "Thanks Hank,
I'll take it from here."

The cop walked off shaking his head.

"Half an hour and confusion reigns in America, who could
cause that says I?"

"Where's the other Welsh git?" asked Mack.

Glen thumbed to the other side of the doors, "We're your lift!"
Eden gave them his best grin from behind the glass doors.

Gurung rattled his keys again.

"You don't think they'll really let you boyos drive in America,
do you? Let's just recap your combined insurance claims for the
past year, it must run into millions."

"I was framed!" said Gurung.

"No, you became the frame, that was the sign you ran into in
Berlin a hundred grand!"

"Wrong side of the road."

"Yes, you were, the sign was just minding its own, so get into
the bastard car."

"What are you then?" asked Jonesy.

"The accountant for ongoing ops," smiled Glen.

"What no Roller pickup for a top gambler?" said Mack.

"Marvelous is in town Mack, enough said?" Glen gave him the
stare.

"Shit!" said Jonesy.

"So, what are we doing boss?" asked Gurung.

"Hey, I'm with the BBC, you lot sort yourselves out," said
Mack.

Glen shook his head at him.

"That's a job on!" said Gurung.

"Oh, for fuck's sake!" shouted Mack, "I thought this was a
BBC freebee!"

The cops stared at the Brits and hoped they would leave the building soon.

"Best get the specs sorted boss before the accountant's department finds out about the small loans from the op's kitty. "said Jonesy.

"Oh, shut up!" said Mack.

"What loan?" asked Glen.

"What kitty, so we've had a kitty all along?" asked Gurung.

"Ah............the good old TV license payers back in the UK, thank you BBC," said Glen.

"And you can shut up as well, you, Welsh wanker!" said Mack.

Eden escorted them to the minibus.

"Oh, for fuck's sake!" shouted Mack, "I'm an executive of the corporation!"

The window buzzed down, and Marvin shouted over to them from the driver's seat, "Get in bus and shut the fuck up!"

Driving into Las Vegas Marvin filled them in regarding the job in hand.

"Dexter recons that they will execute Alice as a sign of their contempt of us, our job is to prevent and react to any attempt, follow the shooter and find the source, no killings just information needed."

"Kidnapping?" asked Jonesy.

"If needed and you get busted during the tail, as always, a low profile, do you hear me in there, Captain Jones?"

"Sir yes Sir!" said Jonesy.

"You are gamblers mooching about having fun, but not too much fun, hear me, Captain Jones?"

"Sir!"

"Mack is with the BBC as normal, you lot are helpful assistants and gamblers on the loose, earpieces 24/7, we have to keep her alive, watch for familiars, all clear?"

"Kit?" said Gurung.

"Under seats, including private protection licenses from the State Department, no wild songs and dances please, cool and professional, yes Captain Jones?"

"Sir!" said Jonesy.

"Women Captain Jones?"

"Given them up sir, too expensive!"

Marvin turned to Mack sitting in the front seat next to him.

"Divorced, sour and bitter, just get him into a punch up and he'll be fine."

"Really?"

"Well not here and not now, we are civilized, yes?"

"Yes boss!" said Jonesy.

"And you Mack, what's the program with the BBC?"

"It's called numbers, it's about calculations and our obsession with luck, we'll be filming winners and losers in that order together with the basics of Las Vegas life."

"And the numbties?"

"Finders, for the winners and the…………"

"Losers?" nodded Marvin.

"What are you doing Marv?"

"Planning committee and working with the State Department."

"Lenny then?"

"Yep, the big Z is still in control, and he's in contact with his old friend and ours the Scottish cultural attaché back in Menton."

"But will he stay in Menton?"

"Lenny wants him away from the zone."

"And your nephew back in London?"

"Aware of the threat to his Great Grandmother, so don't balls it up, clear?"

"Expenses?"

"Yes, Mack as normal."

"So, chasing bandits again?"

"Links as normal Mack, we just pass it on, no direct action please after all, you lot are foreigners, get it?"

Marvin leaned in and whispered so the lads at the back couldn't hear, "Do not lose money to the casinos, do not be an idiot, in the end they always win, clear?"

"A bollockings so soon boss, must be a record somewhere, right?" grinned Mack.

"I'll bail you out if needed, but do not take the piss!"

"But you must be up there Marv, number one on their hit list?"

"A brown man can hide so easy in America, no one notices me, easy peasy."

"You worry me Marv, dead yet alive, here and there, where's your protection."

Marvin nodded to the car in front and nodded to the car following them, "Initial contact group, they stop and fight I run and hide, then return to finish the baddies off with heavy equipment."

"Really Marv?"

"It's how it is, they try, and I react."

"Dexter might be wrong Marv; you might be the main one after all?"

"Then I'll have to die then."

Mack smiled at him, "I'm not worthy Marv, if it has to happen you know my code, yes?"

"Yes Mack, still that west end gentleman's club? Ok let's hope for luck eh."

"Yeah, let's hope Marv, so where are we staying?"

Marvin thumbed to Glen, "Stay in his hotel, low profile remember?"

"That Welsh git owns a hotel in Vegas?"

"Two on the strip and one in the suburbs Macclesfield." said Glen.

"And Eden owns the Grandiose Casino on the main drag." said Marvin.

All faces stared at Eden's grin.

"How the hell?" asked Jonesy

"I built up all the tips Captain, what can I say?"

"Shit!" said Gurung, "So that's the bonus here then boss?"

Marvin grinned at them in the mirror at the back seats, "For good and silent work there will be well earned bonuses, behave and you go up, balls ups and you go down, any simpler explanation needed here gents?"

"Oh, and Glen is the accountant, we found his natural talent at last."

"A multi-national high altitude mountain hotel in the Annapurna's boss?" Gurung grinned at him.

"You have it my little brown friend, providing," Marvin thumbed to Jonesy, "I'll invest in Nepal you'll probably need to call it the Highland Brigade Hotel."

"Yes, boss understood, in Dexter's honor, yes?"

"He'll like that I'm sure," grinned Marvin in the mirror.

"Shit!" said Jonesy, "And you can afford that?" Marvin winked at him.

"And what will the ex-wife say?" laughed Jonesy.

"Fuck off you wanker, normally!" said Gurung.

"Got a way with words has the old woman."

"Yeah, give me your credit card normally!" laughed Gurung.

"Well, all things change, the only certainty in life, now who said that then?"

"Do not mention the name please Gents, some of us are related," said Marvin.

Mack gave them the shut-up face in the back seats, his eyes flicked to Marvin and their silence.

"Yeah, sorry boys, just missing the lessons, that all."

Marvin gave him a grin, "Please stay out of trouble Jonesy, this is a peaceful town, clear?"

Jonesy gave him his best optimistic grin that set everyone off laughing.

# CHAPTER 53 ... Caledonian Hotel ... Rome ... Italy

"So Essential America news, who are these new people, David?" said Augusta down the phone.

"It's a news corporation set up in America, a big money input apparently, from nowhere to the mainstream in just one month."

"Sales?"

"Initially poor but picking up after expensive advertising throughout the American media, newspapers and media glossy mags, famous faces doing the charity roll outs."

"So, do we have a war on David?"

"It's a whispering gallery Gussy, the same as your Great Grandmother used to do, it must be part of the plan to shout louder against the Presidential plan."

"Expensive David!"

"Very, still these people have no limits I think."

"What, too much to lose?"

"Indeed, it must conflict with their current administration, they have a very great deal to lose if it all works out for the President."

"So, it is a war then?"

"Must be Gussy, tin hats time, what do you want me to do for now?"

"Find out more for a start, then we infiltrate and disrupt as usual."

"My God girl, you are of the stamp, aren't you?"

"Not really David, I think of what Nana would do then real it back a hundred yards then plan, still too aggressive mostly, but I'm learning, so keep me informed please."

"There is another fact we should look at Gussy."

"And?"

"Well with you gone their hand would be that much stronger, it must be part of some ones plan I would think, too advanced a thought?"

"No, David, all perfectly thinkable so let me think about that one, Granddad was saying as much the other day, perhaps I should listen to him for a change?"

"You must be a thorn in their feet Augusta, they can't walk far without getting stuck in your media circles."

"American Television then David?"

"It might cost a great deal to move forward but we have to consider cost verses progress in the end."

"A good point David, I'll talk to Granddad and get back to you."

She closed the call and held the phone thinking about what to do, Simon sat on the office chair at the other side of her office, "Did you hear that Si?"

"Yes Gussy, we need experts to help us I think."

"Who?"

"Well, Your Grandparents will be watched as they move about, yes?"

"Err.........well yeah, so?"

"So, I call in favors from friends in France."

"Menton?"

"No Paris, old pals in La Legion."

"But that's risky, can you trust them Si?"

"I'll check with Uncle Marvin first of course."

"And you have Uncle Marvin's number?"

"Yeah, so?"

"And you didn't tell me?"

"Need to know Gussy!"

She stood up in a sudden rage and threw the desk blotter at him, then her teacup, "I'm the need-to-know beetroot head, I'm the boss around here!" she shouted.

"Him, not me Gussy, he said keep it quiet, no one needs to know."

"I do you idiot, so who else is on your call back line?"

He stood and passed her his phone, she snatched it and flipped pages as she searched.

"Generals, Colonels, the Prime Minister?"

"Granny has all the connections Gussy, she insists I make the most of her, she was a great friend to your Great Grandmother in the Ambassadorial service remember?"

Augusta walked over to him and gave him a hug, "Sorry Si, I forget sometimes that you're also connected, thanks darling, please excuse my tantrum."

"Forgiven Gussy, so what next?"

She stared at him as she thought about it all, "Yes, make some calls, lets gather the wagons around us, we need protection after all I think, I'll call Granddad and explain why we don't want his help."

"I wouldn't Gussy."

"Why?"

"Ego, he has a great big ego remember?"

"Grandmother then?"

Simon smiled, "More subtle I think."

She gave him the comforting wink then passed him the phone.

# CHAPTER 54 ... White House ... South Lawn ... Washington

Kelly looked her up and down, Ruth stared back at her without saying anything.

"Jimmy!" She screamed out.

The President turned to his mother "What's up mom?"

"She cannot be seen in public like this, she's too butch for a start, they'll think I'm in a lesbian relationship, do something!"

"How dare you!" shouted Ruth.

Jimmy looked her up and down slowly as she raged, "Ever worn a nice dress, Ruthie?"

"Leggings and a raggedy assed woolly top don't cut it tart!" shouted Kelly.

"Easy mom, she's new to all this, cut her some slack please, so who do we know who can make her look a million dollars?"

"She needs to look good in French fashion or they'll eat her alive, come on Jimmy, do something!"

He stared at Ruth who was getting madder and madder.

"Ever been to Las Vegas Ruth," he smiled as he asked.

"Err............no!"

"Good, two birds with one stone, I like it when a plan sticks out, I know the star of the circus so let's be gone eh?"

"What the hell?" screeched Ruth

Jimmy was on the phone calling for his helicopter, "Yes Johnny, now please!"

"What the hell are you doing son?" asked Kelly.

"So, what would be easier?" asked Jimmy, "Do we go to her or pick her up and bring her here?"

"Who?"

"Yes, mom you're right, I'll get her collected along with her staff, yes, thanks for that!"

"I didn't say anything, who are you talking about?"

"Alice Trueblood Talbot, the owner and managing director of that Paris French fashion house Toulouse, she's in Vegas and she needs protection I'm told."

"By whom?" asked Ruth.

He was looking at her again, "Now that's a better idea Ruth, you go get her for me, can you?"

"Why Alice Talbot, are you mad, why would she come here?"

"Well, you're asking a personal favor and only the one time, make that very clear, oh and a personal favor to me and her Great Grandson."

"Tolly?"

"Yeah, she's his Great Grandmother, so tell her your problem and let her do her thing."

"What Goddam problem?"

"Well, you ain't got the va, va, vroom, and you need some, get it?"

"No, I don't!"

"The wedding the new first Lady, she'll understand and get the deal right off, don't mention the death threat from an assassin though."

"What death threat?"

"It's a predicted movement from someone who wants to hurt us badly, best take a weapon she might already be targeted, yes do it Ruth, switch on please."

"Hold up!" screamed Kelly.

"So, you're sending your new wife into a potential sniper situation?"

"Another day in the office mom!" he shouted over the noise of the helicopter landing on the lawn."

"But that's dangerous son?"

"Welcome to our world mother, we live a dangerous life," he looked at Ruth, "Can you do that for us?"

"Another day in your world, yes?"

"Hey and be careful!" He gave her a kiss then pointed her to the helicopter.

"But I don't have anything to wear!" she screeched over the engine and rotor noise.

"Buy it while you're there, anything you like just make it and you look good."

"So, I don't look good to you Jimmy?"

"I love your look babe, but this is work so get it done, go!"

"Couldn't I just do a shop in town?"

He shook his head and pointed to the helicopter.

Kelly stared at her as she walked away and calmly climbed up the helicopter steps and was clipped in by the load master, he saluted the President then close the door, the aircraft took off at speed.

He was back on the phone, "Listen up, a priority flight to Las Vegas, as fast as you can, deliver her to sight then bring back the people she requires, clear."

"Is she a special agent Mr President?"

"Very special, I need her here as soon as you can with the people she needs, a matter of National security, so go and get it done!"

"Yes Sir!"

The helicopter disappeared over the horizon as he stared at it.

"Are you crazy putting her in a hot zone like that?" shouted his mother.

"Mom, I live in hot zone, if she wants this then she has to earn the jacket and wear it with pride as I do."

"But she's a woman?"

"Yes, thankfully, the woman of my future, this is just the start, she has to work for a living, the same as me and you mommy, we've always been in the slot, remember?"

"But?"

"But what? She's trained for all this, ring Aunty Cal and check her out for reality mother, she is a war hero, they sold her down the river for peace from the press, they locked her up for being good at her job, crazy, eh?"

Kelly punched the UK number into her phone and waited for the pickup, "Caledonia, where the hell are you?"

"I'm back in the US, so what?"

"Yeah, but where?"

"Las Vegas if you must know Erick wanted me here with him for some reason."

"Did you know that it's predicted that Alice will be targeted and killed."

"What, why?"

"How the hell should I know, check it out with your son woman, Jimmy has just sent Ruth to get fixed up with a French wardrobe and to snatch Alice and bring her back here to Washington.

"Yes, I can understand that one she has always been a bit beige and green, she's never had the woman's touch or advice from above, shame really, still she has you now, so good all round, eh?"

"Don't start on me Caledonia, I'm just giving sound advice for her future that's all, you can't roll up to a press release dressed in leggings and a sweatshirt, she has to get real!"

"Agreed woman, no argument from me, how did she take it all?"

"Badly I think."

"Na, she can take it."

"Cal, she worries me, she carries a gun at all times what if she shoots the wrong person?"

"Cover it up dear, what do you want me to say, trust her woman."

"But her UK record?"

"Has been burnt at source, she has an unblemished record of service in the Royal Marines, she retired on health grounds then volunteered for special duties with the department."

"On record?"

"Yep!"

"So, what do I say to the press?"

"The truth, she's your ideal woman for your son, you love her, and you look forward to an early Grandchild, bing, bang, bosh, done!"

Kelly started laughing at her.

"Life is so simple for you ain't it, Caledonia?"

"Happy families take time and effort woman, what do you want me to say?"

"What is your son doing Cal, that would help?"

"I'll ask, but don't expect a clear answer from him, he's so much like my Granddad, it's unreal."

She turned to see Jimmy on his phone again, "Yes Lenny, she's on route, locate Mrs. Talbot and get our people to assist her transfer to here, for me, a personal favor, I have a wedding to plan, and I need the bride to wow the press, understood?"

"Yes Mr President, but she is that crazy brit who caused the mass brawl up in Canada, but I have evidence that she works for British MI6 as an assassin."

"Yeah, I know, so you have an opinion or a warning maybe?"

"Err......no sir, my Laura is a crazy Texan woman and they're all the same sir."

"Give me what you've got on her please Lenny and remember who her British friends are, all perfectly normal in their world man."

"She's about as dangerous as they get Mr President, can you imagine if she loses her cool in front of the press?"

"She won't, and I'll see who ever goes for her in the courts, so a calm warning all round from me please."

"I'll state the facts sir to whoever askes, yes?"

"Yes Lenny, love is all there is, clear?"

"Clear sir!"

"Thanks, Mr Secretary, it's good to have your support sir."

"My honor Mr President."

# CHAPTER 55 ... Penthouse Suit ... The Carlton Hotel ... London

Theo looked at the numbers that Charley had just sent him, he stood up and closed the computer lid then walked to Charley's office, he knocked twice then walked in.

"So, will it work Charley?"

Charley grinned at him and rubbed his hands together in excitement, "Look I've done some robust testing on the system, and it all fills out, the security the reaction times, the lot."

He turned his laptop for Theo to take a look.

Theo stared at the screen, "How long will it take to launch it?"

Charley smiled at him, "That's not the real question here Theo, people's reactions are the thing, this will change the world."

Theo stared at him, "One step too far perhaps?"

"Look Theo, the technology is here, AI has control of misuse and interferences, so if they want it for reality then we can make it happen, you have to sell the system, but for me, it works!"

"But Charley they'll need evidence that its fault proof?"

"We have to demonstrate its capability, there's only one way Theo the big experiment, live for them all to see, I can't see another way."

Theo grabbed Charley's ears and shouted at him, "By God Charley, you will change the world in one click of the computer pad, yes or no, correct?"

"A multilingual voting system for registered voters, if you pay tax then you can vote on any question put to you by the political analyst's, simply agreed or disagreed to any question, what do you think?"

"More testing first Charley, more and more, try to break it first then repair it, then break it again, this has to be the world changer

330

to work, failure would fracture our society, understood, imagine if it failed, what would happen?"

"It works Theo, it's that simple."

"And the consciousness, what do they think?"

"Conny has backed me all the way Theo."

"Yes, but what will happen when we introduce it?"

"If it's acceptable Theo, that's the big thing here, if it's acceptable to most people?"

"Yeah understood, now how do we launch this?"

"A simple phone app Theo, this will make numbers of the masses relevant yes or no and answer from all the voters in seconds, it's a big re-think?"

"Yes Charley, but will it be too far and too fast?"

"Just an option Theo, now they have it."

"This is change that could get us killed."

"Or the quantum leap we have been waiting for Theo, this is fire being discovered for the first time, we can politically cook with gas!"

Theo gave him the face of doubt.

"The big option Theo, for humanity to move forward, we can do this, right?"

"Ok, I'll talk to them and give them the new option, are you ready to face the world Charley?"

"That's you Theo, not me, you! I'm strictly backroom you know that one ......boss!"

"Ok, I'll break it and you repair it yes?"

Charley grinned, "Well you can try Theo."

"A challenge, eh?"

Charley started laughing at him as Theo stared into his eyes, "Possibly unacceptable Charley, do politicians really want an answer from the people?"

"An option, that's all, a television experiment first perhaps?"

Theo stared out of the windows at the people walking by the hotel, "Slowly, slowly, catches the monkey!"

"What?" asked Charley.

"Just an old man's advice Charley, I'll ring Augusta and see if it's possible."

"The flat earth morons will have to be persuaded Theo."

Theo turned to him and laughed, "That's your job, if I can break it then you've failed because that will be the challenge from all of them."

Charley continued to smile at him, "And the legal people, how will that work?"

Theo burst out laughing again, "Yes, how will my brother handle this little bundle, yes, thanks Charley, I'll try him out with the idea first, Mr free the people Collins, let's see how he fights our corner."

"He might reject it boss?"

Theo was still laughing, "Na, he's a revolutionary, he'll love it!"

"Your choice, as an initial name, I thought, yes?"

"Yeah, a good name for it, Charley, yes, your choice! real democracy, this will wake them all up Charley, well done by the way, I knew you could come up with this."

# CHAPTER 56 ... Las Vegas ... Les Grandiose Casino ... Nevada.

Jonesy watched the dancers as they rehearsed their show piece, Adrian was shouting from the lighting box out front, "More sex darlings, shake rattle and bastard roll!"

Jonesy saw Alice as she tried to control Adrian's shouting, she shushed him now and again to try to make life easy for the performers.

Suddenly black suited people walked into the auditorium and surrounded her.

"Red, red, red, contact! we have a contact!"

"Where?" asked Gurung in his ear.

"CIA look alike trying to look smart."

A woman followed on and spoke to Alice as she smiled.

"They're moving out, she is being taken, red, red, red, move your arse, now!"

"Got um!" said Gurung in his earpiece, "They look like company men."

"We would have been told, get Mack and bloody quick, I'll slow em down, ok, on me, I'm moving now!"

Alice walked off with the woman and the dark suits, she had linked arms with the woman.

Jonesy stood in the gangway and stared at them, "Hey! you lot, Union cards, now!"

Alice looked up but didn't recognize the voice, so she pulled back and let men talk to the man doing all the shouting.

"You lot are not allowed in here during rehearsals, not unless you are Union members."

"A Goddammed useless Brit, what you are doing Brit, causing trouble ... again guy?"

The front man tried to push him out of the way, so Jonesy started the fight, others joined in, but Jonesy fought on with gusto, he took a punch in the eye but gave a good rib breaker of a punch in return, but then they jumped him on mass, and he grunted under the weight of these big lads.

# CHAPTER 57 ... The Grand Show Lounge ... Les Grandiose Casino ... Las Vegas.

Ruth found Alice as she watched the show people fuss over details of the dancing, she flopped down in the seat next to her, "You are my last hope, the President sent me, do you know the President?"

Alice looked at her, "I've seen you before, but I can't put a name to you dear sorry."

"Ruth, I was a bodyguard to Caledonia before the marriage proposal."

Alices eyes opened wide as she started at her, "A wedding, wow I love that, so who's the lucky boy?"

"Jimmy Wilson." said Ruth.

The security guards heard what she had just said and looked at each other in shock.

"The new President Jimmy Wilson?" asked Alice.

"Yeah, that's why he sent me to you, I need to look better apparently, dresses, cloths, the works, he said that you could do that for me, he said ask her for a favor for him."

"I'd do this for free little girl, I'd love too, so where?"

"He wants you to come to Washington, you can get all the gear needed there."

"No, no, no madam, we need to go to Paris, I need to get my people around you, this is going to be fantastic girly!"

"Paris, we can't go to Paris."

"Why not?"

"He needs me to be in Washington."

Alice squealed out laughing at her, "No dear, you are the one making the choices, so Paris it is, Alice leaned over to Adrian and kissed him as he was fussing over the dance routine, "I have an emergency Addy, I'm going to Paris, I'll be back before the show, ok?"

"Bastard Paris?" squeaked Adrian.

Alice slapped one of the guards, "Ok, priority trip to Paris, Presidential flight one, make the call, we're on the way to the airport now!"

Ruth looked at her as she stood up, she pulled Ruth out of her seat, "Now dear, no time to lose, move it, let's go!"

Alice shooed the black suited people out of the way as a man from the union started shouting to them.

"Are you putting up with all that rudeness young man, sort it out please." she pushed the guard to stop the man shouting, the fight started as they tried to tackle the violent union rep.

Alice pulled Ruth in the opposite direction and out through one of the fire doors.

She stopped her driver as he walked to her, "Take us to my jet please, now young man."

"But Alice you're booked in here."

"I want to be in Paris as soon as possible, business, understand Roy, now please!"

Ruth stared with her mouth open as Alice pulled her to the Roll Royce waiting at the side of the parking zone.

"But security Alice?" said Ruth.

"Let them catch up, we are away and that's good, we don't have much time so just relax and enjoy, this is your time darling, and you are the princess dear."

Ruth was absorbed by the pure luxury of the silver Roll Royce, when they were going Alice handed her a cold bottle of sparkling water, "Women have to drink more water than men, very important, clear?"

Ruth stared at her in silence as she spoke to the driver, "Roy, I'd like the gold jet please and we need to be booked in to land at the

Charles De Gaulle airport in Paris, they like to know who's coming
and going over there."

"Yes, Ma'am I'm on it!"

She smiled at the shocked face of Ruth.

"You are now a very important person, a person of great
interest, they'll all want a slice of you darling, understood, we have
always to move fast, we outrun the press always, understood?"

Ruth tried to speak but Alice shut her up, "Lesson one, you are
in control, you point, and they fetch, get it, you are the sweetness
and light to their world, you are the power."

"Think Jackie Kennedy, elegant, quiet, the light of their lives,
clear?"

Ruth was overpowered by Alice and her power, "But how will
they all catch up?"

"Who cares dear, let them learn to predict what you as the new
woman wants before you want it, get it?"

"Err.....................no!"

"You will dear, you have the power."

"I marry him that's it!"

"No dear, not it, not it at all, they will look to you for advice for
political answers, even for help, so what do you do?"

Ruth stared at her as she thought about it all.

"So, color, what do you lean towards in colors?"

"Err ......... green normally."

Alice stared at her unblinking, "Blue, yes all the shades of blue,
dark for meetings and shaded for evenings, can you dance dear?"

"Yeah, I dance!"

"Ballroom dancing?"

"Err.....................?"

"Ok, I'll find a teacher while we're there, you are in good hands
darling, the President obviously wanted you prepared, a good
move, could have been embarrassing perhaps."

"I embarrassed him?"

"This is the intro course dear, first stage, get the right cloths, you will not be just another first lady you will be the icon of fashion, all perfectly natural, you'll lead the world dear, ever thought of that?"

"Err............?

"No, I suppose not, well you have time the think, you're young you see, they'll judge you on your cloths, boring or hip, dull or smart, your cloths have to make statements, understand now?"

Ruth shook her head.

Alice leaned over and felt Ruth's bulge where her gun sat in her waist band holster, she took out her own silver short snout magnum and showed her the gun.

"Better for close action, no need to aim just point from the hip in their direction bang and down they go, the noise helps as well, I know six shots are a bit unsafe really, but they understand my determination to protect my man and that's all that matters to me, get it?"

"Oh, I get it Alice, just one question here though, who the hell are you woman?"

Alice giggled as she started to tell her the story of her modeling life back in London and finding the man of her dreams, "He was an animal and I loved that about him and just like an animal he was trustworthy or so I thought."

"So, you killed him?" asked Ruth.

"No!..........he dumped me darling, it broke me in half and I limped home to Canada to hide from the world, I was broken and wanted to die, I eventually married well, just like you he was a politician, we were happy till he played away then I would have killed him if I could have caught him, the Tribe welcomed me back to the ice and I lived as well as I could until my man returned from the hunt."

"Who are we talking about here Alice?"

"Augustus Talbot, my man from the days of modeling."

"But he dumped you?"

"He explained the real reason and I believed him; he was still the one, what can I say? Inuit are like that; the one is the one for life."

Ruth smiled at her, "So this then?"

"What, the wealth? Oh, that's him, smart as a tack and ruthless when he wanted to be, they just wouldn't leave him alone, so he killed them all."

Ruth shook her head as she listened, "I still don't understand Alice, so who are you again?"

Alice grinned, "Caledonia's Grandpa married me, he should have thirty years before as I've just explained."

"So, you are the Queen of the family then Alice?"

"Princess dear let's not overestimate our worth."

Ruth laughed, "You're the real star Alice, come on admit it!"

"Yes! she is!" said the driver "And we have a tail Alice, what should I do?"

"Deal with them Roy, "she turned back to Ruth, "He's one of the old man's trainees, handpicked by Pop to protect me when he died, oh such a bad day."

Ruth squeezed her hand, "What a story you have Alice?"

Alice turned to her again, her eyes were moist, "Now, tell me yours dear, so a marriage to the most famous man in the world? Come on let's hear yours Ruth."

"So, he's Caledonia's Grand Pop then, she talks about him a lot you know."

"Yeah, I know, so do many people, but he's gone, and we have to make up the loss with our own plans, yes?"

"The great planner then?"

"Oh yes dear the greatest planner ever, layers and layers of over planning and secrets, he drove me crazy with all his secrets, he was an adviser to the Queen you know, I never knew that one, just another one of his layers, like a Goddammed English onion! A total inbred when it came to food and wine, all waisted on him, no palette whatsoever, but he did have other charms, one of them was surprise, now that's a gift, get it?"

"No Alice, nor really, but I'll listen and try to catch up if that's ok with you."

"Our relationship changed every day, I can't explain it more than that, every day was different, I suppose that's love, eh?"

"Yes Alice, I suppose its love."

# CHAPTER 58 ... Auditorium ... Les Grandiose Casino ... Las Vegas.

Jonesy punched whenever he got the chance, but these boys were hard men and it took effort to fight them all at the same time, eventually he was losing and one of them placed his foot on Jonesy's head holding him down while others searched his pockets.

The man pulled out the standard earpiece from Jonesy's ear, "The guy's plugged-in man!"

"They've took her mate," shouted Jonesy, "A dark haired woman with thugs, she went out the fire doors, just the two of them, move your arse!"

They cuffed him up and lifted him up to talk, "Who the hell are you really guy?"

Another of them was searching Jonesy's wallet, the get anywhere cards fell out of their multi slide pack, one of them whistled in appreciation, "And he's connected man!"

"Well, who the hell are you buddy?"

Jonesy gave them his toothy grin, "You first yank!"

"Goddam it he's a Brit on the loose, what agency?"

Jonesy grinned on before the man showed him his Presidential security pass, the picture of the White house shone out in silver in his wallet.

"White House eh, so who's the bint?"

They looked at each other for an explanation of what this Brit wanted to know, "Shit!" shouted the man, "She's gone, shit, find her and fast man!"

"Who?" asked Jonesy.

The obvious leader pointed to the fire door, "Get going and follow on, she's top priority, stay back and protect, go!"

"Go where?" asked Jonesy "And why Presidential personnel then mate?"

"I ain't your mate buddy," he looked at Jonesy's cards, "The House of Commons, Whitehall 100, G7, G2, Chequers? What the hell is Chequers?"

"So, who is she then mate?" asked Jonesy again, "Hey! same side mate, come on."

"Who are you first buddy?"

"Captain Karl Jones, Royal Anglian Regiment, and G7 protection unit of the Royal Guard."

"Quite a mouthful guy, red monkey suit normally then?"

"Dark blue actually, but there will be blood stains on it if I don't find out what happened to Mrs. Talbot."

"She's answering a favor guy."

"What?"

The man smiled at him, "Yours first buddy."

"Protect from a possible assassination attempt from unknowns 24/7."

"What with no weapon buddy, what kind of guard has no weapon? "He suddenly felt the click of a weapon being cocked at the side of his head.

"Oh, he has one of those mates, me, not my primary weapon though, still this will do the job." said Gurung.

The man looked up to the little brown face of Gurung over the heckler gun barrel, "A Gurkha?" he whispered.

"Yes!" said Jonesy, "And late as bloody usual."

"Hey, relax he says, this'll be soft he says, I'll take the first shift he says, then all hell breaks loose and he's screaming down the line for help."

"They were big bastards!"

The guard started to laugh at their argument.

Gurung put the barrel on his cheek bone, "Don't laugh when I'm fucking mad, it'll only get me into a killing mood!"

The guard stood still as Jonesy offered his hands to him to take off the cuffs, "And we don't want to see that now do we sir?"

"Earpiece?" asked the Guard.

"That would be nice mate," said Jonesy, "So where did she go with that bint?"

"Bint?"

"The dark-haired woman?"

"Oh, the new first lady, engaged to be married to the President?"

Gurung placed his weapon back into his under-arm sling "What a ball up, I'm blaming you Jonesy, crap as usual, Mack will go ballistic!"

"Not if we find her first, so where did they go then mate?" asked Jonesy.

The guard ignored the question and touched his earpiece, "Airport, going where? Paris! shit! Call it in help from the Air force man, do it do it now, she's priority one man, go bastard go! yeah Goddam it I'll do the paperwork just follow and keep in touch, yes now, go!"

"So, who kidnapped who here then mate?" asked Jonesy.

The guard re focused on the two of them as the dancing started up on stage, "Who the hell are you guys and why the interest in Mrs. Talbot?"

"She's on a number one hit list for VIP assassinations, our job is to divert or find the potential shooters," said Gurung.

"A conflict of interest then man, we protect the VIP from shit heads like you guys."

"What's her name then mate?" asked Jonesy.

"Need to Goddam know man." said the Guard.

Gurung noticed him first, "Oh shit here we go lads, keep your chins down because he'll will be swinging."

"Where the fuck is she you morons?" shouted Mack from the back stalls.

"Paris Boss!" shouted Gurung "The Presidents woman took her."

"And who the fuck is she?"

Jonesy elbowed the guard, "Our boss, better come up with a name and bloody fast mate or he'll take us all, I'm telling you mate!"

"Na, he doesn't look so tough to me man."

Just as the man finished what he was saying Mack was on him and lifted him off the floor by his chin with one hand, "Who the fuck are you?"

"Err............. Presidential security boss!" said Jonesy.

"Who?"

"The bints protection." said Jonesy.

"What bint?"

"The woman who took her Boss."

"Took her where?"

"Paris Boss."

"Shit! Paris? shit! the French have her.........shit! Ok move it! Don't panic, a rethink, that's all we need! "Screamed Mack, he dropped the man and ran off towards the doors.

"Now look what you've caused Yank, World War three with the Bastard French," said Jonesy.

The guard looked from Gurung to Jonesy, "I don't get it guys, why?"

Jonesy ran off after Mack, Gurung stayed to explain, "Because he has a war on with the French mate, simple as, get it?" Gurung ran off following the others.

"No, I don't get it, not one bit do I get it guys!"

The dancing stopped at the back of him, and Adrian started shouting.

"Get in bastard time!" he turned to the security man "And you lot, shut the bastard up!"

# CHAPTER 59 ... Main Hallway ... Casino Stairs ... Grand Entrance

Caledonia spotted Mack as he ran towards her and Erick, she stood in front of him and stopped his panicked run.

"What's up Mack, a problem?"

Mack was sweating with the heat and his panic, he looked from face to face, Erick grabbed his arm as Jonesy and Gurung ran up to them.

"Mack! Cool it man, what's the problem?" asked Erick.

"Err............. they took her."

"Who took her Mack?"

"The dark-haired bint." said Jonesy.

"Who?" asked Cal.

"The Presidents woman, "said Gurung.

Mack turned to him, "The President of America's woman?"

"Yeah, they were secret service agents she was with them and they're in a panic as well, she was in their care apparently."

Mack grabbed hold of him and lifted him off the floor, "More info would have been helpful you shit head!"

"She kidnapped her boss; they went out the fire doors and into a Roller."

"A Roller?" asked Erick, "A silver Rolls Royce?"

"Yeah, top of the range and all that."

"And any idea where she's been taken then?" asked Erick.

"Yes, Paris!" said Cal as she showed him her phone and the call she was making, she walked away from the panic and spoke down the line.

"What the hell's happening pimples?"

Ruth was giggling at her down the phone, "I've been taken over by a mad woman who's going to make a lady out of me, we're on route to Paris to buy clothes for the wedding."

"Does she not realize what chaos she's just caused?"

Ruth started laughing then handed the phone over to Alice, "Hello Caledonia how are things with you and Erick, good?"

"Very good Alice and what are you doing with the new first Lady."

Alice giggled back to her, "Oh come on Caledonia let me have some fun please, let the boys catch up, good exercise for them don't you think?"

Cal burst out laughing then handed the phone to Erick.

"GG what are you doing? You are in a security breach, stay safe at all costs please!"

Alice shouted down the phone to him in Inuit, Erick started laughing, "She's stitching her into her wedding dress Cal, familiar?"

Cal laughed with him as the confused faces stared at them.

"That's her guy!" shouted a police officer at the doors, "Apprehend at all costs, she is wanted for multiple murders here in Vegas, do it go, arrest her on behalf of the Sheriff's department!"

Jonesy turned and started the fight as per normal and punched the police officer coming for them, the chaos erupted as gamblers thought it was a police raid on illegal slot machine cheats, the place descended into complete meltdown as people ran and fought all over the place, Mack was in the middle of it all and swinging at anyone who wanted it, Gurung pulled Cal away and into a side office with an open door then returned to the fray, screaming out the Gurkha attack.

Cal could not stop laughing at the mayhem, Erick followed and cuddled her as she also laughed, "This place is nuts Cal, ok, I agree, you were right let's be gone, yes?"

"Yes, big man, they just don't like me in this town."

He pulled her back out into the casino and side stepped the brawl as it encompassed the whole gambling floor, some security men jumped in to stop the fighting, a machine was pushed over and little in house, gold coins filled the floor.

"Where too then?" asked Cal.

"Well Paris for a start, then we had better be in Washington for the big speech."

Erick pushed his way through the people to breath the warm desert air of an early evening, he was stopped by a police officer.

"My wife you idiot and I'm a Canadian house representative so she would also be covered by an exclusion clause in the diplomatic relationship with our two countries, even if she were guilty of what that fool accused her of."

The office smiled at him, "Sorry sir, she just fit's the facial recognition, sorry!"

"Along with about a million other women?"

"Yes sir, sorry sir."

"Anyway, get in there and stop all that fighting, that's your job, yes?"

"I'll wait for back up sir, we have the local National guard reserve coming to stop the riot, they'll be here in seconds."

"What big speech?" asked Cal as he dragged her to the car.

"The results, win or lose, is the earth moving or staying put?"

"He has no chance you know Erick."

"The first step Cal, his idea will win in the end, they all need to see why it's needed that's all, you see the giant experiment is failing, this country has to expand, or it'll implode, and we'll have a civil war on our hands."

"They need good sense and smart leaders Erick, they need talent, well that's what the old man would have said."

"Agreed Cal, let's go!" he gave up trying to find their car park and hailed a passing cab and pushed her in, "Airport and quick, we need to catch a flight."

They watched the National guard Humvees screaming down the main road to the casino, they screeched up to the main entrance and suddenly solders were everywhere.

"Good luck lads," said Cal as she snuggled into Erick.

"Is she really at-risk Cal?"

"Dexter, what can I say?"

"Well, why, would be a good question."

"Just to hurt us Erick same as usual just to see us pained."

"Who?"

"My mother is trying to find out who is behind all this."

"Could be just smoke and mirrors Cal, just that."

"Daddy says not, big boy, and we're supposed to listen to him now, he's the planner after all."

"Is he though Cal?"

She looked into his eyes, "Mum says that he's the real thing and has planned it all so far, anyway you should know all about it, you're in the privy council after all."

Erick was listening and talking as he watched the car next to them on the freeway as they headed to the airport, the man in the back seat of the jeep in the next lane locked and loaded an AK 47 machine gun and pointed at them.

"Down!" screamed Erick, he pushed Cal down and under the front seat as much as he could before the firing started, then laid on top of her, the car slid sideways at the side of the road, Erick managed to open the near side door and was trying to push Cal out into the ditch, but she wouldn't move.

In the first blast the driver was hit and the taxi swerved off the road into a drainage ditch but the vehicle kept on driving down the ditch, then all came to a stop as more firing came from another car following them, only this time the Jeep was being hit and rolled behind them into the ditch, the taxi came to a shuddering halt as the engine stalled, the driver slumped onto the steering wheel. the slow motion of the action suddenly became real as doors were opened and voices were shouting at them."

"Caledonia, you ok in there, are you hit?"

Erick turned to the voice, "Marvin what the hell man?"

"My boys were following the followers, you guys were the target all along, they look like Mafia people out of New York, do you know any of them?"

Erick stepped out of the wrecked car and pulled Cal out to stand and look at the blasted Jeep, Marvin was now gone and searching the bodies of the dead men for clues.

"Ok Babe?" asked Erick.

She blasted a few quick breaths before answering him, "Yeah, and I'm not carrying, you've got to laugh really."

"I wish I could Cal, so we were the targets all along, what do you think?"

"The cop in the Casino, maybe that was the warning there and then, he had me identified, and he knew the people I killed perhaps!"

Erick hugged her tight, "Are you wounded in any way?"

"Na, just a bit of lost pride, and there's me the ultimate smart arse being shot at, laughable!"

"Tagging us all along then?"

"We're so easy Erick, perhaps we should do what Marvin's done?"

"What die and live a new life? Well not me, I'm fighting all the way Cal, this has got me real mad, those people wanted us dead, well war it is then, let's see them on the other end of a gun Caledonia."

Erick pointed to the dead cab driver, "He was an innocent, now that's wrong Cal."

She stared at him for a moment, "I'm not sure I can any more Erick, I'm just not, I don't know why just that I have to think about it all."

"This shooting upset you then or is it Mexico?"

"Mexico," she started to sniffle as tears fell down her cheeks, she spotted the dead.

Erick was bleeding but didn't realize as he held her.

"You're bleeding!" she screeched out as the blood dripped onto the tarmac.

He looked at his leg, blood was pumping out from a hole above the knee, suddenly he felt the pain and collapsed on the road.

"Medic!" shouted one of Marvin's people, Cal caught the accent immediately but said nothing.

"Wee!" shouted Marvin, "Tout rapidmon!"

She watched the silent communications between them, the thumb over the mouth and the fist in the air.

"These boys are French then Marvin?" asked Erick.

"La Legionaries, brethren, a problem Erick?" said Marvin.

"Why?" asked Cal.

Marvin looked into her eyes, "Because I don't trust anyone else, is that wrong?"

"No Marvelous, just asking that's all, gussy has done the same by the way, just Legionaries."

"Yes, Cal I know, she asked for advice, so I gave her some."

"She asked me, and I said no!"

"Why Cal?"

"English mistrust I suppose and five hundred years of wars."

"Pop's influence more like." grinned Marvin

"And him of course, he didn't trust the French, well only the Americans trust the French."

"His words again?"

"They just pour out Marv, sorry."

"So, was he racist then?"

"Well yeah, he didn't trust the French or the Spanish or the Germans, or even Gypsies for that matter."

"Color?"

"Irrelevant to him, all his angst came from personal experience, and I was on the end of it, sorry."

"No need to be sorry Cal, I just have to hear his wisdom when I can."

"Hello up there, I'm bleeding down here." said Erick.

"A flesh wound Erick, "Said Marvin, "So who did this?"

"They wanted her Marvin, well that's what I think and that would lead me to think that the bad boys in town knew she was here and sent someone to stop her."

"What, they thought she was here to work?"

"Perhaps Marv."

Cal pulled off her summer fleece jacket and wrapped it around his leg then tied it as tight as she could.

Marvin looked at her again, "And were you Cal?"

"I don't any more Marv, done and dusted for that one, understood?"

Marvin looked at Erick for confirmation of her words.

"True Marv, she's done and out of that world."

"Well, someone doesn't believe it Erick, and someone wants her dead, I agree with you, yes it's her they wanted, so Dexter is wrong then?"

"Marvin, we all need protection, this is going to be messy in the end."

"You bet it is Erick, I'm finishing this job so tell everyone to keep out of my way."

"What does that mean Marv?"

"Pop's plan, he said that I have to protect the experiment, or it'll all fall apart."

"The experiment?" asked Erick.

"The USA Erick!" said Cal "The greatest human experiment on the planet and it can't be left to morons to kill it."

Marvin was now staring at her.

She stared back at him, "What ................ bait?"

"Yes, Caledonian bait for the bad people."

"And you'll wipe them away?"

"Completely!"

"No!" said Erick as he was being lifted into the car, "It's a no from me!"

Cal nodded to Marvin, "I'll pay the price Marv, you tie me to the sacrificial post, and I'll sit and wait for the killers to arrive, Pop would have asked, I know that."

Marvin smiled, "They are more important than us eh Cal?"

"His words again Marv and I agree!"

"And Augusta?"

"What do you mean?"

"Will she be a goat as well?"

"No!" screamed Erick from inside the car.

"She's in our world Marv so she has to pay just like us, do you want me to ask?"

"No Cal, I'll ask, I just wanted your input that's all."

Cal stepped into the car and was driven away to the hospital just as the police arrived on the scene, Marvin pulled out his wallet with the golden badge and placed it into his top pocket for all to see, the cop stared at the black man with the badge from the President.

"No, it's not plastic officer, the Presidential application of security to the Nation, black, white yellow, even green if you look hard enough."

"And what is this sir?" asked the Cop.

"An assassination attempt on a Canadian member of parliament, and ambassador to Washington."

"Shit, sir!"

"Very much so officer."

"And the bodies?"

"Mafia men we think, do you recognize any of them officer?" he watched the man's eyes closely to see his reaction to the dead, the man blinked too much for him not to think he knew some of them."

"Err, no sir none of them are familiar to me."

Marvin didn't believe him as he stared into his eyes, "So we have corruption here in Las Vegas then, are you on the side lines wanting to be listened to or fully in waiting for big money to land on your lap?"

"I don't understand the question sir?"

Marvin stared at him for an embarrassingly long time, "Good, so when we start you can point them out to us then, if you're innocent you will be forgiven for having to work with them, believe me we understand officer."

"No comment sir."

"Good, keep it up for as long as you can but remember this, help us and you will be saved, fail to help and that means that you're one of them and we be dealt with accordingly, understand?"

The officer stared at him as the ambulance rolled up.

"I will find the who and the why officer, I always win, tell them if you like, you can jump ship, but you have limited time, clear?"

"But you are sir?"

"The Presidential representative for seeking out corruption of law enforcement agencies and officers and no I'm not internal review, I'm enforcements, get it officer?"

"Sir, yes sir!"

Marvin smiled at him to break the ice between them, he recognized the way the man said the phrase.

"And which of the services were you in before officer?" Marvin read his name badge, "Officer Hallam?

"Marines sir."

"A full service?"

"Eleven years Sir."

"We're proud of you boy, never forget that please, and we want you home officer Hallam, think about that."

The officer breathed out slowly then walked off to the dead bodies.

One of Marvin's men wanted to speak to him, but he shut him up with a look, "Later Vincent, debrief in an hour and we can talk it all out, tell them that I would like ideas as to who and why please."

He whispered in Vincent's ear, "He knows who, we might have to push I think, oh, and tell the lads not to converse while they are here, we don't need to give them clues as to our origins, understood?"

Vincent nodded and walked off to their car in silence, the others gathered and listened to Vincent in a whispered huddle.

When the ambulance had loaded up the bodies and officer Hallam had made calls to the station, he wandered over to Marvin, who was watching.

He tried his best to whisper so as not to be overheard, "It a big thing out here sir, bigger than me for one, lots of people who disagreed out there in the desert."

"I fully understand Officer, I understand the risk, look, just a name and I'll close this world around them, no one will ever know where the word came from, get me?"

"Right from the top Sir, right from the top."

"Uniformed or political?"

The officer razed his hands in the air.

"The very top then?"

The officer nodded then walked off.

"Watch out Marine, fire in the hold, the house is about to blow man!"

The man turned to him and smiled then got back into his squad car and drove off.

"He's scared boss." said Vincent.

"Yep, they all are, imagine being sent to arrest her, the Russian Mafia hit woman in town for action, now who would know that?"

"Facial recognition maybe?"

"No inside info is my guess, we have to find the who and snuff him out, ready?"

Vincent grinned at him.

# CHAPTER 60 ... Downtown Police Lock up ... Las Vegas ... Nevada.

Gurung was chewing a hardened stick of beef given to him by one of the prisoners in the lock up cage.

"What is it?" he asked the long haired Indian.

"Buffalo jerky, nice, eh?"

"Yes nice, so why are you in here?"

"Drunk and disorderly, you?"

"Oh, a disagreement over a one-armed bandit."

"What him?" the Indian pointed to Jonesy who held an ice pack over his swollen eye.

"Yeah him, he started it all, as bloody usual."

Jonesy gave him the one finger salute in return.

"And what's with him?" he pointed to Mack who was soundly asleep on the long bench, his snoring echoed over the cell house.

"Oh, he's a BBC big wig caught up in the fight, I think he might want interviews any time soon."

The door to the cell house opened and a very posh looking man stepped up to the cage, Mack was now up on his feet and staring at the stranger.

"Get me out of here Rupert, this is bloody embarrassing!" shouted Mack.

The door behind the man suddenly filled with police officers, some of them looked beaten and bruised, most had black eyes.

"That's him gentlemen, he's our foreign correspondent over here in America," said Rupert, "There seems to be a dreadful mix up here officers, he's here to interview your police chief in relation to gambling addictions."

"And it's relationship to alcohol consumption." said Mack walking over to the cage door.

"So, he does work for the BBC then?" asked the police sergeant.

"Oh yes, one of our longest serving reporters, a real veteran, always in on the action aren't you, Mack?"

Mack gave him the scowl and the wave to open the door.

"And his friends?"

"Research assistants, here to help him in any way I believe."

"Well that one's staying in here for a start." the sergeant pointed to Jonesy, "And the Indian guy is staying put until we here from his Embassy."

Mack turned to Gurung, "Embassy?"

Gurung gave him the toothy grin, "Political immunity boss?"

"My arse!" grumbled Mack.

The door was opened by the police officer who kept his eyes on Jonesy all along, Mack stepped out and was given the buzzing phone to answer.

"We have a problem Mack," said Marvin down the line.

"Oh, hello Marvelous, how's freedom for you?"

"What, a sore ass this morning?"

"Don't start on me boss because I'm in the mood for you this fine morning."

"The whole lot of them are bent Mack, root and branch corruption, so question one, are the lads safe in the cells, or will they hang themselves by accident?"

Gurung watched Mack's eyes as he spoke down the phone, he turned to Jonesy and nodded to Mack as he watched the panic return.

Jonesy shook his head.

Mack had to think quickly, while he looked at the prisoners through the wire cage.

"Err........................ they all work for me boss, yes, I want them all out and doing as soon as possible, yes get us a lawyer please."

"There's one on the way, a famous face as well so he's on your new protection Rota, such as it is, clear?"

"Clear boss, so when?"

"Now!

"So how famous is he?"

"Patrick you moron!"

"Patrick Collins?"

The police sergeant turned to his words.

Mack grinned at the policeman and held the mouthpiece as he spoke," Patrick Collins is on route for this lot, I would let them out if I were you lads."

"No chance!" said the sergeant, "That one is in here five to ten for sure, I have list of felonies as long as your arm man." he thumbed in Jonesy's direction.

Mack put his face into the sergeants, "He's a fucking war hero, he saved countless American lives for God's sake, cut him a little slack for being drunk, what you've never been on a bender?"

As the sergeant was computing the new information Mack looked at his men, Gurung nodded to the Indian sitting next to him.

"And him!" said Mack, "He's employed by me."

"He's an Indian, what the hell do you want with an Indian drunk?"

"Local color for one and he's a real American for two!" shouted Mack.

The sergeant gulped as he fumed.

Mack didn't give him any time to think about it all as he shouted again, "Is this how America treats war heroes? You treat them like shit, he shed blood for your lot, that's it eh? You can all fuck off now you've saved our babies from bombs and destruction?"

"Shut up!" someone shouted from the doorway.

All faces turned to Patrick as he waved the paper in the air, "Give me some peace please here gentlemen, ok out, open the door please officer."

"And who the hell are you?" shouted the police sergeant.

Patrick handed him his business card, "Persons of special interest sergeant, to the White House, understood?"

"What the hell is this?"

Patrick walked over to him, "They work for the Presidents officer, look I'm trying to be calm her, you can tag them while you process their felonies if you like or hand them over to me as a person of responsibility?"

The sergeant looked at him as it worked its way through his brain, "No way man!"

"Then I will see you and your whole department in court, I hope you have a good law team lined up sergeant, it's funny how police commissioners let junior officer fall into the abyss when they want to slide out of the blame don't you think?"

The man stared blinking at Patrick's words.

"He caused a Goddam fight." the officer thumbed to Jonesy again.

"Witnesses?"

"Yeah plenty!"

"Well, we'll see you in court sergeant, in the meantime I require their liberty."

Gurung elbowed his new friend in the cage cell, "We require your services, well will you help when and if you can, what's your name by the way?"

The Indian smiled back at him, "Yeah sure man, my name is Rudy Blackfoot, you?"

"Call me Gurung, him Jonesy and the boss man is called Mack."

"And your tribe?"

"Oh me, Gurkha Nepali."

"A long way from home guy, army then?"

Gurung nodded, he pointed to Jonesy, "Welsh and the boss is English, no drinking from now on, yes?"

"Err......................... yeah, why not?"

Gurung winked at him, "Any more of those sticks on you?"

"Yeah man, you like?" he reached into his under-armpit bag and brought another for him.

Gurung nodded to Jonesy, so Rudy passed it over to the injured man to try.

Jonesy sniffed it and was about to hand it back when Gurung gave him the cold stare of how dare you insult the man, eat it and shut up.

Jonesy put it in his mouth and tried to chew it.

"Dried in the Nevada sun man." said Rudy.

"Raw then?"

"Yeah, a problem with that?"

Jonesy looked into Gurungs eyes again then back to the Indian, "Err.......no, better than some meat I've eaten, it is meat, yes?"

"Buffalo, five years old."

"And under your armpit all this time, huh?"

Rudy started to laugh at him, Gurung gave him the stare to get it down his pipe and shut up.

The officer came into the cell and started placing electronic tags on their ancles.

"What is this?" asked Jonesy.

"Regulations for release guys, you wear one of these or you stay put in the cell, your choice, that fancy assed lawyer of yours agreed to this until you appear in court, we have a back log of cases you see."

Rudy winked as they were given their belongings back at the counter, "It's a badge of being a bad ass man!"

Jonesy let his wallet cards flop out to the floor for Rudy to see, "And these are mine."

Rudy started to read some, and he leaned over, "What is Chequers?"

Jonesy ignored him and followed Gurung out of the police station, Gurungs phone buzzed into life as they walked.

"Gurung," said Marvin, "Patrick Collins, follow and protect at all costs, close support you Jonesy and the Indian, by the way, what do we need an Indian for?"

"A friend boss and a friend in need at that, he's help I think."

"Ok, you're a smart man, do it your way, keep me in the loop please, is he secure?"

"Not asked Boss."

"Well ask, explain and get him working, he's on the books as of today, you had better get him kitted out as well, the works, he's in the slot, right?"

"Clear boss, and his tribe?"

"Ah, so that's the plan, I like it, good thinking, smart, is he?"

"Very boss and a warrior, we need them, don't we?"

"Yep, sure do, my little mountain warrior!"

Gurung tugged the Indians sleeve and smiled at him.

"Ok, you're in, but you had better be as good as you say you are Rudy."

Rudy showed him his arm scars from the tribal ceremonies.

Gurung rolled up his sleeve and showed the scald dragon scar on his right under arm.

"What the hell is that?"

Gurung stared into the man's soul in silence as the danger became clear to him, "It's a pledge to die for your friends if needed."

"Like a tribe then?"

"Exactly so, we are the tribe who help protect the warm under belly of society, we will be killing corruption and the people causing it all."

"Dangerous then?"

"We take hits from time to time, but we make sure our friends are avenged, we will win in the end because we have big hitters as friends."

"Big hitters?"

Gurung nodded solemnly.

"And I'm in?"

"If you want it Rudy, I am your interface, I'm responsible for your behavior, one drunken binge, one fight not on the books or a killing not sanctioned and I'll be booted out along with you, get it?"

"Why me and why now?"

"A very good question, firstly I suspect that you know a lot of locals, I hear a whisper that the local police are on the take, correct?"

Rudy nodded, "The tribes have invested heavily in some of the casinos and have been burnt accordingly, we no longer trust the white man, he speaks with forked tongue and all that."

"Some perhaps Rudy, but not these, as you can see, I'm not your average white man, just like you I've fought bad men all my life, I worked for the British Government and eventually onto this, a long time for study don't you think?"

"And what have you found out about the pale faces then?"

Gurung grinned at him, "Cut the Indian crap please, look, it's a hard lesson is to go against them in war, Americans are easy, yes they come with all the goodies of war but they don't have the spirit, that magic warrior spirit you and I know about, some are on the inside and take the food from the mouths of children, it's always been like that, but not me and not mine, get it?"

"Brits?"

"It's not the Nation it's the man, my boss says ask you to understand the risk and also the demand we have for silence and security, it's a yes no question in the end Rudy."

"And if I don't?"

"Then goodbye and good luck."

"And yes means?"

"You take orders from me and mine, sometimes confused orders, we obey and do as required in this or that situation."

"Like your friend with the black eye, he took the pain as required?"

"Yes, like Jonesy, start that fight, take that man out, protect these people, follow and observe then report back, always on the end of the phone, clear?"

"A wage?"

"Big enough to choke a horse, if you had time for a horse that is, this is full on my friend, you won't have time for a normal life."

"Well, my life ain't that normal man."

"Ok so clear on the reasons and the actions needed?"

"Yeah...............so do I tell friends?"

"A new world and a new life, I am your new life, follow me and live a life you will have never dreamed of, betray me and mine after you volunteer, and it will be just a short time before your death."

Rudy smiled at him, "As you can see my life is in shitsville, so I say this, I will follow only you, I know you and no one else."

"Understood Rudy, this will do for now, they'll want to see you working anyway before you're fully trusted."

"I feel the same man," he took a little knife out of his sleeve and cut the crease on his right hand bellow the thumb, he handed the knife to Gurung."

Gurung grinned, "We are so similar my friend," he cut the crease the same as Rudy and they clasped hands."

"Brother?"

"Brother Rudy Blackfoot." Gurung handed him a wad of dollars, "Ok, go and get cleaned up and knew cloths then meet me at the Grandiose casino in say four hours, we have a new job so follow and do what I do clear?"

"Err.......... clear, err....... boss?"

"Yes, use that when you want to make a comment, we always want opinions, just a small piece of advice, you have two ears and one mouth, that means that you must listen twice as much as you speak clear?"

"Clear brother!"

Gurung watched the Indian walk away to the town mega store over the road and hoped he had changed a man's life, "And stay out of trouble Blackfoot."

A car horn woke him out of his thoughts, Glen grinned at him from the driving seat of the black limo, Jonesy sat in the back and pointed for him to get in.

"Well, what's with Tonto?"

Gurung looked into Jonesy's eyes, "Another fight so soon, will you never learn white boy?"

"You like him, eh?"

Gurung looked out of the window in silence as he was driven off, "I've been there mate and it's hard to get out of that gully, depression, loss of friends, booze, lock up!"

"Yeah, but you Muslim's don't drink right?"

Gurung tried to grab Jonesy's leg and inflict pain on him, but he was giggling like a little girl, so he laughed with him.

"So, what are the orders, Captain?"

"Follow and protect the lawyer, all the time, no spaces to allow anyone to mess with him, full license, the lot! So, saddle up cowboy."

"So, where's the other one of them," he nodded to Glen the driver.

"In the helicopter, let's hope he don't break this one."

"So, he's had accidents before then? but I arranged to meet Blackfoot in few hours at the casino."

Jonesy started laughing again, "You cannot call him Blackfoot, anyway Glen can spin round and pick him up, the lawyer wants to go to out of town and fast."

"Who is he really?"

Jonesy looked at him and laughed again, "What and you haven't seen the man nicking motors in alphabetical order on that security flick?"

"Shit yes, you're right it's him."

"And he has a scald on his arm, so best warn the Indian to be aware."

"He already is, I think.

"Patrick Collins!" said Glen from the front, "And he's an original so you pair be aware as well, he knows them all and he's the ex-Presidents son, Irish by the way so clamp the gob shut Jonesy, there's a good lad."

Gurung was now laughing at Jonesy's face, "First bollocking of the day Captain?"

"Na.......... second, old Mack is still raging from the first balls up."

"You are just too violent mate; you need therapy perhaps?"

"Yeah, that's a good point, I do like the dancers in the casino."

"Don't!" said Glen from the driver's seat, he adjusted the mirror, "Marvelous is proper pissed with you boy so real the bastard in, there's fighting and there's GBH, got me?"

"Yes sir, noted, but our leader was the instigator on that one."

"Marv says watch and learn from this one, and no pissing about, clear?"

Heads nodded in the back seats.

"This'll be full on I think so no time for wasters."

"Sir!" said Gurung and Jonesy in unison.

# CHAPTER 61 ... University Medical Center ... Nevada

A doctor came into the small room as Caledonia and Erick were talking, they turned and recognized Marvin, with his white coat and stethoscope draped over his shoulder.

Marvin looked at the new bulges under Caledonia's loose coat.

He smiled at them, "So, a change of heart then Cal?"

She opened her coat and showed him the twin hecklers and ammunition clips ready to go, "Seal team six are in trouble if they want him Marv."

"Understood Cal, need assistance? "

"No thanks, he's my only job and this will be to the death if they want us Marv."

Marvin smiled at Erick, "So she's back in the slot then?"

Erick looked at Cal "Tell him Cal."

She shook her head, but Erick nodded again to Marvin.

"I...............had a dream while I was waiting for him to come out of the operating theatre, Pop walked up to me and stared into my eyes."

"And what did he say Cal?"

"To deny your true nature with a lie is a bad move, it will change your life for the worse, defend our people and stop mooching around with a long face, now's the time to bloody grow up woman!"

"And?"

"Then he turned and walked off to the sea, he paddled in the surf like a little child, giggling and running around, but he became younger, and he was a little child on the beach, Bridlington up on the northeast coast of England, his long term love I think."

"Or another message Cal?"

"So, you believe in such things then Marv?"

"Ghost's?"

"Dream sightings, messages for the next world and all that."

He nodded, "Yes Cal, so what's the little child in the water all about?"

"He has GG, that's what he's saying," Said Erick, "Look after your own, she'll be safe in his care."

Marvin looked at Cal for clarification of what he was saying.

"GG is his Grandmother Marv, Alice is already protected by Pop, what he didn't say and is part of his culture is that this could be the warning of her natural demise and he'll collect her when the time comes, they'll play in the surf together just like old times when they were kids."

"And it'll be the summer Marvin," said Erick.

He looked at Cal again.

"Inuit's Marvin, it's not all taught us in schools, is it?" said Cal.

Marvin stared at them as tears came into his eyes, "Next time ask him to visit me, I need direction and I fear the backlash of what I'm about to do."

"You're already dead Marvin," said Erick.

"Yes, but my links are not."

"Ah............. that's it," said Erick, "You have to grow up and stop being a child Marvin."

"But I am."

"Really Marv?" said Cal, "And the Princess?"

He stared at their faces one by one, "Ok, point taken, it'll happen soon, I promise."

"Nana would have given you a proper bollocking Marv, to your face, that woman is your life, make it perfect for her while you can."

"I only came here to see if you were ok Erick, I wasn't expecting a spiritual reading man! Oh and we have a new member, Gurung enlisted his help, a Blackfoot Indian, named Rudy, he says that he has links we could follow, natives Erick, I thought that you could perhaps follow that lead, he's an alcoholic apparently."

"A normal thing for a desert dweller, yeah maybe, and Gurung trust's this Blackfoot?"

"He recognizes a fellow warrior Erick, he goes on feelings, you know what he's like."

"Yeah, and he's normally right, another native with hidden talents, right?"

"Ok, we'll visit the reservation and make enquiries, I'll check him out, so, next move?"

"I'm going to hit them hard as a warning of things to come."

"With the whole team?" asked Cal.

"Err...........................no....... just me, one man and one gun."

"And a woman to back you up Marv?" said Cal.

"Yeah, and a driver for the pickup, yeah!"

Erick stared at him, "It'll change your life Marv, you'll be a grown up afterwards man."

"Maybe Pop's message is the right move."

"Yeah, but he was.................well fearless and bloody dangerous Marvin, as cool under fire as he was in ordinary life, do you have that in your DNA?"

"We'll see Cal, if I don't then it's the end anyway."

"A bit early for a suicide trip Marv," said Cal.

"Surprise, the first trick of taking a position, hard and fast then scoot."

"Better tell her that one first Marv, give her the chance to give an opinion."

"I would prefer to do this on my own Cal, a black man can get in anywhere, they don't even look at my face."

"Distinctive clothing then ditch on site afterwards."

"Like your casino splash then Cal?"

Caledonia looked straight into his soul, "It changed me and Erick Marvin, we ran so fast, and we would have still been running if it wasn't for Pop."

"And now there's no Pop Caledonia," said Erick.

"But he has a Granddaughter Erick, and she can back up anyone who needs her, if it's a war they want then bring it on."

Erick looked to Marvin to witness what she was changing into, "There's your Pop Marvin, she'll ask for peace, and they'll accept or die, simple really."

"Good, I have approval then?"

"Tolly needs to know Mav, best tell him before he sees it on the news headlines, he'll also back you up when the time comes." Said Cal

"And so will Pop Marvin," said Erick, "He'll be there with you, look at your hands before the action starts, then ask him what he would do, he'll answer right there and then."

Marvin looked at Cal again.

"It's the medication, it makes him more spiritual, it brings out the native in him, listen and learn from native Americans Marvin," said Cal "Tolly will cover everything Marvin, he's your Pop now, understood?"

"No argument then, no, is it really needed then from you guys?"

Cal and Erick smiled at him, "Just waiting around for the action to start mate," said Cal.

"But I thought that you were, well busted?"

"Seeing my man shot down changes everything Marv, I'm tooled up and ready for the call."

Marvin stared at Erick," No other way you understand, you can't make a deal that they will stick to, extermination is the only action required and needed.

"Agreed Marvin," said Erick.

"Ok I feel better now I've got it off my chest what I intend to do," he took a bunch of half-eaten grapes out of his pocket and placed them down on the bedside table, "I brought you some Californian grapes but while I was waiting in the traffic, I tried a few, "Err............... there is just one more thing."

Erick looked at the half crushed and eaten grapes, "Just a hole in the leg by the way, I have to let it bleed and heal up on its own crutches for a few weeks."

"Yeah, yeah, they plug it and pull the plug out a little every day, painful though eh?"

"What about the sacrificial goats post?" asked Cal.

"Yeah, where do you think?"

Erick pointed to the room they were in, "We're not going anywhere Marv, they must know that, and no guards, easy peasy really."

"The first salvo I think Marv, then you can take them one by one as they stick their heads out of the trench." said Cal.

Marvin grinned, "You had my plan ready in your minds?"

"Next logical step Marvelous," said Cal, "And no one will be coming out of this room, just us two, clear?"

"Vest's?"

Cal smiled and kicked a parcel under Erick's bed, "Dragon skin number ones and extra ammo if needed.

"My God Caledonia, you are, well..................... ready, yes?"

"Best ring Dexter as well Marv, keep him in the loop, we have people crossing paths now and we don't want a blue-on-blue accident," said Cal.

"A very good point, I'll ring him later, any idea where Augusta is?"

"Yes, Washington following the press corps and seeing that the President is well represented."

"And you Mother Cal?"

"The UK, finding faces, they have another lead back to the city again, the old man would be so mad at those rich armhole's buying power again."

"A name?"

"Not yet, leave that to them Marv, you know what Dexter's like, keep out of his way."

"So, she'll pull their castle down around their ears then?"

"Oh yes."

Marvin smiled as he opened the door, "I'll see you soon then people, if the links are here Cal, let me know please, two birds with one stone right now would be good."

"Agreed Marvelous, thanks for rescuing us by the way and saving our lives."

Marvin nodded and was gone in the same movement.

"Do you want some warm grapes Cal?" asked Erick.

She stared at the window before answering him, "No thanks and it's time to saddle up I think, they would have seen movement, so I think it will be soon."

Erick swallowed hard as he thought about what was going to happen, "Will this shit ever end Cal? It's been the lifetime of our children for God's sake?"

"Yes, and we're the ones who are going to end it, yes?"

"Yes boss, back in the game regardless of anything else Cal, she would have called us wimps you know."

"And we can't run and hide big lad we have to stay and fight, so let's just get that into our heads."

"Recalling friends Cal to help in some way?"

Cal shook her head, "Just you and me big lad, just like old times."

# CHAPTER 62 ... Whitehall ... London ... Top Floor ... London

Tolly pressed the intercom, "Tea and yaba biscuits Jane, I need to conference."

"I'll put the kettle on, a shooting in Vegas though, on CBS channel 3, just come through from the States, oh and Theo wants a word when you get time, he has a big breakthrough he needs to talk to you about before releasing it to the public."

"Anyone we know in Las Vegas?"

"Your parents Tolly, don't be shocked, I think they're ok after all the headlines coming from the press."

I'll ring Gussy and find out the facts Jane, you put the kettle on."

He pressed the tv remote then picked up his phone, but it rang in his hand, "Hello!"

"Tolly!" said George "Ericks took a hit, and your mother is in trouble, they're holed up in a Las Vegas hospital, victims waiting to be put down, I ask to be sent immediately!"

The tv screen flashed as it came on live with the latest shootings coming from Las Vegas, Tolly was silent as he watched the review of the killings and the four-vehicle involvement.

"Are you still there Tolly, we need action and now!"

Tolly watched in silence......................................." George, who are the people doing all the shooting, both cars in a ditch and the shooters have gone but they didn't kill my parents, why leave a job half done, what's happening here?"

"My God you are calm son, I think that Marvin is in onto something over there, we need to ask questions."

"Got you George, ok, pack a bag and head for the airport, do you have a team available to back you?"

"Just Lord Lucan, the others are far too inexperienced for this one."

Tolly thought about the team required ............" Ok, take wives, a break from training, gamblers taking the sights, tell Uncle Rufus to be silent please."

"But follow and observe, yes?"

"Observation at this stage Uncle, mum will have this in hand I would have thought, best keep out of her way, she'll be raging after all this."

"But they're alone Tolly?"

"Would you want to enter her bear cave Uncle?"

"But they have lots of guns Tolly."

"Just get going Uncle, I'll talk to her and get her plan and Uncle Marvin's for that matter."

He cut him off just as Jane came in with the tea and biscuits, "Action started then?"

"Yes, daddy took a hit but he's ok, mum has obviously gone into defense mode so they had better not try her patience or there will be an embarrassing bloodbath."

"A talk with your grandmother would be good Tolls?"

"Uncle Marvin first I think, then Grandpa Dexter, he'll have a handle on this."

"Is the overall plan to make splashes though, you know to arouse public debate and criticism of leaders?"

Tolly looked at her for a while as she poured the tea into the China cups, he looked at his Great Grandmothers expensive China tea set as Jane blobbed the milk and the one sugar lump into each, she put the tea spoon onto the immaculate China saucer and passed them to him in silence, he imagined her being there, (Gun Tolly, this is not time to be dithering, pick up your feet and lets be gone)." His Nana whispered in his head.

"She would have been out of the blocks wouldn't she Jane?"

"Give her some credit Tolly, she was a thinker and a planner, that's something we don't have, people around us are making decisions on their own without consultations to the wider plan, perhaps a chat with Jimmy for clarifications?"

"But Mum and Dad are in danger?"

"Not when she's in the mood Tolly, come on, think it through."

He stared into her eyes and smiled, "You're my secret weapon, underestimated most of the time, but not by me woman, not by me, pure talent on legs."

"Sexy legs Tolly you forgot the missing word."

"Sorry Jane, a slow brain day, ok, Georges is on route, Marvin is obviously up to something that's going to end in a lot of people dead, the American President will obviously have to make a comment at some stage, so what information do we pass on to him?"

"The Dexter's have had long enough Tolls, perhaps time to hear the results and take action here in the UK?"

"The Prime Minister though Jane?"

"Could be in on it all, think about it, is this Imperialist interference from afar to destroy the Presidents plans at source?"

He turned in his swivel chair to stare at the painting of King Charles on the wall, "He doesn't like the idea you know; would he take it too far and plan with his close friends to obstruct the Anglo-Saxon nations?"

"The will of the people Tolly, he needs to hear the will of the people."

He turned back to her and smiled, "What a great idea Jane, genius in fact!"

"What is? What!"

He picked up his phone again and punched in the palace number, "Yes, Whitehall 100 I need a consultation with HRM, yes quickly, cancel all previous meetings please, we have major problems, I need direction, yes withing the hour!", he placed the phone down and smiled at her.

"What Tolly, what are you doing?"

"Seeking the wisdom of Kings!"

She looked at him over the rim of her teacup as she thought about what he was doing, he smiled to her as she caught up with his plan, "Very risky."

"His Mother would have been up to speed and my Great Grandmother would have laid it all out for her, the yes or no decision waiting to be ticked."

She flicked the rim of the teacup, the ting sound echoed as Tolly smiled.

"How am I doing Nana?" said Tolly.

Jane tinged again as he started to laugh, "She was always so very proud of you Tolly, her lead man, her soldier, her knight ready for her fight, perhaps the Americans are wrong you know?"

"Na, Jimmy's right, things have to change or the whole damn thing will fall apart, he listened very closely to Grandpop, and he was always right, Jimmy is the brains of that family, in fact I should have pushed it more here in the UK, now we're just going to be on catch up, same as normal."

"It could fail?"

"Not with the backing of all the Anglo Saxon Nations it won't, so that's what we need, it might frighten Asia though I need to give that some thought, anyway, perhaps we can pull Australia into the trading group as a sweetener to the British establishment, they'll all feel left out with America uniting?"

"But the Chinese Tolly, we could talk to Miami to set the mood over in the south pacific, confuse and deflect perhaps?"

"And talk to Grandpa Dexter? He'll have an opinion on them of course," He smiled at her again, "Right as per usual, I need to talk to the Hoots Mon, let's hope Grandma is in a good mood."

He pressed his intercom for the garage on the ground floor, "Dennis, a full team please I'm going out."

"Where too boss?"

"The Palace and Jane's coming along as a witness."

"Trouble boss?"

"No just a clear the airtime and a touch of reality."

"For whom?"

Tolly listened to Dennis as if he were a stranger, "You're right Dennis I do need a bit of reality as well, thanks for that!"

"I didn't say anything."

"Away in ten please," he cut him off and stared at Jane, "What's my motivation in all this Jane?"

"Your father has just been shot and nearly killed your mother is raging and will cause a blood bath if we don't do something and fast, the killing has started and he needs to jump off the fence this way or that, it doesn't matter we just all need to know, that's it!"

"Because I'm backing Jimmy, yes?"

"Yes, you are babe!"

He looked into her eyes, "And what else have you to say Jane?"

"You've been paying attention Mr Trueblood, 13 weeks and progressing nice."

He stood up and shouted out, "Wow! I thought you were ill."

"Well first stages, mum wants us to call the third child after her."

"And if it's a boy?"

"Well Buzz or something, I don't know."

He winked at her with an agreement, "I like Buzz, a good name?"

"Oh, do me a favor?" she answered in her natural cockney accent.

He picked her up out of the chair and hugged her hard, "I'm speechless woman."

"We need to go Tolly, is that reality enough for you?"

"But what if he admits it, then what?"

"You have to tell your grandfather that we have problem, and it needs his special skills."

"Historic succession changes of the Monarchy?"

"He gets the elbow!"

"We can't give him the boot? no, no, too far down the road Jane, far too far down that long road, Dexter will have to come up with something and fast."

"Attend Prime Ministers question time and ask what the government wants in future relations with the USA, or the US Continent as it will be?"

Tolly smiled at her, "And you, just a council kid out of the East end of this dirty old city, it's not really our business is it, Jane?"

"Nope, but ask anyway, he can't be playing politics behind everyone's backs, it's not in the Government and the Crowns deal, is it?"

"And of course, if this happens then the new continent will have the biggest grain farms and beef farms on the planet, it's a monopoly Jane, that's what's happening."

"Not if we have an input right from the start, the world will be looking at us to make the deal, get it posh boy?"

"So, he's the unelected speaker of the world then?"

"That's what Kings do Tolly, right?"

"Very pushy Jane."

"That's your job boss, give him reality, we have to deal with this monster when it's fully working, get it?"

"And we'll be little outsiders as well, eh?"

"Weren't we always the little islanders causing all the trouble?"

He grinned, "Yes, but we're everywhere?"

"Exactly Tolls, Anglo Saxon nations are everywhere, we are the real majority so tell him to speak up and make the big statement for the world, agreed?"

"Smart arse!" he grinned at her.

She stuck her tongue out at him then thumbed to the door to get going.

His mobile phone started buzzing so he picked it up, "Yes Dennis so where is he?"

"He's out of the palace boss and looking to ride out in the park, the security people are buzzing round him, what do you want me to do?"

"Stay on site and tell the King that I would like to accompany him on his morning trot out, I'll be there in ten if I rush."

"Ok boss, I'll pass it on."

Tolly cut him off and looked into her eyes, "Too public Jane?"

"Na, a good time to yabba, you can do this Tolly, you just have to bring him round, right?"

"Yeah, right!"

She pointed to his working wardrobe in the corner of his office and his riding gear, she watched him change into jodhpurs and jacket as she thought about it all.

"Nana would like it this way you know, out there taking exercise as you work for the crown?"

He grinned as he tied his tartan tie then grabbed his riding hat, "I'm still behind Jane, she would have been there by now."

"This is how she did her work though Tolls, horses and yabba, remember?"

He smiled as he thought about the rides with the Queen and the Royals in the great park at Windsor.

Jane was on the phone, "Change of plan Billy, he needs to get to Windsor great park and get someone to saddle up Benbow for him please, he's conferencing on horseback today."

Billy was giggling on the other end of the line as she cut him off, "Ok, clear on what we want and need Tolls?"

"Do you want to ride out?"

Her face betrayed her horror, "Certainly not, I'm a city girl remember? Just don't piss about and make the deal, right?"

"Clear Ma'am!"

She pushed him out of the door and returned to her desk.

# CHAPTER 63 ... Les Grandiose Casino ... Las Vegas ... Nevada ...

Eden looked for the Indian man at the entrance of the casino, he tooted the horn of the limo to get people out of his way so he could park in the casino parking slot, people milled around staring at the long dark car and waited for the VIP to step out.

A man in a sharp suit stood in front of him and smiled, "Did Gurung send you guy?"

Eden focused on the man, he didn't look like an Indian, more the stockbroker on vacation, Eden buzzed the window down and was hit by the Nevada heat, "You don't look like an Indian boyo?"

"What's a boyo man?"

"Well not you for a start."

Rudy looked for the scald on the man's arm and smiled when he saw it as he got out and shook his hand, "So branded eh?"

Eden side glanced at his own arm then realized what he was being asked, "You have to earn one of these boy, so the first job is to contact and support friends in need, clear?

Rudy shook his head, Eden pointed to the car for him to get in.

Rudy watched every move this man made to try to understand who and what he was.

"So, a haircut and some cloths and you become a local, yes?"

Eden put his foot down and headed south out of the city.

"It seemed the right thing to do, Gurung gave be a grub stake, so I changed, the right thing to do?"

"Oh yes boy the right thing to do, so the job in hand?"

"So quickly?"

Eden turned to him, "They picked me up off the street, I was a beggar, believe that?"

Rudy nodded, "But a valued beggar?"

"History my friend, my military background made waves when I quit, too valuable to leave on the street you see, I suspect that you're the same, yes?"

"Not really, I ain't military in any way man."

"A native though, yes?"

"Well yeah, but not from around here, Blackfoot from up north."

Eden grinned at him, "Well I'm taking you to meet another native, now he's a big boss in Canada, I'll let him explain, your job is to help in any way you can."

"But I also have a plan Mr?"

"Call me Eden, Welsh you see."

"Welsh?"

"Yeah, from Wales."

"Wales?"

"West of England, Wales."

"English then?"

Eden smiled at him, "Geography not a strong subject at school then?"

"Reservation schools' man, the tribe is poor, we can't pay for fancy teachers."

"Ok, just so you don't upset folks, especially the Jocks!"

"Jocks?"

"Ok, we are all different tribes, me Welsh, the English heartland and Scottish northern, across the Irish sea to the west is Ireland, both north and south, very important to understand differences, get it?"

"Trying man."

"You have to find him and his wife, they're in hospital, he was shot and now he needs help, his name is Erick, be respectful he's a Canadian Indian."

"I'm cool with that man."

Eden pulled into the hospital yard and parked up "Erick Trueblood, ward 231, present yourself and ask for further instructions."

"I ain't army man!"

"No one thinks you are boy, just follow and listen to instructions, they know more about you than you think, follow and be of use, clear?"

"Err...........clear boss?"

"No that's Erick, he's your boss."

Eden watched him climb out and walk into the medical Centre, he smiled and drove off.

# CHAPTER 64 ... University Medical Centre ... South Nevada

The medical students came into Ericks room and were asking questions about pain levels from the gunshot wound, "So how did it feel to get shot Sir?" asked one of the white coated junior Doctors.

"More shock than pain I suppose, I didn't feel it for quite a while until the blood started to drip, and once I looked at the blood the pain hit me, strange, eh?"

The door moved again as another person came in and joined them.

Cal immediately cornered him with a gun to his head, "And you are?"

"Rudy, err............. Gurung sent me to help you guys in any way I could."

All eyes watched Cal as she replaced the heckler back in her under arm sling.

"I'm his security folks, this was an assassination attempt, they won't get a second shot at him, understand?" said Cal to the shocked faces.

"Any more questions people?" asked Erick, "As you can see, we're all a bit tense as you can imagine after being shot."

The medical students shuffled out one by one in numbed silence as Rudy stood and waited for instructions, he watched Cal as she readjusted her weapons and saw the familiar brand on his right arm, Erick pointed to his own and waited for silence.

"Understand the connections here Rudy?"

"Err.........yeah, I just don't know what he wanted with me, I ain't mussel man, I'm just an Indian trying to dry out."

"The first day is the hardest, after today it's easy, but you have to remember, you are just that one drink away from being that drunken bum again, one drink and you're back in that stinking cell with all the rest."

"Easy on him Erick," said Cal "He's new to all this, welcome lad, so Gurung head hunted you, so he must have seen something of value in you, give your self-credit for impressing him, after all Gurkhas are not easily impressed."

"I don't understand what he is, what is he anyway?"

"A loyal friend willing to die for you and all his other friends, simple really don't you think?"

Rudy nodded as he tried to understand these people.

"What tribe are you, Son?" asked Erick.

"Blackfoot, Northern Nevada."

"Not your range though, is it?"

"We live about 40 miles east of here the tribe invested in one of the casinos and got ripped off, I'm here to find work and work them out for the revenge."

"How much?"

"Too much for us to admit to, and too much to go home without."

"So that's the drinking then, end of the road, eh?"

"Just about, the next was a shoot em up at all costs situations."

"Suicide eh, not yet son not yet."

"That's what Gurung said, not yet, when I told him my story and you sir?"

"This is my Wife Caledonia, and my name is Erick Trueblood, yes, Indian too, Inuit from the icy north."

"But she's a ............"

"White woman, yes she's a headhunter from the north Atlantic, dangerous women up there so beware!"

Rudy stared at her, she opened her coat to reveal the twin hecklers and ammo pouches.

"Shit guy!"

"They will sonny!" said Cal.

"My private protection and she's very good Rudy, if there's any shooting happening just drop to the floor and let her do her thing, she will wipe them away, fools die, don't you think?"

"Yeah, any fool trying it on with her sir I can see that."

"So, Erick," said Cal, "Why send him to us, what has he in mind do you think."

Erick stared at the new man, "He has a story we can use Cal, Gurung is smart."

"Hey, I just want our money back, that's it!"

"And he's our way in then?" Said Cal.

"She speaks like the Queen of England."

"Related, can't you tell." grinned Erick.

Rudy's eyes widened as he stared at Caledonia.

"So which casino are we talking about Rudy?" asked Erick.

"The Golden Spur on the main drag, the Dugan brothers, mean sons of bitches and they have connections."

"French then?" asked Cal.

"Err.............. I don't think so, why?"

"Because we might have another way in if they are."

"Well, I never heard them speak French, I think they're American from the west coast."

"Not south like Carolina or some place?" asked Cal.

"I don't know Maim."

She looked at Erick, he smiled, "We'll check that one out Cal, perhaps helpful."

"I don't get it." said Rudy.

"So how did the rip off go then?" asked Erick.

"Err.............we wanted to invest here as well other places we have casino's all-over west Texas and southern Nevada."

"But here you were swindled."

"They have muscle, and they use it against those without back up from New York."

"Ah, the picture clears, New York Cal."

"We have Lord Longmore on route apparently big boy, perhaps a little entertainment for him?"

"Yes, entertainment," he turned back to Rudy, "So, would you be happy with your money back or do you still want an input in this place fully knowing the risks involved?"

Rudy stared from face to face as they looked at him making his decision, he didn't know what to say to them.

"I like the idea Erick and what's more he'll like this place, I'm sure."

"So that's the plan then Cal, Rudy here tells his story to Lord Longmore and askes for investment, Rufus will love that, and I assume that the gorilla will be with him and back him up if there's any drama."

"Oh yes, he'll love all that, mixing with gangsters, well he is one I suppose."

Erick started laughing, "Yep, he'll love all that, so clear on the plan now Rudy?"

"Err.............no not at all clear, so who's the gorilla and who's Lord who ever?"

Cal was now on the phone as she ignored his question, "Eden, yes it's me, come back and pick up Rudy, then take him and collect Lord Longmore and co from the airport, Rudy has a story and a problem, he'll ask if Rufus can help in any way, we like that idea understood?"

Eden was laughing on the other end of the line, "And the gorilla is his backup then?"

"Well obviously Eden, hey! And do not offer your services by the way, George will work out the plan I think, we have other fish to fry so warm up the little girl, we're sick of hospital life, London I think, we'll be along when we've had a chat with Marvelous."

"Yes, Ma'am on my way over."

She closed the call and watched Rudy's face and his total confusion, "Now listen up Rudy, these people are premier league players, follow instructions to the letter and learn your new trade."

"But I don't."

"You will, look and learn, watch and do as they do."

"What tribe are they?"

Erick burst out laughing again.

Cal looked at him, "The London cockney tribe, you might need some translation tips so listen up and ask questions when you get the chance, clear?"

Rudy shook his head as he stared, his eye bulged in total confusion, "But why a gorilla and who's George?"

"Just open your eyes son when you meet them, best not call him that though."

"Who?"

Cal couldn't help laughing and Erick joined in, Rudy looked on confused.

A toot from a car horn outside and Erick pointed to the doors, "And be careful, don't get shot, it bloody hurts!" said Erick.

Rudy walked out in a daze as he thought about these mad people.

# CHAPTER 65 ... McCarran International Airport ... Las Vegas ... Nevada

Eden welcomed Rudy with a grin, then drove him off at speed, "Ok, this is your ride, can you drive this motor?"

"Err...........yeah, I suppose, but why where are you going?"

"I'm flying out in about an hour, that's me," he thumbed to the little private jets as they drove past the giant hangar buildings, I have a London pick up to make."

"But I don't know these people."

"You'll soon see who you need to pick up, wave the plaque at everyone and see who turns up, yes?"

Rudy looked at the crown and mace plaque at the side of him, "What the hell is this?"

"Lord Longmore's coat of arms, so be respectful and don't call George a gorilla or you might not have a head, clear?"

"So, who is my boss again?"

"George is your boss, so be respectful, he gets touchy sometimes."

"But who are you again?"

"A Welsh boy, that's all he needs to know."

"So what flight is he on?"

"British Airways."

"What time?"

Eden laughed, "No idea, just keep alert and wait for the word, you are a blue team member, clear?"

"So what team is Gurung in then?"

"Oh, come on man, red team, the same as me, stop here mate!"

Eden jumped out and went to the boot, "Park up in the VIP suite, and look smart, he likes smart people even if he isn't."

"Who does?"

Eden was walking off, his large army bag over his shoulder, he disappeared into the crowd and was gone.

"But what the hell man?"

He thought about his night in the cell and his day in the company of crazy people then he was shocked to see British Airways airplane coming into land and understood that his time to shine was upon him, he tightened his tie in the mirror, grabbed the plaque and walked to the airport arrivals lounge, with the Beatles greatest hits humming over the cool air overhead.

# CHAPTER 66 ... McCarran International Airport ... Customs and Arrivals

"Why does he always have to do this Bren, what is it a bad childhood or something?"

Brenda snuggled into him as they waited at the customs counter, "Now my lucky number is 7, remember, so 7 goes on number 7 slot machine and 7dollars and no more or less."

"Are all Irish like this Bren?"

"Yes, and we come with the emerald-colored blood in our veins, think lucky and you'll be lucky, get it?"

"Must be disappointing though Bren when you lose all the time?"

"I don't lose, I won you didn't I, and look at you, magnificent, a wash and a shave and you could be a Hollywood star out on his vacation."

"Irish charm, eh?"

"Full on big man."

Yoshi walked over to a man in a suit who was waving a plaque and stood in front of him.

The big Japanese man looked down on the sign holding man with the red suntan, he walked over to him and gave him his best smile, the pointed vampire teeth shone in the spotlights.

# CHAPTER 67 ... Arrivals lounge ... McCarran International ... Nevada

Rudy looked at the people coming through the giant arrivals doors he showed them his plaque and hoped for someone to say something, a big oriental man stood in front of him and blocked his view of the people, he tried to look around him but was blocked out.

Suddenly there was a crowd of them looking at him, "Lord Longmore?"

The hairy man now stood and stared at him, "And you are?"

"Err.......... new to the game, Rudy, Gurung sent me."

"What are you, son?"

"Indian, Blackfoot plains."

"Wow! "Said Brenda, "A real Indian, wow, glad to meet you my good man, so are you the driver?"

"Yeah, he said follow your orders Mrs. Longmore?"

"No dear, that's Lady Longmore," she pointed to the Japanese woman walking towards them."

George looked bored, "So where is the little shit Bren?"

A police officer stopped Rudy as he tried to walk off and lead them to his vehicle.

"Some form of identification on you sir?"

Rudy's eyes betrayed his panic, "Err just doing a favor for a friend."

"And the friends name is?"

"Gurung, err.......... Erick and his white wife Calhoun or something."

"Caledonia?"

"Yes, that's her, Caledonia, his wife's from England."

The cop turned to the people, "Yeah, he's real."

"Stop pissing about bollock brain!" said George.

He grabbed hold of Rudy, "And where did you meet Gurung?"

"Err.........police lock up, last night, he gave me a job and here I am."

"Typical!" said George, "So why?"

"To get the Tribes money back from the casinos."

"Oh for........."

Rufus stopped George as he was about to swear, "How much mate?"

"Err......too much not to go back home with."

"Do you see George, Gurung gave us the plan there and then, that boys clever eh?"

"And how the hell are you going to help? We already have one job so shut up and let's be gone."

Rufus tugged on George's shirt, "You take red, and I'll join blue with this bloke, I feel lucky know what I mean?"

"And do what?"

"Get his money back while we're sorting out targets for her, obviously?"

"Her?"

"Yes her, well she must be back in the game if her old man's just took a round from them surely?"

"And you see the way?"

"Yeah, I see the way, so you take the reds and I'll tag along with this boys crew and see what I can find out."

George looked at Brenda for an opinion, she put the imaginary hook in her mouth with her finger and pulled it sideways, "Old Marvelous is a clever man George, he's just given him the hook to start the action, I like it."

George growled as he walked off to the doors and the desert heat.

Rudy rushed in front to open the limo doors and start packing all the cases in the boot.

He stood in front of Rudy as the cases were being loaded, "So where are Erick and Caledonia?"

"Well, they were at the hospital, but they were on the move somewhere else, so I don't know."

"So, your orders were?"

"Pick you guys up and follow orders from Lord Longmore, he said that the Lord would work out the plan and to follow and introduce him to Las Vegas."

Rufus grinned at George, "You see, all planned out so leave this one to me and the Indians."

"And the Japanese Rufus?" said Kiki.

"What a good idea Darling yes, high rollers from out east wanting to gamble responsibly, yes, great, let's go."

George turned to Yoshi, "Do not let the moron out of your sight, red call out if it gets sticky, clear?"

Yoshi nodded then walked off to finish the loading into the giant boot space.

"So, the Welsh?" he stared into Rudy's eyes.

He pointed to the heliport across the road, "One of them went in there, err.... Eden?"

"Why?"

Rudy shrugged to him is silence, not knowing what else to say to the man that was obviously called the gorilla, he watched the hairy man very closely and the burn scar on his right arm, he tried to check them all out for the sign but his was the only one he could see.

George looked at him as he tried not to be too obvious, "You know what that is then son?"

Rudy showed George his tribal scars, "Ceremonies of trust."

"Exactly lad, ceremonies of trust, let's hope Gurung was right about you."

Rudy watched the gorilla's eyes and knew he was a killer.

"You have to earn it son, no other way."

Rudy nodded then walked around to the driver's side and climbed in.

Brenda asked the question with her eyes as she stared at George.

"Yes Bren, he knows what the results of betrayal are I think."

Rudy drove off and into the traffic in silence, Brenda leaned forward and whispered in the driver's ear, "So where are you taking us Rudy?"

"The Grandiose Casino on the main strip, you are all booked in I was told."

She sat back and elbowed George, he watched them in the mirror as George spoke down the phone but didn't understand what they were really saying.

"Yes, I can see for myself, the fannies Aunt, so what's to do?"

"Ok, clear, and Fauntleroy?"

"Ok, will do, so yours then?"

"Ok but it's your fault if is go's westward."

"Look you know what he's like, so be prepared you French git!"

Brenda watched Rudy's eyes as he listened to George, "Confused Mr Indian?"

"Err....... what tribe are you Maim?"

"Me.........Irish............him.......... a cockney geezer."

Rudy looked and he could hear what she was saying but didn't understand one bit of it all, George cut the call and leaned forward, "Take us to the hotel mate, then you're with the nut for the rest of the day, clear?"

Rudy looked at them, they were speaking English, he shook his head.

Brenda pointed to Lord Longmore who was now asleep and dribbling down the side window, she leaned forward and whispered again in his ear, "Listen up son, follow, protect and be ready to hit the floor if he and his mates start shooting, leave the guns to the buns, clear?"

Rudy nodded but really, he just wanted them out from the car and into the Casino.

"Guns to the buns," he mumbled.

# CHAPTER 68 ... Les Grandiose Casino ... Las Vegas

Lord Longmore stepped out of the Limo a different man, he was now wearing a silver jacket and loud Bermuda shorts with golden crocks on his feet.

He wife was dressed as a Japanese woman and so was the big Sumo wrestler Yoshi.

"Ready folks?" he grinned at them.

He walked off, the entourage followed Yoshi carrying most of the luggage.

Brenda hooked up to George and was giggling as they entered the aircon coolness of the casino, George pointed to Rufus for Rudy to follow as he turned away and disappeared in another direction.

As they trudged through the slot machines Rudy spotted Gurung, he was playing on a slot machine.

Rufus ignored him and walked on by Yoshi, however handed him a small leather case then walked off with the rest.

Gurung pulled Rudy over to talk, "Ok with it all mate?"

"Who the hell are these people man?"

Gurung ignored him, "We need you to get into your casino, it is yours, yes?"

"Err......... we own most of it just not the profits."

"And you want that, yes?"

"Yeah, we want it or our money back."

"Good, follow me then."

"But I was told to follow the Lord guy."

"We'll meet him later, now probs."

The familiar Welsh man drove them away down the strip to the Golden Spur casino, Jonesy was sitting up front and handed Rudy the side cutters.

"What for?"

"Cut the tag off boy, they can follow us all electronically get it."

He noticed that Gurungs ankle tag had gone, the Gurkha smiled at him then took the cutters from Jonesy and cut the tag off Rudy's leg.

The car came to a halt then Gurung stepped out with the tag.

Rudy looked into the mirror at the driver.

"He's going to find a stray dog and attach the tag to it, so at least they know where we are eh?"

Rudy started laughing at their idea, then suddenly Gurung returned and got back into the car.

Jonesy looked at him in silence, "I found a cat, that'll do, won't it?"

"And break the night curfew, you wanker."

"Ah!"

Rudy was still laughing at the idea and them, "This is Vegas, night is day and day is night." Said Rudy.

"See," said Gurung, he thumbed to Rudy.

Jonesy tutted and turned back to the windscreen.

"Today, you're our front man, you can get in, then we'll sort out the situation, understood?" said Gurung, "It's just not fair, is it?"

"What?" asked Rudy.

"Bullying! Not fare, so that's plan A, then tomorrow we have plan B rolling.

Rudy looked at Glen in the mirror and received the pearly white grin in return.

Rudy watched Gurung open the leather case, he took out a long-curved knife and placed the cold blade on his forehead.

Rudy stared in silence and Gurung silently went through his personal habit of welcoming to the Goddess of war.

"What the hell?" said Rudy.

"Shush mate!" said Jonesy, "He's welcoming the lady of the hour so shut up."

Gurung licked the blade before sharpening the edge with a little sharpening stick then nicked his thumb to draw blood before returning her to the sheath, he breathed out slowly then noticed Rudy looking at him.

Gurung smiled at him, "Sorry, the Goddess Khukuri is a vicious woman and lusts blood, we have to be careful my friend."

Rudy continued to stare at the Gurkha.

"He's the lead out man, so he's first through the door, clear?" said Jonesy.

Rudy nodded as Gurung slid the sheath into his inside pocket.

"And what do I say to these people?"

"Err.................my money or your head on that table, which is it?"

"That's a bit direct mate," said Gurung.

"Ok, eloquence it up a bit if you like, but that's the message, yes?"

"Well yeah, that's the message."

"Are you going to kill them?" asked Rudy.

"Deaf ears mate," said Jonesy.

Gurung nodded.

"I bit violent though?" said Rudy,

"Just ask the question, no answer or they get funny, and we kill them all."

"Shit," said Rudy.'

"Do you have another way then Indian? We are always open to new ideas, "said Jonesy, he waited for Rudy to say something, but nothing came back.

"Leave it to the headhunter and for God's sake do not get in between him and the targets, stand away and you might not get splashed.

"Splashed?"

"Claret mate, understood? oh by the way, Marvelous wants you to be the next owner of this casino, ok with that?"

Rudy narrowed his eyes as he looked at the back of Jonesy's head, "What is this, really?"

"We're starting a war mate, and you're the first shot so to speak."

"With his Mafia buddies?"

"Spot on that man, then we see where the wood worms come out of all the timber mate."

"And you kill them?"

"You see, the plan's easy, eh?"

"Shit!" said Rudy "And then they come and kill me?"

"They try son," said Jonesy, "That's when the big guns arrive and clear them all out, bing bang bosh, dust to dust ashes to ashes."

"How many?"

Gurung shrugged, "Best to clear all the weeds before re-planting don't you think?"

"Shit! that's a plan?"

"Do you have a better one mate? Now's the time if you have."

Rudy shook his head at the mad men.

Jonesy locked eyes with him, "Now if you've lied to us about numbers or something then you are in deep do be do, my advice is to say nothing and just get us into that office for the new negotiations involving more Tribal investments, after all you're the money man aren't you, give it your best impression of wanting to help their cause, get it?"

"How much am I investing?"

"You have 150 million from the land buy back scheme from the Government and it's burning a hole in your tribal councils' pockets."

"But?"

"You want to be the new owner, get it?"

"And they'll want our money?"

"Bang on that man!"

"The hook?"

"The barbed hook!" said Jonesy.

"But you want their signature on this," Gurung pulled out a land deed sale document, they sign it and we the witnesses sign it, they agree to receive the money and hand over the casino to your nation, then they can go on living, failure and they get buried in shallow sandy graves.

"You're asking a lot from me here?" said Rudy nervously.

"Do you have the balls son, that's all we're asking, well do you punk?" said Jonesy.

Rudy grinned at then and took hold of the document, "They've ignored this before, we have one of these already!"

"Not today mate, signature or claret, simple as."

"But they have muscle on site though? You do know that right?"

"So do we son and we're ready, get it?"

"So why are you helping me and my little Nation?"

"We're putting the first wedge into their system Rudy," said Gurung, "Bullying gangsters, drug dealing scum are on the road my friend you are just the first to start."

"But my people will be in the front and center of all this?"

"And would they back down Rudy, and let the white man get away with all this.................again!"

Rudy gulped with emotion, "No............we ...............kill them all!"

"You know it makes sense mate!" said Jonesy, he flicked his phone and spoke into it.

"Yes, boss agreed, we're on route, plan A is rolling, yes call in Glen please, we need that lift, we'll meet you on sight, Oh, so how do we exit?" he listened to the new instructions as they were given to him, "Ok and Mack will follow on then? Ok Marv will do, and if it goes tits up?" Ok, nearly there, is he ready?"

Jonesy nodded to Gurung, "Exit change, we wait for the plods and this wanker."

Glen grinned at him, "I bring in the cops, and you boys claim self-defense, "he pulled out a sheet paper, "Your lines captain and we need your words to be exact, clear?"

"Oh bollocks, I hate acting."

Gurung giggled in the back seat, "Unless there's a woman involved?"

Jonesy studied his lines with his middle finger insult, facing Gurung.

"The bastard FBI?"

Glen laughed, "That's Marvelous for you, more troops arriving, what can I say, I'm not the planner lads, and you give me the excuse, get it captain?"

"Why don't you ask him to do this?"

Glen thumbed to Gurung who was now fondling the leather case in his hand, Jonesy nodded his understanding of the Gurkha and his primary weapon.

"But who's winding him in when it's all kicked off bollock brain. This could end up being a claret bath house, get me?"

"Mack will be there in the end, or so he tells me anyway."

"Tight timings again though, are we sure it won't get confusing?"

"That's me, I'm the cop on site, understood boyos?

"Oh bollocks, always complicated." snarled Jonesy, he glanced at Gurung on the back seat who now had his eye shut and mumbling something, "Oh bollocks here we go!"

Rudy stared again at the mad men as he watched their jaws tighten with determined action in their heads and blood.

"Shit man!" Rudy felt like the mouse in the trap waiting for the bar to snap his neck.

Gurung pulled out the cardboard box from under the seat and passed Jonesy the machine gun and loaded clips.

"Prepare for war and you will have peace," said Gurung, "And a failure of the peace means revenge!"

Gurung passed him a plastic bag, he read the tag, US Marine body armor.

"Insurance Rudy, we need you alive mate, underneath all your clothing please."

Rudy's hands were now shaking as he took off his jacket and shirt, Gurung helped him by passing him the protection vest and holding his jacket, he smiled at him.

"I'm not ready for all this sir."

"Well, that's a shame because we are, so prepare to be part of the plan," said Gurung, "And always remember, if the shooting starts, you drop to the floor and you won't get hit, with him it's always quantity and not quality.

Rudy looked at him confused, Gurung nodded to Jonesy who was still studying his script.

# CHAPTER 69 ... Windsor Great Park ... The gallop

King Charles watched Tolly as he galloped up to him and the horse stopped snorting and breathing.

"That old nag needs s rest Tolly?"

"Na Benbow is as fit as a fiddle, he's just a bit fat."

The King looked at him as he turned the horse to take a look at Toll's mount, "I heard a story a long time ago about a horse that killed her ex-husband."

"Nana?"

"Yes, your great grandmother, true, was it?"

"Oh yes, Satan was his name, an old gelding from the blues a Royals, he was murder on legs, all the bad habits of a spoilt brat!" laughed Tolly.

"Mummy liked him and didn't believe it was true you know."

"He stamped him into a mulch on the barn floor, there's still a stain there in fact."

The King burst out laughing at his casual talk about a murderous horse, they trotted off without talking for a while then the king turned to him, "So to what do I owe this special occasion Mr DGI?"

"A little conference Your Majesty, Grandpa and co have the grumps with you if the rumors are right in what I hear."

King Charles started laughing again, "Yes the right hump apparently, I'll lose some trust I think, and you have an opinion Tolly?"

"So, the Kings council is dead then sir?"

"Oh no, just lacking two members, returning to the high seas perhaps."

"And you realize what will happen sir?"

The King pulled up his horse, "Now look here Mr DGI, I realize your importance to the crown but some things I will not give in easily, one of them is Canada, no way, understood?"

Tolly grinned, "I wonder what she would have said to all that?"

Charles started laughing again, "She would have shot me I think?"

"Never sire, never!"

"Yes, but your grandfather promised to execute me did you know that?"

"Na, just him showing off, besides grandma would have shot him first, he does get excited sometimes, forgive his stupidity please sir!"

"Forgiven already Tolly, I've told them as much, perhaps I took wrong advice I think, I should have talked more about it all, still the die is cast now I think?"

Tolly smiled at him then started his horse off into to a walk, the King followed.

"So!" shouted Charles, "What's this all about then?"

"Err............your new positioning sir, the speaker for the world, the killer lines and the hard questions put to the new systems."

"I don't get what you're saying Tolly, explain please."

"We are now not used by them sir, I closed it all down as you requested, my mother is now out and retired along with my father who is now going back into politics back in Canada, he likes the new plan by the way."

"But he and the American are staying in the council, right?"

Tolly grinned, "So, do you get the need now sir?"

"Oh, I get the need all right, what I don't get is your last statement, so what is it you want me to do now?"

"Speak up for the system that's lasted the longest, ours, sir!"

"But isn't Monarchy against all that is recognized as democratic?"

"Not in the UK, here it works, here it works well, no communist uprising and no monopolies taking over, our Monarch stops all that dead right?"

"Do I, so when is that?"

"The future sir."

"What are you talking about Tolly?"

"We want you to speak out for us and the Commonwealth of Nations sir, we want you to be our voice of common sense and straight talking against the big economies of the east and now the America's will buy and sell us, after all they are creating a monopoly, correct?""

"To be the referee?"

"Exactly sir, the ref with his pea whistle saying what's right and what's wrong."

"But why Tolly?"

"Because there is no one else sir, you are the last survivor of an ancient state, the Monarchy that's changed the world, your people gave us our state our history and our future."

"But I thought that I was blocking the new uprising of democracy Tolly, some say I am too old an institution to survive, the old and greedy way?"

"Wrong sir, you and your family are our future, we need our history to continue not like the Russians who murdered millions, and the extermination of the Tsars."

Charles pulled up the horse again, "And speak to the world in a political speech, do you understand what you are asking me to do Tolly?"

"Yes Sire, I'm asking you to jump into the political ring and give us reality."

"And if I fail as an un-elected piece of ancient trash, then what?"

"Oh, you will be elected sir, that's the first stage in fact."

"What the hell are you saying here Tolly?"

"We have new systems coming online sir and we want to bring you into the world with a National then a European vote to be the chairman of the table of Nations, you already represent the commonwealth so why not other Nations?"

"Not right Tolly, advice from my ancestors were to always keep out of the cock fight, its degrading and deadly for the line of succession."

"I disagree sir, so much so that I have already started your progression to a parliamentary seat in the house of Lords to speak for the Nation."

"On what, the gardeners say so?"

"No sir, the vote of the Nation, 70 million people will take a vote for you to be our spokesperson and our representative here in Europe."

"Impossible!"

"Not so sir, we now have the means and the technology to achieve this in one vote within one hour of voters pressing the apps on their phones."

"And a no vote Tolly?"

"Well....... you become a gentleman farmer sir and retire to the country in peace and quiet."

"So....in or out then?"

"Yes, your Majesty in our out of the public eye, a real job at last."

"Hereditary?"

"No sir, the democratic choice of millions based on achievements or the public love of one respected and trusted person."

"So, an actor could do my job in the end then?"

"But you already are your Majesty?"

The King burst out laughing at him, "And you see this working then Mr DGI?"

"A regulator for madness your Majesty, the very same as normal!"

The King galloped off as the clumps of earth splattered the path from the horses' hooves, Tolly galloped after him to get his reaction and not give him a break in discussing the options.

"So?" shouted Tolly.

"No!" shouted the King.

"Dexter's option sir?"

The King was laughing again, "Isn't this bullying?"

"A three-letter word begging with Y sir, no other option on the table!"

"And you will protect and serve as normal?"

"Always Sire, you know that!"

"And the army?"

"Waiting for the decision at last."

"So, you've spoken to others about your plan?"

"Not my plan your Majesty."

The King pulled up again and waited for him to catch up as he stared, "So who's plan was this?"

Tolly grinned in silence.

"An old man's plan, made many years ago, correct, and the next logical step, right?"

Tolly nodded and grinned

"Hereditary entrapment?"

"Yes sir!"

Charles waited to come closer then slapped Tolly's hand in agreement, "No other way I suppose?"

"None your Majesty."

"Ok, I'm interested, so let's see how the voting goes first eh?"

"You have doubts sir?"

King Charles turned to him again, "And you don't?"

"None, you are loved by millions, but possibly not so much by my grandparents if they hear the whispers so far your Majesty."

"I think that Colonel Dexter needs a vacation, don't you?"

"Yes, sir, agreed then!"

"So, you followed the disagreements from the palace then Mr DGI?"

"It's what I do for a living Sire!"

Charles laughed then kicked off into a gallop again as Benbow and Tolly stood and watched.

"Sunday night live Your Majesty, BBC one, the new world horizon, best to keep an open channel!" Shouted Tolly to the clods of mud flying in the air.

The King waved as he rode off shaking his head in disbelief.

# CHAPTER 70 ... Les Grandiose Casino ... Texas Holdum Table

Yoshi held the tray of chips as Rufus asked the questions, the dealer was staring and answering his stupid questions one by one.

"And this gold one is what?"

"A thousand-dollar chip sir."

"And I can only use it in this casino, correct?"

"Yes, sir we have an agreement with all of the others on the main strip sir, the chips are good everywhere."

A gambler at the table was getting heated up as the big Jap was overshadowing him.

"God dammed slinky eyes, get out of my light man!"

The imperceptible look from Rufus let Yoshi do his thing, he stepped onto the man's toe, Rufus grinned at him as he squeaked.

"25 stone, heavy eh mate?"

"Get off my foot shit head!"

"What's that in pounds Miss?"

"Dammed heavy I would say," said the dealer.

"So, what are the rules again?"

"Well sit-down sir, I'm sure these guys can take you through the systems."

Yoshi received the wink from Rufus and stepped away from the table.

"Well, I like this table, you go and get something to eat Yoshi and bring me a pastie when you've finished, oh and a larger and lime please."

Yoshi placed the tray on the table and walked off in silence, the faces of the gamblers watched the big man walk off.

"Not his sport lads, he's a sumo champion, he got the red card for being too violent, stupid really don't you think?"

"Japanese blubber on legs then man?" said the gambler.

"You can tell him that one when he comes back mate, he likes people to have an opinion, and your name young man?"

"Err.......... Red.......... you?"

"Well, it's Rufus.......... Lord Longmore......Earl of the Isles ......County Sheriff of Wiltshire....... Duchy of Devon and Dartmoor."

"Yeah, yeah, yeah, we get it, you're a smart ass!"

The faces around the table started laughing at him until the immaculate Japanese woman floated over to him and kissed his ear.

"Give me an hour please Darling, I just need to learn how to play this game," she floated away to the restaurant in silence."

The dealer coughed to get them all back to the game, "Ok, minimum bet is 10 dollars Mr Lord, ok with that?"

"That's one of these yellow things, yes?"

"Yep!" she shuffled the deck then started dealing out the cards.

"Only 2 cards, that's at bit stingy isn't it, miss?"

She rolled her eyes and carried on, "Your blind bet sir."

"How much normally?"

"Just the one sir, we don't want you flat broke too early."

He smiled to the other gamblers and threw a handful of the yellow chips onto the table.

"That's a hundred bucks so a double up of 2 hundred dollars continuation bet please gentlemen," said the dealer.

"Shit man, that's hard for us little guys to keep up," said the gambler, others laughed at the crazy Englishman's stupidity.

"Sorry, I just get bored easily, don't mind me, I'll just join in your game, so are you in sir?"

"Shit man!" he threw in his 2 hundred dollars' worth of chips.

The dealer laughed as she dealt out the three flop community cards.

"So, 2 kings, good right?"

The dealer rolled her eyes again, "Silence is best sir, or these guys will skin you alive."

"Surely not, they all look like very nice gentlemen."

The table burst out laughing at him.

"So, is this pot mine now then?"

"No sir, we have two more rounds of betting first so are you still in?"

"Yeah, what's that phrase they use on TV err .... .... all in!"

"So soon sir, are you sure?" asked the dealer.

"Yes, this pot is mine, are you lot out?"

The gamblers scowled at him thinking he was a bluff artist, they tried to work him out most dropped out but one of them continued and challenged his all-in call.

"What you got buddy?" he threw his cards down.

Rufus grinned, "All the same color, hearts, good, eh?"

The gamblers started to laugh at him.

"What?"

"You lose Mr Lord of the realm a 2 and a 3 don't cut it buddy, my ace wins it."

"We still have two other cards to play gentlemen, the turn and the river, remember?" said the dealer woman.

She flipped the cards over one by one as the faces watched the red cards shine in the lighting.

"That's a 7 flush, Mr Lord wins gentlemen."

"Shit, that's two hundred bucks of my money in his pot, Goddammed rip off British shit!"

"A proper mardy arse then?" grinned Rufus.

The man tried to grab him in anger but the large hands of Yoshi lifted him off the floor and slammed him down onto the card table, the chips scattered as the chaos started, punches flashed out and the table was up ended by Rufus, elbows started fights with other tables and the casino descended into total chaos, people grabbed at the loose chips on the floor and scrambled away only to be punched by flying fists of losers, someone's cigar started a fire when vodka was thrown and a table set alight, alarms started winding up as more and more people started fighting, a bottle was tipped over to spread the flames onto the plush carpeting, in seconds the place was in flames and Yoshi pushed away all comers from hurting Rufus, Kiki handed him his lager and lime, he sipped as he watched the mass brawl continue despite the flames growing higher all around them.

"Didn't they have pasties then darling?"

"No Rufty, just pizza and I know that you're not keen on American pizza.

A chair flew over his head and smashed into the mirror behind the bar, Rufus ducked.

"Seven years bad luck I think for that, eh Kiki?"

"No, My Lord, you are the bad luck, they just don't realize it yet."

He smiled at her, "Having fun darling?"

She smiled back, "It reminds me of the last time we were involved in a mass brawl, back in Tokyo, remember?"

"And I fell in love Kiki, that very night, I remember that, fun, eh? So, all right, which way is it out of here?"

She pointed to the fire alarm sign and the direction arrow, the overhead camera moved to his direction and followed his stare, he gave them a wink then walked off, Yoshi was the rear guard against any ongoing punches.

Rufus clapped his hands as they reached the hot desert air, the sound of fire engines and the National guard troop transporters screeching to a halt in front of them, the place becoming full of army uniforms, Rufus linked arms with Kiki and walked off down the strip, "Which one next Darling?"

She thumbed to the Desert Mirage across the road and glittering lights she giggled.

Yoshi followed on in silence following the ongoing plan.

# CHAPTER 71 ... Room 3232 ... Les Grandiose Casino Hotel ... Las Vegas

The black waiter brought in the drinks on a silver platter and placed them down on the center table, George watched him as he stood up.

"Ok Wanker, stop pissing about and give us the latest."

Marvin gave him his best pearly white smile, "Eager then Tarzan?"

"Where is she, knob head?"

The door knocked as Marvin thumbed to the door, "Should I let them in Sir?"

Brenda stood up and pushed him to sit down on the sofa then walked over and opened the suite door to let them in, Caledonia gave her the theatrical kisses to her cheeks as Erick followed her in on his crutches, he let them fall to the floor then flopped onto the sofa next to Marvin."

"It hurts, eh?"

"Shut up!" grumbled Erick.

Cal handed him the drink then swerved the glass away from him and took a sip, "Alcohol, no, no, no Mr Iceman, medication, remember."

"Is this her nursey nurse mode then Erick?" asked Marvin laughing.

"Shut up!" said Erick.

"So!" said George, "What the hell is happening in this town and why?"

"It's a Mafia holiday resort," said Marvin, "And as such is a main target for shall I say the first round of offences, you see Pop said weed kill or they will choke democracy and they are so here we are, any other questions?"

"He has Pops way of speaking bullshit," said Erick.

"He's right though, this is the place, and we've been here before remember?" said Cal.

"Shit!" said Erick.

"So, something similar I thought, yes?" said Marvin.

Erick growled at him as he reached for a drink before Cal could stop him and took a slug of the whisky, "I don't like the risks in this town, why not one of the other gambling towns?"

She snatched it off him and placed it back on the table.

"Well, what the hell are you two doing here anyway, facial recognition err....der!"

"This is the most famous, this is the top floor man, so these are the people we want gone." said Marvin.

"And top politicians will be here as well you know?" said George, "What about them?"

"That's the very point George, "Said Marvin, "We want them to be exposed, just like her last little visit to Vegas, we need headlines splashes all over America."

"But why?" asked Cal.

"It's the old man's plan Cal, the very same as before, embarrass, shame and then get rid of the scum in full public view."

"But who.........................?

Their conversation was drowned out by police sirens wailing down the strip to the far end.

"What the hell's that Marvin?" asked Erick.

"Oh, that's just plan A at a critical stage."

"And?" asked Cal.

"Oh, just new owners taking possession of one of the older casinos."

"Yours?"

"Well, no not really, well, Gurungs idea really, the Blackfoot tribe now have their casino, they might have to give it a bit of a hoover up however."

"Rudy?"

"Yes, nice kid I thought, you?"

"But they'll go for the whole tribe in revenge?" said Erick.

"Hopefully yes." Marvin grinned at him.

"Now that's your plan eh Marvelous?"

"The President wants native involvement changing hearts and all that, they are voters after all."

"Yes, they vote don't they Marvin."

"So, what are we here for then?" asked George.

"Ah.......... plan B tomorrow, we need another little splash."

"Of blood?" asked Cal.

"It gets headlines Caledonia as I said we need world press to grab this one."

"Who?" asked George.

"The police chief, and the mayor, they have a meeting in the morning, we'll disrupt their tea and fancy pants."

"Where?" asked George.

"Town hall, main street that's that end of town," he pointed the other way, "What, no good?"

"Bonkers!" said George.

"Rufus will be doing the research as we speak."

Another police car screeched by as it motored in the other direction.

George thumbed to the police on the street, "Rufus?"

"Yeah...........he's    causing    a    diplomatic    incident, ...........................again."

"Where?"

"Oh, didn't I say?"

"No, you did not Marvelous," said Erick "It's just like listening to the old man Cal, he's a genetic bullshit monster."

"Yeah, and I'm really impressed, well done that man!" said Cal, "So we just what?"

"Kill the police chief Cal and I'll do the rest."

"Which means?"

"I bring in the Feds to sort out corruptions of State and police institutions, historic complaints and bad moves by officials running this little town."

"The press again then."

"Yep, where is Augusta by the way?"

"No!" said Erick, "She is not coming here to this shit hole, no bastard way!"

Cal shushed him before asking, "And she will be the bait then, yes?"

"And you Cal, we want you to be arrested for the Police chiefs murder."

"Shit no!" said Erick.

"Now that's a bit radical Marvelous Marvin?" said Cal.

"Courts Cal, the big high court case to help sell it all to the people."

"Shit!" said Erick.

"They still have the electric chair in this State Marvelous," said George, "They'll execute her, fried bacon on a stool, shaved head, feet in water, power outage all over."

"Shut up George!" shouted Brenda, "You're not helping."

"No, he's right, they'll kill her as quick as possible, bing bang bosh, dead on a slab!" said Erick.

"And we break her out of prison well before that, the people are angry and want justice sorted out, bad guys deserve to be killed, stealing our tax dollars and buying casinos with it all."

"What the hell has he been smoking?" said Erick.

"Revolution Erick, he's talking the French revolution aren't you Marvelous Marv?" grinned Cal.

"Big enough for you yet everyone?"

"Shit, he's gone fucking stark raving bonkers!" said Erick.

"And the death scene end of Marv?" asked Cal.

"Restructure and re-brand the United States of America."

"As?" asked George.

"The democratic revolutionary continent of the America's, the United Continental States of the America's, the UCSA, any questions?"

The room erupted in shouting and screaming, then died down as everyone thought about the consequences of a revolution on the American land mass.

"And you can control a revolution once it starts rolling Marvin?" said Cal.

"We fight for democracy, or it dies in the hands of tyrants."

"So, you're calling all peoples of the continent to come together as one vote, supporting your ideas?"

"If we don't do something fast then this idea will fail out of public boredom and will be lost for another three hundred years when they will come back to our conclusions, it has to be done!"

"How?" asked George.

"Didn't I say?" said Marvin, "I perhaps should have mentioned Theo's new invention."

"What invention Marv?" asked Cal.

He stared at her and ignored her question, "I just have to ask though Cal, can you do this?"

Her eyes watered as she thought about it all.

He watched her eyes, "Hey, no probs, the old man would want me to do it anyway, so I'll be the executioner this time, yes?"

Erick stared in silence at this sudden change and waited for Caledonia's answer.

# CHAPTER 72 ... The Golden Spur Casino ... Main Street Las Vegas

Rudy sat behind the giant table as the brothers stared at him from the other side.

"Just 150 million and you think you can buy this place for that dog shit amount?"

"Oh, I'm not giving you 150 million, that's the investment in infrastructure after you're gone, no, no, you must be confused or something Sandy, after all we have already bought the place off you guys fair and square."

Sandy started laughing at him as Rudy pulled out the paper for them to sign, "Look guys, sign this and all will fall into place, easy right?"

"And if we don't?"

"Well, the alternative is messy, I would advise the former guys."

Sandy jumped up and pulled Rudy across the table with his shirt collar.

Gurung unsheathed his Kukri and chopped off the man's hand, it was still holding onto Rudy's shirt as the blood spurted out over the table, the man screamed out in shock and horror.

Rudy couldn't take his eyes off the horror as gunshots rang out when Jonesy shot whoever was near to him, bangs echoed through the casino, Jonesy killed all the security staff standing around the negotiating table before they realized they were dead.

Gurung chopped Sandy's head off in one sweep then took down the second brother with a chop to the collar bone the man sat is deep shock unable to move with horror and pain.

"Sign the paper sir or the Gurkha will make sure you have no hands as well mate!" said Jonesy, now replacing a fresh clip into the Glock.

Rudy recovered slightly then moved the paper over the table through all the blood for the man to sign.

Gurung lifted the man's hand up to the pen on the table with the kukri, "She seeks your blood, I would do it soon or I'll lose control of her sir."

He turned his face to the little brown man as he listened to the strange voice, "Who the hell are you people, you're all dead, we're protected man!"

"Not very well I think mate," said Jonesy.

Mack suddenly walked into the room and smiled at Gurung, "Well done, so has he signed yet?"

"No boss, he suggests that we are in trouble."

Mack moved around the table and took the man's good hand, then placed the pen between his finger and scribbled out a signature then crossed it with a flourish, "Things that happen in Vegas, stay in Vegas, correct?"

Gurung went to chop the man's head, but Mack stopped him, "No, we need a witness, he'll pass on our best I think, yes?"

Gurungs red face gave away his madness, he chopped down at the man's signature hand and took off all his finger.

The man was screaming in pain and delayed shock.

"Stop!" shouted Mack, "Put the lady away soldier! Her job here is done, clear that man?"

Gurung came back from the world's end with a smile and some deep breaths.

"Ok, lads!" shouted Mack, "You can all come in now!"

The film crew crashed into the room and started filming the blood of the dead men, Mack faced up to the camera, "We have just missed out on seeing a takeover of a casino as the previous owners have signed it away to the new owners."

He moved aside to let the camera man move around the table and continued to speak to the sound man, "An attempt was made

to kill the new owner as negotiations dissolved into gang violence
but friends of the Tribe held their own and fought the Mafia
people, here right in this room, the blood you see is theirs, spilt in
the pursuit of money, another example of the greedy City of Las
Vegas, the Native Indian Tribe of Blackfoot are the proud owners
of the Golden Spur, perhaps a re-brand then sir?"

The BBC sound man placed his microphone under Rudy's
chin.

Mack kicked Rudy's foot under the table to bring him round
from the shocked horror.

"Sir, you have a new name for the casino?"

"Err............. yes.....................err.........the ....... White Buffalo!"

"Lucky is it Sir, the buffalo I mean?"

"Yes Mr?"

"Macclesfield York, from the BBC sir, we just happened to
be here and caught a little of the gun fight, what really happened
here?"

The camera was now in Rudy's face, "Err.... we paid them, we
bought the casino in good faith in cold hard cash, but they
wouldn't stick to the deal and pulled out taking the money and
calling it lost in the system, so I came here to negotiate but they
started shooting."

"So, they attacked you then sir?

"The White Buffalo took them, it's an old legend sir," said
Rudy.

"Is that nature you're talking about then?" asked Mack.

"Yes," Rudy was coming around now from the shock and was
now speaking with ease.

"Yes sir, Mr BBC man, luck has a lot to do with seeing the
White Buffalo, once in a lifetime in fact."

"So, is there a lesson here for our viewers sir?"

"Well yeah, greed can get you killed, be fare, play fare and nature will be generous, cheat and she helps you to your grave!"

Mack turned back to the camera, "Well……. insights into life in sin city, play fare and you will be lucky, cheat and the end is near."

"And cut!" shouted the sound manager, "Nice one Mack, ok folks were up town next, saddle up everyone, the police want to come in and take notes of the action, we didn't see a thing, right?"

"Ok, can it all please team, we're out of here, go!"

Mack patted Rudy's shoulder then was gone with all the other BBC people.

Rudy focused on Gurung as he cleaned the blade of the Kukri then touched his for head with it before replacing it back in its sheath.

Gurung locked eyes with him, Rudy tried to close his mouth as he stared at the Gurkha but failed, he watched the horror in his eyes and mind over again and again.

Glen grinned at them from the outer office, "Ok officers, we need evidence of a crime please, weapons, the lot.

One of the officers recognized Gurung and especially Jonesy, "The Indian and the English guy's Lieutenant, they were involved, yes?"

"Ask em Reynolds check em out."

Gurung and Jonesy were now holding up their carry licenses to show the police officers, but the officer focused on the man's head on the table and the blood everywhere, one of the officers caught the smell and was sick at the door.

"So, what happened here Captain Jones?" shouted Glen.

"A change of ownership, the Indians have got their casino back, real sore mate."

"So, who did the shooting here?"

"Me, self-defense mate, as I said these people wanted us dead," He waved his carry license to the on looking police."

"So, this is in fact an FBI matter, yes?" said Glen, nice and loud.

"Err............ yeah, these blokes are from out of town, unlike our friend here, he's a local, they tried to bully him out of his right to own and tried the old-time gangster fraud, to take his money and tell him to fuck off, not good, eh?"

"So, you are FBI agents then?" asked Glen trying to prompt Jonesy to speed up his statement in front of police witnesses.

"Err............ yeah, the er............... Native council called us in on the fraud, these two brothers caused a lot of pain in this town."

Glen finished his words silently as Jonesy spoke.

"So, we have to close the site I suppose, for the FBI to investigate, yes?" he nodded his head to get Jonesy to finish up his scripted statement.

"Err...........yes, we have to tape the scene off, FBI only people, so clear out please!"

Glen breathed out slowly having heard Jonesy finally say the magic words, "So this is an FBI crime scene, yes?"

"Yes," Said Jonesy, "National security only!"

Glen turned to everyone, "So out people, we're out of here, the FBI have this one covered, out!"

"But lieutenant?" said one of the police officers.

Glen focused on the man, "And you want a slice of this shit?"

"Err, no sir, but?"

"Scrub your report gents this is not of our concern."

Suddenly men in dark suits arrive and started ushering people out of the room and the corridor.

A medical team followed with stretchers and body bags; Glen held the door for them before disappearing with the other police officers.

"So, I forgot to ask at the airport, so who made him into a cop here then?" asked Gurung to no one.

One of the medic's answered him in an English accent, "Marvelous had him seconded from the Royal Marines, a training swap they call it, their bloke is over in the UK doing the London Royal duty thing."

"And you are?" asked Jonesy.

"Oh, do me a favor, shut it!" said the man then started on the work in hand by strapping up the man's hand with his missing fingers, the man was sobbing in pain.

"You guys are fucking dead man, and them Injun's are also fucking dead!"

"He has a plan mate." said Jonesy.

"Yeah, and he's going to tell his mates all about us," said Gurung.

Jonesy gave the man a kick, "Be gone arse hole, I'm bored with your company already!"

He walked out of the room but was sick at the door as he realized he had walked in the blood of his friends.

"Gangster's, eh?" said Gurung.

"Yeah, wankers more like, little kids playing at being big and tough," said Jonesy.

"Yeah, and they now have damp pants!"

"So, Rudy, you need to talk to the general manager now, clear?" said Gurung.

He handed Rudy the phone off the desk, "The sooner the better I think, give him the good news and a pay rise, yes?"

Rudy's pulled his eyes away from the slaughter to the Gurkha and nodded in silence before taking the phone off him.

Rufus now stood in the doorway staring at the action, "A bit over the top wasn't it chaps, gruesome and all that?"

Jonesy looked at him, "A message, do you want to add anything Lord Longmore?"

Faces turned to see who he was talking to."

"Lord Longmore, who do you think he is?" he stared at Gurung.

"We need to protect his tribe now My Lord." said Gurung.

"Yes, but for how long, you lot have just started a long and bitter war, they will come when they feel safe and it'll be nasty," said Rufus.

"You have another idea then boss?" asked Jonesy.

Rufus shook his head, "It can't be you lot who do the protecting, I'll make a call and cover them with out of towner's."

"Who?" asked Gurung.

"The military have top ranking Indian officers, perhaps they can help?"

He scribbled a number he was copying from his phone and dropped the card on the table.

"Rudy, ring that man, he's a General, Indian nation by the way, tell him your story and ask advice, oh and you also have another investor in your casino," he grinned.

"You?" asked Rudy.

Rufus nodded, "I'll take up any slack in the restructuring, 30% silent ownership, ok with that?"

Rudy looked around at the blank faces then nodded.

Gurung gave him the grin and the nod to speak.

"Err...............yeah, err................ cool, but what restructuring are you thinking of?"

Rufus sat down in front of him and smiled, "Now I heard over the radio that you lads have a good name for the casino, the white buffalo, yes?"

"So, what about, let me enhance that a little!" he swept his hands in the air, "Picture the colored sign flashing out there, the Indians chasing a buffalo and suddenly the white one comes and takes a gander at them, well what do you think?"

He looked at Gurung in confusion, "What's a gander, and who the hell is he?"

"He's Mr 30% and he has the money to take them all on," said Gurung.

"And do what?"

Rufus flicked his fingers in front of Rudy's face, "Well we need a 500-bedroom hotel for a start then I'll call up a mate and have French cooks here to give the place class, got me mate?"

"Who's mate?"

Gurung and Jonesy laughed at the nutter talking to the Indian.

"Hey!" said Rudy, "Don't leave me with him."

A Mexican bandit walked in on the conversation and looked around.

"Well Zorro, what do you think?" said Rufus.

"A lot of blood boss, is that normal?"

"Yeah, yeah, Indians, know what I mean here mate?"

"Whose mate?" asked Rudy."

Zorro pointed to Rufus, "What they need here Rufus, is bandits as security guards, what do you think?"

"No!" said Rudy, "This is the White Buffalo, no bandits and no cowboys, this is part of the reservation, we own this, and it will be done by our rules understood?"

"Wooden Indians at the doors then?" said Zorro.

"Yeah, wooden Indian and slots in a line," said Rufus, "Hey with Indian pan pipes playing in the background?"

"No!" said Rudy.

"Hey, and free peace pipes?" said Zorro.

"Leave it, no drugs, remember?" laughed Rufus.

"Oh yes boss, nearly forgot there."

Gurung and Jonesy walked out laughing then their phones buzzed in as the action started again, "So where's Councilor Collins, "Asked Marvin.

"Err....in the hotel Boss." said Gurung.

"Find him and protect him, yes?"

"But we......."

"Find him now, move your arses.... now!"

"Can I come with you guys?" shouted Rudy from his new office.

Gurung put his head back in the room, "And he's your tribal protection 24/7 for as long as you like, he'll fit right in with your people.

Rudy stared at the Mexican bandit, "But he's a............a bandito?
"

Zorro's gold tooth glinted as he grinned.

"He's also a native of this land so cut him some slack." said Gurung.

Zorro thumbed to the Gurkha, "An Indian?"

Rudy focused on his grin, "Err............... yeah, but not from round here."

"So, he cut these guys up with a knife?"

Rudy just stared at all the blood on the floor and people's footprints walking it all over the place, "We need a clean-up first."

"Yeah, messy huh?" said Zorro as he looked around.

The door closed and Rudy was left with the bandit and the smell of death.

"You get used to it Injun, in the end." said the bandit.

"And who are you really?" asked Rudy.

"Well just a friend who's here to help in any way I can."

"Yeah, but why?"

"I'm his hotel manager, we have many hotels, this will be another one, a native American classic, the white buffalo legend has been born, we just need to enhance the dream, get me boy?"

"Who's get me boy?"

The gold tooth glinted in the light as Zorro laughed.

# CHAPTER 73 ... Room 3232 ... Les Grandiose Hotel ... Las Vegas

"What new invention?" asked Erick.

Cal passed him her buzzing phone, "Ah, the man himself, ask him Erick."

Erick looked at Theo's face on the phone then pressed green, "Yes Theo!"

"New York City is the first, the experiment is ongoing and will be rolled out to the whole country when we check it all out and prove its reliability to the observers."

"Theodore, just tell me what the hell you are talking about?"

"The democratic vote Erick, for everyone, instant results of questions asked."

Erick turned to the grinning face of Marvin.

"New York, yes?"

Erick turned away, "Ok, explain for me please Theo, because this is the first, I've heard of it." he walked away to the other side of the room as Theo explained the new democratic system to him.

"And you and your people are convinced that this will work, yes?"

"Register with the Government and you can vote on your phone or online anywhere in the world on any National vote declared by the President at any time, day or night."

"Millions of votes in seconds?"

"Billions of votes counted in seconds Erick, this is real democracy at last, no waiting around for the peoples vote, almost instant questions answered."

"Woo Theo, and this is above board and reliable?"

A complete waste of breath asking Theodore, the people might like the idea, but the politicians won't," said Erick, "You're removing the leadership from the decision-making process, it won't work!"

"But Erick, this can work!"

"Shelve it Theo, we have more work for you so put it on the back shelf for later talks, clear?"

"What if I sell it to the UK, then what?"

Erick started to laugh, "You have no chance, Theo!"

"But what if?"

"Ok, you sell the idea to the Brits, and I'll talk it through with the Americans, yes?"

"Seventy million people Erick, not to be sniffed at, right?"

"You are bonkers Theo if you think that they will go for that."

"So, I can try then?"

"Waste of time Theo, so has she found the man yet?"

"Err.......... you won't like it, Erick."

"Come on, just the name."

"Cabinet office!"

"Oh no!

"Yes, no, Erick, Elizabeth is fuming and, on her way, over."

"Stop her Theo, not now, we have a war brewing over here, one step at a time please, tell her from me, to stop and think, let the planner re plan, ok?"

"Well, yes Erick, clear, I'll pass it on to them, but will they listen?"

"Yes, from me they must, we have another plan rolling and rule one is not to cross over and confuse everyone, understood?"

"Ok Erick, I'll pass it on."

Cal grinned at him as he closed the call, "And, Caledonia?"

"You can't keep all the plates spinning Erick, sometimes they fall off and smash on the floor, it's nature."

"Cal, phone your mother and call her off until the timings are right, clear?"

"He's taken over," said Marvin.

Erick pointed to Marvin, "And you can give me the plan, right here and right now!"

"Wee, Chef!"

"And I noticed your French people don't mix, so why is that Marvelous?"

"Because I don't trust your lot Erick, I've learned the hard way on that one."

"Give him a break Erick," said Cal.

"You, phone.... now!"

"He's become the politician Marv, he talks to them all, best listen up please."

"With your support then Cal?"

"I think he's an idiot Marv, but he has the passion so who am I to stop him, I just protect and serve like always."

"No phobias then Cal?"

"Oh, lots of Marv but he is more important than me and he will get there with our help, we need you as well Marvelous, to make it happen."

"Make what happen?"

"He's going to be the next Prime Minister of Canada; he's driving them to the voting polls as we speak."

"Cal!" shouted Erick, "Phone her now, this minute!"

She stopped and picked up her phone and walked into the bedroom, Erick turned to Marvin.

"So where is your better half?"

"Well, she had a recall from London."

"Tolly?"

"Yeah, he has a new idea and wants her on board for the launch."

"Do I have to squeeze every little piece of information from you Marv, out with it please."

"He's downing the King and changing over to a new type of Monarchy!"

Cal's head came into the room, "What!"

"He's changing the Monarchy."

"Has he gone nuts Marv?" shouted Cal.

"What the hell Marv?" said Erick.

"An old argument about who runs the country, same as folks."

Erick pointed to Cal again, "Get on that bloody phone and find out Caledonia, now!"

She punched in recall and waited.

"Is it me Marv, am I dreaming all this?" said Erick.

Marvin grinned again, "He's calling on a board of interested parties to talk it all over, he wanted the Princess there to take notes."

"Where's Patrick Marv?"

"Why?"

"Because this all smells like an Irish idea to me!"

"I don't get you Erick?"

"Well, I do, find him Marv and bloody quick."

Marvin took his phone out and shouted at Gurung, "Find him and protect, yes?" he cut the call and stared at Ericks thinking face as he stared at the window curtains.

"But why Diana Marvelous, what the hell's happening here man?"

"It's classic Tolly Erick, what do you want me to say man?"

Erick stared into his eyes as he thought about it all, "Ah.... manipulation, he's putting the thumb screws on King Charles and proving a point, what do you think?"

"How?"

"By taking him through the process step by step."

But Charles might just step out and tell them all to stick the Monarchy where monkeys put nuts, this could be his chance to escape man, think about that one if you dare."

"Shit! you're right, Charles could just pack it all in and let them form a republic."

"And your son would be the new Oliver Cromwell, stirring them all up again with the military takeover in the background, generals in his pocket and all that."

"Shit! your right Marv, he's lost the plot man!"

Caledonia's head appeared in the doorway again, "Got him on the phone, so what do you want answering Erick?"

He was with her in two strides he took the phone from her, "Ok baby, give me the story in your head please."

"Oh, hiya Pa, what's up?"

"I hear a real nightmare of a story coming from the UK, easy my mind can you Tolly?"

"Oh, the Monarchy question, yes?"

"Yes, the Monarchy question as you call it, so what the hell is happening?"

Tolly started laughing at him.

"Cut that out son and explain to me please, because I think that you might be going through breakdown or something?"

"Cool it Pa, look we're asking the people to make a choice, finally we have the mechanisms to do just that, we give them the choice and they choose, right?"

"Are you nuts, what if they say goodbye to the King and all his people, then what?"

"Calm Father, calm please, look, Uncle Theo came to me with a new piece of equipment, and I said yes, that's it!"

"A 70 million people vote Tolly, are you lot on drugs, do not let it get out of hand son, do you hear me?"

"Too late Pa, done and dusted!"

Erick flopped onto the settee in a panic, he handed the phone to Cal, "Ask him, I can't take any more!"

She took the phone and spoke down the line, "Baby, what the hell have you done?"

"We tested the new system mum, that's it!"

"That's it, what's it?"

"Oh, didn't I say?"

"No, you did not say Tolly so what happened?"

"Well, when I conferenced with the king and his councilors, he mentioned that he didn't feel like a King who could count on his people for confidence, well just as Uncle Theo phoned, karma I would call it."

"You are getting me wound up Tolly, what are you talking about?"

"We gave the British people the chance to vote, question one, do you want the King to be involved in politics in relation to world events and two do you want him to speak for the Nation on the unification of the America's?

"Shit Tolly, why?"

"Well Grandma started it all rolling really."

"Tolly, you are really winding me up, clear and concise please, what the hell have you done?"

Mother, calm please, we have the technology so I launched it on the net for all of the UK to vote on those two subjects, it was a vote of confidence for King Charles, we simply provided the options and what would happen without our Monarch, I gave them some history from the last time it happened."

"1642?" growled Cal

"Yes, the English civil war, very nasty by the way."

"Yes Tolly, I am my Grandads little listener as well, I've listened to him for years about it all, that's why he was a monarchist, he understood the alternatives I suppose?"

"Well yes mum, well I simply gave them the history and we called for the National vote."

"And Tolly, what next?"

"Oh, they voted yes and yes!"

"Yes, bloody yes what?"

"Oh, they want him to speak out for the ordinary man in the street, 75% voted, fantastic mum you should have been here, it was pure historic, I tell you this, the hairs on my neck stood up as the vote came in, wow, eh?"

"Tolly, listen to me now, are you still there, look get one of the golden guns out of my office draw and shoot Theodore for me please."

"Mum, you don't understand the changes this will enforce within our society, safety, security, politics' the lot mum."

She slammed the phone down on him and flopped onto the settee next to Erick.

"Bloody Theodore Smirnoff, he's bonkers Erick, he'd already sold that thing to Tolly, they voted on the Monarchy."

Erick put his fingers in his ears, "Well, did he win?"

"Yep....70% vote in the affirmative."

"Which was what?"

"Do you Brits want me to speak up for the ordinary people of the world and on your behalf, yes and yes they said."

"Good God Cal, our Son very nearly lost the country, does he realize that fact?"

She snuggled into him and laughed, "We're too old for all this cobblers Erick, let's get back to the ice where we belong! The kids have taken over the asylum.

He started to laugh at her words.

"What?" said Marvin, "Did I miss something here?"

Cal looked at his face and started laughing at him.

"What?"

Cal screeched out at his question and his face.

"But why did he want Diana in on the game?"

"Oh, do wake up Marvelous," said Cal, "There are two brains in that office."

"I still don't get it, what?"

"Jane you moron, she's pushing you to get it done, what would Nana say? Go get her and bring back your new wife you moron!"

"Jane?"

"She will be shopping with Diane, the dress the home things that women always need around them."

"But me and the Princess have always done it our way, and it's none his or your business."

"Well Jane disagrees perhaps Marv?"

Marvin stared at them in shock, "She didn't say anything."

Erick put his finger in the air, "No Cal, you're wrong, she will be in Paris with guess who?"

"Yes Erick of course she is, this is Grandma pushing and Jane would have made the invite to the wedding party of the decade with the new first lady of America."

"Alice?"

"Err.... der Marvelous, well get going big lad."

He stared at them in silence as it swilled around his brain, "But I have work to do?"

"When Marv?" asked Cal.

He looked at his watch, "Well now I suppose," he stared again at them while he thought of what to do next, he changed focus from Erick to Cal and stared at her.

"Oh no Marv, she will not be involved at this stage!" said Erick.

"A driver, that's it!"

Cal grinned at him, "And you can do this?"

"One man and one gun, I can do this, in fact I have to do this, you just drive, my lads will cover us as we move, ok with that Cal?"

"No Marv!" she is not involved," screeched Erick.

She tapped his bad leg and laughed, he cried out in pain, "Just driving Erick, no drama, he's good at all this, in, out and onto a plane yes Marv?"

He nodded, looking at Erick.

"Hold on, we have a full team in town why her?"

"Because of plan A Erick, remember?"

"Shit and you're still on that mad plan?"

"The only plan Erick and as of now, we have no choice, do you hear me?"

Erick picked up his phone, "I can stop you Marv, if I want you know?"

"But you won't, will you Erick, we need her and her alone, get me man?"

"They could just kill her Marv?"

Cal opened her coat and showed the Hecklers.

"They'll shoot you Cal, out of fear of what you might do, this is America, shoot first and ask the time after, understood?"

"A politician's wife after Erick?"

"With a limp because her hip was shot out?"

"I want to do this Erick, in fact if I don't the old man will haunt me, get it?"

"That bloody old man again, will he ever die?"

"The plan Erick, we need to do this," said Marvin.

"For the experiment?"

"Yes, Erick for the experiment that is more important than us, are you ready for that?"

"Shit .... get going, so what do I say to the gorilla?"

"That they have her locked and bolted, and she will be executed when the dust settles."

"Shit Marv, that's a stupid plan man!"

"Everyone is ready Erick, it's now down to me to start the rolling plan, clear?"

"Marvin, I hope this works, because if it doesn't then all hell will break loose."

"It will anyway Erick, no other way, well do you know a better way? Will they move over and leave us alone, no, will they talk and listen, no, well this will do the talking."

He patted the magnum under his arm pit.

"Oh, come on man, that's just six, tell him Cal, come on woman, give some professional advice."

"His plan Erick and I must pay a price, look, we have to go, ok?"

He stood up and pulled her out of the settee, he hugged her tight, "No risks, take the heat and get locked up, silence, no comment to anyone until Patrick shows up, clear?"

She took the Hecklers and threw them onto the settee.

"I won't need them, Erick."

He looked at Marvin as he panicked, "My God you're just like the old man Marv, he was always so confident, remember?"

"Got yer Erick, try to relax, then make the call, yes?"

"This is just bonkers people!"

Cal kissed him and walked out; Marvin didn't even look back as he walked out."

"Shit!" shouted Erick as the door closed, he turned and looked at her weapons on the settee, he gave it a kick with his good leg, "Shit!" Then flopped back down to do some thinking and planning, he had watched the old man in the past draw circles in the air with his finger as he planned out situation, he tried doing the same but gave up in the end, then he thought of Canada and the changes that were going to happen, he reached for his note pad and pen then started to write out an opening speech for the senate hearing that was about to happen in Washington.

"Why the hell am I doing this?" Pop's croaky voice came to his mind and made him laugh out loud, (Because you're our man, so pull your pants up and get it done before someone else kills the idea)" Ok Pop, I'm on it! What about Cal though?" (Oh, do me a favor?) The old man's voice made him laugh again as he thought of all those lessons he'd been thrown into without a care in the world for his safety, "Yes Pop, will do! Understood, they are more important than scum like us, got ya!"

# CHAPTER 74 ... The Sultanate Palace Hotel ... Las Vegas ... Room 10

Patrick was playing chess with the girls, three brains verse his, he made a quick move to make them panic, his wife laughed at his grin.

"Come on daddy don't be too aggressive with them."

"Too aggressive? look at where they have me, surrounded and waiting to take my Queen."

Suddenly there was a knock at the door, her eyes flashed panic through the room.

"Room service Chuck, let's be calm, eh?

She moved to the table and checked her weapon then went to the door, "Who is it?"

"Marvelous sent us to keep you entertained." said Jonesy.

She looked to Patrick, who laughed, "Jail birds darling seeking advice perhaps?"

She unlocked the door and let them in, Gurung walked in with pizza boxes and Jonesy followed with the drinks, wine, beer and fresh orange juice.

"We thought that we'd bring the party to you if that's ok?"

The girls jumped up and ran over as they squealed out in excitement just as the door knocked again, all faces turned to the door, Jonesy grinned.

"Err.... aren't you boys doing a job here?"

"Na.... the Welsh have arrived, we watched um in the car parks, I hear the sounds of a Welsh male voice choir in my ears, can't you?"

Carol was up and at the door as the second knocked four times "Come on open the door I'm carrying all the stuff," shouted Griff.

Carol opened up and the line of men walked in Griff, Glen, Eden, Robbie and Winston Churchill smiled at them.

"What the hell?" asked Carol.

"The troops Chuck, and a couple of spares."

Patrick looked around at them, "A bit obvious isn't it, gentlemen?"

"One minute we were in an airplane waiting for the drop, routines say's the pilot," said Winston, he thumbed to Griff, "Then I looked round, and these blokes were doing the same, who are you, say's I, no response, what are we doing say's I, no response, where are we going? says I."

"No response!" said the girls in unison.

"Is this normal Mr....... whoever you are?" asked Winston.

"Yes Griffyd, I like him, a black man and an English speaker, very good, why the other gentleman though?"

"A safe breaker by all accounts Patrick, the best, say some, Elizabeth sent him to keep him out of trouble."

"He gets himself in trouble then?"

"Oh, all the time she recons."

"Well, that will have to stop err......?"

"Robbie, sir!"

"And why do you call me sir, Robbie?"

"I've admired your work sir, from a distance of course."

Patrick looked at Griff for an explanation.

Griff smiled at him, "The gorilla thought it good to show him your car thefts in alphabetical order video, he can see that you're a ledge Patrick and so assumes correctly we think."

Jonesy coughed into his hand to get Patrick attention.

"Yes Captain."

"Can we resume sir, outer perimeter and over cover?"

"Ok, all take a seat please gentlemen, I'll run the plan over you quickly then Captain Jones and Gurung can go back to work, I was told to tell you by another black man to and I quote, do not get into trouble and do not cause a fight please!"

Jonesy grinned at him, "Sorry boss, old habits and all that."

"Listen up lads, "said Patrick, "I'm the lawyer and Griff as always is my research man, we stand together in the dock to prosecute the enemies when and if, clear?"

"Oh, I remember him now, "Said Winston, "Alphabetical order, fantastic so now you're a lawyer?"

Patrick focused on him, "And Clink Eastwood might be governor of California so repeat after me, do you feel lucky punk? In a Jamaican American accent, ok.... go!"

The girls encouraged him to have a go, they waved their hands to get him to speak.

"Err......do you feel lucky punk?" said Winston.

Patrick looked to his girls, "Good?"

"Yes Pa, good, he sounds just like Uncle Marvin," said Willow.

"Thanks darling," he focused back onto Winston again, "So, the plan, what do you think?"

"You want me to impersonate this Uncle Marvin, yes?"

The women gave him a round of applause as they laughed.

"Good!" said Patrick, "Sharp, the gorilla said you were at least sharp, so I want you to be the second Marvin, movement, cloths, the lot."

"Should I ask why?"

"Not really, err.... what is your real name by the way, George gave me some stupid name, off his head obviously?"

"Winston Churchill Mr whoever you are?"

The women started laughing, Patrick shushed them up, "Please don't insult his family ladies, remember your own odd names, he is our star and an ace in the hole after all."

Winston stared at him in confusion.

"Can we eat at least?" asked Carol.

"Oh, sorry, get some plates please girls, and glasses, let's eat first eh."

"An answer to my first question would be polite Mr?" said Winston.

Patrick focused on him again as the girls ran off to get the plates for the pizzas.

"Yes, sorry Winston, an explanation is required, eh? I don't mean to be rude, it's just that I live in America, it's part of being a local, blunts questions, brash behavior, eating with one's hands, no insult intended Winston, it's just that George said that you had hidden talents and one of them was impersonation, a good mimic he said."

Winston stared at him in silence as he waited.

"Ah, sorry again, so, I'm Patrick Collins, this is my wife Carol, and these are my daughters Willow, Jenny and April, these gents are all for our protection on and off site, Captains Gurung and Jones are perimeter over watch, and what we call the Welsh boys are Griffyd, Eden and Glen, your close support.

"I don't understand, so I now need close support Mr Collins?"

"Well, yes, you see everyone wants to kill Marvin and are we're here to protect him."

"So, I have a bull's eye painted on the back of my neck then?"

"A bit more subtle than that Winston and you might meet a friend while you're out here in Las Vegas."

"And you'd bring your family into all this sir?"

"My family are always close to me; I've learnt that lesson already."

"But the risks?"

"It's the world we live in Winston, by the way, Rufus is in town, and he'd like a talk with you, ever been to a casino?"

Winston shook his head as he started to sweat.

Patrick nodded to Carol, "When we've eaten you can follow Chuckuluk and she'll give you your outfit to wear, later you can go and visit Rufus for the yaba daba doo, yes?"

"And he'll explain the plan to me?"

"No, that's my job after we've eaten, ok with all this."

"A stupid question already but obviously why Welsh, a bit strange?" asked Winston.

"All about language actually, they are native speakers, so, never been to Wales? The spoken word over there is impossible to understand, imagine being an American and trying to find a translation while on the move and listening in to their convo's, get me?"

Winston grinned at him, "Cleaver sir."

"Patrick, Winston, just Patrick, calling anyone sir highlights their higher position and we don't need to give free information away, clear?"

"Err yeah, I see."

"You will catch on Winston, just talk to Rufus, he'll give you the lowdown in the sit rep, yes?"

"Yes boss!"

Patrick smiled at him, "So, brought up with Rufus then?"

"Err.........I'm a lower life form, err....... Patrick, me and him slept in gutters sometimes, no other abode, understand me .........err.... boss?"

"Well, we all have something in common then Winston, all of us in this room have hit and lived at the very bottom, we are all dirt bags learning to be real, it's all perfectly normal my friend."

"Am I?"

"What, a friend? Yes, Winston, we are all friends, loyal companions, we cover each other's back the same as you and Rufus used to do, he'll explain, I'm sure.

The girls came back with the plates and the glasses, and the sound level became confused as the pizzas were dished out and consumed.

"So, will this get me killed boss?"

"No Winston it will not, we just need an actor and that's you, ok with that?"

Winston took a bite of pizza and nodded.

"I like your family boss."

"Do you play chess?"

"Yeah, Rufus taught me, I'm good I think."

"Well, that's good then, you can take my slot because the girls have got me in a Russian clamp and I can't get out, perhaps you could still survive?"

Winston grinned at him again and moved over to the chess table, the girls took up their positions and waited for his move while eating pizza.

Patrick gave Carol the knowing smile, she nodded in agreement to his new and improved plan, then turned to her girls to see if they could nail him down.

He made a rapid move by sliding the rook down to the corner of the table, "Check, ladies!" he started laughing at them.

"But how?" squealed Willow.

"Always protect your back four, he was leading you into an embarrassing check mate called fools mate, the back was wide open, your move, get it?"

The girls looked at their father who was just laughing at them, "Pa! that's cheating?"

"That's the rule girls, come on three brains verses one, same as, grind him down, come on, you have more pieces you have to be cruel to be kind girls."

Winston squealed out laughing at their faces and rubbed his hands together.

Carol nodded to Patrick in agreement, she also liked the new man on site.

Robbie smiled at the action as Patrick focused on him, he held his hands up, "Hey this is a foreign land, I'm no good out here."

"Again, George said that you could be useful in the coming days, you see we need information, only it's in the police headquarters, how hard can it be?"

Robbie choked on his chili covered pizza.

"We need evidence for the prosecution, you can provide that can't you Robbie?"

"Err.......... when?"

"Let's see, tonight 0200 to 0500, plenty of time to take photos of reports and such, Glen and Eden will get you in, you just have to break whatever security they have and take photos of files."

"High security?"

"No just metal office cabinet's full of history, we need it you see, secretary's open files and even desk top books, that's it, well, can you do that for us?"

"Err............... yeah......err....... boss! But I don't have a .........?"

Patrick handed him a brand-new hi-tech camera phone, "No need to focus just point and snap, every file cover and then every page of selected files, then just press send to the recall number one on the top and it's gone, ok clear with all that?"

"Err.......... yeah, I suppose, so American locks, yes?"

Patrick nodded.

"But I know nothing about American locks."

"Chub, Yale, where do you think they were invented?" said Patrick.

"Ah, yeah, got ya, so my lock picks will do the biz then?"

"Perhaps, but if not, you'll have to improvise, can you do that and not leave a trace?"

Robbie grinned, "My middle name boss, just out of interest again Patrick, why do you call your wife Chuckuluk?"

"Because she is a native of this land and Carol is her second name her first is?"

"Chuckuluk?" said Robbie.

Patrick nodded and smiled at him, "We're simple folk Robbie."

"I don't think that Mr Collins, hold up a mo, so where will all the cops be then? because even the night shift would normally be there.

"Not so tonight, Robbie, they might be very busy in fact, things happen fast around here."

Robbie searched the faces looking at him for some clues, blank faces smiled back at him, "Not my part of the plan, eh?"

"Yes Robbie, not your part, clear?"

"Very clear Boss! But what does the name really mean?

Patrick looked over to Carol.

She smiled at him, "The direct translation means the small ice cube in the dark ocean."

"Like the iceberg that sank the Titanic then?"

She screeched out laughing at him, "Bang on that guy!"

"Oh, how did you get on with Elizabeth and Dexter?"

"Completely bonkers, both, I didn't understand them most of the time, do they have another language or something?

"Oh yes, another language all of their own Robbie, same here sometimes, you just have to live the history and you'll catch on......in the end." she giggled and moved away to see how the girls were doing.

"Check!" shouted Willow.

Winston burst out laughing, "Ok, I'm going to castle!"

"Too late, you moved the king before."

"Not me, I didn't move the king, no, no, you lot are very tricky," he moved his queen in front of his king, check!"

The girls jumped up and started shouting at him.

"What?"

"That's illegal!"

"No, it ain't, I'm from Brixton and it's all perfectly legal down there!"

They looked to their father to judge the situation, but he burst out laughing at them, "No, he obviously knows the origins of the game."

"Yeah, Brixton where it was invented!" screeched Winston as he laughed at them.

"You just made that up!" screeched Willow.

"No, scouts honor!"

"But were you ever in the scouts?"

"Ah, you might have a technical clause there girls," he screeched out laughing.

"Isn't this supposed to be a silent game?" asked Carol.

"Not in Brixton it's not, loud man, the same as dominoes!"

# CHAPTER 75 ... Du Salon ... St Michel ... Paris ... France

Alice marched through the outer glass doors and screeched out laughing at the girls behind the giant counter, "Good news mon angels du Paris, we have a wedding rolling and we're here to make a statement, come on let's open the champagne and get the party started!"

The place erupted in squealing and shouting as the designers and dress makers ran across to gather her up in their arms, Alice was held in the air by her friends in the industry as they screeched.

Where is my boy, Michel?" shouted Alice.

Diana and Ruth stood behind her with mouths open as the chaos continued before Michel came out of his office bleary eyed and ran over to Alice, she was passed over to him as she kissed his cheeks, while in the air she pointed to the brides.

"I have two for you Michel, a gigantic one and a quiet one, this lady is going to be the first lady of America and that lady is going to be the richest woman in the world, so do your magic mon Ami!"

The crowd surrounded the two women and whooped at the new projects.

Alice clapped her hands, "Ok, obviously the dresses, then the makeup but we also need fashion sense and education, plus dance classes, perhaps even etiquettes you'll have to close the salon Michel, we have a lot of work to do."

"But Alice I have customers! I have a shoot to do, I have the house wanting my clothes, Alice?

"Yes, but you have two of the biggest jobs you have ever had Michel, so get the grey matter working and let's do this!"

"But Alice?"

"Ok, but if you hurt me to the bone Michel, I'll leave and that will be that!"

"No, no, no, Alice no, we are closed to the public as of this hour," he clapped his hands in the air, ok troopers let the party start!"

Ruth was ready to run as the women took hold of her and took measurements of all her sizes, fingers clicked as they put them into the computer for recording and analysis and potential pattern groupings, they mumbled on and on in French.

"Zonglais, Michel!" shouted one of them.

He babbled on and on in French to them then stood before them, "All actions and translations will come to you ladies from me or Aunty Alice, agreed?"

Ruth was overwhelmed by it all, but Diana was in her element, "Come on Ruth, this is dream land, anything you want, shout out and it will appear."

"This is not me Princess!" said Ruth.

"Princess?" shouted Michel.

Alice grinned in silence as he did a double take to her, she nodded, and he did a little dance to a silent musical sequence.

Alice giggled at him and all the others who took a close look at Diana.

"Du sang de bleu et la Grande Bretagne!" shouted Alice, "A la premier Dame de la Ameriques! Comprendre mon ami? So, tout rapidmont, alez!"

"Impossible!" said Michel.

"Non mon ami, possible, due fame et tres famous, comprendre mon petti garcon?"

Michel gulped air as his dream entered a golden age, but this was for real, he started to cry but Alice got hold of him and gave him a shake, "Alez Michel, La President du Ameriques com et vous?"

He slapped his own face to come round from his dream like state then started to dance again."

Alice put her hands on her hips, "Michel.......... alez!" she shouted.

It was as if someone had lit a fire under him as he ran off to collect samples of cloth.

"My God this is heaven Ruth!"

"Like hell it is?" said Ruth, "Now what the hell's going to happen?" she jumped in the air with shock as Alice opened the first bottle of champagne.

"Shit!"

"Great!" said Diana.

Alice poured the liquid into the wide glasses and grinned for ear to ear, enjoy ladies this is going to be epic, right?"

# CHAPTER 76 ... Chelsea ... Central London ...UK

The black Range Rover was parked on the curbside the engine was ticking over as Lord Halifax came down his house steps, he was going to shout at whoever was making all the fumes but thought better of it as he glanced at the driver, the blacked-out windows blocked his view of the passengers in the back seat.

Suddenly the rear window buzzed down, and Elizabeth whistled to him, "Percy, want a lift chap?"

He was shocked at her sudden appearance, "Err............Elizabeth, I thought you were.............?

"Away with the fairies?" grinned Liz.

"So where is your husband?"

She thumbed to the front seat and the blacked-out window, "He's got a mood on him this morning."

He smiled at her, "A normal day in the office then Liz?"

"Not really Percy, get in please!"

"But Liz I normally get my coffee on route to the office it just down the road."

She held out a plastic cup with the straw sticking out.

"Going cold Percy, come on get in the motor."

He opened the door and climbed in, Dexter ignored him on the front passenger seat, "Do you know Elizabeth, your mother fumed from time to time at your pretended cockney accent, all that money spent on elocution lessons she would say, she's turning into a cour blimy laddet!" he laughed nervously.

She handed him his coffee and smiled, "And what would she have done with you Percy?"

"In what way Liz, I don't understand?"

She tapped the drivers head "Go to the river please Richard."

Lord Halifax side glanced her and Dexter, "What's going on Elizabeth?"

"We've just borrowed a yacht from the manufacturers, it's down in docklands, you'll love it, I'm sure."

"I don't like the water Liz, so drop me off, could you?"

"Ten million to buy I'm told, we're checking it out for the future sail away, oh come on Percy just go with me on this please."

His smile changed to a panic as he watched Dexter's ears getting red, he remembered the signs of him getting angry.

"Elizabeth, what is this, a kidnapping?"

"No!" said Dexter, "A good old-fashioned murder down in the Thames where all the rest are!"

"But why?"

Elizabeth held his hand and smiled, "We've found you out Percy, all of your sins have come to the surface, he's a little tiffed if you know what I mean?"

"But Liz?"

"Ok tell us all please Percy and I promises that he won't drown you down at traitors gate in the Thames, because that's his only plan."

He stared at Dexter's head as the ears began to glow.

"Now Percy, you know us, I'm the peace maker today, he wants your head on a spike, but I can reel him in if you speak up, clear old man?"

"But I was a friend of your father Elizabeth, why?"

Dexter turned in his seat, "People have been killed because of you!"

"Calm husband," said Liz, "Cool down Hamish, we can discuss this calmly I'm sure, there is no need to be nasty, he gets so worked up these days Percy, PDHD I think plus I've stopped him drinking and that has to be good don't you think?"

"It wasn't my idea Liz, I shouted against the idea, but I was out voted right from the start."

"Who's idea Percy?"

"Err...........................I can't Liz............I can't betray my boss, I'm not a traitor!"

"Only to your friends then eh?" shouted Dexter, "You sack of shit!" he turned to grab hold of Lord Halifax, but Elizabeth grabbed his hand and turned it into a painful finger lock, Dexter screeched out in pain and anger."

"Just look what you've caused Percy, I'll have to get some strong stuff down his neck now, that's all your fault."

"I can't Liz!"

The driver locked eyes with her in the mirror, "He has only one boss Liz, so he's giving it to you there and then."

Lord Halifax looked at her in a panic again, she let go of Dexter and smiled at him, "Thank you Percy for that anyway."

"No Elizabeth you cannot do what you are thinking of doing, please!"

"Thank you, Richard, I understand now, so! Dexter!" said Liz, "Would you kill a King?"

"In a heartbeat Liz!"

"Why?"

"Well because he betrayed us all, he's turned into Charles the first, backstabbing, stitching us up like this, he's probably got us on a red file ready to be put down as we speak."

"Over stretched his authority then?"

"Yes, completely Liz and just like his name's sake he has to be put down."

The Rover stopped at the traffic lights as she stared at Halifax, a cyclist leaned on the car as he took a break in the London traffic, she buzzed the window down and snatched the coffee from Halifax then threw the lot over the cyclist and buzzed up the window as they pulled off.

Dexter giggled on the front seat as they drove off," Oh dear, now Elizabeth's getting steamed up, you are running out of time Percy and her patience, that poor bloke took her for granted you see and being rude, I imagine he doesn't know why she did that eh?"

"Rudeness Dexter, I can't stand rudeness," she turned to face Lord Halifax, "Now listen up Percy, we won't stand for being back stabbed even by our King, clear, you can pass it on if you like, and also, if we suddenly have people following us, we will click into silent mode and kill him, now do you understand how angry we are?"

"He didn't want this Liz, he just didn't want the Americans to take Canada, well not on his shift anyway, he's against it all.

She smiled at him and held his hand again, "Now listen up Percy, this is reality, we are a democracy, it's not the King who decides, it's all of us, understand, if he fiddles, we will destroy him, not me and Dexter but the whole Nation, they are watching Percy, you have to explain these things to him, understand? You see, as my father used to say as a mantra, they are more important than us scum bags, they matter more than you me or even him, clear Percy, tell him our views please, we are gone as of now, if he wants us back then he will have to find us and ask politely, all clear so far?"

Lord Halifax stared into her eyes, "But the country needs you, he needs you Liz, you and Dexter are big players, they all follow you!"

"He smiled in our faces and stabbed us in our backs Percy, it will take time to come back from this, better give him the good news of what will happen next if he doesn't get a grip of his monarchy, the people will throw him out!"

"But Liz that just leaves the Australians and the Gurkha's!"

"You can keep the dingo's Percy!" said Dexter.

Liz grinned, "Just the Aussies then, good luck mate, the lads will always follow him, I don't know why, he's such a monster really."

Lord Halifax stared at her with his mouth open in shock, "This has never happened before, never!"

"The Queen was loyal to her people Percy, he is not, simple as that, get it?"

She tapped the drivers head, "Stop Ricard, and let him out please."

The Range Rover stopped on the curb as the door opened, Halifax was reluctant to get out straight away, "But Elizabeth, you just can't do this, what will happen next?"

"Disloyalty has a price Percy, he has to understand that Charles the first learnt the very hard way, he needs education Percy and that's up to you, so go, we are no longer involved in his business let him crap his pants like all the other monarchs who tried to betray their own people!" She pushed him out into the rain and slammed the door, the Rover wheels spun off into the traffic as the cyclist came up to him and started shouting.

"You miserable bastard, that was disgusting!" The man shouted at him.

Lord Halifax grabbed the man by the collar, "You! Shut the fuck up before I tear your rude head off, that was so rude leaning on our car like that, where do you think we're living?"

The man cycled off in shock, his bad day continuing as he mumbled and fumed.

Dexter passed her the phone and smiled, "Enough?"

"Yes, we made our point I think, don't you?"

"Yes Liz, so now phone our grandson and get him working, yes?"

She stared into his eyes and instantly knew his plan, "Well yes, that's the way, yes!"

"And let him earn his corn Liz, we are done, ok?"

"Yes, haggis bollocks, we are done................... docklands please Richard and silent about all this please!"

"Absolutely Elizabeth, it's my day off anyway.... should I talk to Tolly?"

"Yes!" said Dex, "And give him what happened, we're done and gone, understood?"

"But do you need anything before you leave boss?"

Dexter's eyes met hers, she smiled back at him, he turned back to him, "No thanks lad, we have all that we need, perhaps a plan for you in the future?"

Richard grinned, "I haven't found the right woman yet boss!"

"And when you do lad?"

"Well........................... I'll be away with the fairies just like you, boss!"

Dexter patted his shoulder, "One day you'll have to lad, so prepare, the lassie is first, after all they're more important than us, clear?"

"Clear!" he locked eyes with Liz on the back seat, "But you are very lucky boss!"

"Oh, I know that one lad, find one that will love you know matter what, it'll be a hard but interesting life after that, but you'll be a man my lad!"

"And where will you go boss?" Dexter returned the look that silenced his stupid question.

Liz started laughing at the question, "Do me a favor!"

Dexter joined in their laughing.

Richard watched them get into the little rowboat, as Dexter took up the oars.

"But I thought that you had a boat?"

"We do darling, but haggis Needs the exercise, it's down river a little."

"Where?"

"Graves end!"

He didn't want to ask any more daft questions as Dexter rowed away into the center of the River Thames, "But Graves end is miles away," he whispered to himself.

Elizabeth waved and smiled at him, "Bye, bye, for now!" she shouted over to him.

He just had to bend over and laugh, "Bonkers!"

# THE END ...

Book Twelve up next ... PURE MALACE ...

# Don't miss out!

Visit the website below and you can sign up to receive emails whenever Percy Stevenson publishes a new book. There's no charge and no obligation.

https://books2read.com/r/B-A-GXFY-ZTPTC

**BOOKS 2 READ**

Connecting independent readers to independent writers.

Did you love *The Ghost Planner Book Eleven ... The United Continent of the Americas ...*? Then you should read *The Ghost Planner ... Book Nine ... Sin's of the Just ...*[1] by Percy Stevenson!

[2]

In this ninth book in the series, we witness how Tolly Victor Trueblood has grown, and along with his sister Augusta, they become part of the system. Still, they have to fight bigotry and fear from above as politicians panic in the face of the Dragons breath threat, fear of a governmental takeover is rife in Parliament, so the new Prime Minister has a plan to arrest them all, but his plan is flawed in its execution, long term heroes and Dragon men are arrested, Augustus Talbot realizes that they are being attacked and has to devise yet another plan, so he calls Theodore and Patrick from their normal lives to help, this is a time of panic, so all talents

1. https://books2read.com/u/4jEjzl

2. https://books2read.com/u/4jEjzl

must come back and help. Helen is no longer in power as her health fails and this is the trigger for the actions to start against them all. Patrick has to remind them all of the laws of the land as he ties them up in legality.

Augusta kills her lover, in the same old madness inherited from her mother, which complicates the whole problem, Augustus has to make a personal visit to sort out the problem in the same old way, and Alice finds out some more of his complicated history as they arrive for the demonstrations in central London.

# Also by Percy Stevenson

**THE GHOST PLANNER SERIES**
The Ghost Planner ... Book One ...The Female is More Deadly Than the Male ...
The Ghost Planner ... Book Two ... Promotion
The Ghost Planner Book Four... Men Of War...
The Ghost Planner ... Book Five ... The Wilson's
The Ghost Planner ... Book Six ... Brethren
The Ghost Planner ... Book Seven ... Revolution
The Ghost Planner ... Book Eight ... China
The Ghost Planner ... Book Nine ... Sin's of the Just ...
The Ghost Planner ... Book Ten ... The New Man in the Big Seat
The Ghost Planner Book Eleven ... The United Continent of the Americas ...
The Ghost Planner ... Book Twelve ... Pure Malice


**Standalone**
The Ghost Planner ... Book Three ... Talbot's dream ...

# About the Author

He has lived in Loughborough in Leicestershire, UK, for most of his working life but has also lived and worked in France.

Now retired and starting this new career, the stories can finally come out of friends in the trade and on the mountains of Europe who have given him some wonderful characters in passing.

Milton Keynes UK
Ingram Content Group UK Ltd.
UKHW012322290524
443431UK00001B/40